ZANE PRES

Sexpionage

Dear Reader:

Lesley E. Hal's *Sexpionage* is sure to thrill readers as it lives up to its title: intrigue, suspense and plenty of sex. It's a steamy mix of erotica and ecstasy with the plot of a detective novel.

Voluptuous Bianca Brooks finds herself in a compromising situation once she wakes up in a Dallas hotel room with a dead man, later revealed as a criminal mastermind. Not only is the man a stranger, but her last recollection was that she was in Paris. The scene leads her to become a storyteller to the FBI whose top mission is to find Bianca's lover, Jordan Lei aka The Tarantula, wanted for serious crimes all over the world. Known to use women to accomplish his illegal activities, it appears Bianca also falls into his trap as he knocks her off her feet and whom she finds irresistible. She can't seem to get enough of him, so she stays in his web, becoming entangled in a world of crime and secret missions covering the globe. No matter where Jordan's next move leads to, Bianca is compelled to accompany him while simultaneously trying to keep her fledgling events planning company, Pleasure Principles, afloat. This novel with international appeal, daring adventures and shady characters is full of twists and turns, and loaded with surprises that will keep you guessing.

As always, thanks for supporting myself and the Strebor Books family. We strive to bring you the most cutting-edge, out-of-the-box material on the market. You can find me on Facebook @AuthorZane or you can email me at zane@eroticanoir.com.

Blessings,

Zane

Publisher
Strebor Books
www.simonandschuster.com

ZANE PRESENTS

Sexpionage

A NOVEL
LESLEY E. HAL

STREBOR BOOKS

NEW YORK LONDON TORONTO SYDNEY

Strebor Books
P.O. Box 55471
Atlanta, GA 30308
www.simonandschuster.com

ISBN 978-1-59309-690-8
ISBN 978-1-50111-900-2 (ebook)
LCCN 2016948699

First Strebor Books trade paperback edition March 2017

Cover design: www.mariondesigns.com
Cover photograph: © Keith Saunders/Keith Saunders Photos

10 9 8 7 6 5 4 3 2 1

Manufactured in the United States of America

For information regarding special discounts for bulk purchases,
please contact Simon & Schuster Special Sales at 1-866-506-1949

The Simon & Schuster Speakers Bureau can bring authors to your live event.
For more information or to book an event, contact the Simon & Schuster Speakers
Bureau at 1-866-248-3049 or visit our website at www.simonspeakers.com.

Credit of this accomplishment goes to my beautiful beloved mother,
Dora L. Hal, who is now my angel. It's been a hard few years,
but I think I'm ready to get back to living and making you even
more proud of me. I'll miss, love and cherish you always.

Prologue

When I woke up, my head ached as if I were having open brain surgery without any anesthesia. My hand instinctively went to the back of my head, causing me to wince when I came in contact with a big, nasty lump. Disoriented, and reeking of alcohol, I found it difficult to remember what had taken place the previous night. The pain intensified as my eyes acclimated to the sunlight that flooded into the room. A quick peek under the crisp, white linens revealed that I was completely naked. As I investigated my surroundings, the Dallas skyline loomed outside of the floor-to-ceiling windows. It was then that I realized that I wasn't in Paris anymore ... nor was I in bed alone.

Headache notwithstanding, and suddenly filled with excitement, I shook Jordan's shoulder to get him to wake up. I must've been drunk out of my mind not to remember the earth-shattering, sex-filled night that I knew we'd had. Playtime for us was always filled with so much passion and necessary roughness which hopefully, would explain the bump on the back of my head. I was so busy trying to wake him that I didn't notice that his skin felt cold and clammy. As I rolled him onto his back ready to straddle him, it was then that I looked into his face and saw that his glossy eyes were wide open and his pupils dilated. My eyes doubled in size as I gaped at the gruesome discovery. The man in my bed wasn't Jordan. I wanted to scream, but it felt as if my vocal cords had been paralyzed.

Somehow I managed to get out of the bed and really take in my surroundings. I was in a hotel room—that much I'd gathered from the insignia on the comforter. What I didn't understand was how I had gotten here when the last place I remembered being was in Paris. The room had been destroyed as if there had been a struggle. Upon closer inspection of my not-so guest of honor, there was no denying the single gunshot entry that left a small hole in the middle of his forehead. Blood blanketed the left side of his pillow and had leaked down the side of the bed. A few droplets had made it onto the floor. I couldn't bear to look at him or the crimson-soaked pillow as he stared into nothingness with those haunting, vacant eyes. Panic gripped me as I frantically tried to figure out what the hell was going on. None of this made any sense. I had to get dressed and get the hell out of dodge. Unfortunately, no sooner than I had that thought, the doors to the suite flew open. The room was immediately filled with the Dallas SWAT, FBI and police.

"Get on the floor now!" shouted a big, burly chick who sounded and looked like a man.

"But I didn't do anything!" I protested as I was manhandled and thrown face-first onto the floor.

Someone put their knee in the small of my back. "Ouch! Is this even necessary?"

My arms were pinned tightly behind me as another person roughly slapped the handcuffs on. "I don't understand what's going on. Can't you see that I'm being framed?" My pleas fell on deaf ears as I was yanked back onto my feet.

"You have the right to remain silent. Anything you say can and will be used against you in a court of law. You have a right to an attorney. If you cannot afford an attorney, one will be appointed for you," the big bitch that screamed for me to drop to the floor stated as she Mirandized me. Her eyes gleamed approval as she discreetly licked her chapped lips while taking in my bare breasts and then the rest of my nakedness.

"Wanda!" a black male with mesmerizing gray eyes called out.

Man-chick stopped her gawking long enough to give him her attention. "What is it now, Agent Carter?" She rolled her eyes not bothering to hide her annoyance.

He handed her my discarded clothing. "Don't you think you should have her to get dressed first?"

She signaled for the assisting officer to uncuff me and shoved my clothing into my hands. "Here! Put these on."

As I was being led out of the suite flanked by Agent Carter and another officer, a familiar face appeared within the crowd of spectating hotel guests and staff. Her show-stopping beauty and confidence caused them to stop leading me to where-the-hell-ever as she introduced herself to them as my attorney.

A Month Later

I sat in a dull and gloomy interrogation room filled with nothing but married, sex-deprived-ass men who all wore badges. The only other woman present was my attorney,

Aliyah S. Talal. Having her on my side meant a distraction for various reasons. Men were mesmerized and distracted by the hourglass-shaped Arabian goddess with sparkling emerald eyes. They overlooked that the shrewd, ruthless vixen knew her way around the law among other things. When it came to beautiful women, men couldn't care less about her fancy degrees or the intelligence she harbored. All that interested them was getting to sample a taste of what was between her legs.

But today, all eyes were on me and with good reason. I was caught in a hotel room with a corpse who was later identified as Sherman Val Easterman, a known mastermind who was wanted in twelve states for various crimes. All evidence found against me was circumstantial, of course. There was never a weapon recovered. I'd never had a run-in with the law, but they were wrong. As far as they knew, I had no reason to harm the deceased. No motive whatsoever, but I couldn't afford the bad press that this could bring. That would mean allowing Pleasure Principles, my premier event planning company, and all of the hard work of creating it, go down the drain. My staff depended on me for their livelihoods. They shouldn't have been made to suffer because of my extra-curricular activities.

The reason I was even being incorporated into this mess was because I was linked to a man who had committed some serious crimes against banks and other fine establishments all over the world. Per my attorney, I was to dress to tease for the occasion. I wore a gray, pinstriped, mid-thigh-length skirt suit with a split that gave a tantalizing view of my sexy legs. To soften it up, I'd added a pink ruffled blouse that showcased my cleavage beautifully along with a white gold chain and diamond, heart-shaped pendant. Without much effort, the pendant found its resting place between my luscious double-Ds whenever I moved. Then back to hard and killing it with the finale: a pair of the fiercest stilettos to ever walk the earth. My makeup as always was flawless, as well as the God-given tresses that flowed nicely down my back. I slowly licked my luscious lips with the intention of toying with FBI Special Agent in Charge Garza and his crew. I gave the horny bastards a seductive toss of my honey-highlighted hair, a movement that displayed a little extra cleavage as intended. The necklace did its job superbly by nestling itself between my breasts. Without even having to look in the mirror, I knew it was a beautiful sight from the way they were all salivating. I repositioned myself in the chair and slowly crossed my shapely legs. In doing so, the men all received a bird's-eye view of heaven.

This wasn't lost on Special Agent Garza as he gathered his composure to start his so-called interview that was really an interrogation. "Ms. Brooks, I'm not playing any games with you. You're lucky that we're even giving you this opportunity after being caught in the predicament that you were. Now unless you talk, you may as well kiss your fucking freedom goodbye."

"You mean a predicament where everything is circumstantial, don't you, Agent Garza? My client was drug tested and it was discovered that she was under the influence of Rohypnol and other substances, which are used to impair a person's memory and render them unconscious. Not to mention that no weapon was ever recovered proving that Ms. Brooks wasn't the one that caused Mr. Easterman's demise," Aliyah spoke out of turn.

He ignored her and looked at me trying to put on the persona of a bad cop. "Now are you going to talk or what, Ms. Brooks?"

His tough-guy bravado didn't scare me one bit. Instead of quivering in fear, I took advantage of the situation using my best God-given weapon ... feminine wiles.

"Did you say my ... *fucking* freedom?" I leaned back a little further and crossed my legs to the other side. "Oh my goodness, the injustice of it all."

The Special Agent in Charge turned beet red. "I'm going to ignore that last remark, Ms. Brooks, but let me tell you a thing or two about your so-called knight in shining armor. The NSA has listed him as one of the most dangerous hackers in America and it doesn't stop there. The FBI has placed him on the most wanted list for a shit load of other federal crimes he's committed. Jordan Lei aka The Tarantula uses people, mainly *naïve women* who are foolish enough to think that he gives a rat's ass about them to do his dirty work." Agent Garza got in my face. "I bet you thought you were the exception, didn't ya? You're nothing to him but a—"

My lawyer banged her fist down on the table. "You will refrain from insulting or threatening my client, or this meeting is over. Take what you can get because my client sure as hell is taking the full immunity granted in return for her cooperation. So you decide, agent, how do you want this to play out?"

Agent Garza glared at my attorney. If looks could kill, well, let's just say that at that moment, she would've been drawing her last breath. "I'm going to press record on this video recorder . . ." he said, ignoring Aliyah, "which makes this official and on the books, Ms. Brooks."

"Of course, but first, I'd like a glass of iced water. And when I say glass, Agent Garza ... that's exactly what I mean."

"This is not Club Med for crying out loud! From the way I see it, you're gonna have to settle for either a Styrofoam cup or a bottled water."

Aliyah stopped him again. "Given how big of a deal this is and not to mention the risks my client is taking, I don't think a glass of water would be too much trouble for one of your agents here to handle."

I could tell by the way he gritted his teeth that Agent Garza was trying his best not to lose his temper as he gave the order to grant my request.

A few short minutes later, the agent who went out to comply with my request returned. "I hope this will do, found this set in the break room."

I was given a crystal pitcher of iced water accompanied by a matching flute. After pouring a glass full, I gingerly took a much-needed sip, making sure to put on a show. After taking the glass away from my matted fire-engine-red painted lips, the room grew silent. I produced an ice cube from my mouth sucking it slowly and allowing the cold water to drip onto my exposed cleavage. I then used the same ice cube to caress my neck allowing a whimper of a moan to escape from between my lips. My lawyer was doing her best not to laugh at the drooling fools sitting around the table. From the looks on their loopy faces, I knew they envisioned me sucking their dicks with the same amount of passion.

I took in a deep breath. "Umm ... that was ... so ... *satisfying*. Thank you," I whispered breathlessly.

Agent Garza cleared his throat. "Ms. Brooks, enough with the shenanigans already." He loosened his tie and turned on the recorder. "State your name and the relationship you have with The Tarantula."

Showtime! I uncrossed and crossed my legs again for good measure. "I'm Bianca Brooks, the girlfriend of Jordan Lei, whom you all refer to as The Tarantula," I stated for the record.

Agent Garza leaned forward with his elbows resting on the table. "Whenever you're ready."

"Umm ... okay! I don't know if it was love or the intoxicating sex that had me so caught up. The things this man would make me do to be rewarded with the most scrumptious dick I'd ever had the pleasure of knowing is—"

"Ms. Brooks!" Agent Garza interrupted.

"Umm ... ahem ... okay! Like, for example, I did something that wouldn't make mama proud just to meet him in Aspen, Colorado for an unforgettable weekend at one of his friends' lavish chalets in the mountains." Then I abruptly stopped. "I want to make one thing clear before I go on. Do not, and I repeat, do not try and assassinate Jordan's character. Trust me, when I say, that would be a lost cause. Please, understand that despite everything, I love the man I fell for. The fact that I'm about to reveal intimate details, should be proof enough that I'm more than willing to stick to my end of the bargain." Once I saw that he caught my drift, I began telling an entire room filled with strangers about the most gratifying, yet tumultuous, eleven months of my life with the man they called The Tarantula.

Chapter 1

I'd met Jordan at a banker's convention in Chicago. The chemistry between us that night would not be denied. When I saw him enter the room, I dropped my champagne flute, obviously due to being rendered speechless. As you can imagine, my mouth had other ideas as it hung shamelessly wide open. Vain as always, my friend Shelia placed a napkin under my chin to catch any runaway drool. Jordan was a mouthwatering, muscled-bound caramel god that stood a towering six foot seven inches. Needless to say, he took my breath away. His slanted brown eyes took precedence over his prominent Nubian King features and gave way to his Chinese lineage. His Caesar cut was an ocean of dark waves attached to sideburns that were anchored by a deep set of dimples that masked his devious intentions well.

"Girl, are you okay?" Shelia shook me out of my daydream when she used the napkin to dab at the corners of my mouth.

I licked my lips to make sure they were still glossy and captivating. "I am now."

Shelia followed my line of sight and soon become entranced in his magnificence herself. "Damn, girl, I was about to light into your ass about this champagne you spilled on my Choos, but

I'mma let you make it, though. Oomph! Oomph! Oomph! They don't make 'em like that anymore, do they?" She continued to stare dreamily.

"No, they don't." I agreed without taking my eyes off of the man who had imprisoned my soul.

We both stared at the object of our affection as he made small talk with several of the bigwigs in the banking industry. Working the room like a smooth operator, he made it a point to shake each of their hands as he regaled them in conversation. His eye contact was on point as he wore a look of poise instead of intimidation. As if he'd put a spell on the entire ballroom, everyone seemed to be enthralled by his urbane good looks and air of confidence that bordered on arrogance. Everyone, no matter their position, wanted to make his acquaintance, but none more so than me.

I glanced over at my competition to size her up. Shelia was the woman to have if you preferred the trying-too-hard type. She was beyond gorgeous and had the most beautiful butterscotch skin that I'd ever seen on anyone without makeup. Her crowning glory, however, was her head full of bouncy cinnamon natural curls streaked with caramel-blond highlights. The hairstyle and color made her appear angelic-like until you got to know her. She stood five feet three inches with the Coke-bottle shape that celebrities paid thousands to have—but not Shelia; she got hers courtesy of her evil-ass mama. With all of those attributes going for her, the one drawback were her crooked-ass teeth, also inherited from her mama. Thankfully, Shelia was correcting that problem with braces, but problem with that was who wanted metal scraping up against their dick and skinning them alive? I guess she either never heard of, or was just too cheap to go with Invisalign. As usual, Shelia dressed like a woman on the prowl va-va-voom style and leaving very little to the imagination. Her butt looked like it was about to pop the seams of her form-fitted, black satin cocktail dress. As for me, I'm a natural born sex kitten. I don't require all of the cosmetic bells and whistles that women are dying to have these days. You see, I ooze seduction—smooth, café au lait, blemish-free complexion; oval-shaped, chestnut-colored eyes, an hourglass figure, legs for days and ample bosom.

"Trust me, gentlemen. . ." I ran my hands over my curves. "There ain't a damn thing fake about any of this."

I knew without a doubt that I had this man on lock, being that there were few women of color in the room. Shelia and I were the pick of the litter from the ones who were present. Unless he fancied cream in his coffee, and even then, there was no real competition. Well, there were these four other women that could've given us a run, but they were so bourgeois that they wouldn't have noticed if Jesus, himself, had entered the room. Besides, it looked as though they were having a little spat with the chick in the off-the-shoulder, fitted white gown. She was definitely a looker, but she couldn't hold a candle to me. I gave them one more second of my time watching them claw and hiss at one another. This was the very reason I didn't put any energy into having too many female friends; women were nothing but drama.

I turned my attention back to Shelia. "I'm sorry about the shoes, girl. You know my pussy woke up the minute she sensed the prime dick attached to that gorgeous specimen of a man."

"Girl, I swear you're a nympho." Shelia laughed.

"Don't trip, you undercover freak."

"Hey, I never professed to be a nun, so get it right." Shelia clicked her long, lacquered nails together. We both laughed as the waiter walked by with another tray of champagne.

By this time, Jordan was looking my way, and of course Shelia took notice. She adjusted her double Ds and refreshed her lipstick.

There was no need for all of that. I knew I was looking good without even having to break out a mirror.

No sooner than he'd made it over to us, Shelia immediately stuck out her hand. "Hi, I'm Shelia Billings, and you are?"

"Jordan. Jordan Lei . . ." He turned his attention toward me. ". . . and who might this lovely vision be?" I could tell this pissed Shelia off, but I had to give it to her, she put up one hell of a front to hide her embarrassment.

"Oh, that's my good friend, Bianca Brooks."

"Bianca ... " I loved the way he pronounced my name. " ... making your acquaintance makes this function worthwhile, oh—and yours too, Shelia." Jordan kissed both of our hands. "What are two stunning ladies like you doing at a stuffy old party like this?"

"I'm the one who's in charge of this stuffy old party," I announced as I handed him one of my ever-present business cards. I had to let him know that I wasn't just another pretty face. "I own Pleasure Principles Event Planning. I specialize in all kinds of *pleasurable* gatherings." I winked at him.

"And I'm a real estate broker," Shelia volunteered quickly. "If I'm not being too forward, where is Mrs. Lei tonight?"

I had to give it to my girl; she was persistent as fuck.

"Unfortunately, there isn't a Mrs., yet, that is." Jordan gleamed that gorgeous smile of his at me.

"Well, in that case, would you like to have a seat with me?" Shelia batted her fake lashes at Jordan.

"Please don't take offense, Shelia, but I was actually hoping to get to know Bianca a little better, if you don't mind."

The retreated look that appeared on Shelia's face was that of ice water being thrown in it. "None taken." She gulped the rest of her drink, and fluffed cleavage once more to show Jordan what he could've had. "Bianca, I'll catch up with you later, girl. I'm going to find Reggie and Cody."

After Shelia's departure, Jordan literally devoured me with his eyes. There was a room full of people, but we had suddenly developed a severe case of tunnel vision, where nothing, or no one else, mattered but us.

His silence, and stare down, was so all-pervading, that it caused me to get a little nervous after an unhealthy amount of time had passed. "What? Do I have a boogie in my nose, or something?" I responded jokingly.

"I'm just imagining how you would look riding my dick, while I watch you in motion from the mirrored ceiling in my hotel suite, not too far from here. I've already gotten what I came here for. Why don't we ditch this party? There's no use in sticking around." He caressed my chin.

I didn't know if I should've been insulted, or embarrassed, because he'd read my mind. "Excuse me?" He nearly caused me to swoon when he smiled at me showcasing those dimples, but I couldn't allow that to distract me.

"You heard me," he said, not backing down.

Jordan was so narcissistic. So audacious. A winning combination that always got my fire lit, but I had to be responsible about this. "But I—this is my event." *Damn it!* I hate that I stammered giving him full advantage.

"Let your people handle it." Before I could make another attempt to stand my ground, Jordan was whisking me through the crowd, and toward the front of the mansion. I saw two of the ladies that were bickering earlier, still going at it by the grand double staircase at the entrance as we walked out.

He gave the valet the ticket to retrieve his car.

Was I was really about to leave my event—with a man I didn't know? I stood there debating with myself.

Chapter 2

*J*ust looking into his eyes, I knew I was headed wherever he was going. The valet pulled up in a sleek black Aston Martin One-77 and stopped in front of us. After being tipped, he ran over to help me open the door, and then closed it once I was seated inside of the lustrous beauty.

As we drove, Jordan was suddenly at a loss in the art of conversing, which was surprising after being so lively earlier. We rode in silence arriving in less than ten minutes later at the Ritz-Carlton.

After handing over his keys to yet another valet, Jordan walked me through the exquisitely decorated lobby that offered stunning, wide-sweeping vistas of Chicago's Magnificent Mile. When we got on the elevator, he used a special key to go to his floor.

The continuation of noncommunication was beginning to grate on my nerves, and irritate the hell out of me. "Where are we going?"

"If you have to ask, maybe I should go back and reintroduce myself to your desperate friend. Shelia, was it?" Jordan answered, while still staring straight ahead.

The elevator opened into the presidential suite, which featured two-story, floor-to-ceiling windows that offered views of the majestic Lake Michigan. There was also a media room and a spiral staircase that separated the bedrooms from the common areas. The setup practically mimicked the one in Dallas, save for the view of the lake. The skyline was breathtaking, as luminous lighting from the buildings played a part in the seductive scene sprawled before us.

Jordan pressed a button on the elevator which allowed it to stay open. Before I knew it, I was up against the wall being drowned in kisses, as his quick-witted hands roamed over my luscious derrière.

I broke away long enough to ask, "Damn, you're not wasting any time, are you?"

Instead of responding to my question, his hand roughly yanked my dress up, and tore off my lace thong. My clit was throbbing so hard, that I didn't give a damn if he completely ripped off my fifteen-hundred-dollar designer dress, just so long as he put out the fire.

His tongue thrust its way back into my mouth, drowning out my throaty moans. "You want this, don't you?" he breathlessly asked, once the kiss ended.

"Yeeesss," I replied as best I could.

He led me off of the elevator, before releasing it to go back down. We left a trail of clothing as we made our way inside of the penthouse. I stood with my back to the window as I watched Jordan, watch me. I gasped when my uncovered back and ass made contact against the cool windowpane. I hardly had time to catch my breath before he was upon me again with more kisses.

Everyone, including Special Agent Garza, hung on to my every word. A few of them had handkerchiefs dabbing at their foreheads. The room was a cool seventy-two degrees, per my request, which let me know the heat wasn't from the temperature, but their libidos.

"Are you getting this, Agent Garza?"

"Uh, yes. Yes. Yes. Go ... go on," he urged.

Now, what in the hell does my first fuck session with Jordan have to do with the information needed to capture him? Horny motherfuckers. I laughed to myself.

The lights reflected off of Lake Michigan, causing the water to sparkle like black diamonds in the night. Jordan wrapped my right leg around his waist, and plunged deep into my saturated pussy. I hoisted my other leg around him, with the goal of feeling every inch that he had to offer. Jordan held me tightly, and although I hadn't seen his dick, I knew it had to be glorious from the way it felt. Then reality hit me. We were having unprotected sex! I pushed back to unravel myself from around him, but—

The loud gasps coming from my captive audience in the room interrupted me. I stopped long enough to let them get ahold of themselves. One would have thought that these clowns had never got caught outside in the rain without a raincoat before, but then again ...

"Humph." I rolled my eyes and continued.

"No! No! We have to stop!" I regrettably said while still trying to get out of Jordan's grasp.

"No. Not now." Jordan never missed a beat. He did something spectacular that made his dick seemingly curve and hit my spot. Seeing that he had me, he finally let me out of the all-consuming Kung-Fu grip. We abandoned the scenic view the window provided, as he continued having his way with me until we toppled over onto the sofa. My tongue followed my body's lead as it snaked its way down his torso, and then finally arriving at his belly button.

He stood, taking me along with him as he hungrily devoured my breasts before kneeling to get a taste of heaven. He stared, admiring how wet I was for him. His fingers traced my swollen and beckoning lips before sliding them inside. The sounds my pussy made, and the whimpers escaping from me, propelled him in his mission. Jordan separated the moist milky folds of my vagina with his tongue taking turns wiggling it teasingly on my clit and thrusting it deep into my soaked canal.

"Mmm ... " he moaned as he enjoyed the sweet creamy treat he was rewarded with. For the finale, he showed his gentle side. He caressed my face adoringly, while staring deeply into my eyes. I wasn't trying to fall in love. I was just trying to fuck all night if possible.

Returning the favor, I took a little adventure of my own, and was surprised at how flawless, from the color, to the solidity, that his dick was. I licked around his shaft, sucking his balls one at a time before giving him some deep throat action. To get him off even more, I relaxed my throat muscles and began making vibrating noises as I fondled his balls and massaged his taut ass.

"Ah yes, suck that ... aww damn." Jordan held the top of my head with one hand. Once I felt that he was about to unload, I leaned onto the sofa and opened my treasure allowing him to go on an expedition.

Jordan stuck his finger inside, swirled it around, and then put it in his mouth. "Umm, you're so sweet and ready, but first. . ." He flipped me over and positioned me on my knees with my ass in his face. He licked my clit from behind.

I gripped the sofa nearly breaking a nail. "Ooh ... that's my spot!" I screamed. Before entering, he propped my right leg up on the back of the sofa, and eased his way in. Jordan held me firmly around my waist while I fingered my clit creating an intoxicating but stimulating feeling.

"UMMMMM, yes ... that ... feels ... soooo good!" I sang his praises.

Jordan spanked my ass. "I'mma tear … this cunt … up! Come on … work that … fat ass!" *Smack!* Jordan took his dick out momentarily and flipped me upside down.

"What the—"

Smack! Smack!

"Shut the fuck up and follow my lead!" Jordan commanded as the gentleman from a minute ago left the building and was replaced by a hoodlum. I obliged and ended up being power drilled into weak putty. The blood rushing to my head coupled with an orgasm was nothing short of amazing!

Agent Garza stopped recording. "Okay, Ms. Brooks, this sounds like an interesting story, but none of what you just told us can help build a case against The Tarantula."

"If you'd let my client continue, I'm sure you'd find that you could use some of what she has to say. Sexing women senseless is part of his MO; you even said as much yourself," Aliyah explained.

He shook his head surprisingly agreeing with Aliyah, and then pushed "play" on the recorder again. "All right, continue."

Chapter 3

The first time I had learned of Jordan's role in banking, we were at my house. We'd been making love as usual, but this time our passion was lacking the intensity that it normally had. The covers had lay crumpled, and pooled around us. Being saddled with ADD, I had become restless. The king-sized bed had made us seem even further apart, with the only sound coming from the tick-tock of the clock hanging on the wall. Something had to give.

I had sat up and turned on the lamp that was sitting on the nightstand. "Baby, what's the matter?"

He had done the same and faced me, placing my hands in his. "There are some things about me that you need to know, if we're to continue seeing each other."

I had pulled my hands away from his. "Oh, God. Please spare me the you're-married-and-how-your-wife-doesn't-satisfy-you-anymore-and-let-herself-go speech."

He had chuckled and shook his head. "No. It's nothing like that at all."

"What then? You're on the DL? On the run? Have another

woman? Baby mama drama? Live in your grandma's basement? Sick? What is it, Jordan?" I had searched his face frantically looking for answers.

He had drawn me close. "Baby, please, calm down, and listen to me."

I had taken deep, calculated breaths to steady myself for whatever he was about to disclose. "Okay. I'm listening. Now spill."

He had exhaled. "It's about the line of business that I'm in."

"I know, banking. What's the problem with that? It's a respectable business."

"Damn it, Bianca, could you please allow me to get out what I'm trying to say without any more interruptions?" Jordan had snapped.

I didn't mind his drill-sergeant behavior during sex, but the suspense while waiting on his big reveal had me feeling really anxious.

"I have a lot of unfinished business," he had admitted.

I had looked at him sideways. I didn't know what the hell this man was talking about, but I was all ears. "What do you need to finish, Jordan?"

"What I started," he'd said calmly.

I had jumped out of bed, breasts swinging in the wind, my nakedness exposed for the world to see, being that my terrace doors were wide open. I had yanked open my nightstand drawer, grabbed my Clonazepam pills, and downed two with no water. "Enough with the beating around the bush already; just tell me, damn it!"

He had taken a deep breath and blown it out slowly. "I'm into banking, but not in the capacity that you think I am. Before I go further, I need to know that I have your complete trust. Your loyalty has to be to me, if we're to go on."

I had exhaled unnecessarily loud. "Okay, if you want loyalty, I can be as loyal as a fucking dog, just as long as it doesn't get me killed."

He had turned on the charm and my pussy had started to

percolate at the sound of his melodious voice. His left eyebrow had arched mischievously when he'd noticed me squeezing my thighs together. It was something I did whenever I was trying to quell the yearning between my legs. "Now why would I put your sexy ass in harm's way?" he had asked as he leaned over to retrieve the edible oil from the nightstand that we'd given each other massages with earlier. I had watched as he poured some into his hand, and proceeded to stroke his massive rod into steel with it. His manhood had glistened like a bar of freshly polished gold, and damn if I wasn't one distracted bitch.

In my own little one-track-minded world, his member was behaving as if it were a cobra. His hand suddenly had become the basket it was hovering over, and he was the Pied Piper. Following his invisible commands, my hips had swayed from left to right as I had squeezed my breasts and let a moan escape my salacious lips. I had licked them to keep from drooling, but it was all a waste of time. The sounds coming from the imaginary pipe had been so intoxicating and too harmonious for me to ignore. The only thing I could think about was taming the snake that was charming me relentlessly. I had glided over to the bed and kissed my way up his thighs. As soon as my mouth was about to make contact with its intended target, he had pulled back.

"No more of this until you listen."

I had immediately sat up, pouty lips whining. "But baby."

He'd had seriousness in his eyes that I'd never seen before. "Bianca, this is important. I need you to show me that you'll remain loyal, regardless of the situation."

Still in character, I had continued on with my charade. "Whatever you say, daddy, but just so you know, I've been a naughty, naughty girl. I can be really good, though ... if you give me my candy cane." I'd twirled my hair around my finger and behaved like a spoiled little brat. When it had looked as if he were relenting, I'd attempted to fill my mouth with his rock-hard sweetness again. No sooner than I'd made contact, he'd pushed me and I nearly fell off of the bed. As graceful as a cat, I'd caught my balance and recovered just as quickly.

"Jordan, that was highly uncalled for!"

His demeanor had gone from menacing to caring within five seconds flat. "Come here, baby."

I had gone to him obeying his command when he'd patted his lap. I'd climbed on the bed and straddled him. When he'd eased himself inside filling me up with his pleasure pole, I had liked to have passed out, it felt so right. Jordan had gotten me to where I was about to cum, and abruptly had stopped.

"Jordan!"

"Now listen to me," he'd said, easing himself in and out at an agonizingly slow pace, driving me further down the road of insanity. "I have a friend that's in the banking industry, and we have a very lucrative side business. I need you to set up accounts in the Cayman Islands and Switzerland in your name."

I had stopped grinding my hips and looked Jordan in the eyes. "Why do you need me, and who is this associate?"

He'd stopped pumping and gave me a you're-asking-for-too-much look. "That's more than you need to know at this time."

"The hell it is if you want me to get accounts in my name." I had tried to get up, but he'd held me in place and started back to working me over.

Continuous strokes had been used to coerce me into doing something that I was totally against. "Come on, I need you, Bianca."

"And I need my ... I've ... ooh shit. . . lived this long without ... umm ... without going to jail ... and I'll be damned if I let someone else p-p-p ... put me there."

Jordan had plowed deeper still, and moaned in delight for what we were creating.

"Oh, babe ... that feels sooo ... good." I had rotated my hips in a circular motion trying to get the orgasm that was about to peak.

"Damn, girl, your pussy is soaking wet." Jordan had drawn in deep breaths, pounding me nearly into a state of unconsciousness. When it was getting to be too much, he'd pulled out.

"Joooordan!" I had panted from frustration. Trying to catch my breath, all while trying to control the urge to stab him in his left eyeball with the pair of scissors that was sitting on my nightstand, had become a tough task. "Damn, why do you keep doing this to me?"

After he had forced me off of him and gotten out of the bed, he'd made his way into the bathroom. "Until I get what I want ... ," he'd gripped that succulent shaft of his, and shaken it in my direction like it was a ruler, "... to hell with satisfying you with this dick."

I had sat in disbelief as I heard water running. Still needing to be satisfied, I'd reached over and pulled my vibrator out of the nightstand to finish the job. I had hit the power button, and nothing. I had shaken it, tried again, and still nothing. Finally, I had opened the back of the toy and discovered that the batteries were gone. "What the—?" I had searched through the drawer and couldn't find any spare batteries. The shower had turned off, and I couldn't have cared less if he'd caught me with my B.O.B. I needed those damned batteries yesterday!

The bathroom door had opened and steam billowed out. "Looking for these?" Jordan had tossed the batteries I'd been looking for into the trashcan. He was naked and dripping water all over my fucking white-as-snow rug.

Livid couldn't have described what I was feeling. "Jordan, we need to talk."

"Of course we *needed* to talk, but now I have other things to do," he'd said as he'd dried off and slipped back into his clothes.

"Things like what?"

"That's none of your damned business, Bianca." Jordan had walked out of my room, leaving me in a bad place.

"So, you didn't learn anything about his connections? Is that what you're telling me, Ms. Brooks?" Agent Garza demanded to know.

"If you'll let Ms. Brooks gather herself, and finish without interrupting, you'll get whatever information you're looking for, *Special Agent in Charge,*" my attorney said, mocking his title as she spoke on my behalf for the second time.

Chapter 4

That was not the last time we saw each other, but I sure thought it was. Jordan didn't come around for a couple of weeks. He didn't return any of the numerous texts, or phone calls that I'd made trying to reach out to him. So instead, I threw myself into my business. I worked like a madwoman trying to forget the way his hands burned my skin whenever they touched me, but it was useless. Usually, being in seclusion behind the glass doors of my glitzy and very feminine-designed office did wonders for my psyche. However, this time around, the mirrored desk that I just had to have due to the touch of glamour and elegance that it provided made me ill. I could see how despondent I looked in my reflection. The wingback, purple-velvet guest chairs had me wishing that Jordan was sitting in one with me riding him like so many times before. Was it the left chair, or the right chair, the last time? Hmm ... whichever it was, we'd had a hell of a time in it.

Looking above my head into the lights of the chandelier brought back memories from our first encounter at the Ritz. The lovely lavender-gray-colored walls that I loved were now making me feel gloomy. The charcoal sheer window treatments reminded me of the negligée that I'd worn for him to celebrate our one-month anniversary. Fresh flowers that were meant to add life to the room sitting in the beautiful crystal vases reminded me of a funeral. Oh my God, I was one pathetic chick. There was no use in denying it; my addiction to this man was unlike anything that I'd ever experienced in my life.

Suddenly, the black-and-glass French doors to my office swung open. Of course I couldn't wallow in self-pity for too long with my best friends-slash employees being anywhere within a 500-mile radius, especially with their offices being just down the hall from mine.

"Girl, get over it! Another dick will come along that'll be just as good. Hunty, Jordan will be a distant memory in no time. Trust me, I've been there, done that, and got a T-shirt to remind me not to ever go there again." Cody sashayed his way in with his luxurious hair that he prided himself on. It whipped behind him while he held a magazine. I was sure it was about fashion since he was a true clothes whore.

"I know, but it's more than that. We've connected on so many levels that go way beyond just sex."

"Chile, good dick will leave you confused as hell. Take it from a bitch who knows," Reggie threw in as he sat in one of the chairs that I was just daydreaming about riding Jordan on only seconds ago.

"Okay!" Cody cosigned Reggie with a high-five. "I bet you won't catch this diva, going through behind some dick." Cody threw the *Vogue* magazine he'd been reading on my desk. On the cover was supermodel Giovanna, wearing a gorgeous red gown.

"Now *she* is all that." Reggie eyed the cover hungrily. "No offense, Bianca, but if I could come back as any bitch, it would definitely be Giovanna, hunty."

Cody snatched the magazine from Reggie's hands before he

could pick it up. "Naw bitch, you said you would want to come back as Beyoncé! I'm the one who said I would come back as Giovanna!"

While they argued over foolishness, I gathered my purse and keys from my desk, and logged off of my custom, blinged-out MacBook with the company's logo encrusted in pink and purple Swarovski crystals. "Who in the fuck cares about Giovanna's love life? I sure as hell don't. You all are fussing over who'll come back as her, like she's the second coming or something. Anyway, I'll check back in with you all later."

"She is!" they both shouted in unison.

I shook my head knowing that it was a lost cause to argue with them over something as stupid as being reincarnated as their favorite diva. I left them and the conversation as I made a beeline for the door. Of course, they stood and followed me out into the lobby. I walked as fast as my six-inch stilettos would allow without breaking my neck. The idea was to get away from them, but they had me beat easily by a mile.

Cody stopped in front of me and placed his hands on his slender hips. "If you want us to shoot by once we're finished here, give us a ring, girl."

"Yes, hunty, you know we don't mind being a shoulder to cry on over a good bottle of wine and some takeout. You know how we do!" Reggie called after me as I sidestepped Cody, and continued on my way hoping that they would take the hint that I didn't want to be bothered.

I sat with my left hand gripping the steering wheel of my Range Rover as if my next breath depended on it. My right hand held on firmly to the vibrator as it hummed against my clit. My eyes rolled to the back of my head as I was nearing what I hoped would be a satisfying climax. "Ooh yes! Umm! Ooh ..." No sooner than I was almost there, I jerked a little and lost the spot. "Fuck … this!" The droning sounds continued after I took my frustrations out on the toy, threw it in the passenger seat before it bounced and fell on the floor.

I softly banged my head against the steering wheel aggravated with myself. Who was I fooling? I thought about how Jordan had left me hanging, as though I meant nothing to him. "Who the hell does he think he is that he can interrupt my life like this?" I screamed to no one in particular.

An abrupt knock on the window nearly gave me a heart attack. "Shit!" My hands flew to my chest as if to catch my reckless, beating heart.

"Oh shit … my bad," he said, letting on that I wasn't the only one traumatized.

Quickly recovering, and realizing that the baritone voice didn't belong to Cody, or Reggie, I stared into some of the prettiest yet familiar gray eyes attached to a *le beau* ideal, standing right before me. "Fuck!" I mumbled more to myself than I did my intruder. I hurriedly pulled my skirt down, and tried to make myself decent before cracking the window open. "Yes?" I asked with attitude. Although, I was wishing that he would fuck the shit out of me on the hood of my Range. Or, at the very least, he could bend me over in front of it and take me from behind. In other words, if he were here to satisfy my raging lust, then, and only then, would he graduate from persona non grata to *hello, daddy*.

His eyes immediately went from mine to the passenger side, before landing on the floor where my sex toy continued to buzz. "Sorry, to have startled you, but I'm sure you'll find the reason for my impromptu visit to be very beneficial."

Anyone else would've been ashamed that they were caught masturbating in their car, of all places, but that was them, and this was me. I wasn't a least bit embarrassed. I leaned over and picked up the toy, turned it off, and threw it in the backseat where it landed with a thud. "Sure, but make it quick. As you can see, I have things to do."

"Oh yeah, I can *definitely* see that." I watched as he walked his sexy ass over to the passenger side and got in. He had his say, which turned out to be very beneficial, and left me his card. Before getting out, he had one more thing to say, that also proved to be advantageous given my current situation. "Now that you have my numbers, you can call me *anytime*, for *anything*, especially when you get tired of Bob."

A dubious and dumbstruck expression was the look I wore on my face. "Who in the hell is Bob?"

He chuckled, showcasing a set of beautiful teeth before answering. "Oh, you know him, and very well, I might add." The mocking and accusatory tone in his voice was beginning to grate on my nerves. "Bob is your battery-operated boyfriend that's been relegated to backseat riding." He laughed. "Remember...," he said before getting out of my car, "you'd rather have me be with you, than against you." He got out of the car, straightened the jacket of the sexy tailor-made suit that hugged his body deliciously, winked, and left me alone with nasty ideas that featured him. I watched as he strutted off. He had a come-hither gait like Denzel Washington, and President Obama, that was full of confidence, very macho, and I'm sure along with everything that was him, got him more ass than a toilet seat.

I looked at my "B.O.B." laying in the backseat and laughed. I started my car and drove home wondering whom to call that could give me some serious inches. My unexpected visitor, I was certain, was more than capable of finishing the job that I'd started. Of that I was sure, but with him, I needed to tread lightly. Then my neighbor, Brandon, came to mind instantly bringing a smile to my face. Just the thought of him had my foot mashing the gas to get there faster.

Once I made it home and looked across the street, I saw his girlfriend's Mercedes sitting in the driveway. I suddenly wanted to throw a brick through that slut's window. "Ugh! Share the dick, bitch!" I screamed in the direction of his house, and stormed toward my own.

I struggled with my keys trying to unlock the front door. They fell a few times, but I managed to finally get in. I dropped everything on the way to the bedroom, trying to get to my little black book. I had to have some dick before I hurt some damned body. My target was none other than that egomaniac son of a bitch, Jordan.

I almost had a heart attack upon entering into my bedroom and seeing a naked man. He was lying on my bed, but his dick was standing at full attention. I had to rub my eyes to see if it was a mirage, or just maybe I'd finally lost my damned mind.

"Are you going to come in here, or just stand there gawking?" Jordan stroked himself and I could've sworn drool escaped my mouth, and dribbled down my chin.

The pent-up anger I had from not being able to go over to Brandon's, and then, the parking lot incident, all vanished when I zeroed in on the object of my desire. His dick was erect, colossal, glistening, and calling my name. *Bianca. Biancaaaa* ... it beckoned. It was as if I were being transported telepathically. I literally glided across the room before coming to a stop and dropping down to my knees. I inhaled deeply, capturing his masculine scent. No words were spoken nor needed. I spread his thighs apart, snuggled between them comfortably, and let my tongue do the talking. I sucked in both balls in one effortless swoop. I juggled them in my mouth before licking the base of his dick, and taking all of him in.

Allowing his length to hit the back of my tonsils turned me on even more.

"Ooh, baby. Umm, I missed you. Missed you so much" was his husky response to the pleasure I was giving him.

Jordan bit his bottom lip while caressing my head as I went deep throat dicking. His phallus slid down my esophagus with ease. He knew that he was now in the mouth of a master. His hips thrust faster as he marveled at my superb gag reflexes.

"Shh ... you're good, bae. Yeah, suck that shit ... just like that," he said as he rotated his hips. "Ooh, yeah ... that throat feel good, bae." His toes popped as his grip on my head made my eyes turn Chinese. In no time flat, I had Jordan spurting like the fountains at the Bellagio in Las Vegas. I watched in amazement, because his streams were just as magical.

"Damn, you're so fucking beautiful. I must've been on something serious to be able to walk out on you and that salacious mouth." Jordan's voice was raspy. His chest rose and fell with each deep breath he took, which only made me even hotter. I was still tripping about him being in my bed, especially since I didn't recall seeing his car outside, or giving him a key to my place.

But none of that mattered. I was going to take full advantage of the moment. "I'm sorry, for making what you needed seem unimportant. Everything about you is ... very ... important to me. Everything, Jordan. Whatever, you need ... me to do ... I'll do. Just don't ... leave ... me again," I said between planting kisses on his sweet dick.

It seemed as if that were music to his ears. His eyes became even tighter as he busted another delicious nut.

After he recovered from my ravenous mouth wolfing him down again, he came serious. "Are you sure you're ready to get involved with me one hundred percent?"

My eyes connected with his. "Yes, I was about to lose my mind trying to find a substitute of you."

Jordan pulled me from between his legs and into his embrace. "A substitute?" He laughed. "Girl, you bet not be giving my pussy away to anybody."

I held on to him tighter when he made claim to my body being his. Everything at that moment was so right. Until he ruined it.

"I'm a cat burglar. Well, more like a multifaceted thief," he said out of nowhere.

I jumped back and looked at him as if he were crazy. "What did you just say to me?"

Jordan laughed. "Not in the traditional sense." He pulled me back into his arms. "I have an inside connection with a lot of the big boys in the industry. We have an alliance. You see, we all make money through the banks and then stash it in overseas accounts. But, I have other associations with people that specialize in high-end commodities, like cars, art, and jewelry, etcetera. You name it, and more than likely, I've dabbled in it. "

"Which is why you want me to get accounts in the Caymans, and Switzerland?"

He patted the top of my head like I was a kid being rewarded. "That's my girl. You catch on quickly."

As much as I wanted to be with him, I couldn't throw caution to the wind. "Jordan, I have worked my ass off to establish what I have. I can't afford to get caught up, not now anyway."

Jordan ignored what I said and explained the way things worked in his world. "I use key loggers to capture passwords and to gain access into the accounts of corporations and individuals. Once I manipulate their proxy, and or stateful inspection firewalls, I create dummy accounts. I'm able to do this with the assistance of my inside connections. After breaching, I transfer the money I take into offshore accounts. I never keep any starter account active over forty-eight hours, and I never take from the poor. Only the fat cats." He laughed.

I had to get up. This fool was crazy. How did I know he wasn't setting me up to take the fall?

"Bae, look, let me explain what it is that I do." He took my hand trying to urge me back into his embrace.

I reluctantly took a seat next to him on the bed, so that I wouldn't be sidetracked by the feel of his skin against mine. "Please do."

"With the help of key loggers, I can copy keystrokes for passwords, etcetera. Once I have that information downloaded, I gain access into the systems. I need key loggers because passwords, and or security measures, are ever changing. So, even if they change security passcodes every day, I can still breach. Once I'm in, I can do or take anything I want undetected, but the window for that is small. Armed with the information that has been passed on to me, within a matter of minutes, I can create a replica and work it at my leisure. Once I find all I need to know about their encryptions, and modes of security, I then make my move."

"So, let me get this straight: you're a thief and you want *me* to set up an account in *my* name, for the feds to come knocking down *my* door. Am I reading you correct?"

Jordan attempted to pull me toward him again. I cringed at his touch. "Bianca, I wouldn't do that to you."

"I have worked too damned hard to let some dick—." I exhaled a deep breath. "... as good as it may be—I can't allow you to destroy my life, Jordan. I don't know what you were seeking that night at the gala, but if it was a weak woman, you picked the wrong one."

Jordan brought his hands up to his face and respired. "By the time they realize something's up, the money's long gone and the account is extracted from their records and tapes without a trace. Like I said, I have inside connections."

"I ... I can't—how did you get into this line of business anyway?"

"It's a long story, but I'll give you the short version. Before moving to the States, my father was heavy into gambling, which is part of the reason for us coming here. Anyway, from that ruthless world, he met a lot of people, but developed a friendship beyond gambling with these two cousins that were caught up in the 1983 New York Lottery scandal. The cousins, along with a relatively famous man in New York, who was accused of being the mastermind, set into motion what has become the Numbers Game. What the authorities never found out was that my father was the real mastermind behind the scam. Once he learned the role the cousins played in the lottery, he said it was a no-brainer on how to steal the largest jackpot at that time. The plan was to make it look as though the winner had a stroke of good luck on his side. They plotted to rig the daily number, a three-digit game the New York Lottery offered at the time. The cousins owned the vending company that supplied the machines that the numbers were picked from. All of the balls except threes, and nines, were weighted. This was a sure way that the drawing was almost sure to be a combination of only threes and nines, and it worked. According to the media, it was the unusual betting patterns that alerted authorities to the possible scam. My father believed it was someone that one of the three trusted who blew the whistle. Luckily, for my father, he never met with anyone, but the cousins, and used an alias in order to keep his real identity hidden. That story fascinated me in ways that I can't begin to explain. As a result, I've researched heists and bank robberies, but more importantly, how they got caught. I wanted to best the old man. Unfortunately, he never got to see me become the clever and always elusive man that I am today."

"I was just starting my career as a rookie at the time, but I remember the Numbers Game. Who would've thought that Jordan Lei was connected to it via good ole pops? Wow. I tell ya, the fruit sure don't fall far from the tree," Agent Garza belted out and scratched his head in wonder.

Aliyah rolled her eyes heavenward at Agent Garza's interruption, and gave me the nod to continue.

I didn't know how to respond to Jordan's reveal. I was raised to believe that it was hard work that got you the rewards. "I want to relate, but I can't seem to find a way that I can."

"That's the beauty of it, Bianca! I don't want you to relate, but participate without really participating at all."

I took a deep breath trying to take in what he was asking. I knew if I answered wrong, that I could lose him, and I didn't want that. I was facing a catch-22—damned if I did, and damned if I didn't situation. "But, why use my real identity?"

"Everything has to check out with identification systems. You'll have offshore accounts where the States won't have any jurisdiction. You'll be fine. Trust me."

I got up and peered out of the window. "Who else?"

"Who else what?" he questioned.

"Damn it!" I turned to face him. "Who else is in on this operation that you're running?"

"I have my associates," Jordan damn near mumbled.

I stared at him long and hard. "Your associates?" I laughed. "Is Jordan Lei even your real name?"

Jordan got off of the bed and walked over to where I was now standing and taking in the view. "Please, allow me to reintroduce myself. I'm Jordan Lei. I make my living by robbing banks, high-end art galleries, stocks, bonds, and other ventures that I find to be very lucrative."

I chuckled lightly at the audacity of this man. "So, you're like what, a modern-day Robin Hood, or something? Better yet, are you going to rob me too, Jordan?"

He turned me so that I was facing him again. "I'm also the man that makes you scream out my name—" kiss "... shudder at the thought of me—" kiss "... have wet fantasies while in your meetings—" kiss "... can't sleep or eat when I'm not around—" caresses my arms "... I'm the man that can satisfy your every desire like no other—" kiss on the forehead. "... because you throw caution to the wind just to be near me." His hand softly traveled up my leg and rested on my pleasure button.

A soft moan escaped my lips. "Ooh ... "

" ... I'm also the man that drives you insane just from a simple touch or whisper in your ear—" Kissed me. " ... my breath on your neck causes you to cream with anticipation of what I'll do to you next—" Kissed me. "... I'm the man that causes your body to respond to me involuntarily, directly or indirectly—" Licked on the nape of my neck, followed by a kiss and sucking combination that I was sure left a passion mark behind. " ... I'm the man that can fix whatever ails you just by looking at you, arouse your intellect, and satisfy all of your desires—" Deep, hungry French kissed me. " ... Bianca, I'm *your* man. I'll never put you in harm's way." Caressed my cheek. " ... I'll protect you like I would the most precious of diamonds." Knelt in front of me. " ... Bianca, you're the rarest of any jewel that I've ever taken—" Pushed me up against the window. "Trust me, bae." Kiss. "Believe in me." He placed my leg on his shoulder and rubbed my kitty until she was purring. "Look at you, just as wet as you can be." Inserted one, two, and then finally three of his fingers and stroked me slowly. "You want me, don't you, baby? Don't be shy now. Go ahead and admit it. You want to give in to me, don't you?"

I didn't respond, but he took my quivering and wetness as his answer. "Don't fight it." He blew warm air on my pleasure button causing it to stiffen and stick out even more. "Just let it be," he said before removing his fingers and devouring me ferociously.

"Oh, Jordan. I'll do it!" He caught my pearl and suckled on it gently causing me to shudder. "Got damn it, I'll do it!" I felt myself drifting into oblivion. This wasn't about an orgasm, but about having a lowdown to the nastiest of pornographic desires fulfilled.

Jordan stood with me still riding his face. My back pressed against the cool windowpane receiving all that he had to give with me being the main course.

Chapter 5

I lay spent in Jordan's arms. No words were needed for what I was feeling. I would do just about anything for that man, as long as he kept doing what he did so well to me.

"So, where do we go from here?"

Jordan patted me on the arm so he could get up. He walked out of the room, and returned a few minutes later with bottled drinks and his laptop. "Okay, this is what's next." He rubbed both of his hands together in anticipation of his latest coup ... me.

Jordan set up three bank accounts over the Internet with my information. He said that way I could deny any knowledge of the accounts since they never would have seen my face, or have me on video coming into their establishments. He also reassured me that the IP address being used couldn't be traced, since it was being bounced off numerous towers all over the country.

"Okay, we're all set," he said as he leaned over and kissed my nervous mouth.

I watched as Jordan wrote down information that he obtained from my accounts. He then logged on to Wrotham International, an investment firm, and accessed different portfolios of individuals and corporations that he had listed on some electronic device. He connected it to one of the portals in his computer. Once he got into the portfolio, he would enter in a sequence of numbers that scrolled through accounts. The numbers were moving so fast, that I couldn't keep up if I tried. Jordan wrote down information frantically. I couldn't understand what he was doing, but I did understand the dollar amounts he was transferring over into the accounts he'd gotten in my name. He looked at me and smiled.

"And to think, I'm only taking a small percent of what his account is actually worth. This money won't be missed, at least not for a while, anyway. I've studied his spending habits, thanks to Jim Reynolds, one of my insiders at Kingdom Bank."

"Jim Reynolds?" asked.

"Yes, good ole Jimmy. He's one of my go-to people. Good thing is, he has just as much to lose as I do. Being that you also have just as much to lose, it would behoove you not to go getting any ideas in that pretty little head of yours." He slapped the side of my thigh. "Capisce?"

My head snapped around nearly causing me whiplash. "Excuse me?"

"I have a lot on the line here, Bianca, and I can't have you, or anybody for that matter, going soft on me. So, yes, you are my lady, but I don't love anyone more than I love Jordan Lei." He pointed his finger at his chest.

"What happened to you're my woman and 'I'll never put you in harm's way,' Jordan? Like you said, I have a lot at stake."

Jordan never looked up from the computer. "Sure you do, which is why I know you're going to be a good girl, and keep your fucking mouth shut." He then leaned in and kissed me before I could pull away. "Rule number one, Bianca: never do dirt with anyone, who doesn't have anything to lose." He looked at me and winked. "Relax, sexy, we're a team now. I wouldn't do anything to hurt you as long as you do the same by me. We're going to be like Bonnie and Clyde, but don't worry; our story won't end in a hell storm of bullets like theirs did." I sat staring at the man that just rocked my world and turned me into a white-collar criminal all within an hour. Was I that desperate to have Jordan's touch, that I was willing to risk it all? I answered that question immediately. *Yes, I was.*

Jordan did a few more transactions and closed the computer. "Jim will have all of the information for the transfers tomorrow. Your account with Kingdom is done."

My curiosity got the best of me. "How much did you put into that account?"

He showed me the figures from each account he took from at Wrotham International. The number floored me.

"Oh my God!" I blinked rapidly. "Who? What—"

"Calm down, bae." He laughed, and I can only imagine why with the way my mouth was hanging open. "It's ours, well, except for Jim's cut."

"So, what does that leave me?"

"Thirty-four percent. For this one, I'm even willing to split the pie equally, and since the accounts are in your name, you should get the extra piece."

I was still trying to digest what he'd just told me. "When can I get my cut?"

"As soon as we move it to Switzerland."

"How?" I had to swallow the golf ball-size lump that had formed in my throat. "How long will that take?"

"Don't worry. It will be sooner than you think. Maybe even tomorrow. Better yet, I can have Jim to arrange a cash payment to you," he assured me.

I grabbed the drink he'd brought in, and gulped it. The burn from the unexpected alcohol surprised me. I looked at it before asking, "What was that?"

"Pineapple juice, with plenty of rum." Jordan unplugged the laptop and put it away.

Then it all hit me just as hard as the unexpected rum did. "Oh, my God, I'm rich! I can't believe it!" I jumped for joy and laughed till my head hurt. I dived into Jordan, who fell back onto the bed with his arms wrapped around me.

"It's overrated. Being a millionaire, that is. Sure, you can buy anything you desire, but once you've done that, the thrill is gone. It's just a means to a never-ending cycle of want, and before long, becomes about ego."

I stopped laughing long enough to become serious. "So, how long have you been a part of the millionaire's club?"

"I was sort of born into it."

That halted me for a minute. "But I thought—I don't understand?"

Jordan sat up with me still straddling him. "My father lost it all to gambling and drinking. I saw my mother go from socialite to a has-been when my father lost the family's textile dynasty. Being exiled killed her—literally. It was bad enough that she had to fight for her position and respect, but once my father lost everything, all fingers pointed to her. Let it be told, she was the reason, even though my father was notorious for his gambling habit long before ever meeting my mother."

Jordan's eyes filled with tears, but they never fell. I could see anger in them that was no longer hidden. "You blame your father for your mother's death?"

He dabbed at his eyes and sniffed loudly. "You damn right I do. He was a dreamer when he didn't have to be. He had everything at his disposal the day he was born. At the time, my mother had just discovered that she was pregnant with me, when they had to flee to the U.S. as a result of his gambling."

I embraced Jordan when his anger became too much. He held me tightly and continued to never let a tear fall. Instead, he made love to me for the rest of the night. The good sense that God, and my parents, gave me, fled as I took pleasure in the moment. Everything in me was screaming that something wasn't right with his story, but at that moment, I didn't give a damn.

After that, Jordan convinced me to open up numerous accounts, all in my name. I lost count after a while. I was so into the loving, and the added bonus of money, that I would've done just about anything to make him happy.

"I have someone I'd like for you to meet," Jordan said one late night while we were having dinner out on my terrace.

I dabbed at the corners or my mouth, and placed the napkin down next to my plate. "Oh, really? Who?" I asked before taking a sip of wine.

He threw his napkin on his plate, and pushed back from the table. "In due time," he threw over his shoulder as he left me out on the terrace. When I heard my alarm beep, signaling that Jordan had opened the door, I ran to catch up with him.

It was close to midnight as we drove to a Kingdom Bank located in downtown Dallas. No one was there, and strangely enough, not even security. Jordan had an access badge that he used to let himself in with. We were met in the lobby by Jim Reynolds whom he had been telling me about. Jim ranked high in authority at the bank, and made it known that by the time he was finished with the business he and Jordan had, that he would soon be president. He was trying to set up the current regional director to take the fall for his misdeeds.

"Jordan! Glad you could pull in some more accounts." They shook hands, and clapped each other on the back as we walked to his office. "Here are the papers confirming our transactions from Switzerland, Caymans, China, Australia and Paris."

Jordan took a seat at Jim's desk, while looking over the documents with a keen eye. "Everything appears to be in order." Jordan then placed the papers into his briefcase. "What about the dormant accounts?"

"Like taking candy from a baby." Both Jim and Jordan laughed heartily.

Jim sized me up, and from the glint in his eyes, I could tell that he approved. "So, are you and this beautiful lady taking a *vacation* anytime soon?"

Jordan looked over at me and smiled. "We haven't discussed a *vacation*, but I would love to see her on the white sands of Anguilla, looking sexy in a two-piece of the same color while sipping on something sweet. In short, I think I've finally found the one, Jim." He winked, and I blushed like a teenager in love for the first time. It was to the point that I couldn't contain my smile. Then again, that was only part of Jordan's charm.

"I think you've made a wise decision, but one will never know fully until after a *vacation*." Jim finally took his eyes off of me long enough to voice his stamp of approval ... I thought.

They talked for a few more minutes before Jim became serious. "That ever-present thorn in my side, Chante Michaels bitch, is starting to use her brain."

"Whatever gave her a reason to, after all of this time?" Jordan questioned.

Jim exhaled and leaned back in his chair. "I suspended Chad Wertheimer, and penned the missing money from the dormant accounts on him. I wanted to send his father a message, since he wanted to stall us out on the Wall Street matter."

Jordan irately sprung up from his seat, and got in Jim's face. "This shit was supposed to fly under the fucking radar! I told you, leave Wertheimer to me." Jordan paced back and forth. I could see worry etched on his face for the first time.

"But, I thought with a little fire—"

Jordan shut him up abruptly. "Until the auditing of the dormant accounts, you had better pray that nothing is uncovered, or the Wertheimer situation won't be the only thing that I have handled."

"And I promise you, nothing will be. I just went with the assumption that using his son would speed things along." Jim moved to the far side of the room to be out of Jordan's reach. "Anyway, the matter is now under investigation, but don't worry!" Jim raised his hands in surrender. "I have everything under control. They can launch all of the investigations in the world, but money talks, and bullshit walks," Jim stated with much audacity from his safe haven. From the looks of it, he and I both knew that Jordan was about to go nuclear.

After a few intense moments of silence, Jordan surprised us both when he snapped his fingers at me signaling our departure. "You just better make damn sure you do. I'm not going down because of your fucking stupidity."

"Don't worry, I got everything under control. Seriously, I do," Jim said, hoping to quell Jordan's temper.

"I'm not worried, but you, on the other hand, should be." With that, we walked out.

Agent Garza stopped the tape. "So, you've actually been in the presence of Jordan and Jim Reynolds together conspiring?"

I took a sip from my glass of iced water. "Yes, I met him on a few occasions."

"We have Mr. Reynolds, Mr. Pringley, along with some of the other board members from Kingdom, in custody awaiting trial.

I'll have some photos for you to view later. Hopefully, you'll recognize some of these men as coconspirators. With Sherman Val Easterman dead, the only piece of the puzzle missing is Jordan Lei, The Tarantula," Agent Garza made known.

I cringed at that name. "Could we not call him that, please? It's bad enough that I'm giving you information that's probably going to get him locked up for the rest of his life."

"I'll try to remember that," he responded halfheartedly while wearing a smug smile on his beefy flushed face.

I continued on with my story wondering if I was doing the right thing.

Chapter 6

"Bae, how does it feel having the world at your fingertips?" Jordan asked as he drove his latest high-end luxury car, a red Bugatti Super Sport, along the George Bush Turnpike. Looking straight ahead, I answered, "Kind of scary, to be honest."

"Is it because of the way we're obtaining the money?" he asked as he zipped along passing cars.

I took a moment to answer as I ran my fingers across the cool onyx, Louis Vuitton Calypso GM messenger bag that I was holding. "Yes, and I'm afraid that we're going to get caught."

"Never that. Besides, they have nothing on you."

I looked out the window. The images become a blur just as fast as they materialized. "What about the accounts in my name?"

Jordan caressed the side of my face. "What accounts?"

"You know the ones with—"

Jordan briefly placed his finger up to my lips. "Shh ... those, my dear, have been purged."

My mood suddenly took an upswing. "As if they never existed?"

"Exactly. Like I told you, once they have served their purpose, good as gone, thanks to my connects."

I breathed a sigh of relief. "So, when do you think it'll be safe to move my money back to the States?"

"The thing is, we have Uncle Sam to contend with here. You have to be able to account for everything that's over ten grand in your account. You can do with it as you like; just be mindful of how you move with it."

I turned, so that I was looking at his handsome profile. "Trust me, I know all about Uncle Sam, but I have my own business. That should account for something."

He took his eyes off the road for a brief second when he looked over at me. "Can your business justify the amount you have sitting over in the Caymans? Let's not even start with the others you've acquired."

Sighing deeply, I wondered if I would ever get my money all in one place. Having to do wire transactions all the time made me nervous. Even though, Jim had assured me that as long as I used his bank, I would be fine. "I can't say that it does."

"Maybe you should consider relocating with me. I'm retiring after this. I hadn't decided on where yet, but when I do, it'll be in a place where I don't have to worry about being extradited back to the States."

We exited the toll and came to a stop at a red light. A woman with a stroller was crossing the street in front of us. Looking at her got me to thinking about what was important. "Sounds tempting, but I have a business, and people depending on me."

"Who says you can't run your business from wherever you are? Or, better yet, give it to your friends as a token of your appreciation," Jordan explained as the light turned green and we took off at lightning speed.

My life consisted on me making everyone else happy. Maybe it was time that I looked out for me, for a change. "Okay, I'll give it some thought." But then my conscience kicked in. Here I was, really considering his proposal to fulfill his dream, while giving up on mine.

Jordan pulled into a bank parking lot. "Good, wouldn't want to start my new life without you by my side."

I looked around puzzled. "Why are we here?"

"Oh, I have a brief meeting. It'll only take a few minutes if you don't mind waiting in the car." Jordan grabbed the onyx messenger bag from my lap, put his shades on, slid out of the car and headed inside of a Texans Mutual bank.

Before I could even sort through my thoughts good, Jordan was headed back out with a different messenger bag.

He leaned over and gave me a kiss as he got back inside of the car. "I told you that I would only be a few minutes."

I only smiled in response. I knew something was up; he was too chipper. Jordan rarely displayed that side of him, unless he wanted something.

He traced his fingers along my lips until a smile emerged upon them. "I have a proposition for you."

Even though I knew something was coming down the pike, I still had a queasy feeling that it had a lot to do with whatever it was that he was about to proposition. "What is it, Jordan?" I answered with an unsure tone to my voice.

"I have a business dinner tonight with some major players from Spain, and I need for you to run a little interference for me."

I turned completely around so that I was facing Jordan. "What *kind* of interference, Jordan?" I responded dryly.

He took hold of my hands. "I want you to work your magic on them. If it leads to more, then I want you to oblige."

I snatched my hands away quickly, and the queasy feeling only intensified. "I am not a prostitute, Jordan!"

His demeanor, and the look on his face, was as if he'd just asked me to contribute a cake to the local bake sale that the church was having. "I never said you were, but you are the best, and I know we can come out on top, no pun intended, if you went along." He chuckled.

"Hire some strippers." I unbuckled my seatbelt and attempted to get out the car, but he caught my arm. "You had better let me go before I act a fucking fool," I demanded in an authoritative tone.

He leaned over me and opened the door. "Gon' then. Get the fuck out!"

Then I thought about my car not being there, and not wanting to call Cody, or Reggie, to drive way out to Plano. They despised that high-ass George Bush tollway. I closed the car door, and buckled myself back in. "Just take me home ... now!"

Jordan sped out of the bank's parking lot. We rode the forty-minute drive in silence until he got to my cul-de-sac. "All right, you're home; now get the fuck out of my car and forget you ever met me."

I sat looking at him in disbelief. "After all that I've done for you, really?"

He drew in some air and then exhaled it slowly as if he were trying to calm himself down. "You said you were down for me, but every time I ask anything of you, there's a problem, Bianca. What the fuck, huh?"

The insolence of his suggestion, the arrogance dripping from each of his insulting words, and the overall tactlessness had me wanting to rip his head clean off of his thick-ass neck. "But you want me to act as a whore, Jordan. *A whore!*" I emphasized in case he wasn't getting my gist. "Who would ask their woman to do such a thing?"

Jordan's eyes squinted as more inconsiderate words left his contemptuous lips. "Every man would if they knew what was at stake. Trust me, I know exactly who, and what *you* are. In fact, I have it on pretty good authority—no need in being ashamed of it, bae. Hell, I love a freak in the sheets." Then he scrutinized me for a moment longer as tears began to form. "In case you hadn't noticed, Bianca," he said as he dabbed at my eyes, "emotions have no place in my line of business."

I wasn't about to let him belittle me any longer. "Business? Is that all I am to you is *business*?"

"Damn it, Bianca, I don't have time for this bullshit!" he screamed, causing the car to shake.

"How many of your other associates put their women on the line for *business*?"

Jordan exhaled again, then looked me square in the eyes. "I'm not going to answer a fucked-up question like that just to make you feel better. Mistresses—"

I flew off the handle at the mention of being referred to as that low-on-the-totem-pole title. "So, now I'm your *mistress*, Jordan?" I had to laugh to keep from shedding another tear over this incredulous, egotistical jackass. "Apparently, you only view me as another unenlightened notch on your bedpost, and nothing more. Now that I've seen the light, I want nothing more to do with you, you opportunistic, pompous-ass jerk!" I got out of his overpriced car, which was nothing more than an extension of his already humongous dick, used to screw women around even more. I didn't even give him another glance as I ran to my house.

When I opened the door, I was pushed inside, and slammed up against the wall nearly having the wind knocked out of me. Before I could register what was happening, Jordan made his position clear.

"If you thought you were getting rid of me that easily, you got another thing coming, bitch."

Struggling with him was as pointless as a dull knife. "Let go of me!" I yelled, and tried to kick my way free.

Jordan rough-handled me, as he held my arms above my head with one hand, and tore off my skirt with the other. His kisses were hard, but passionate. Once he had me free of my skirt, and panties, he unbuckled his pants, and pushed himself inside of me with urgent strokes.

"You like that?" he panted in my ear.

"Jor ... ooh ... yes!" was my stupid-ass response. His take-charge action had me screaming for him to fuck the shit out of me.

Jordan pulled out, and yanked me around. My face was now kissing the wall. He picked up where he left off, ran his finger up and down my butt crack before inserting one, then two into my asshole.

"I want you to take all of me. This will be your ... last ... time," he grunted.

"No it's ... not. Fuck me, ARRGGH ... harder! Take this pussy! It's yours. All yours, baby." By this time, my makeup had left an imprint of my face on the wall.

Jordan pulled out of me again, wet his fingers with spit, and stuck them back in my ass before easing himself in. At first, he was slow until he felt me getting into it before upping the tempo. He held me in place, fucking the living daylights out of my ass. My fingers had found their way to my clit. I felt complete euphoria nearing, the breaking edge of a serious orgasm. I felt that familiar get-ready-for-it tingling sensation beginning to stir. I stood on my tippy toes to match his thrusts. I threw it back at his ass with just as much exuberance. The feeling traveled up my legs and lingered. It created a friction that sent me soaring straight to the moon. I trembled, and moaned louder as my juices began to flow. He inserted his fingers inside of my vagina, while I was still massaging my clit. The experience of being pleased in three places at once was mind-boggling.

"OHH! I'm cumming! Mmmm ... shit, I'm cumming!" I screamed.

Then it was as if the world had stopped turning. He pulled out and laughed. "I'm glad you thought you were." He continued to chuckle at my expense.

I was at the point of no return and couldn't be held responsible for my actions. "Jordan, now is not the time for you to be doing this shit to me!"

Jordan was zipping his pants back up. "Now you see how I feel." He was about to walk out the door when I became a madwoman, dived onto his back, and tried to claw his eyes out, but he grabbed ahold of my hands to prevent that from happening.

Somehow, during the tussle, Jordan ended up on top of me. "You want it that bad, huh; you want this sweet dick?"

"Yeah, I fucking want it, and I'm going to have it!" I was sure I looked like a crazed freak of nature with my hair all over the place. "Let me go!" I continued to struggle.

Jordan held both my hands over my head again. After he got me where he wanted, he used one of his hands to rip my top off. In the process of freeing my delicious apples, he tore my bra. "Umm ... forbidden fruit my ass," Jordan moaned while sucking and devouring my breasts.

"You can't ... keep doing this ... to me. Please, don't—" He released my hands and slid down between my legs. I was left breathless when his tongue glided across my pearl before suckling it. "Oh my! Oh my! Ooh, Joooor ... daaaann!"

He threw my trembling legs over his shoulders, put up a men-at-work sign, and wore me out. I got the orgasm I was fighting for and many more.

We lay spent on the floor, but of course, he had to ruin that. "Bianca, I really do care about you but—"

"But what, Jordan?" I was in full diva mode and still pissed about his proposition.

"My companion has to be down for whatever, whenever. There is no room for emotions, questions or derailment, when it comes to a job needing to be done. You have to throw caution to the wind, bae, and just trust your man."

I sat up, so that he could see that I was serious. "I am down for almost anything, but I can tell you now, prostituting myself for you, is where I draw the line, Jordan."

Jordan got up completely, I guessed to call himself leaving again. "Okay, I see that your mind is made up."

"You know, this leaving act is really getting tired. So if you must leave, then leave, damn it. See if I care." I began picking up my tattered clothing that had been scattered all over the foyer's entrance.

"Are you sure that's what you want? Because once I walk out of that door, that's it, Bianca, and I mean it." Jordan went to my guest bathroom to get himself together.

My pussy twitched as if to say, *bitch, you bet not let that good dick walk out on us again!* Then my breasts began to tingle, as if they were stating their case too. I have never been the one to beg for sex and wasn't about to start now. I could find someone else to light my fire just as good as, Jordan, couldn't I?

Hell naw! was the reply I got from my conscience, or was it my lower region?

I heard the shower come on and shortly after, the toilet flushed. I couldn't just let Jordan walk out on me again. I remembered how I felt trying to fill the void that I felt the last time he'd left. I was faced with making one of two choices. One, I could do as Jordan asked. Two, I could always wait on my neighbor's girl not to be around to get it on with him until I found someone of my own. I wasn't feeling either of those choices, then I thought I could troll the Internet dating sites, bars, or join one of those exclusive member-only sex clubs. Nah, just thinking of those options bored me. Besides, I'd been there, and done them all. I wanted what I wanted, when I wanted it. No ifs, ands or buts about it. I guess it was clear as to what I had to do.

When Jordan came out of the bathroom fully dressed, I swallowed my pride and said what was on my mind.

"Jordan, I'm used to being the one calling the shots in a relationship, regardless of the kind it is. I've never been the submissive, but there's something about you that—" I was having a hard time. It felt as if I were signing on the dotted line of a contract with the devil. "I can't see myself without you, and if it'll make you happy, I'll meet with your associates." I swiped at the lone tear that had escaped my eye.

"Are you sure?" he stopped long enough to ask.

"What time are we doing this?" was my answer.

Jordan looked at me sideways, as if he didn't know how to take me. "Eight o'clock at Del Frisco's, located inside Le' Ameritage Hotel. Oh, and tonight, you're going by the name Priscilla, and you'll refer to me as Marques."

I took in what he'd said and began making my way toward the stairs. "Okay, I'll see you at eight."

Jordan caught up with me, grabbed my arm, and stopped me, before I could make it to the landing. "Are you dismissing me?"

"I need some time alone to figure out how much exactly did you pay for my soul, and where the hell I was during the negotiations." I left Jordan as I ascended the stairs to ponder on what he'd done to me, and the lengths that I was willing to go through just to show him that I was the one.

Chapter 7

A gent Garza stopped the recorder again. "You mean to tell me, that this man had you *prostituting* yourself?"

"Don't answer that, Bianca!" my attorney shouted before directing her next remark at Agent Garza. "She's here to help you, and I ask that you remember that."

He stared at both of us as he pushed the "record" button.

At eight o'clock sharp, I was at the restaurant to meet with Jordan's acquaintances. From what I'd recalled from listening to them on a phone call with Jordan earlier was that they had thick Spanish accents, but spoke perfect English.

Upon entering, the maître d' met me halfway. "Hello, I have an eight o'clock dinner reservation with a Mr. Vicente Valdez, and a Mr. Antonio Martinez," I explained nervously, as I scoped out.the restaurant.

Without going back to his post to look at his list, he gestured for me to follow him. "Ah yes, Ms. Priscilla, they're right this way."

The restaurant was filled to capacity with people laughing and talking as they dined on fine food and drinks. I looked around admiring the fifteen-foot ceilings, six-foot elk-horn chandeliers, classical art work, and hand-painted murals. A magnificent fireplace dramatized the ambiance of the dining room. The aromas filling the air from the steaks, and other delectable dishes, made me really want to enjoy my dining experience, and I would have, had it been under different circumstances.

Getting into the flow of the restaurant was interrupted when the maître d' announced my arrival while pulling out a chair for me to have a seat. "Gentlemen, I present to you, Ms. Priscilla. We hope to provide you all with an unforgettable dining experience with us this evening. If you need anything, your personal waiter will be more than happy to oblige your every request."

"Thank you," we all said in unison.

"Enjoy." The maître d' bowed gracefully, and left us.

"Senorita Priscilla." A strikingly handsome man kissed my hand. "I'm Vicente Valdez, and from what I see, Marques' description of you doesn't do you justice."

I almost didn't respond to the name, but luckily, I caught on quickly, or the whole operation would've been over with before it began. "Thank you, Senor Valdez," I said while adjusting myself in the seat he'd pulled out for me.

The other man stood, took my hand, and brought it to his lips repeating the gentlemanly kissing tradition. "Senorita, I'm Antonio Martinez. It's an honor to be in your lovely presence tonight."

They both smiled like I was the main course on their menus instead of what the restaurant was serving. Jordan had yet to show his face, and I was beginning to feel that he wouldn't. It was so unlike him to be late, and that worried me.

"I've taken the liberty of ordering you a special drink. Special, because it's not on the menu." Vicente chuckled. "A Screaming White Orgasm, and we'd *love* to see you have one." This time, Antonio joined in the laugh with him.

"That just so happens to be one ... of my ... my favorites." I hoped smiling concealed my lie about the drink and everything else about my identity that wasn't the truth. "Thank you." I took a sip of the creamy concoction. My eyes rolled back when I took the drink from my lips. "Mmm ... " It was actually scrumptious.

My eyes darted around the restaurant hoping to spot Jordan. When I didn't see him, I paid closer attention to my dinner companions. Both men were sexy with heads full of jet-black wavy hair, intense dark eyes, and hairless faces. They looked to be in their mid to late thirties. I guess if I had to do them, I could.

Antonio must've picked up on my nervousness and the fact that I was looking for "Marques" to make an appearance.

"From the looks of it, Marques won't be joining us tonight." He broke the silence and tried to get me to relax by placing his hand on my leg which I removed quickly, but without seeming rude.

"I was under the impression that he would be. Maybe he got stuck in traffic or something," I responded to distract him from trying to touch me again and to reassure them of Jordan's punctuality.

Then Vincent's eyes seemed to glaze over with yearning. "If it's all the same to you, sexy lady, I'd like to take this meeting to our suite."

"Yes, we ordered dinner to be served there as well. I hope a medium steak dinner with all the trimmings suits your palate," Antonio seconded.

"Just the way I like it." I swallowed hard to get rid of the lump that was rapidly forming in my throat. Now I was really beginning to wonder where the hell Jordan was.

Antonio called the waiter over before we left. "Another round of Courvoisier Erte."

"Will the lady be refreshing her drink?" the waiter asked.

I stopped the waiter before he could take away my half-filled martini glass. "No, I'm good." *Here we go*, I thought as I cussed Jordan out in my mind.

After Antonio and Vicente received their refreshed drinks, we were about to step onto the elevator when my phone rang.

I quickly answered it. "Hello?"

"Good job, baby." It was Jordan.

I tried to act as though I were speaking to someone else. "Hey, Shelia, I'm glad that you could get back to me so soon."

"Now listen," Jordan said, getting straight to the point, "the food ordered to their suites will be served by me."

"Oh, how nice." I smiled to throw them off. "I look forward to seeing you. It's been awhile."

"Bianca, they have never seen me in the flesh before, but that doesn't mean that they hadn't seen pictures of me. Make sure they drink the Courvoisier that's going to accompany their meals. I've injected enough Rohypnol in it to put their big asses out for the night. So whatever you do, do not drink *any* of what they're having."

I was relieved to know that my baby was working behind the scenes. Now my confidence was through the roof. I strutted like a proud peacock and joined them on the waiting elevator to go to their suite. "That sounds like a plan. Is there anything else?"

"Yes, dazzle them, do whatever you have to, but you bet not give them none of my pussy. You got that?"

"I wouldn't dream of it. Thanks for calling." I grinned while pushing the "end" button on my phone.

"I love seeing a woman smile," Antonio complimented as the elevator doors closed.

I flashed him a megawatt grin as the elevator made its way to their floor.

Once the elevator opened, I allowed Antonio to lead me by the small of my back down the hall to an adjoining suite. Of course, the door was flanked by two big, burly bodyguards standing at attention. I acknowledged the two human towers with a head nod as we entered and they responded in kind.

"Wow, this is nice." I admired the room as I took in the pewter and topaz color scheme, with a deft blend of contemporary and traditional furnishings, and art work. The breathtaking view of the city's skyline completed the suite's decor.

Vicente was not one for words once the door was closed. He pulled me into him and went straight for my breasts.

"I have to have some of your sweet American poussie." Suddenly, it was like I was being attacked by an octopus. His hands were everywhere. His breathing was labored, but he managed to moan and flick my ear with his slimy tongue.

Totally grossed out of my mind, I shimmied out of his grasp. "Damn, can a girl finish her drink and at least have some dinner first?"

Antonio seemed to be the voice of reason between the two. "Yes, Vicente, treat her like a lady." He licked his lips hungrily. "We have plenty of time to enjoy her later."

Thank God that the doorbell rang interrupting them when it did.

"Room service!" was announced from the other side of the door.

Antonio went to let Jordan in. His facial features were disguised around the eye and nose areas, but he still looked damn good. He was followed by a glamazon of a woman. The bitch was playing that Arabian goddess role to the hilt, with that horsetail swinging behind her and that thick-ass mascara enhancing her emerald-green eyes. I almost blew his cover when the green-eyed monster, better known as jealousy, surfaced.

Antonio led me to an exquisitely decorated table to be seated for dinner, but I couldn't seem to take my eyes off of Jordan, as he played his role of waiter.

When he went to pour the Courvoisier, Vicente placed his hand over his glass.

"Is there something the matter, sir?" Jordan asked with a British accent.

"I still have a glass in the parlor that I have yet to finish. I'd hate to waste a good drink by getting another," he explained.

Never one to let them see him sweat, Jordan spoke up. "Well then, please allow me to go and get it for you, sir."

The woman took over serving us. Jordan returned less than a minute later with the drink Vicente didn't want to go to waste.

"Here you go, sir." Jordan handed the half-empty glass to him upon his return.

Vicente took a generous gulp from his drink the moment it touched his wandering hands. Once everything was served, I watched as Vicente and Antonio dug into their steaks savoring each bite.

"Umm," Vicente moaned as he flirted with me with his free hand under the table. "I don't know which is better." He looked my way displaying a mischievous smile on his ruddy face.

"Ahh!" I jumped when Vicente's fingers found their way inside my panties.

Jordan's head whipped around so fast that I thought he was going to kill Vicente on the spot. "Is everything all right, Ms.?"

My eyes indicated for him to point his direction under the table. Jordan understood what I was saying and gritted his teeth. His mystery woman snickered quietly to herself, but I caught the bitch in action. I'd deal with her ass later.

"Is there *anything* else you gentlemen would prefer?" She put thick emphasis on the word "anything" and probably meant it— job or not.

This whore evidently didn't know who the fuck she was pissing off, I thought as I seethed silently while plotting her demise.

Vicente looked her over taking in her long ponytail, hourglass figure, double-D breasts and bronzed complexion. The walking buffet teetering around on the legs of a supermodel gave him an instant hard-on that he placed my hand on top of. It was nice and bulky. Had it been under any other circumstances, and had I not known what it was like to be with Jordan, I would've given him a whirl.

"Are you on the menu?" He laughed, evoking an even heartier one from Antonio.

Jordan lightly expressed amusement in the statement, so not to draw suspicion to himself. He then topped their drinks off, while they went about finishing serving us our meals and left.

"I know you were expecting Marques to join us, but he wanted us to take a *load* off tonight, if you know what I mean," Vicente hinted flirtatiously.

They roared with laughter as they made a toast to the evening we would share, and the business they'd discuss the following day with Marques. They gulped their drinks down and refilled their glasses. After knocking back the refills, they both tried to shake off what had gotten ahold of them.

"I ... I feel—" Before Vicente could finish his sentence, he fell facedown into his steak dinner. Antonio tried to come to his aid, but collapsed flat on his ass before he could even take a step.

I hurriedly left the table, grabbed my phone and called Jordan. "It's done." I disconnected the call and went in search of their belongings. I saw the Louis Vuitton Calypso GM messenger bag like the one that Jordan had earlier. A laptop was sitting by a desk in the living area just off of the dining room. I opened it to see if it password protected, and it was. I'd let Jordan worry about that. I reached inside the messenger bag and pulled out a manila folder, a vintage 1953 *Playboy* with Marilyn Monroe on the cover, a newspaper, breath mints and a few flash drives that I set on the desk along with the computer.

There were two thuds heard out in the hallway. Shortly afterward, Jordan, and his bitch, entered the room.

Jordan immediately pulled out a device and went for the flash drives that I'd retrieved. He looked at the computer, and took another device out of his pocket. It resembled a flash drive and after examining the computer, he put it in one of the outlets on the side. The computer lit up and numbers started scrolling with a password invalid warning popping up every so often.

"What about the guards?" I stopped looking through the messenger bag and asked.

"Handled." Jordan's sidekick hollered over her shoulder as she pulled Vicente's face out of his plate and cleared his airway passages so he wouldn't suffocate. She then proceeded to check the pulses on both men to ensure that all was okay.

The green-eyed monster reared her ugly head again, and I had no control over it. "Jordan, who is this bitch, and why couldn't she be the one you had to run interference?"

Jordan looked at me as though he couldn't believe that I was questioning him—something he'd told me there was no room for on a job.

"Bianca, now is not the time to let your insecurities get the best of you. Help her drag those goons in here, so I can get what we need uninterrupted. You'll know who she is, soon enough."

Reluctantly, I did as I was told and helped her haul those heavy-ass men inside the suite, which was no easy feat by far. By the time we were done, we were both sweating profusely, and if that wasn't bad enough, my back was aching something awful.

"They, too, were given some of the tainted Courvoisier Erte. They thought they were getting a taste of their bosses' expensive liquor without them being the wiser, while on the job," she explained with amusement in her voice.

This ... BITCH! I wanted to scream out loud. "How did you convince these apes to take a swig?" I asked instead, and surprisingly, with a calm demeanor.

"Oh, you know Jordan can be quite persuasive when he needs to be," she answered nonchalantly.

No this bitch didn't! Damn the pain in my back. "And how would you know that?" I questioned, now standing with my hands on my hips ready to rock and roll.

She laughed. "Hmmm, wouldn't you like to know?"

This bitch was trying it, and just didn't know her ass was about to be traced in a chalk outline in five ... four ... To hell with the bodyguards we'd just dragged in. "Bitch, don't play with me."

"Ooh, I'm so scared." She laughed again and turned her back to me. Big mistake.

I grabbed that long-ass, horse-hair ponytail, swung her around, and covered her mouth so that Jordan couldn't hear us. She put up a good struggle; I'll give her that. Only she couldn't break the hold that I had on her, thanks to the martial arts classes my parents made my sister and I take three days a week when we were kids. Unfortunately for her, I never stopped training throughout my adult years.

"Now, I'm going to ask you one more time, you insufferable cunt: who are you, and what are you doing with *my* man?"

"We work together from time to time. That's all. I swear." She choked back tears as my grip tightened.

"Is everything okay in there?" Jordan called out from the room of the suite where he went to search through their things while the files downloaded.

"Yes, honey, we're fine," I answered back and yanked down on her hair harder, threatening to pull all her weave out as my grip tightened. "Tell 'em you're all right."

"We're tying up some ... some loose ends," she managed to squeak out.

I released my hold on her hair. She stood, and gasped for air like I'd been choking her.

Agent Garza stopped the recording. "So who was this other woman? We don't have any females in custody in connection with the Taran—er ... I mean, Jordan Lei."

My attorney gave me a look.

I cleared my throat to buy me a little time. "I never got her name," I lied.

Garza pushed his chair back and went on a tirade. "Do you expect me to believe that as dependent as you were on Jordan, that you didn't get the name of the lady that helped you in that hotel room that night? That's bullshit and you know it! What are you trying to hide from us, Ms. Brooks?"

Aliyah spoke up. "That's exactly what she's telling you, Agent Garza."

It was Garza's turn to get smug. "Attorney Talal, it was per our agreement that Ms. Brooks would tell us everything that she knew. Withholding any information kills the deal. I think it would be within her best interest not to try and dick us around."

Aliyah, not to be outdone, also stood. "Agent Garza, your assumption would be correct if my client wasn't cooperating. Ms. Brook, is giving you very pertinent information that if it doesn't give you Jordan Lei's whereabouts, it will definitely give you more ammunition against the others that you already have in custody. Let's not forget, that she just gave you two more most-wanted list criminals, Vicente Valdez, and Antonio Martinez.

Both are ruthless drug lords and they dabble in the same rip-off business as Jordan Lei."

Agent Garza turned another shade of red. "But this isn't about the others, Valdez, or Martinez. I want that damned Jordan Lei like I want my next breath, and she's withholding information trying to protect that arrogant S.O.B.!"

Aliyah sat back down and entered some information on her laptop. Once she was done, she looked up to address him.

"Agent Garza, I understand that you're a possible appointee as director of the FBI, the coup de grâce of your career pending the outcome of this case. If you accomplish the capture and conviction of The Tarantula, it would catapult your chances of accomplishing that goal. While I admire your tenacity, it's not my client's duty to see that you get a golden parachute to ascend into that position. Now, unless you want this interview to end abruptly, meaning before I finish this sentence, then you'll refrain from the threats. My client has just given you two men on your most wanted list. Now, if that's not cooperation, then I don't know what the hell is. It would be a shame for me to let the current director know that you're bypassing pertinent information on other high-profile criminals just to get your hooks into one. Now, wouldn't it?" Aliyah was stern and from the looks of it, Agent Garza knew not to fuck with her.

Agent Garza, not wanting Aliyah to make good on her promise, relented. It would take too much time to get orders from a judge. By the time he did that, I could have been long gone and he knew it.

"Ms. Brooks, I hope you would accept my most sincere apologies."

"I accept."

Chapter 8

*O*nce we left the hotel, Jordan had me follow his car to a house that I'd never been to. It was nestled in a well-to-do gated community that you had to get clearance from security in order to gain entrance. We drove for another few minutes before stopping at two grand, black, wrought-iron gates opening to an astounding, French country chateau.

Jordan jumped out of another of one of his many candy-apple-red and black sports cars and opened the door for that bitch, while I sat in my Range Rover fuming. The fucked-up part about it was that he didn't even bother to extend me the same courtesy. It wasn't until he was damn near inside the house that I decided to get out and run to catch up with them.

Instead of explaining himself, he hit a button on a remote that was on his key chain. The walls parted like the Red Sea, revealing a secret room that resembled a CIA command center. There were all types of computers and gadgets, enough to put any electronic store to shame. For the first time, what I was involved in took root and finally hit me.

To make matters worse, the bitch I wanted to strangle went to work right away. Oh yeah, she was very familiar with the way things worked around there. That reality, in itself, really took my fucked-up attitude to a level of detonation. They went about their business on the computers as if I wasn't even there. I enviously watched as they worked in synch with one another. Their movements were sexually motivated—well, at least in my mind, they were. The body language. The closeness. The intimacy. The glances. The smiles. It all made me nauseous as I stood there like a useless, and desperate, attention-seeking fool. Who was this bitch, and why was she all up on my man like I wasn't even in the vicinity? I could only imagine what the heifer did when I wasn't around.

I was feeling myself about to combust as . . . "JORDAAAAAAN!" leapt from the bottom of my being, and burst forth through my lips creating a piercing, foreign sound that chilled me to the core.

He hesitantly let the black leather and chrome chair swivel around so that he was facing me. Finally, I had his undivided attention.

"Don't you see that I'm working?" His annoyance dripped off of every word.

I knew it was because I was wearing my insecurities like a tightly fitted bustier, but at that moment, I didn't give a damn. "Who is she?" I pointed toward her, and questioned again.

Jordan ran his hands over his head, inhaled and exhaled deeply. "She's one of us."

"One ... one of us?" I threw my hands up frustrated with the way he was talking at me, instead of to me. "Are you serious—no bump that. Are you fucking her too?"

Jordan stood, and walked over to me. Mystery bitch never took her hands off of the keyboard. I was waiting for her eyes to leave the monitor and look my way so I could knock them out of her skull and fuck her up. He placed his hands on my shoulders giving them a gentle squeeze. The move was followed by soft caresses before tilting my head in a position to kiss. Jordan's lips were tantalizing. His touch was nothing short of mesmerizing. I was in a zone as his hands explored my yearning flesh. My eyes searched his for answers that weren't forthcoming.

"Do you trust me, Bianca?" he whispered as his head dipped to kiss my exposed cleavage.

All I wanted was for him to tell me what the hell was going on, but it could wait. "Fuck me," I answered instead.

Jordan smiled as he ran his fingertips along my lips. His hands traveled down, tweaking my nipples along the way before finally drifting up under my skirt. He slid my thong to the side and massaged my engorged clit. I didn't care that someone else was there with us. I just wanted what I wanted. To hell with that bitch; Jordan was *my* man.

He worked up a delicious friction causing me to open my legs wider as I stood bracing him for support. I worked my hips in synch with his touches. My eyes closed, and a deep moan escaped from somewhere deep within me. Between my thighs became drenched with the sticky essence from making my kitty awaken from her slumber. I was in a world of my own when I felt my shirt being lifted in the back and a tongue licking and relieving my thighs of the creamy nectar that had collected between them. My thong was slowly tugged until it pooled around my ankles. Jordan's fingers found their way inside my saturated pussy, but the other things that I was feeling were impossible for him to be doing all at once. As if to answer my question, the next sensation threw me overboard. The tongue that was on my legs was now competing with Jordan's fingers as it tap danced on my clit. The orgasm I experienced was so powerful that it knocked me to my knees, but that didn't stop my assailants from assaulting me further.

I opened my eyes in time to see Jordan taking the thong

completely off and spreading my legs wide open. That bitch didn't waste any time getting between them and putting on a hell of a show.

I wanted to put her in a choke hold with my legs, but what she was doing felt so damned good that I couldn't muster the strength to do so if I tried. Instead, I wrapped her ponytail around my hand and steered her head in the directions that I wanted it to go to get maximum satisfaction.

Jordan replaced her when he grabbed me by the ankles and put them on his shoulders and gave me what I'd been craving. She surprisingly brought her lips to mine kissing me gently before thrusting her tongue inside of my mouth. I could taste myself as our kiss deepened. Her hands squeezed my breasts and her mouth eventually left mine to suckle on my hardened nipples.

That was the first time I'd ever been dominated by two people, but it wouldn't be the last.

"Do you recall where this house was located?" Agent Garza asked.

"Sounds like it's one of Pringley's homes due to the secret wall, but who knows," another agent answered.

"I do recall it being on Lobello Drive in the Preston Hollow area of town."

"Definitely, Pringley's place," the agent confirmed. "We already got this one on the books, but knowing that Jordan conducted business there means we'll need to get a crew over there and have forensics to do a deeper analysis on the confiscated computers. At first we were just looking for Pringley's dealings, but now we have to go even deeper, because we know how Jordan likes to *think* he can extract things." The agent looked me dead in the eyes, smirking at the shocked expression I was sure I had on my face due to his last comment.

"Well, get on it right away, Agent Smithscoff. After you get the search warrant, make sure they search every nook and cranny of that house. Oh, and to make it easier, get the plans so you'll know exactly where that secret room she's talking about is hidden."

"I'm already on it, Sir." The agent left the room with his things in tow.

Agent Garza turned his focus back on me. "So, Ms. Brooks, let me get this straight. You, Jordan, and the '*Bitch*,' since you can't seem to recall her name," Agent Garza used his fingers as quotation marks, "had this threesome which leaves me wondering ..." Garza slammed his opened hand down on the table in frustration. "What in the hell has this got to do with my case!"

"Agent Garza, you said that you would hear my client out regardless of how you arrived at the dance just so long as you got there. Remember?" Aliyah reminded him.

"While I'm sure that the others in here have no problem hearing of Ms. Brooks' sex life, I, on the other hand, have better things to be doing with my time."

Aliyah stood. "Well, Bianca, I guess this concludes our business with *Special Agent in Charge* ... Garza. Hopefully, he can get his man without any help from you. Oh, and by the way, I wish you would try to have anything rescinded."

Agent Garza watched as I stood and went to grab my purse in order to leave on Aliyah's orders. "You can't do this. We had a deal, damn it!"

Aliyah faced Agent Garza. "We can and we will. Before you get all indignant, let me remind you of something." She whispered in his ear and that caused him to turn a deep ruby red. "Now try me if you want and that position will just be a figment of your imagination once I'm done."

Garza's whole demeanor changed after whatever she'd told him. "Ms. Brooks, I tend to get a little beside myself being that I am very passionate when it comes to my job. I promise to try and control myself better. Please, I'd like for you to continue, if you don't mind."

I looked over at Aliyah and she gave me a nod to go ahead. Whatever could she possibly have said to make Agent Garza dance to her tune had me unnerved.

I sat down and got as comfortable as the situation allowed before continuing. "And for the record, Agent Garza, I told you, I never got her name."

Chapter 9

I woke up from a deep slumber in an unfamiliar bed completely naked. My body was achy and stiff. Moving was more of a task than it should've been. Once out of bed, I stood in the bathroom mirror looking at the red welts that I didn't recall being on my body the previous day. Puzzled, I slowly hobbled over to the shower and turned the water on making it as hot as I could stand it. I needed the pulsating streams to massage my muscles and rejuvenate me back to my normal self.

After a much needed and relaxing shower, I found my clothes carelessly thrown on a chair in the room. I couldn't put my dress back on, so I looked in the dresser and found a pair of men's jogging pants and oversized T-shirt. Luckily, they had a drawstring and would have to do until I got home. I walked down the long, winding staircase in stilettos with my tattered belongings looking for the command center from the night before, but like magic, it had disappeared into thin air. I pushed on the wall thinking that it would gain me access and even looked for a control panel, anything to tell me that I wasn't tripping. Finding out was important, because I was definitely beginning to question my own sanity.

During the search of the missing command center, I was startled by an older white man dressed for golf.

"You must be Bianca, the event planner from Pleasure Principles, but for now operating under code name *Priscilla*," he whispered with a chuckle in his voice. "Did you sleep well?"

Bewildered, I scratched my head while looking at the man as if he were from another planet. "Umm ... yes, I'm Pri ... I mean, Bianca. Who are you, and where is Jordan?"

He chortled like I'd just told him a good joke. "You don't remember, do you? To jog your memory, you can call me Pringley. I thought I'd made quite an impression on you when we met before." He stood smiling a few moments, I guess to see if I would recall knowing him. Finally, he gave up, but not before holding up his finger as though he'd forgotten that I'd asked him two questions. "Jordan left a few hours ago. He told me that you were still asleep. So I delayed my tee time and decided to wait for you."

Now I was pissed. How dare he leave me unattended with this old-ass coot? "Pringley, thank you for the information, but do you know what time Jordan will be returning home?"

Pringley's eyes roamed over my body keenly before answering. "I wouldn't have the answer to that unfortunately."

"He does live here, doesn't he? Aren't you the butler or something?" I probed further.

He shifted his weight from one foot to the other. "Dear, you misunderstand; you see, this is my humble abode. Jordan is a business associate of mine."

I'm sure embarrassment blanketed my face. "Excuse me for the mix-up. I was under the impression that he lived here, but since he doesn't—" I started for the door.

"Care to join me for lunch, or at least have a cup of coffee with me? You look like you could use some," he called out before I could leave his presence. "You have to be famished, after last night." He covered his mouth with his hand and snickered thinking that I didn't hear or see him do it.

Was this old geezer trying to hit on me? I turned wearing a pasted grin on my face. "Thank you, but I really need to be getting home."

Pringley nodded his head as if he understood. "I see. Your keys are on the table beside the door and your car is waiting in the spot where you left it." He then went about his business in the opposite direction from where I headed to the front door. Then it hit me; Pringley was the banker that I had thrown the party for in Chicago. After remembering his spare-no-expense speech, the palatial estate in Chicago, the very bodacious tip that not only Pleasure Principles as a company but all the staff received individually, and now this ostentatious estate, he really did leave an impression on me. Yes, I would say that Jordan really was stomping with the big dogs.

I hurriedly walked out of the house, jumped into my Range Rover, and hightailed out of there, but not before dialing Jordan.

He picked up on the first ring. "Bianca, I'll need to call you back." *Click!*

I hit my steering wheel. "Shit! I should've taken Pringley up on his offer for coffee, so I could pick his brain and ask who the hell that bitch was, and if she left with Jordan."

Chapter 10

The moment I pulled into my driveway, Jordan was in his car waiting.

He got out and walked to my side of the car and opened the door for me. "Hey, I just got here." He leaned in for a kiss, but I dodged it.

I got to my front door, paused before unlocking it, and faced him. "You know, I'm a lot of things, but a doormat isn't one of them. How dare you leave me at some stranger's house."

Unperturbed, Jordan reached for the keys, unlocked the door and nudged me inside. He led me to a seat on the sofa, but I refused to sit.

"Jordan, I asked you a question, and you are going to answer it," I demanded.

His smile was so wide it resembled that of a clown. The way he ignored my pissed-off mood really rattled my cage. "You know the Spanish guys we hit last night?"

I rolled my eyes heavenward. "How could I ever forget being fondled by two octopuses?"

He grabbed my hands and tried to get me to sit again, but I pulled back. "Louvre."

"The museum? What in the— you know what, I don't even care to know what the hell you're talking about the Louvre for." I threw my hands up in surrender since it was apparent that I wasn't going to get anything that I wanted to know answered.

Continuing to ignore my feelings, he shouted. "I have the blueprints that actually have all of the original escape routes for the Louvre! This is monumental, since it's been remodeled in some areas and those routes did not make it back onto the current blueprints, and are now considered secret tunnels. Do you know what that means?"

"What? You're going to steal a painting? While you're at it, why not go for the *Mona Lisa* or better yet, a Marquise de Pompadour, since I'm your mistress and that painting is more fitting for what I am to you. They should fetch a pretty penny on the black market," I answered sarcastically.

Jordan's smile fell and darkness came over him. "Don't you *ever* for as long as you live mock me, Bianca." Then the darkness retreated, and the light in his tight eyes reappeared. "I don't know how many times I'm going to tell you that you're not my fucking mistress, but if that's what you want to be, it can be easily arranged."

For some reason, I wasn't fazed by his displeasure or imminent threat of leaving me if he decided to play that card again. "If you want me to respect you, then do the same for me, damn it. And if you think I'm going to help you take anything from the Louvre, you're sadly mistaken, mister."

Instead of responding the way I thought he would, Jordan changed his tone, and laughed out loud for what seemed like an eternity. He wouldn't stop, and I didn't know what he found to be so amusing. "A painting? You underestimate me, Bianca, because I wouldn't need the blueprints to take anything from the Louvre." He continued his giggling fit.

I asked the most obvious question. "Why have the blueprints if they're not needed?"

He finally stopped, cleared his throat and adjusted the jacket to the suit that he was wearing. "Only a fool would steal anything out of the Louvre, but luckily for me, I know one. A very rich one, that's willing to pay top dollar for those plans."

My day had been confusing so far; leading me further into the fog wasn't going to change a thing for better or worse. "Humor me. What does he need them for?"

Jordan shrugged his shoulders. "Maybe he's foolish enough to risk stealing some of the world's most guarded treasures. That's his business and not my concern except for where it concerns me."

"I can't even remember most of last night, so you'll have to excuse me for having such a hard time following you. Can we cut to the chase and get to the point already?" I snapped, becoming impatient with the riddles.

Jordan finally stopped fidgeting with his jacket and took the damn thing off. "Like I said, he's foolish enough to try the Louvre. The paintings, artifacts or whatever he plans to take won't be easy to get rid of, so that makes him a fool, unless he has a buyer in which I suspect that he does. I have some unfinished business with the buyer of these blueprints. His name is Easter and a pudgy, little fuck maggot is what he is."

I laughed at the description of Easter. "What did he ever do to you to be described so lovingly?"

"He tried to set me and some very good friends of mine up to be killed is what he did. Anyway, back to what I was saying, I know that he will keep the plans in a secure place like a safe. That's where we come in with part one that's going to make him wish that he'd never double-crossed me."

I was starting to catch his drift, but I was still confused. "So, I get it. You're going to sell him the plans, then steal them back from him?"

"Not hardly. Documents can have undetectable tracking and other devices put on them like the Trojan horses that infect your computer. I will have those plans telling me every move they make. When he places them in a safe, another tracker will automatically lock in on the code with its sensor. The GPS will let me know exactly where the safe is located. Knowing Easter, the way that I do, he will take extreme measures like using his fingerprints to avoid anyone cracking his safe's code. The blueprint will be covered in undetectable transmitters for this very reason. My sensor will transmit data to me every time he touches the document via a special computer that will generate a very thin, skin-like film for me to place on my fingers matching his prints exactly. If it comes down to it, I can also lift his prints from the safe. Another advantage to knowing him is, I'm confident that once he has the plans, he won't make a move on the Louvre immediately. He's a perfectionist, but he's also a procrastinator, which will give me the time that I need."

Jordan's ramblings left me even more bewildered. "So I was right; you're going to steal the plans back from him?"

Now he was the one frustrated. "Were you listening to me, Bianca? Apparently, what he has in his safe is what I'm after. The blueprints, although valuable due to being the originals, are just the bait that I'm using."

"Okay! I get it. You only went after Antonio and Vicente for the blueprints, but why if you don't need them?"

"The man who wants to buy the blueprints undercut me a few years ago and went behind my back in order to broker a deal with your dinner companions, Antonio, and Vicente, for a job in Bangkok. They helped him get the jump on us in order to take everything before he met up with us to complete the job. He almost got us iced with the people that we were working for. For that reason, and a few others, he has to pay. Once he buys those prints from my associate, and try to execute the job on the Louvre, it will not only be a day of reckoning, but one of déjà vu. Easter will be executed on the spot for trying to pull another fast one. Plus, I'm making sure to invite our Spanish friends and have them under the impression that Easter was the one who set them up at the Le' Ameritage Hotel. So you see, everyone will be getting their due in blood for crossing Jordan Lei."

"Couldn't you just have said that?" Instead of waiting for another long-winded answer, I got up and walked into the kitchen to find something to eat. I was starving, and wished again that I had taken Pringley up on his offer for food.

Jordan followed behind me. "You have to learn the business if you're going to be a part of it. Nothing is simple when it comes to what I do."

After pouring a glass of orange juice and taking a huge gulp, I pulled a breakfast bowl out of the freezer and popped it into the microwave. "I'm not looking to get technical, so it shouldn't matter."

Jordan took the glass from me, and finished the juice off. "You have a right to be as involved as you want, but don't pull another stunt like you did last night just because I have another woman working with me. She's not the only one—just so you know from here on out."

With my left hand resting on my hip, I leaned on the counter. "Speaking of other women, are you going to tell me who she is?"

Jordan ran his hand over his head. "I told you who she was last night. If you forgot, then I'm sorry."

I drew in a deep breath about to blow my top, but calmed myself just as quickly. "If you had told me, I damn sure wouldn't have forgotten."

Jordan laughed as he left me in the kitchen when the microwave beeped. "That's another thing; nothing is repeated more than once, especially identities," he called over his shoulder.

Chapter 11

*L*ater that night, I waited for Jordan to wrap up a phone call. When he was done, he sat next to me on the sofa and pulled my feet into his lap. I was nursing a glass of Cabernet after a few rounds of marathon sex that was concluded on the floor.

"So?"

Jordan exhaled loudly, probably wondering if he should give me the extended version or not. "Things are coming together better than I would've ever imagined. There's a very high-profile wedding in two weeks. The security is going to be insane, but that won't be a problem for us."

"Why would we care about security if we're attending a wedding?"

"Because we're not attending to offer well-wishes; we're going to score."

I looked at Jordan knowing I should've known better. "Besides the ring, what could you possibly want from a wedding?"

Jordan placed my feet on the sofa and stood. "Since it's for a prominent family like the Wangs, it's going to be a who's who type of event. It will be a media circus and everyone will come wearing nothing but the best jewels—for starters. However, the bride's ring is my primary target, but not more so than the purchaser of it, which will be her father-in-law. It's more about what it represents than its value."

I laughed at Jordan's reason for pulling a heist at a wedding. "No one could've told me that Jordan Lei has a sentimental bone in his body. Did the ring belong to someone you hold dear?"

The look on his face was not one of amusement. "Elizabeth Taylor's jewelry collection set an unprecedented record of being auctioned off as the highest in history for Christie's. The Joie De Vivre diamond sold for over eight million dollars to a private Chinese collector. He's giving the ring to his son to present to his bride. Once I have the ring in my possession, he's going to show his hand because of his pride. Which is what I want him to do so that I'll be able to finally settle another old score."

I needed a refill because this was too much to handle in the course of a day. First, the Louvre, now a damned wedding; this guy seriously needed a vacation. After refreshing my drink, and bringing him a glass, we resumed our conversation.

"This is the second old score of the day, Jordan. What did this collector person do to you?"

Jordan didn't answer me. Instead, he went into my office to his laptop. I joined him to see what he was up to.

"I asked you a question."

He continued setting up his computer by fitting it with other hardware that I wasn't familiar with. "I'm getting my team together. You'll know more the day of." And with the wave of a hand, I was dismissed.

From the wedding, I learned about Jordan and his "connections." The security detail for the wedding was going to be bananas like he'd said, but what he didn't disclose was that he was the one providing it. When protection was hired, an interview was conducted at AHS Protection Agency. The collector's people came to finalize the paper work and to see if the company was up to his high standards. A dummy office was set up on another floor. Before a face to face, the calls were intercepted and rerouted. The real AHS Protection Agency was never notified of the job, so that would be their argument. It would stick because when the phone records were examined, it would show that no contact was ever made relieving them of all liability. The owner of the company owed Jordan a favor and was only too glad to return it. I never knew what the score was that Jordan had to settle, until things were set in motion.

"The Wang wedding is still under investigation, especially since the insurance on that ring is substantial. I had no idea that The Tarantula, ahem ... Jordan, was in on it. When I spoke with Mr. Wang, he wasn't of much help, but now I see why. AHS Protection Agency looks like they're going to be cleared of any involvement from what I was told by the investigator at the insurance company that provided coverage for the ring. The insurance money will be at least three times more than what he paid for it since the owners were such iconic figures." Agent Garza got up and walked around in a circle mumbling to himself. "Since Mr. Wang isn't cooperating, I can only assume that he's going after Jordan to get his ring and will still receive a nice payday in the process. I can't see him letting the insurance company know if he does succeed in getting it back." He paced some more. "Now I'm starting to get the information that I've been looking for. Ms. Brooks, you may proceed."

"I'm glad." I was relieved that I was making some leeway.

Chapter 12
Day of the Wedding
Two Weeks Later

The wedding was going according to plan. Guests arrived dressed to the nines and wearing valuable jewels that were insured and normally locked away in a vault for safekeeping. Everyone that was anyone was invited to celebrate the marriage of Da-Xia Qian, and Ming-Hua Wang. I wore a red, bob-styled wig, an earpiece, black skirt suit with a white button-down shirt and six-inch Louboutins. The guys were all dressed in black suits with their guns concealed behind their jackets, dark shades and earpieces. We all looked like a part of the Secret Service.

Per the request of the family, cell phones and other electronic equipment were not permitted inside of the church. The guests had to pass through metal detectors and other security measures before even being allowed inside. Who were these people that they needed all of this protection, and at a church of all places? I asked Jordan when we were going over the job and he told me that they were very important and wouldn't give me any more than that.

Since the break of dawn, I played my part as personal security for the bride. I had no idea that a Chinese wedding was an all-day event. On the day of the wedding, both families performed a hair dressing and capping ritual for both the bride and the groom. Then the groom, along with servants, musicians and others, came to the bride's home, which was decorated in red, to play the door game. Since I was the bride's personal guard, I was already there with a few other "security" personnel. Following tradition, when the groom arrived, the bride's friends tried to prevent him from getting inside the house. I was glad that Jordan had informed me of everything because I wouldn't have expected any of this and would've blown our cover. The groom claimed his bride, gave gifts to the family and then took her back to his home that was also decorated in red for the tea ceremony with his parents. There were a host of other traditions to follow, and it's a very detailed and organized event down to the wedding night and the following three days afterward. Before the ceremony even began, I was in need of a strong and serious drink, straight up with no chaser, with all of the hoopla that was going on.

The wedding was performed in keeping with Chinese custom, but was preceded by the writing of three letters and then followed up by the six etiquettes. From what I'd learned from Jordan, it's a very long courtship that's prearranged by both families. The colors in the church for the nuptials were very vibrant as was the bride as she stood elegantly in her red gown. The priest conducted the vows in both English and Chinese. Had I been there under legitimate circumstances, I would've really enjoyed the ceremony. As the service progressed, I was beginning to wonder why in the hell was I even there. I hadn't seen Jordan since he'd left me the previous night.

After reciting the vows in Chinese, he then said, "Da-Xia Qian, do you take Ming-Hua Wang to be your lawful husband, to have and to hold, from this day forward, for better, for worse, for richer, for poorer, in sickness and in health, until death do you part?"

"I do," the bride professed lovingly.

The priest then said a blessing over the wedding bands. "And now the rings." The couple was about to exchange them when suddenly, the priest reached over and snatched the groom's hand and took the ring before he could put it on his bride's finger. In one swift motion, he tore off a facial mask that resembled an older Chinese man and his clerical collar that had a voice scrambler attached to it. People began screaming as gunshots were fired into the ceiling of the cathedral.

He pulled a gun out of his robe and held it up high for everyone to see. "Listen, nobody moves, nobody gets hurt. Do as you're told and you'll leave the way you came, less a few items, of course." He looked around with his eyes coming to a stop, resting on the father of the groom. "If you think you want to be a hero, go ahead and try. We're already in a church; we can easily arrange for this to go from being a wedding to a funeral ... easily."

The groom stood frozen at the altar. His bride cried hysterically while I relieved her of all the jewels that she was wearing. The father, whom I assumed to be The Collector, recognized Jordan and immediately shouted out.

"Unfortunately for me, I spared you once too many, but trust me when I say, that I will not make the same mistake of allowing you to continue to draw breath. You will *not* continue to defy me and on this day of all days." He had to catch his breath and wipe the spittle from his mouth. "You ... imbecile! You're like the one you called father and that *ha guay* (nigger) you had for a mother!" His face was filled with rage, but he dared not get up from the pew he was sitting on since he had a gun being aimed directly at his head.

Jordan, unfazed by the threat, walked over to the older gentleman, and punched him in the face. His wife begged for Jordan not to hurt her husband. He snatched the old man up by the lapels of his suit. "That's the spirit, old man. I saved you the trouble of wondering so you'll know exactly who to come looking for." Jordan roughly shoved him back down onto the pew. His wife instantly went to his aid to comfort him while crying and speaking something that I couldn't decipher in her native tongue.

"This is not over, *chigger* (chink/nigger)!" The Collector said sternly to Jordan's back before going into a coughing fit.

Jordan turned around facing him again. "Of course it's not, but by the time this chigger is done with you, you're going to wish it was."

The Collector screamed obscenities at his back as he walked off.

The rest of the "security" team worked feverishly relieving the attendees of their precious jewels. On the outside, sirens could be heard. The media that were waiting in the wings for the first snapshot of the couple must've heard the gunshots and pandemonium that was taking place inside. I was nervous wondering how we were going to get away, but Jordan didn't break a sweat. I'm sure the church was surrounded as I wondered again, why I was there.

Jordan must've noticed the signs of panic on my face when he massaged my shoulders to assure me that everything was going to be OK. Before having me to follow one of the "security" members, he took the jewels I had taken from the bride and the rest of the wedding party. He took special care of the diamond ring and kept it with him. We went to the back of the church where I was given a backless red dress, another wig and other accessories to look the part of a guest attending the wedding.

"Take off every other stitch of clothing you remove and place them inside of this bag," a short, stocky guy that was holding a bag out in front of me ordered.

When I was done, I handed the bag containing the discards to the same man who had given it to me. I noticed that we all were dressed like the rest of the people in the church and would blend in effortlessly. There were threats being made to the congregation, but I wondered by whom, because all of the "security" was accounted for. Jordan was already dressed and was being fitted with another prosthetic. This time he looked like an older, but distinguished black man with salt-and-pepper sideburns.

"Okay. Let's do this," I said.

The next thing I heard was complete chaos. People were screaming and the commotion was so overwhelming that I reacted like a deer caught in headlights. I was pushed forward by one of the "security" personnel from the back of the church and into the stampede that was started as if out of the blue. We all became actors running for their lives with the rest of the people. The police instructed the crowd to the side of the church while other law enforcement stormed the cathedral after making sure everyone was out. There were cops, SWAT, firemen and ambulances everywhere.

My nerves made me a very believable character when the police asked if I'd been hurt. "My jewelry! They took my jewelry!" I cried while being led over to a section where statements were being taken from everyone.

Once I was no longer being watched, I slipped off to the designated location where Jordan was nearby waiting for me in a red Ferrari 458 Italia.

Chapter 13

*O*n the ride home, Jordan was silent, and appeared to be fuming about something. I didn't care to know what it was, so long as I got home and back to resuming my life as a law-abiding citizen. When we got to my house, Jordan whipped the car into my driveway and revved the engine. I took that as a sign that he wasn't in the mood to talk and to get out.

I opened the door to do just that when Jordan hit the steering wheel repeatedly. "Damn it! Damn it! Damn it!"

I turned around to see what the uproar was about. "What's wrong?"

Tears were in his eyes when he looked over at me. "Nothing. I'll talk to you later."

I sat a minute longer, deciding that now wouldn't be the time to probe him with the numerous questions that I needed answered. The moment I stepped out and was at a safe distance, he burnt rubber trying to get out of my cul-de-sac.

After a long, leisurely shower, to wash away the day's event, I made a hot cup of tea with a lemon wedge and honey in order to have a relaxing evening. Everything was fine, until I turned on the television and saw that the wedding was breaking news. I watched intently to see if they had any suspects. Surprisingly, the only lead they had was AHS Protection Agency who had been advised by their attorneys to reserve comment. The consensus was that it was as if the guests had been robbed by ghosts posed as security that vanished into thin air. With that bit of news, I was finally able to take a deep breath, but I still couldn't relax. Damn it, my tea was now cold.

A Week Later

*I*n Amsterdam, at a coffeehouse that also served other specialty items, Easter sat with a man he had idolized since learning about him years earlier. The guest of honor was surrounded by a flock of bodyguards, more than what Easter had at his disposal. He made a mental note to get him a few more men to watch his back. For the longest time, no words were spoken, at least not to Easter as the man drank his java and smoked on a special cigarette that was still illegal in some parts of the States. He puffed on his stick enjoying the feeling that was overtaking him. He gestured it toward Easter, who eagerly took a long-winded pull and immediately began to choke. His guard patted his back making Easter feel inadequate in front of whom he considered as close to royalty as he would ever get. The man's eyes held amusement at the scene playing out in front of him, while his lips never cracked a smile. Easter held up his hand signaling for the man to stop beating him on the back.

Once the cigarette was consumed, the reason they were there commenced. "I understand you have a strong dislike for a certain spider," the man spoke with a heavy accent.

Easter adjusted himself in his seat which was hard to do since his feet barely touched the resting point. His Stacy Adams kept slipping making it hard for him to catch a firm grip which was the root of his seating issue due to its height. He adjusted the jacket of his black leather suit with snakeskin patches that had him sweating up a storm, but he tried to play it cool.

"If The Tarantula is the spider you speak of, then I would love nothing more than to squash him with my bare hands," he responded while dabbing at his drenched brow with a handkerchief held between his slender, delicate, ladylike fingers.

The man looked at Easter's small, ladylike hands, shook his head, and had one of his guards to light him another special cigarette. He dismissed his talk about squashing The Tarantula. That was a task that the tiny man would never be able to live up to. "I hear that you have other business that I would be interested in—yes."

Easter looked around and leaned in just in case someone was lurking. "Yes, I have in my possession the original blueprints for the Musée du Louvre. I understand that you like collecting rare treasures, hence the name."

The man rubbed his chin in deep thought, pulled on his smoke and exhaled before answering. "Nothing gets by you, I see; smart man you are." The sarcasm was lost on Easter as he puffed his chest out with pride. "Hmm ... Musée du Louvre, a big order to fill." He took another toke from his cigarette and blew smoke in Easter's direction. "I've never met such a little man with such big ambition. I like that. No room for error!" His voice rose a few octaves, then went back to its regular level. "You do know that punishment for betraying me is how you say ... merciless."

Easter swallowed hard and then choked on the smoke he inhaled. The same guard patted him on his back causing him further embarrassment. He shook the guard off and wore a menacing scowl on his face that only would've intimidated him if he'd had a mirror.

"Enough!" he shouted loudly and drew attention from the other patrons. "Look—" He leaned in to his guest again trying not to show the fear that he had instilled in him with his last words spoken. "I'm a man of my word; ask anybody."

"And that I shall," the man said without flinching.

"This isn't going to be done overnight, you know. Planning and strategy have to be on point along with the right team to pull this kind of job off without a hitch. Now, I know you're serious, but you have to cut me a little slack here. I mean, this is the fucking Louvre we're talking about, and not some small-time art gallery. I will get you the pieces you want for your collection without fail. Just give me a chance."

The man stood from his seating position and shook Easter's hand. "I'll be in touch."

"Thank you, sir! You ... you won't regret it!" Easter watched as the man walked out the door with his guards covering him from front to back.

Easter was floating on cloud nine thinking about the possibility of helping The Collector take down The Tarantula, once and for all. Then he remembered his guard embarrassing him in front of his esteemed guest.

"You!" He pointed at the man.

"Sir?" the colossal man answered with a Barry White baritone voice.

Easter gestured for him to stoop to where he was at his level, and when the giant did, as he was instructed, Easter pulled back as far as his little arm would allow, and punched him with all of his might. "You're fired!" When he saw that he had spectators, he jumped off of the stool and kicked him in the shin. "Fucking cunt!" He signaled for the other two men who shrugged at their fallen comrade as they followed behind their miniature, overdressed boss who strutted out of the door like a proud peacock with his chest poked out.

Chapter 14

*I*t had been a week since I'd heard from Jordan. I was beginning to worry, thinking that The Collector had made good on his threat. To take my mind off of it all, I decided to drown myself in work. In order to be able to account for my sudden influx of cash, I had to make Pleasure Principles the premier event planning company I always knew it could be. I placed pricey ads in nationally distributed magazines like *Bridal*, *O*, *Vogue*, *Elle*, *People*, major newspapers, billboards across the country and even a commercial that ran during prime hours of the day. I had a major overhaul done on my website adding all of the bells and whistles it needed to make it pop. Per Reggie's suggestion, I even hired a marketing firm used by A-list celebrities. Cody worked miracles on the social networking scene and it all seemed to be paying off. I logged on to my computer to see if the event coordinator from the African American Museum of Arts had gotten back to me with a date and time to go over the plans for their fiftieth anniversary when Reggie barged into my office.

"Are we still sulking over that same dick that dismissed you the last time you were in here looking like hell?"

I laughed at his truthful remark. He was a welcomed distraction, but to make sure I was on point, I looked into the sterling silver, oval, double-sided makeup mirror that I kept on my desk. "You liar, I do not look like hell."

He took a seat in one of the chairs in front of my desk and crossed his legs. "Oh, you look fine on the outside, but giiiirrrl, I can tell that on the inside, you're a hot mess. I know it has something to do with that tight-eyed dick you been messing around with. Now, say that I'm lying so I can go and get ready for my funeral because that must mean I'm dying. You know a bitch has to be casket sharp, hunty!" He snapped his fingers.

I couldn't hide anything from Reggie, so I decided to tell him what was going on, but left out the parts about me being involved in illegal activities. I wasn't afraid that he would betray me intentionally, but under pressure, Reggie and Cody were better off being left in the dark.

"I hadn't heard from him all week, and this time I didn't even do anything."

Reggie adjusted himself in his chair and cleared his throat. "Seven whole days and not a word from you . . ." He pretended that he had a microphone in his hand as he sang Toni Braxton's song. "Come on, girl, and pout those lips like Ms. Braxton, and get into the groove with me. I can't take it, won't take it—" Once he saw I wasn't budging, he gave me the eye and stopped his impromptu performance.

"Ugh, girl, you need to learn how to have some fun to get you through!" He popped his lips and rolled his eyes. "But anyway, let me tell you something about a man that likes to play games like Mr. Tight-Eyed Dick. For one, he's a control freak based on what you say about him. The minute he can't have his way, what does he do?"

"Call himself leaving," I responded solemnly.

"Mm-hmm, call himself leaving like you're some damned child. You need to stop letting that man trample all over you with that bullshit. Hell, do him one better and you be the one to leave. Stop wasting your time waiting by the phone and go get you some replacement dick. His ain't the only one in town. Trust me, I'm talking from experience. Now, I ain't had no tight-eyed dick, so he could have some ole ancient Chinese secret spell cast on ya ass, for all I know. But girl, boo, go get you some of that good ole thug-a-licious hood dick and call it a day. Okay!" Reggie snapped his fingers in Z formation.

I couldn't help but laugh at that fool, but for as crazy as he was, he was right. There was nothing, and I mean absolutely nothing, like thug loving. It was time I stopped being at Jordan's beck and call, and get back to marching to the beat of my own drum, instead of his snake-charming-me-delirious ass. "After I get through finalizing the details on this birthday party for Mr. Buchanan, and confirming that date and time for the meeting with the African American Museum of Arts, want to go and grab a bite to eat?"

Reggie stood and put his hands on his hips. "Hunty, you ain't said nothing but a word, and while we're at it, let's go dick shopping too. It's time for you and the doll . . .," he pointed to himself, "to try something new."

We were in the midst of having lunch at MOOYAH, when who walks in but Jordan. I put my burger down and dabbed at the corners of my mouth. "Damn it!"

Reggie stopped chewing and followed my line of vision. "Girl, who is that?" he whispered.

"Jordan," I mumbled as he made his way over to our table.

"Baby, he is one-olla-fine!" Reggie exclaimed, but in a hushed tone. "But if he get out of hand and try to be cute, I don't mind putting an ass whopping down!" He slapped the table causing it to shake and our drinks to nearly topple over.

Jordan was wearing jeans and a fitted T-shirt with motorcycle boots. I'd never seen him as dressed down as he was now unless he was naked. Just thinking about him in the nude had my pussy meowing. No scratch that—more like roaring.

Jordan stopped in front of our table. "Bianca, can I have a word with you?" he said, totally ignoring Reggie.

"Ahem!" Reggie cleared his throat. "Umm, hello! Am I invisible up in this bitch or what?" He dramatically patted himself down just to be sure.

"Uh . . .Jordan, this is one of my best friends, Reggie. Reggie, this is Jordan." I made room for him to sit, but he didn't take the subtle invite to join us.

"Bianca," he said, letting me know that he wasn't taking no for an answer.

I made an attempt to get up, but Reggie wasn't too happy with my puppy dog behavior. "The last time I checked, your father, Mr. Brooks, lived in Atlanta. I sure as hell don't see a ring on your finger to be getting demands snapped at you."

To deflect a situation from occurring, I hurriedly stood and like a scolded child, followed Jordan out to his parked Harley. I could just feel Reggie burning a hole through my back with his laser-beam eyes.

I stood with my arms crossed in front of me trying to show an appearance of being pissed off while waiting to see what he had to say. We stared at each other unnecessarily long before he decided to speak his peace.

"I'm sorry for not being in touch, but I had to lay low in order to take care of some things after the wedding. Besides, the less you know, the better."

I chose my words carefully to avoid us arguing out in public, but threw in some seduction. "I'm sure you can't get into the particulars here, so why don't you come over tonight, so we can discuss it then."

For the first time, Jordan cracked a smile since he'd walked all serious into the restaurant. "Sure that's all you want me over there for?"

I returned the smile. "Oh, I can think of a few other things."

He placed his helmet on his head, getting ready to leave, but I had a burning question to ask. "How did you know where I was?"

"I have my ways," was the answer he gave before cranking up that beast of a bike and driving off.

I stood there for a few minutes longer, but there was no use in going back inside Reggie was on his way out and not looking too pleased with me.

"Reggie—"

He threw his hand up and kept walking. "Girl, save it for somebody who gives a damn."

I followed behind trying to get him to stop. "How are you going to get back to the office? You rode with me, remember?"

He stopped abruptly and snapped on me. "Hunty, don't try to worry about me now. The Doll always has a way to get from point B and back to A. Trust!" He held up his arm and snapped his fingers extremely loud like he was about to break into a dance move.

As if summoned, Cody pulled up. "Where he at?" he asked Reggie.

Reggie opened the car door and got in. "He hopped his conceited, tight-eyed ass on his bike and left, which was for the best. Trust!"

Cody pulled at the band that was holding his hair together. His honey highlighted on chocolate-brown tresses fell forward into a beautiful layered wrap hairstyle. "I was ready to *ruuuuumble*! Don't let the delicate look fool you. Okay!" he snapped.

Ignoring Cody's hyper ass, I tried to reason with Reggie. "I'm sorry about what happened. Can we at least talk?"

Reggie strapped on his seatbelt and glared at me. "Until you develop a backbone when it comes to that rude, obnoxious and inconsiderate muthafucka, hunty, we ain't got nothing to talk about unless it's work related." He tapped the dashboard twice. "Ms. Thing, take me away from this!"

Cody shrugged his shoulders and drove off in his nebula gray pearl Lexus LX SUV, leaving me looking after them.

Chapter 15

There was nothing I could do to get Reggie to talk to me so instead of going back to work, I made an appointment at Pampered Divas. After the luxurious whole body spa package, and a mani-pedi, I was ready to top my night off with some sexual healing.

Jordan arrived around eight looking damn good in some Armani jeans and a fitted, button-down shirt. I greeted him with a kiss that led to me being pushed into the wall and devoured like a Popsicle on a hot summer's day. The silk robe I had on was pulled off in one fluid motion. Good thing I was naked underneath; this was just the kind of greeting that I was hoping for.

His lips traveled to my dark nipples and twirled them around like cherry stems before moving on to the main course. His tongue tangoed with my clit, as his lips massaged my labia, pulling on them passionately before lifting me onto his shoulders so he could really get down to business. Once he had me secure, he stood and turned me into an all-you-can-eat buffet. I used the wall for support as I enjoyed being his evening snack. His fingers got lost in the plushness of my soft ass cheeks as he squeezed them like Charmin. As the heat got more intense, we worked our way over to the sofa where he continued his assault, only this time from the back. I was leaning over the sofa stuck between the world of rhapsody and the state of semiconsciousness.

Taking charge, I grinded my pelvis in a circular motion to assist with his face and tongue fuck. "Ooh ... baby, I've missed you so much!"

Jordan's apologies came out in a sea of grumbles, but I understood him perfectly. My fingers found their way to my clit and the other hand reached around me in search of his zipper to unleash the dick I'd been craving all week. While I was trying to get at him, he slipped his thumb inside my ass and worked it counterclockwise in synch with his tongue that was still dancing inside of my pussy. What I felt next was nothing short of spectacular.

"Oooooooh. Joooordan. Ohmygoodnessgracious! Arrrghhhh!" I screamed as an orgasm paralyzed my entire body before releasing it to jerk in mini spasms.

Jordan wanted in on the action. He quickly unbuckled his jeans and practically leapt out of them. His hand pressed against the middle of my back to hold me in place while he tore open a condom with his teeth. His dick went on a treasure hunt and dug for gold when he buried it deep within my quivering walls. I was still coming from the oral interaction, and now I was just about ready for liftoff.

"Ahhhh!" The notes I were hitting were so high, that if my neighbors hadn't known any better, they'd have sworn that opera's demanding diva, Kathleen Battle, was giving a one-night-only concert while shattering a few of my wineglasses at the same time.

Jordan didn't let up; he was relentless in trying to make up for lost time. He fondled my breasts, pinched my nipples and sped up the tempo. His thrusts had my pussy speaking in tongues as cum ran down my inner thighs. I gripped the sofa pillow, trying to hold out as another orgasm mounted about to tear through me.

The pressure was too intense to go on another second longer, but luckily, Jordan, was ready too. We exploded together, releasing the wild kingdom beasts within.

"Damn you, Bianca!" Jordan fell back onto the sofa breathing hard and sweating profusely. "Shit yeah!"

I didn't have the stamina to do much else, but stay leaning over the sofa trying to gather the strength to stand upright. I took in a few deep breaths and allowed myself to collapse onto Jordan's chest. "I needed that."

We showered and enjoyed another epic fuck fest that started out in the bathroom and went on a tour through my home office, den, and the kitchen. It finally ended in my bedroom around five a.m. I think we more than made up for the entire week of not being together.

"I'm too stiff to move," I complained as I tried to get in a comfortable position.

Jordan laughed, but helped me get right. "I know you may not want to talk about jobs right now, but I owe you an explanation."

He was right; I didn't want to hear about any of that shit, but curiosity was getting the better of me. "No time like the present."

Jordan sat up and pulled me into his arms. "The day of the wedding, a few things went wrong, but I couldn't afford not to go through with the job."

"Things like what?" I questioned. As far as I knew, no one had gotten caught. Plus, he had gotten the ring and Wang's attention.

Jordan exhaled, leaned back into the fluffy pillows, and closed his eyes. "The getaway wasn't as clean as I would've liked it to be. I'm worried that we may have left clues behind."

I thought about the news and recalled them saying they had no leads except for AHS Protection Agency, which would ultimately lead to nowhere. I hadn't heard anything else about it since.

"Clues like what? Am I in any kind of danger that I should know about?"

Jordan cracked up as if Martin Lawrence had just walked into the room and started doing standup. "Baby, I'm just fucking with you." He squeezed me tightly, but continued laughing. "Seriously, I accomplished what I'd set out to do. Wang aka The Collector is definitely opening himself up the way I thought he would. He's put a hit out, and will pay big money to whoever brings me to him dead, or alive."

"Jordan, this is no time to be joking around." I delivered a love tap to his chest. "I'm terrified of what could happen."

He grabbed my fists before I could land another blow. "Let me let you in on what's really going on with The Collector. He's the one who cheated my father out of everything, and left the Leis destitute, and my mother exiled."

I gasped when it finally clicked. I'd been so caught up that I didn't realize it until now. "Xing Ho Wang, the real estate developer, and The Collector, is the same person?"

"Make that *billionaire* Xing Ho Wang, the real estate developer, and yes, they are," Jordan spat like saying his name left a nasty taste in his mouth before continuing. "It wasn't always like that, according to my family. Xing and my father were best friends, more like brothers at one time. My father was the one chosen to marry his sister, Su Ming Wang, but instead of honoring tradition, he ran off to the States, met and married my mother who, when he returned to China, was pregnant with me. It was a sheer embarrassment to the Wang family. It was like my father had spit in the face of the Wangs when they learned that he was married and then to a black woman of all people. As a result, for years, the once like family turned into mortal enemies."

I mustered the strength to sit up and really listen to what

Jordan was saying. Since knowing him, this was the most he'd ever revealed to me about his family. "Su Ming Wang must've been hell on the eyes or something."

Jordan laughed. "No, she was actually very pretty from what I've heard. It was her ways that wouldn't allow him to commit himself to her."

I was confused now. "What do you mean, her ways?"

Jordan took a deep breath as if he were trying to compose himself. "She ... she wasn't umm ... pure."

"Oh, she was a whore?" I said, meaning to be crass. How else could you relate to information like that without being anything but?

Jordan nearly choked on a cough while trying to suppress his humor, but lost that battle. "Yeah, I guess that's the word I was looking for. She was a big raging whore from what my father told me."

We had a good laugh at Su Ming Wang's expense which was sad since I knew nothing about her other than her being a slut.

Jordan stopped laughing and continued on with the story. "My father was notorious for his gambling, and Wang found a way to use that to his advantage and avenge his sister's '*honor*.' Jordan used his fingers as quotations upon mentioning the word *honor* in the same sentence describing Wang's plan of retaliation in his sister's defense. It caused us to laugh again.

"One night, my father was leaving from a high-stakes poker party given by a mutual wealthy friend, when Wang accosted him and gave him a choice."

I pulled the covers tighter around me when I realized that I was shivering from the wind coming in through my open terrace doors. "What choice could he have given?"

Jordan grew quiet again and I could've sworn I heard him sniff back tears, but it happened so quickly, that I couldn't be sure.

"He gave my father a letter and in it, he wrote that if he didn't take a dive, and relinquish everything over to him, that he would have my pregnant mother killed. In China, he would've gotten away with it too since the Leis had had little power compared to the Wangs. He knew my father's love for my mother would leave him susceptible to whatever demands he made. The family knew which is why she was exiled because in a sense, she was to blame. My father had finally lost the regard they once held him in and seeing that was the undoing of my mother.

"Before I was born, my parents moved to New York since it was home for my mother. My father was always trying to get us back to the wealth he'd lost by getting into one scam after another. After years of struggling to make ends meet, coupled with depression, my mother took her life with a bottle of pills when I was only twelve years old. My father took her death hard and blamed himself since he hadn't lived up to his promise of providing her with a lifestyle of privilege." Jordan took a deep breath and continued.

"After my mother's death, our relationship became strained. Despite our relationship, I did well in school and received a full ride to NYU. I spent a lot of those years blaming my father for making everything so hard, especially when he became a violent alcoholic. We clashed often and things had gotten so bad between us, that during the last year of his life, we weren't even on speaking terms. He eventually drank himself to death. I regret how things ended. I loved him. He was my father, after all. I fulfilled my duties as his son and removed his belongings from the only home that I'd ever known. That's the day that changed the course of my life forever."

I held Jordan close and tried to comfort him. "I can't imagine how you feel. I'm so sorry."

This time I knew I heard the sniffles. "I found the letter from Wang while I was cleaning out the apartment. It was crumpled inside the pocket of the coat my mother had gotten him for his birthday the same year of the blackmail. I could tell that it was my father's way of punishing himself which is why he kept it as a reminder. I always wondered why he never got rid of that old coat, but that day, it all became clear. I was in such a rage when I realized that I'd made my father pay, when all he was trying to do was protect his wife and unborn child." The tears finally broke and flowed silently.

I wiped them with the back of my hand. "Now, I understand your need for revenge, but you have to try and forgive in order to live in peace, Jordan. I'm sure that's what your parents would've wanted for you. Not this," I explained as best I could.

Jordan bounded out of the bed and looked at me with fire blazing in his watery eyes. "My mother died anyway as if he pulled the trigger, and my father because of the guilt. It's because of that, that I will have no peace until I get every penny he took from us back and he's no longer breathing."

I could tell that Jordan was fighting the urge to break down and just have a good cry, but the man in him wouldn't allow it. The story he'd told me before about the lottery scam, and now this, had me confused. Plus, being that I was in lust, I couldn't make heads or tails past physical gratification to know fact from fiction, and personally, I didn't give a damn.

"I got—" He had to stop again to compose himself. "I got his diamond and he's not going to rest until he gets it back in his possession. Unfortunately, for him, I won't either until he's left with nothing. Especially, his life," he reiterated.

I decided to change the subject and ask about the wedding. "When we left out of the church with the rest of the crowd, what happened to the other jewelry?"

"A few of my men stayed behind and went underground. The

church has secret tunnels that haven't been used in years, which was the escape route we would've used had things not worked out as I planned them."

Then I remembered the people still obeying someone while we were all changing in the back. "Who was left behind shouting out orders and shooting?"

Jordan seemed to relax as he got back in bed and leaned back up against the headboard, and clasped his hands behind his head. "No one, except technology." He laughed out loud. "The men with the guns trained on the people in the upper pews were holograms. I had a tech; you met her, working sound effects, etcetera offsite. No gun was ever fired in that church and what smelled like gun smoke, was nothing but pop rocks. My problem is with Xing Wang, not God." His laughter pierced the air again when he thought about his handiwork. "When the doors of the church flew open, the part of our team that was mixed in seated with the congregation started the stampede and of course, everyone else followed. That little ingenuity allowed us to filter in with the crowd undetected. Meanwhile, the Joie De Vivre and other valuable jewels were being smuggled out in the opposite direction."

I was flabbergasted. "I am—I don't know what to say."

Jordan leaned over and kissed me. "Don't say anything; just give me that diamond between your legs."

Chapter 16

Two weeks later over breakfast on my terrace, Jordan was busy on his phone while I looked over into my neighbor's yard to see what he was up to. Instead of getting a glimpse of his rock-hard body, I saw his girlfriend leaving wearing that freshly fucked look. Before I could roll my eyes, I heard Jordan ending his call and quickly gave him my undivided attention.

He laughed while shaking his head as if he'd heard a good joke. "He did just as I expected. The Louvre blueprints are in a Beaverton 1000 burn safe."

"How do you know that?"

"The GPS has been sitting on an address in Paris for the last four days. That safe isn't going to be easy to crack, but I can do it. I'm waiting on the film sheets with his fingerprints to come through and then we're off to Paris."

The bacon I was about to bite into suddenly lost its appeal. "We? Jordan, I have a huge event coming up. I can't go to Paris."

Jordan took a sip from his coffee, leaned back in his seat and stared at me. I couldn't make out what was going through that manipulative head of his and he wasn't going to make it easy. He just continued to glare at me with his eyes becoming tighter than they already were—if that were even possible.

"Jordan, did you hear me?"

He put his coffee down and finally answered. "Yes, I heard you. The more things change, the more they stay the fucking same."

Nigga, please was the look I was sure that was etched on my face. "Why is this relationship so one-sided?" I questioned.

Jordan wiped his mouth, threw the napkin onto his plate and forcefully pushed his chair back and walked inside. I sat out on the terrace a moment longer before going in for the inevitable. When I stepped in, Jordan was half dressed and had his back to me. I tried to wrap my arms around him, but he wasn't having it.

He forcefully peeled my hands from around him and turned as he pointed his finger in my face and yelled, "Don't!"

I tried again, but was met with the same aggression. "Bianca, I'm not in the mood for your bullshit, all right!" He turned his back on me and continued getting dressed.

"What is it with you? I can't believe you're being so inconsiderate of what I do."

He took a calculated breath before facing me. "What you do is no comparison. I opened my heart to you, and this morning, you just trampled all over it. You don't give a damn about me, Bianca. All you care about is getting laid, but that's about to come to an abrupt halt. I have someone else in mind that doesn't mind being there for me when I need her to be."

A sinking feeling came over me. "Her? As in that *bitch* from the night at the Le' Ameritage?"

"She is not the only *her* that I know." Jordan tried to sidestep me, but I wasn't giving up that easily. I shoved into him, causing a lamp sitting on the nightstand to topple over before he connected with the wall.

Once he regained his balance, he charged at me. "Arrrggh!"

We tussled all over the room. I tried to slap him, but he was too quick and caught my hand before it could do any of the damage that I was hoping for.

"Have you lost your damned mind?" he yelled at me once he got my arms pinned down.

At this point, my anger had better authority over me than the common sense to try and rationalize what I was doing. I continued trying to fight him knowing he had the upper hand due to size, strength, his maneuvering techniques and training. He blocked every move I made before finally lifting me into the air and throwing me onto the bed. I tried to get up and come for him again, but what I saw in his eyes halted me in my tracks.

"I don't hit women, but I swear if you even look my way again, I won't hesitate to make an exception today."

Common sense had finally made its way into my thinking process, but I still wasn't done making my point known. "Why are you doing this to me?" My face was drenched from the avalanche of tears that decided to flow without my permission. "Why do you always have to issue an ultimatum when I can't do something for you?" Instead of going for him the way I wanted to, I took my aggression out on one of the pillows that decorated the bed.

Jordan shook his head and regarded me like I'd lost my mind. "Look at you, Bianca. You're not stable. I need a partner who knows how to keep a cool head and not wear her emotions on her sleeve." He stared at me a bit longer before saying another word. "I'm heading to Paris. I'll talk to you whenever, if ever."

He turned to leave and I behaved as the unstable bitch he'd just accused me of being. I leapt onto his back and tried to dig my claws into his skin, but he threw me off of him before I could do any damage. This time I landed on the floor instead of the soft bed.

He rushed me before I could recover, picked me up again and tossed me back onto the bed. "You wanna fight me?" he said as he unbuckled his pants. "I know exactly what you want."

As mad as I was, I did want it. Carnal urges won the battle as I ripped the buttons off of his shirt and bit into his flesh just enough to cause pain without breaking the skin. Like a vampire, I went for his neck and repeatedly bit him.

"Ahh," he gasped.

The bites left behind huge red welts for any bitch he was thinking about hooking up with to see. Not to be outdone, he took over when he did the same damage to my breasts. We were both bruised black, blue and red, but still going at it hot and heavy. I got on top kissing my way downtown and engulfed his inches into my ravenous mouth. Inhaling deeply to capture his masculine scent heightened my experience and made me feel closer to him. I took him all the way in and relaxed my muscles to control the gag while humming a delicious tune, igniting a spark that ran electric pulses up his spine as I continued pleasuring him to no return.

Jordan's breath caught in his throat as he grabbed my head moving it back and forth to match his strokes as he fucked my face. It wasn't long before he unloaded his frustrations down the hatch. When I removed my lips from his deflated dick, he exhaled long, deep breaths.

"I believe I have more than proved that I'm more than capable of being in control."

Trying to catch his breath and recover, he was only able to shake his head yes.

Chapter 17
Three Days Later ... Paris

After landing, we briskly walked through terminal 2A of Paris' Charles de Gaulle Airport to meet up with up with a contact. In grand Jordan style, I was dismissed and told to peruse Hermès that was located inside the airport while he conducted business. Being a shopaholic, I was only too glad to get away from his uptight ass. Before I walked into the store, I saw Jordan shake hands with a tall, white man sporting dark shades, goatee and a bald head. He appeared to be in his forties and very fashionable judging from his white, skinny-leg suit that Cody and Reggie would've wrestled him down to the ground for.

Almost an hour later with nothing else to do, I slowly browsed through the scarves trying to pass time since I'd already made my purchases. I was about to go over to the fragrance counter when I caught sight of Jordan heading in my direction.

He leaned in and kissed me. "Looks like we're in luck. My connect says that the address on my tracker is registering in the Trocadéro area which is heavily toured. The bonus is that the dumb fuck has his safe in the high-rise where we're now going to be staying in a room that's located directly beneath his. There's no turning back now, Bianca. Are you ready to step inside of my world?" Jordan asked as he relieved me of my bags.

"As ready as ever," I replied as I followed him out of the store and through the terminal.

My heels clickety-clacked on the tiled flooring as Jordan pulled me along the expansive airport. We stopped at Europcar to get a rental. Jordan spoke perfect French as he gave his reservation information to a young, busty blonde. A few times I caught her blue eyes ogling my man. Remembering what Jordan said about me wearing my emotions on my sleeve, I decided to let her make it.

"*Au revoir*, Monsieur Travis!" she said a little too excited for my taste and calling him by an alias.

"*Au revoir*," Jordan replied back over his shoulders as we walked out of the terminal and was met curbside with a black Porsche with red interior.

A nice-looking guy jumped out of the vehicle. This time, I was the center of attention. "*Salut ma belle!*" He helped me inside the car. His hands touched and lingered longer than necessary, but I didn't mind.

"*Otez vos mains de ma dame!*" Jordan spoke very fast and harsh. Whatever it was had the young man rattled.

He waved his hands back and forth frantically as he stepped away from me and the car backward. "*Je suis désolé! Je suis désolé monsieur!*" Jordan got inside the car mumbling to himself. I'd never seen him get jealous before, but I had to admit that it was a turn-on to know that I mattered. I eased my hand into his lap and massaged his dick through his pants. It responded immediately to my touch.

I was about to unzip them when he stopped my action and handed me a piece of paper. "Here, plug this address into the GPS."

I looked at the address, then the GPS system which was totally in French. "Jordan, I don't speak or read the language."

He took a deep breath and punched a few of the keys. "There, I switched it to English."

I did as I was told and put the address 5 Avenue Albert de Mun into the system. During the drive, I took in the city and its ancient beauty. The Eiffel Tower loomed ahead of us. I was in complete awe. Then there it was—the Musée du Louvre palace. I immediately thought of all that I'd heard about the treasures, specifically the Holy Grail, according to Dan Brown, author of the *The Da Vinci Code*. I was dying to tour the inside and see the spectacular magnificence up close and personal. I'd heard that you could view the museum from the underground lobby of the pyramid through the glass. That was great because I would like to have seen if that tomb was really there. Unfortunately for me, Jordan had other plans and sightseeing wasn't one of them.

The GPS signaled that we had arrived and I was thrilled that both monuments were still in viewing distance. Jordan tipped the valet before coming around to my side to lead the way to our new residence for the next few days. He took my hand and led me through the lobby where we were greeted by a doorman. Despite the luxurious lobby, I was still skeptical about our lodging. Chandeliers hung in sequential order all leading up to a larger one that was dramatically suspended in the middle of the ceiling as if floating on air. Silk tapestry adorned the windows and exquisite furnishings decorated the rest of the space. A petite, cinnamon-colored woman with bouncy, reddish curls welcomed us from behind a massive, glass-encased desk with gold finishes. While Jordan transacted business, I enjoyed watching people walking in and out of the building as they went about their day.

After he was done, Jordan came over followed by a bellhop with our two bags. "We're on the seventh floor." He busied himself with his cell.

I didn't know how he wanted me to respond to that dry-ass statement. So I said the first thing that came to mind. "Lead the way."

We got on the lift and went to the floor that we would be calling home for the next few days. When we entered our unit, I breathed in a sigh of relief when I saw that it matched the grand style of the lobby and was decorated just as superbly. I flopped down on the purple velvet sofa and watched Jordan as he tipped the bellhop. I then walked around inspecting every inch of the space. He still wasn't really speaking which was beginning to grate on my nerves. Hell, I could've stayed across the pond if he were going to ignore me the whole time.

Thirty minutes later, I was still trying not to let my emotions show, but this was ridiculous. "Jordan, are you going to continue behaving as though I'm not even here or what?"

"Isn't that what you did to me when that punk was sniffing around my pussy at the airport?"

Bingo! I knew it! He's jealous. "I took it as him being nice. It's not like I knew what he was saying to me."

Jordan poured himself a glass of wine and finally took a seat next to me on the purple velvet sofa. "You don't have to know the language to know when a man is interested. Body language is the same no matter what part of the world you're in, and you know it."

I shook my head in response. "Okay. You got me there, but what about Miss Prissy at the car rental counter? You don't think I noticed her being overly helpful."

Jordan held up his drink. "Touché. Now go and refresh yourself; my team Triple S will be here shortly."

Chapter 18

Jordan's crew of three joined us in the room a few short hours later. When that bitch walked in behind the white guy from the airport and another guy, I liked to have died on the spot. I tried to make the best of the situation and remembered that I was there to do a job, but once it was done, Jordan had some serious explaining to do.

Garza stopped the tape. I was surprised that he hadn't interrupted me way before now. "Ms. Brooks, did you get the names of any of his people, specifically the woman?"

My attorney shifted nervously in her seat. "The names I got were all code names. The man from the airport went by Snake— I assume because of a nervous condition of constantly darting his tongue out like one. The other guy was identified as Sledge, and what stood out about him besides his doe-like eyes, was the mole on the left side of his face resting on his cheek. Oh, and now that I think of it, they called the bitch, Seven." Aliyah cleared her throat unnecessarily loud.

"But I know that couldn't have been her real name," I interjected. Jordan informed me of who they were while I was getting dressed.

Dismissing the lie from earlier about not knowing the bitch's name, Garza immediately began flipping through his files as did the others in the room.

"Triple S is a name associated with our guy, Ramon Benavidez," one of the agents shouted.

Garza stopped looking and rubbed his chin. "Ramon Benavidez. Ramon Benavidez ..." He pondered. "Our ninety-eight-million-dollar embezzler who only got a year after spilling his guts?"

"The one and only, and get this," the agent said excitedly, as he scanned the file with his index finger, "when Benavidez gave names and relationships in order to strike a deal, he revealed that he and Jordan Lei went to NYU together."

Garza walked over to where the agent was sitting and picked up the file. "Benavidez has a tattoo on his back of a sledgehammer ... interesting. Are you thinking what I'm thinking, Agent Carter?"

Agent Carter and the others all agreed that the man that went by the name Sledge in Paris was none other than Ramon Benavidez.

Garza came over to me with a page filled with mug shots. "Even though I should hang your ass out to dry for lying about the woman, I'm willing to look over it since you slipped up and gave us way more than you meant to." He slammed the paper down in front of me and whispered in my ear. "Don't try to bullshit me again, Ms. Brooks. You're not as cunning as you think you are." He then straightened up and fixed his tie. "Can you tell me which of these men is Sledge?"

I looked at Aliyah with shock and worry, but she discreetly nodded her head signaling that it was OK. I thought back to how Jordan constantly berated me because I led with my emotions. *Hmm ... I knew he should've let Sledge's shifty ass go for a swim with the sharks instead of just firing him. Now he's cut a deal to serve Jordan's ass up on a platter in exchange for his freedom. Punk-ass motherfucker,* I thought as I scanned the images until I came upon his traitorous face that seemed to mockingly leap off the pages at me.

Without hesitation, I stated, "That's him." I pointed to a man with dark, low-cut, curly hair, doe-like eyes and a mole on the left side of his face resting on his cheek.

Garza's smile couldn't be contained when I accurately identified Benavidez. "Agent Carter."

When I saw the agent who put the clues together stand, the moment I caught a glimpse of those alluring gray eyes, my throat instantly went dry causing me to choke. I grabbed my glass of water and gulped down the contents, refilled it and took another sip. Our eyes connected instantly. Quickly, I lowered my eyelids as if there were a sudden need to inspect my fingernails.

His gray eyes went back to Agent Garza. "That's my name."

"I'm going to need you to take a little trip downtown and pay Mr. Benavidez a visit at the Lew."

Agent Carter gathered his files and was headed out the door when Garza gave him another set of instructions. "Make sure you're *very* persuasive."

"That's who I am ... Mr. Persuasive." His deep baritone voice mesmerized and tantalized my senses making me wish that we'd met under different circumstances. He had the right handle; he could've persuaded me to do anything.

Garza then turned his attention back to me. "Continue on, Ms. Brooks."

Within minutes of their arrival, sketch pads and equipment were strewn everywhere. Since I was the technically challenged newbie, I sat back and watched them work. My role, as I was told, would be the distracting eye candy ... again.

"Look to your right ... pause, then back to me ... pause, and then to your left ... pause," Jordan instructed Snake. "Okay, your coordinates are looking good and lining up perfectly. There's a camera built right into the bridge of your glasses that spans to both lenses. Whatever you see, it sees and transmits it back to this computer. As a result, Seven will see footage of everything on the right side of her screen. Make sure you get a good look at his place and pay special attention to the area where the safe is located. Are you with me?" Jordan asked while taking down the coordinates.

Snake stopped fidgeting with the glasses long enough to answer Jordan. "Yeah, I'm with you all the way, baby."

"Good. Easter won't think twice about you wearing glasses since you always have. Plus, according to my Trojans on the blueprint configurations, he has a biometric Beaverton 1000 burn safe. Normally, his fingerprint along with a code is needed, but just to cover all bases, I want you to get a good look into his eyes and keep them in focus for at least thirty seconds. But the longer, the better. I want to get a shot locked in to duplicate his eye coordinates in case we need a retina scan," Jordan explained to Snake.

Snake took the glasses off and became serious. "If we're going to do this, we only have one chance to get it right. The moment that Easter gets wind that he's being robbed, he won't show any mercy. I'm going to ask you for the last time: are you sure about this?"

Jordan looked at his team with certainty. "As sure as I am about my next breath. If any of you want to bow out, now is the time to do it. Easter didn't honor the code when he snubbed us all on the Bangkok job. Why should we? If he's foolish enough not to think that I wouldn't strike, then he's a bigger idiot than I thought him to be."

The bitch stopped typing and challenged Jordan. "Who's the fool if you believe that there's honor among thieves?" She stood and eyed everyone in the room. "I didn't come to Paris to go home empty-handed. So, if one of these pussies wants to back out, then that's a bigger slice of the pie for me."

Jordan looked over at Sledge who hadn't said a word until he noticed that all eyes were on him.

"I'm in," he answered casually.

"If this is too much for you, Sledge, now is the time to speak." Snake gave him a chance to take an out, but after being called a pussy, he had a point to prove. "I said I was in, damn it. Now, let's get this shit handled!" he said with more enthusiasm.

"Good. I'll send The Collector a little tip on our dear friend Easter before we leave. Postage from Paris just makes it seem ... more ... official."

The expression on Jordan's face was one of extreme pleasure due to whatever calculated evil he had in store for his enemies.

Chapter 19
The Setup

*B*ehind closed doors in our bedroom, Jordan walked around me one last time before I was to leave on the arm of Snake. I wore a sexy, electric-blue, just-above-the knee Alexander McQueen draped dress that flowed over my curves like water and a pair of provocative heels. With a beach wave, honey-blonde wig with auburn lowlights, green contacts, and facial prosthetics used to change my look around the eyes and forehead area, I hardly even recognized myself. The lady that stood in the mirror with Jordan was simply gorgeous. Any man, unless he was blind, would be crazy not to take notice of this buxom bombshell.

Standing behind me with his hands caressing my arms for reassurance, Jordan talked me through what to expect. "Don't think too much about it; just go with the flow and everything will be fine," he said before lifting my hair and kissing the nape of my neck. "Snake will not let anything happen to you and neither will I. I'll see everything that's going on through his eyes and so will Sledge and Seven," he assured me once again before releasing my hair as it fell around me like a cloud. "Are you ready?"

I nodded my head. I was actually feeling quite adventurous and looking forward to the impending meeting. "Don't worry, babe; I know what to do."

Jordan leaned in and kissed the side of my neck. His eyes were locked in on mine through our reflections in the mirror. "I can't wait to get you all to myself." He squeezed my arms again before letting his hands travel down the front of my torso and underneath my dress. His fingers found their way inside my panties and played tag with my clit.

"Ooooh. Umm ..." I moaned seductively as my knees nearly buckled.

No sooner than I was about to come, he removed his hand and stuck his drenched fingers inside of his mouth to suck my essence off of them. "Now, you have something to look forward to." He popped me on my rear. "Go get 'em with your sexy ass."

Snake and I used the service elevators, and then walked down a long corridor and out the back of the building where a parked black Mercedes-Benz rested. Snake ran a detector around and under it. I don't know what he was looking for, but I waited until he was satisfied.

"We're clear," he said to me, signaling that it was OK to get inside of the car.

We both stepped in. I put on my seat belt and waited on him to start the car. "Aren't we the meticulous one?"

Snake's tongue darted in and out a few times before responding. "In this line of business, you're dead if you're not." He pulled off without another word.

Snake drove the long way around passing the Eiffel Tower. At nighttime, the lights made it more stunning. The city was even more alive with people dressed for a night on the town. I people-watched wondering what their plans were for the evening. I often did this type of thing when I was a child. So here I was using my imagination to plan people's evenings based on what they were wearing. Before I knew it, we were pulling up in front of the building we'd just left. We were met by the same valet that had helped me out of the car earlier. As we were about to exit the car, Snake squeezed my hand and mouthed for me not to worry. I retrieved my clutch as the valet opened my door. This was all done in case our target had someone up front to alert him of our arrival.

We cruised through the lobby with me draped all over him like a cheap suit, since I was supposed to be his horny companion for the night. I could tell that Snake was enjoying me being all up on him. To my dismay, he got into character even more by caressing my ass when we got on the lift with two other couples. We arrived on the eighth floor, and were greeted by two other men. Snake slapped skins with them before going in for a one-arm hug.

A mountain of a man embraced Snake last. "It's good to see you back on the radar again. You had me worried for a minute there."

Snake gave him dap. "I was never off the radar, just cooling my heels. After being in this business for over twenty years, don't you think I had a little down time coming to me?"

A man with the face of a bulldog joined in on the conversation. "I thought I was going to have to call the Calvary to come rescue your old ass." They all laughed.

Snake ended the mini roasting session. "I'm sorry that I have to break this reunion up, but Easter is expecting me and I don't want to keep the little guy waiting." The retort evoked a laugh from the group. "Plus, I got X-rated things I want to do to this hot bitch on my arm. I'm sure you understand my haste, gentlemen." He brazenly grabbed a handful of my ass.

I let out a naughty giggle and let my hand grope his crotch in response. To my surprise, he wasn't wearing any underwear and was working with an average, but still nice package.

He adjusted himself so he wouldn't salute everyone. "See, she can't wait, either."

Both men looked me over with gluttonous lust dancing in their eyes wishing they could take me somewhere and bend me over. Not even on my worst day would I have them.

The one with the bulldog face rubbed his goatee while undressing me with his beady, red-rimmed eyes. "Hell yeah, I understand perfectly."

Snake smoothly switched the subject from me back to the business he had with Easter. "I sure hope you're in on this big job Easter's planning. It'll be like old times, my friends." They slapped hands again with Snake.

"That's why we were here, but he didn't give us a definite answer as of yet, but I'm sure we will be," the one who was eye-fucking me said to Snake.

Bulldog face spoke up next. "Well, we haven't eaten in about two hours and this French food doesn't hold us for long, so we're on our way to see if we can find a buffet of snails or something to terrorize." He laughed. "Talk to you later, Snake. Pretty lady." He winked at me before walking off.

We watched until they got on the lift and the doors were closed with the numbers going down. Snake then walked the rest of the short distance and knocked on the door of our target.

The door opened, and a little pipsqueak of a white man was revealed. I was expecting a John Travolta or a Tony Soprano type to be the other side of the door. Instead, Danny DeVito's twin, with an awful tan that made him look like he could pass for Hispanic or African American, was standing there. The little maggot wore round-rimmed glasses, a horrible brown toupee and was overdressed in a tux, of all things.

"Going somewhere special?" Snake asked, taking in his attire after he let us in.

He spread his arms out. "Every day that I wake up with the ability to take a deep breath is special. So, I dress for the occasion to celebrate God's blessing," he guffawed, really feeling himself when he shouldn't have been. "But in all honesty, I happen to have dinner reservations with a beautiful woman within the next hour." He stepped back and allowed us entry.

Once inside, he showed us to the bar, where he poured ready-mixed martinis.

Snake declined his offer. "You know I never touch anything that's going to cloud my judgment when I'm discussing business, Easter. It hasn't been that long, has it?"

Easter responded by making a tsk sound before putting the drinks down and walking us over to the sofa to have a seat. "I didn't think you'd mind drinking with an old friend." Then as just realizing that they weren't alone, he responded, "Where are my manners? Who is this lovely, tall being that I behold before my eyes?"

Snake eased his arm around me. "*Heather*, and she's my date for this evening, but you don't need to worry about her. She's just the chosen accessory that I decided to wear on my arm tonight. She won't be a problem for us. Isn't that right, babe?"

I was about to kiss him until that damn tongue darted out repulsing me. So instead, I opted to go for the crotch again to avoid tossing my cookies all over Easter's pretty white sofa. "Umm ... not at all, papi," I responded as seductively as I could using my perfected-over-the-years Latina accent.

Snake squeezed my hand because I was making his soldier rise for battle again. "Cut it out, babe." He tweaked my nipple and gleamed at me. "Now is not the time."

Easter had to catch drool from oozing out of his mouth when he caught sight of my plump nipple peeking through my dress. "Wha ... wha ..."

Snake snapped his fingers to bring him out of the trance that I had him under. "What's the plan?" He glanced at his watch and got straight to the point. "As you can see. . ." He felt me up some more causing Easter's eyes to grow as big as saucers as they watched Snake's hand disappear under my dress. To drive him mad with lust, I moaned like he was doing the damned thing when he was only touching my thigh, but Easter didn't know that. "I don't have a lot of time; as you can see, she's purring for me," Snake said as he removed his hand from under my dress and placed his fingers in his mouth. "Damn, you taste good."

Easter bit his bottom lip to suppress an escaping moan. After failing, he eased back in his chair to hide his diminutive erection. "Having the beautiful supermodel Giovanna, I can certainly understand your urgency."

Ugh, here we go with this Giovanna bitch again. Is there no escaping her? I wondered as I groaned inwardly.

Snake choked back a cough. "*The* Giovanna?"

Humph! How typical, I thought as seeing how men—no matter if they were gay or straight—worshipped her.

Feeling the power shift, Easter puffed his chest out and smiled broadly. "Of course it's *the* Giovanna and she's my date for the night." He smiled broadly.

Snake scratched his head. "You're one lucky bastard. I'll tell you that, but let's get back to the point of this meeting."

Finally! I breathed a sigh of relief. Cover or no cover, there was no way in hell I was going to sit there and listen at them go on and on about Giovanna. For as beautiful as she was, there was something unnerving about her.

Easter was filled with joviality. His shoulders shook from laughing so hard. He went into a hacking fit before he was able to settle down and get back to business. "As you can see, no hired guns are around, and I'm usually guarded like the president. See, I trust you, Snake, and I hope you feel the same way about me." He sniggered at the thought of trusting a snake. "Ahem ... Bangkok was bad business for us all. I don't have to tell you that." He cleared his throat some more and immediately started coughing again.

Snake was about to get up to keep him from choking when Easter's hand shot up.

"Need me to get you some water, man?"

Easter declined while clearing his throat before continuing. "Ahem ... before I let you in, I got to know that you don't hold Bangkok against me."

Snake reacted as though he were offended. "Look at me, Easter." Easter looked in Snake's direction, but not at him. "No, look me in the eyes so that we can be on the same page once and for all about this Bangkok debacle." Snake leaned forward and Easter did as he was told. "We go back in this business together since day one." He held up one finger. "I've always had your back and you've had mine. When have I ever let you down?"

Easter shifted a bit, but held eye contact long enough for Jordan to get what he needed. "I ... I know what we have, but The Tarantula. He's another story. You're loyal to him. Hell, I was too at one point until he thought he was in charge and started to change. I'm my own man, Snake. I don't need a self-righteous prick like Tarantula telling me when I can take a shit or how to think!" His finger rested on his temple to show that he had a brain like we didn't know; even if it was pea-sized, he still had one.

Snake stood and began pacing. He made sure to take in every inch of the room. There was a door with a biometric lock on it. It had to be where the safe was located. He then turned his attention back to Easter. "I thought I was the only one feeling that way about Tarantula. Actually, I was okay with it since we always accomplished the jobs and got paid down the middle. Where

Tarantula fucked me was when he thought he had the right to whatever he wanted, even if it was my woman."

Easter peered at Snake incredulously before breaking out into a hearty roar when he was met with the same look. "So it's true? I'm freaking thrilled that everything is finally out about The Tarantula and Seven; I couldn't stand watching you fawn all over that bitch while she two-timed you with him. It was freaking ridiculous."

Snake shot me an uneasy glance in the hopes that I wouldn't blow my cover. I sat poised and ready to endure whatever it was that was about to be revealed.

Snake shook his head with a pained expression on his face. "You mean to tell me that you knew?"

"Everybody knew ... well, except you."

Snake threw his hands up. "Of all the jobs I'd pulled over the years, you'd think that I would be up on being two-timed. Especially, someone I considered like a brother, at that."

"Hell, she had you so far gone that you wouldn't believe me if I showed you footage of the two of them. You beat Bo into a coma when he tired, so excuse me for not wanting to meet the same fate, my friend. He's never recovered from his head injuries brought on by you, you know."

Snake hung his head remembering the rage that had taken over him that day. He'd felt so guilty for what he'd done to Bo. He'd secretly made huge deposits off of every job into his account to keep him and his family afloat since the man could no longer form a sentence, let alone earn a living. No thanks to him.

Easter knew that Snake was flashing back down memory lane as he sat in silence for what seemed like an eternity.

"Every time I think about what I did to Bo, I ... I ... I feel like such a fool." He breathed deeply and slowly released it. "What can I say? She was my only weakness and they knew it. That's why I stayed away. I had to get my head right after they betrayed me. They treated me like I was nothing, after all that we'd been through. So you want to talk about loyalty?" Snake's voice elevated. "Tarantula doesn't know the meaning of the word, but this is a new day. I came to Paris because it's time that I got my dick wet again, and the only way to achieve that, is by doing what I love. I need to feel that surge running through the blood in my veins again, and this job is the only thing that can give me my life back, man." His voice held such fury as he spoke. I didn't know if he was for real or putting on a show, but he was damn convincing, whichever it was.

Easter clapped his hands like he'd just been entertained. "I'mma let you in on a little secret." He stopped his round of applause long enough to clear his throat before leaning forward like there was someone else besides us in his suite. "Word going around was that I'd left the business after the botched Bangkok job. Also, rumor has it, that I double-crossed you all and needed to lay low. When the truth is, I never left. I just got smarter and decided to put my focus on bigger scores and work for myself. I got this apartment after that fiasco, which turned out to be a huge loss for us all— well, except for the one who got there first." He scratched his head and cleared his throat again which were big indicators that he was lying about what really had happened in Bangkok. "I'm convinced that it was The Tarantula, but that's another story. Pulling this off will be the biggest blow to The Tarantula's over-inflated ego, and I can't wait to be the one to do it." He rubbed his hands together looking like a little troll doll. "There were whispers about the Louvre score even then. According to those murmurs, the score is going to be astronomical if it can be pulled off. Since then, I've made Paris my home and connected with the buyer that was looking for someone to pull the job off. He's very particular with what he wants."

Chapter 20

Snake's eyes gleamed interest in Easter's story. "So, who's this mysterious buyer?"

"Now, you know I can't give you that information, but once I get the goods of his choosing, just know that we will be able to retire if we want to."

Snake's tongue darted in and out a few times while he sat taking in all of what Easter was selling him. "Fair enough, but how much are we talking? Surely, you can give me that much at least."

"You always were a man about the details, Snake, but to answer your question, the bounty is in the high-seven figures, my friend." He smiled cunningly. "Just to let you know, the Louvre, and taking down The Tarantula, have become my missions in life. I've accomplished most of my goals while getting to know some good escape routes from the Louvre, in case those blueprints didn't come through. I've studied their security measures and uncovered a few blind spots in the process." Easter happily divulged. "Plus—"

"Blind spots?" Snake interrupted.

"Yes, blind spots. The palace is heavily secured, but like anything else, it has its flaws and weaknesses. Focusing mainly on the assets, while leaving 'spots.'" He used his fingers as quotations. "Their vulnerability is what I'm going to use to get the job done."

Snake shifted his body weight when he leaned forward to get where Easter was going with his findings. "So, let me get this straight: you know the changing of the guards, which is the easy part. You have an idea of what measures are being taken, but what you don't know, is what you can't see like the lasers that I'm sure they have in place. Plus, I know there has to be silent trigger alarms on each painting and other valuables in the place."

Easter chuckled in response. "Of course they do, Snake, but as you should also know, I'm well versed in the art of stealing much like your hero, The Tarantula. When I was able to stomach his arrogance long enough, I actually learned a lot from the bastard. The Louvre is very secure and you're right; I wouldn't have been able to see the lasers during business hours except in the case of the valuables, which are always activated. As I told you, I've been studying. I took a detector and went to the museum after midnight when I knew all security would be in full force. You can see the lobby of the pyramid through the glass ceiling which would be the ground outside. I stood on it peering down to see if I could find any lasers and as suspected, I didn't."

"Easter—"

Easter jumped up and practically threw a temper tantrum for being interrupted. "Give me some fucking respect!" His arms flailed about crazily and spit flew from his angry, contorted mouth. "I'm better than The Tarantula, and you will respect me, damn it; and this is why." He held up one shaking finger. "It was I who successfully got away with Matissio's *Pope* and two other valuable paintings during a heist at a premier art gallery last year. Me! Not him, but *me!*" His hand flew to his chest pounding it fiercely. I was hoping he was going to knock the wind out of himself so we could just take what we needed and leave.

Snake and I looked at each other confused, then back at Easter, who was indeed throwing a fit. Snake held up his hands in surrender letting the little imp have the floor before he had an aneurysm. The scowl on his face was that of a spoiled child, and it nearly killed me not to bust a gut.

"For the last three years ... " The look in his eyes dared Snake not even think about interrupting him again. Again, it took all that I had to control myself. "*Nothing* has consumed me like the Louvre. She's the last thing on my mind when I go to sleep at night and the first thing when I wake up in the morning." He waited to see if Snake was going to object. When he saw that he wasn't, he proceeded. "The lasers aren't visible to the naked eye and since there's no law against looking, no one paid me any mind. First, I used the detector and got somewhat of a read, but after viewing the specs' proximity, the readings had to be coming from the glass. We all know there's a sizeable amount of space between the ground and the floor of the museum. Not one to have only one trick up my sleeve, I then put on a pair of what looked to be regular eyeglasses, and that's when I saw them. I examined as much as I could to see how they were running and the sons of bitches changed positions every thirty seconds it seems. There's no learning the sequence in order to crawl through like *Tarantula* would normally do. That's old school and played out, just like he is." He laughed. "My next thought was to figure out a way to freeze them, but thought, that would more than likely trigger a silent alarm leaving us vulnerable. Just when I was about to give up, I saw a blind spot. To make sure this spot wasn't a glitch in the system, I went back sporadically for six months disguised differently every time and discovered it was permanently blind.

"And that's not the only thing; the guards delay the lasers to prevent them from going off as they make their rounds. I managed to get locked in the museum for ten minutes once everything was shut down. I put on my glasses and saw other blind spots that were the same circumference as the one I scoped for six months. I tripped the alarm on purpose to see how fast the response time was, and what else would be activated to know what we were up against. That one incident gave me just as much insight as the rest of my research. I conducted a few more alarm triggers to see if something new would occur, but they all yielded the same results. I know the camera positions, timing, layout and the rhythm of the lasers and how they are placed. During this experience, I did some checking around on the backgrounds of a few guards, collecting detrimental dirt that I don't mind exposing if we have to get in through them as they're making their rounds, if all else fails." Easter seemed to be power-drunk. "Let's just say, I'll be better prepared than the great Tarantula ever was."

I was waiting on him to take a bow after his long-ass spiel. Snake raised his hand like a kid in school to make sure it was OK for him to interject. Easter nodded his approval.

"As a man, I just felt disrespected, but as a mastermind, I apologize for making you feel inept. However, I would appreciate it if you'd stopped making comments as if I was Tarantula's bitch. He's your hang-up, not mine." Snake threw the ball back in Easter's court.

Easter hesitated, undoubtedly thinking before he said the wrong thing. He knew by the look on Snake's face that he'd used his one and only lifeline and not to try him again. "Sorry ... er ... umm, Snake. You know I get passionate when it, umm ... comes to umm ... you know to ... to pulling off a caper."

"You're straight. I just wanted to make myself clear so there would be no misunderstandings." Snake motioned for him to continue with a gesture of the hand.

"As I was saying, I know where each piece is located, its cataloging information as well as its significance. The whole enchilada. The only piece missing was the original blueprints, which have information that the newer ones wouldn't like old underground tunnels, and even older water exits. I finally commandeered them, but at a hefty price. Validation has already been made to ensure that they weren't fakes. It wasn't easy, but luckily for us, everyone has a price."

Snake folded his arms over his chest. "If you were able to get them validated from someone within the museum, couldn't you have just as easily gotten the prints from your source?"

"There's too much red tape involved, and I don't need a paper trail. It's like I said: everyone has a price, especially when it comes at the expense of their life."

"Can I see them?" Snake asked. The thick cloud of tension that was hovering over the room, as well as my need to laugh, was now slowly dissipating.

Like a giddy kid being given permission to play with his new favorite toy, Easter didn't waste any time scurrying as fast as his stubby legs would take him to the door with the biometric lock. It opened to an empty room with a huge vault inside. Snake waited giving Easter the privacy he thought he had while going through all of his security measures that included a retina scan, like Jordan thought it would. Without raising suspicion, he took a quick survey of what was inside the vault while Easter turned his back to retrieve the blueprints. From where I was seated, I could see most of everything that was taking place.

When they returned to go over them, I was still sitting in the same spot twirling my hair. While Snake browsed the blueprints, Easter tried to be slick and throw a few flirtatious gestures my way, as though he didn't just act a baby in front of me. I smiled and batted my eyelashes like the airheaded bimbo I was supposed to be.

"Looks authentic to me," Snake approved as he scrutinized the document before handing it back to Easter. "I have the perfect crew for the job you're trying to pull off. I met these youngsters some years back when we were all hired by a giant corporate suit to get copies of a prototype before the first e-reader was introduced to the public."

Suddenly, Easter's short arms started whipping about wildly as he jumped to his feet. "Whoa ... wait a minute, rattlesnake! Did you pull it off and who was this suit?"

Snake chuckled. "You know the rules. I can't divulge that information and of course it was a success. Why do you think one company is now dominating the market when it comes to those things?"

"And some youngsters helped you pull off a job like that?" Easter asked skeptically.

"The Kids, as I now call them, were damn phenomenal in that expedition. The girl's name is Delilah, and man, talk about having knowledge, balls, moves and skills, this chick can't be touched. The guys, Stanley and Kirk, are nothing to sneeze at either. They remind me of a younger version of Triple S, and you know how in synch and in demand we were before Jordan fucked up that chemistry, but never again. What do you say?"

Easter sat down and leaned back into the sofa while rubbing his double chin. "Snake, normally I go with my own men, people that I know personally, and a girl ... shhh ... that's Tarantula's kind of thing. As my father always said, never send a girl in to do a man's job."

That was it! I couldn't contain the laugh that finally made its way out of my mouth. Snake rubbed my leg, indicating that I needed to put a lid on it. Tears sprang into my eyes, but I managed to stop before I became a howling fit.

Easter's look of lust for me was replaced by one of *how dare she*. "I see the *lady of the night* has heard something amusing. Do you mind sharing what it is?"

"I—"

Snake interrupted by holding his hand up before I could explain. "Never mind her; she's just my chosen arm accessory for the night. As I've stated earlier, if I'm to be a part of this, they are the ones that I work with."

Easter leaned forward with his hands positioned in his face as though he were praying. His leg began to shake. "I need you, Snake. This kids team you have, I ... I don't know. Let me get back to you on that. This job is being done for a very important man, and I can't afford to have any screwups or I'm dead, literally, man."

Easter's pleas went over Snake's head as he gave his conditions once more. "If you want me, those are my terms, and they're nonnegotiable."

Easter drew in a deep breath and looked over at me, then back at Snake. "Okay! Fine. As long as my man Novikov can be on the team, then I can live with that."

Snake smiled slightly at the victory while nodding his head. "The name Novikov doesn't ring a bell, but I see no problem with it as long as he respects my team." He paused for a brief second. "I have a question for you, though, Easter."

Easter arrogantly responded as if he hadn't given Snake enough control over *his* mission already. "And what might that be?"

"How is this going to be the undoing of The Tarantula?"

As if he were bipolar, Easter belted out a hearty laugh becoming excited all over again. It was like he just hadn't acted a fool a minute ago. "Who do you think came up with the plan? He's slipping, and having too many pillow-talk sessions with the women he entertains. I sent a woman I knew he couldn't resist to seduce him, and like the hound dog that he is, he took the bait and after one drink too many, he revealed the seller to her. I contacted the source and made him an offer that he couldn't refuse. The money I paid for the plans will seem like peanuts once we storm the Louvre and get The Collector what he wants."

I choked when I heard that name. Both men looked in my direction. When they saw that I was OK, they continued their conversation.

"So the man that has you petrified is that rice-eating son of a bitch, Collector?" Snake asked Easter.

"You know him?"

"Yes, I know of him. He's powerful, I'll give him that, but he bleeds like every other man when punctured or shot."

A surge of energy renewed Easter's confidence after hearing that Snake didn't fear The Collector. "I like where this is headed; maybe we can do a little side action *if* you know what I mean. In the meantime, I need to get going to meet with a prime piece of ass that's attached to the one and only Giovanna. Every man's fantasy. Unlike The Tarantula, you can guarantee that I won't be getting wasted and giving away the keys to the kingdom. I'm telling you, he's losing his touch, Snake."

Snake shook his head while thinking Easter would fuck over Lucifer at the prospect of making an extra dollar for himself. "I've always said that cunt and booze would be his downfall." He laughed. "And yours too." *Dirty little motherfucker.*

Easter went over to the bar to get his abandoned drink. "I'll drink to that."

Chapter 21

*A*fter Snake's chat with Easter, we left the building, got back inside of the car and drove to Champs-Élysées where there were plenty of restaurants and nightlife activity. I was ready to party, but I couldn't seem to get The Collector's name out of my head. I wondered if Snake knew about Jordan's vendetta, but thought it best not to say anything. I'd bet all of my newly acquired riches that Jordan was lining all of his enemies up to take each other out. He was playing a dangerous game that had me wondering if I was a sitting duck.

According to Snake and Jordan, Easter would have us followed just to be sure that he wasn't being double-crossed. Suffice it to say that he was right. I spotted a white male appearing to be in his mid-to-late thirties with long, blond hair with another man who had a very bad toupee when we'd left Easter's. Not surprisingly, they were now sitting a few tables over from where we were dining.

Snake laughed while he sipped his after-dinner coffee that he was having with a decadent chocolate piece of cake for dessert. "I see we have company."

I savored the warm Crème Brûlée I'd just spooned into my

mouth. "Umm ... yes, I've noticed that too." Then I did a double-take and shielded my face without being too obvious. "Oh shit, it's Vicente and Antonio!" They suddenly had appeared.

Snake used the butter knife and caught what he could of their reflection. When they approached the table, and spoke with him without recognizing me, I inwardly breathed a sigh of relief.

"Look at this punta. How's it going, Worm?" Vicente said.

Snake laughed. "Is that the best you can do?"

"Trying to double-cross us again? I guess the last lesson taught you wasn't effective enough."

Snake wasn't in a bantering mood. "Can't you see that I'm trying to entertain this beautiful lady?"

Both men looked at me and for a moment, I thought my cover was blown. "You need to be thanking her," Antonio spat.

Snake's hand disappeared under the table. "And why is that?"

Antonio saw Snake's movement and smirked. "Because she just saved your pathetic life." With that, they left us with only Easter's two goons watching us.

"What was that about?"

"Nothing for you to worry about. They're just upset about the Bangkok job."

"Oh," I said, but was thinking that Snake was hiding something.

After dinner, we went to a few nightclubs on Champs-Élysées and needless to say, so did our uninvited guests. The entire street was festive with tourists and Parisians having a ball. To get my mind off the goons following us, the things discussed about Jordan's playboy lifestyle and The Collector, and Antonio's and Vicente's reemergence, I immersed myself into the atmosphere while staying true to my character of being an airheaded bimbo gone wild.

We danced and drank the night away. I learned that Snake had some nice moves on him to be a white man in his fifties. What annoyed the hell out of me about him was that damn tongue that would dart out just for the hell of it. If anyone was paying attention to us, they would have thought he was a nasty, long-tongued, pussy-eating freak, but if only they knew. Just when I got over his disgusting habit, his lips were damn near inside of my ear canal as he gave me some instructions letting me know that it was time to switch it up and get back to the safe house. First, he had a couple of ladies to distract our unwanted guests and then gave me a slip of paper.

Then, per his orders, I went into the restroom, read the note, balled it up and made a beeline for the third stall. Before going in, I made sure no one was else was there. Once inside the stall, I flushed the letter down the toilet. Next, I took off my heels, stood on top of the toilet and removed the air vent. I felt around until my hand made contact with what I was looking for. I then busied myself by discarding the wig, prosthetic face coverings, contacts and the to-die-for electric blue dress. I stuffed them all inside the oversized snakeskin hobo that I retrieved from inside of the vent. It held my new ensemble—a super-short red dress, fishnets and thigh-high boots. After quickly changing, I gave my hair a shake and toss to achieve a seductive but untamed look.

After making sure the coast was clear, I stepped out of the stall and checked my face to make sure nothing was amiss. The door swung open startling me, as three drunken white girls staggered in on wobbly legs trying to hold each other up while laughing like they didn't have a care in the world. I breathed a sigh of relief, and left them to their throwing up or whatever they were going to be doing. When I passed Snake, he was still at it with a dead ringer of me from the looks to the dress that I'd just taken off. He saw me and slyly pointed his finger at our guests who were still rooted at the bar watching "us" intently. Snake then gave me a thumbs-up before lifting my double into the air and twirling her around.

A welcoming cool breeze smacked me in the face when I exited the club. I wandered down Champs-Élysées to the Grand Palais where a white Range Rover was parked with its hazard lights on. I took the keys out of the hobo and let my hand run over the Beretta 950 Jetfire, a just-in-case precaution that was lying peacefully in the side pocket of the purse. There was no one that looked to be a threat lurking about since our guests thought they still had us in their sights. However, that did little to quell my paranoia. Doors locked, I quickly programmed the GPS and left for the safe house. Thank God it was in English!

Chapter 22

When I walked inside, Jordan was at the computer sitting awfully close to Seven. Sledge was nowhere to be found. I wanted to go off after what I'd heard and now this, but Jordan beat me to the punch.

He turned his chair around to where he was facing me. "Before you get upset, nothing that Snake said was true. Well, except for the part about the pillow talk, but I knew who she was working for. I set the whole thing up so Easter would take the bait," Jordan explained.

I looked over at Seven who sat quietly, still watching the activity on a bank of computer monitors. Bitch wasn't so vocal now. "What about her and Snake?"

"Inseparable. When it comes to a job, we do what we have to do to get it done." Just then, Sledge let himself in.

Jordan turned his attention to him. "Well?"

"The layout is the same as this flat which we gathered from the video. The floors are marble, but underneath them is some serious inches of concrete and steel. With the vault, that's another five or so inches, give or take a few. We're roughly looking at about thirteen inches of concrete and steel to get through and that's just me guessing. C-Four is definitely out of the question. This has to fly under the radar. Which brings me to plan B." Sledge clasped his hands together. "I have access to a Stealth 5800 laser beam circular saw. The motor is quiet. The cut is clean, but it'll take some time. Either that or we can use a compression detonator. It's not as noisy as C4, but it can still be heard nonetheless," Sledge explained without stopping to take a breath.

"The front door seems the more logical choice," I said to get Jordan's attention back on me since I'd been dismissed without a word. "He's a temperamental dweeb; how hard can it be to get past him?"

Jordan threw his hands up in frustration. "Looks are deceiving and you wonder why I —" He raised his fist in the air, then brought it crashing down on the table like he wished it were me instead. "Bianca, when I want your opinion, I'll give it to you. Understood?"

This was a job. I had to remind myself. Fuck that! "To hell with you, Jordan!" I stormed off into the room and slammed the door. *Why in the hell was I even here?* I wondered.

The next morning, I woke up to voices and unfamiliar sounds. Jordan's side of the bed hadn't been slept in and I was still fully dressed. My head was pounding and all I wanted to do was go home. I sat up and tried to decipher what was being said, but it was a lost cause with all of the other racket that was going on. There was nothing left for me to do but get a hot shower, some food in my stomach, and try my best to get through the day without stepping on any toes.

After showering, I dressed comfortably in a black velour track suit with a pink T-shirt that had black cursive lettering that read *Pleasure Diva*. I pulled my hair up into a playful ponytail and took one last look in the mirror.

As soon as I stepped out of the room, I looked around until I found Jordan on a ladder with Sledge and Snake passing him some type of devices. In the second bedroom, there was a circle of black things stuck to the ceiling that Jordan was placing within a precise space of each other with the help of some electronic laser.

"Good morning, all," I said in general, receiving dry responses back. I left them to whatever they were doing and went to get a cup of the coffee I smelled brewing. The moment I walked into the kitchen, who did I see but that Bitch making her a cup.

"Top of the morning." She smiled sweetly at me.

"Hmph," I grunted and went about making me a cup.

She leaned against the granite counter, sizing me up. "You know I'm not the enemy, right?"

I was about to pour in some vanilla creamer and stopped. "Excuse me?"

She faced me and placed her coffee on the counter. "I said we don't have to be enemies. I understand your angst, but face it, honey, we had a hell of a night our first encounter." She laughed. "We were closer than close, and from the way you took to me that night. . . well, I thought we were past you letting your claws come out whenever I just so happen to be around."

This bitch had lost her damned mind. For one, I didn't know what the hell she was talking about let alone arriving at a point of being friendly with her. "Let me get a few things straight, darling. I don't like you." I held up one finger. "I don't trust you around my man." Another finger. "And whatever happened that night couldn't have been all that great because I don't remember any of it." The last gesture I gave her was the *fuck you* finger.

Roaring laughter escaped her. "You may not remember it, but you damn sure enjoyed my sweet sap that coated your tongue. Hmm, you couldn't seem to get enough." She chuckled. "You have a problem with me and that's fine, but let me get something straight with you, *darling*." She pointed her finger in my face, but quickly snatched it back when I reached out to break it off of her hand. "I was here before you, and guess what?" She paused for a dramatic effect. "I'll be here when you're long gone. Just like the rest, *darling*, you're nothing special so get over yourself, and things will go a lot smoother for you in the process." She picked up her coffee in an attempt to let her words be last, but somehow a handful of her hair found its way into my hands.

I lunged and initiated the attack causing the hot java that she was holding to burn us both. The biggest mistake I made was reacting to the scorching liquid and giving her time to get the best of me when she pulled a move I didn't see coming. With little effort, she flipped me over her back and onto the floor. She straddled me with her fist hovering inches just above my face when Snake grabbed her.

"What in the hell is going on in here?" Jordan shouted as he pushed through and stared down at me menacingly.

I didn't feel the need to explain myself so instead of responding, I got up to leave when Snake finally got that bitch up off of me. No sooner than I was up, that I was nearly knocked back down onto the floor by Jordan.

"What the fuck, Jordan?" I said as I pulled from his firm grasp. Snake was comforting Seven like her ass was the one pinned to the floor about to be pummeled to death. Before I could utter a word, Jordan roughly grabbed me again and shook me a like a rag doll. "I told you I don't have time for all that emotional shit, Bianca!"

"Let go of me!" I screamed as I struggled to break free of his hold, but he was too strong.

"Move out of my way!" he hollered at Snake and Seven as he dragged me through the apartment by the hood of my jacket and shirt while kicking and screaming, creating damage to anything in our path. I saw Sledge wearing a smirk on his face as if he were enjoying the show. We didn't stop until we were behind the closed doors of our bedroom.

"What the fuck is your problem?" Jordan demanded to know.

My ponytail had come undone and hair was in my face, making it hard for me to see anything. The pain from the carpet burns on my back was unbearable. "I don't have a problem," I snapped while trying to get the hair out of my face so I could assess the damage done to my aching back.

Jordan's hands gripped their way around my neck tightly as he lifted me back onto my feet before swinging me onto the bed. His weight pressing down on me made it hard to breathe. "After we leave here, I don't ever want to see your deranged ass again. You got that?" His grip tightened when I didn't answer fast enough. "I will—"

"Yes," I was able to get out some kind of way. After receiving his answer, he released his clutches from around my neck. I gasped and coughed for air while trying to catch my breath, all the while finger-combing the hair out of my face. I couldn't believe what had just happened. There was nothing left for me in Paris. After catching my breath, I lay there scared to move as I watched Jordan watching me.

When the stare-down match ended, I wouldn't know. I rolled over wiping drool and hair from the side of my face. I looked around the room to see if Jordan was still there, but I found myself in bed alone. After recalling what had taken place between Jordan and me, I felt around my neck and winced at the stiffness and pain that resided in it. With my sore back being of major concern, I slowly got up and pulled my luggage from the wardrobe. I packed the few things I'd traveled with along with the electric-blue dress and heels that I had worn the night before.

The next thing on my agenda was to pull myself together and comb my hair so that I would look at least halfway presentable when I left for the airport. I took care to examine my back in the bathroom and see if there was anything that I could find to soothe it.

When I came out of the bathroom, I found Jordan sitting in a chair with his head resting in his hands. Our eyes locked in on each other, but I was in no mood for another stare down. I went to my suitcase so that I could leave without incident.

"Where do you think you're going?" His voice was raspy and deeper than normal.

I didn't have anything to say to Jordan. Instead, I focused on adjusting the handle on my luggage, but damn it, it was stuck and not cooperating. He came over to where I was struggling with the handle and placed the luggage to the side. When I tried to walk away, he caught me around my waist and pulled me into his embrace.

He rested his forehead against mine. "I'm so sorry, baby." Visible tears that he didn't try to hide ran down his face and dripped onto mine. The good cry that he needed was finally getting its due.

In an attempt to comfort him, I reluctantly wrapped my arms around him. "I forgive you." No words were needed after that. Even with tears streaming down his face, he was still aroused by the closeness of our bodies.

His hand found its way to my face where he stroked it lightly. They then traveled down to my sore neck. He tilted my head to the side to get a better view. When he saw the angry red prints from his hands and the carpet burns on my back, he couldn't deny what had happened. The bruises he'd left behind served as a painful reminder of what he had done to me. His head dropped in shame.

"Bianca." My name was barely audible when it came out of his mouth as he fell to his knees in a heap of misery. "I don't know what came over me. I ... I've never done anything like this before. I'm so sorry," he cried.

I cradled his head against my abdomen and let him get it all out. My thoughts were conflicted; I knew why these jobs were so important to him. They were a means to an end. Jordan was trying to get his family's dignity, money and respect back from the one who had taken it. But did that mean I had to endure what I'd been getting from him? Abso-fucking-lutely not!

An hour later, we were all seated at the dining room table inside the safe house listening to Snake's evaluation of Easter's apartment.

"The flat is the same floor plan as ours and since we're directly below him, going through our ceiling into the room where the safe is would be the best in. He definitely has a Beaverton 1000 burn safe. From what we know about burn safes, we need to first pump in liquid CO_2 with a two-way solenoid injection valve to offset it, but it has to be precise. Otherwise, everything in the safe will burn hence the name.

"And if done right?" I interrupted from where I was perched next to Jordan. I figured if I was going to be in, then I needed to know as much as I could absorb.

Snake had a don't-disturb-me-again expression on his face like he was still upset with me for fighting his precious Seven. He took in a deep breath and continued. "If done right, everything in the safe will freeze if we snap the cold chip, but this is *if* we have to break into it. Hopefully, the fingerprint and code detectors on the blueprints gave us accurate information, but we're always prepared with plan B," he explained.

Jordan stood and took over. "There are a total of four men guarding his place as we speak. Two at the door and I'm assuming the other two are inside." He pointed. "Seven, you're going to run interference from your post here in the room by being our eyes with the building's surveillance system and elevators to offset any surprises. Sledge, you're taking over the tail. I already have Snake's crew, the Kids, on him as we speak in order to avoid suspicion. You're in charge of them, but you are to report directly back to me for direction if anything comes up."

Sledge was dressed as a tourist wearing a backpack. He also sported Justin Bieber's old look with a windswept-styled wig and dork glasses. He was leaning back on his chair swigging on a warm beer that he'd been nursing since the meeting started. "I can handle that." His reply was a little too nonchalant for my taste, but who was I to make any noise.

Jordan's attention lingered on Sledge a little longer before continuing. "Snake, you're with me in the foxhole." Lastly, he pointed at me. "Bianca, you'll be assisting and working the slider camera to see what's happening on the other side of that door while we're in," he concluded.

I didn't want to appear stupid by asking what he meant by a foxhole, especially in front of that bitch. "Okay."

"Does anyone have any questions?" He looked around at the four faces at the table. When there was no response from us, he clapped his hands loudly. "Okay, let's get to it."

Everyone checked their weapons and other equipment to make sure everything was in order. The rest of us were all dressed in black fitted clothes, but the stretch cotton material made them comfortable. Since we knew there would be a retina scan, Jordan wore the contact lenses that duplicated Easter's to a tee.

In the bathroom and sitting at the vanity, I pulled my hair into a tight chignon with no loose strands and finished off my look by applying the deepest of red matte lipstick. I sat a moment longer looking at my reflection in the mirror and wondering who was the girl staring back at me. Since meeting Jordan, I'd compromised my integrity by engaging in illegal activities that I never would've thought of otherwise. Humiliated. Disrespected. Now physically abused, but yet here I was once again rising to his occasion. Maybe Reggie was right; maybe I didn't have a backbone.

Chapter 23
The Take

*E*aster, like most height-challenged men, loved nothing more than having a tall, modelesque beauty to flaunt around on his arm. As predicted, Easter was only too glad to see that the beautiful Giovanna was interested in him the day they'd locked eyes on one another while dining at Le Clos des Gourmets. Giovanna had received a bottle of what she was drinking, compliments of Easter. To show a token of her appreciation, she'd invited him over to her table where they'd enjoyed each other's company over wine and delectable French cuisines. After their brief encounter, they had become inseparable ever since.

Fast-forward to two months later, Easter was to escort Giovanna to L'Opéra Bastille to celebrate her birthday. The spoiled beauty wanted to attend a ballet and much to Easter's loathing of all things opera, he knew he had to grant her wish if he wanted to remain on her good side. Sledge reported back to Jordan that the limo had just left Café de la Paix where they'd had dinner and was en route to the opera house.

Jordan looked at each of us signaling showtime. Snake and Jordan activated the circular saw that in a few swift circular rounds was able to get through the layers of the floor faster due to the compression that was done earlier. Afterward, they removed the circular cut just big enough for us to fit through in the ceiling. I waited for them to hand each other the equipment needed. Snake was the first one in to make sure it was OK for us to follow. Next, Jordan reached out for me as I climbed the ladder and joined Snake. Following hand signals, Seven removed the ladder and went back to her post at the bank of computer monitors.

Snake and Jordan communicated via sign language and Seven transmitted back to me through the bluetooth as she watched them from the monitors made possible by another camera identical to the one that I was using.

Per Seven's instructions, I was to stick the almost invisible camera unit that was attached to a thin see-through, cylindrical tube through the bottom of the door. The video surveillance allowed me to see everything that was going on within the perimeter of the room outside of where we were. I watched to see what the guards in place were up to and caught a visual of them sitting on the same sofa that I was on during my visit. They were engrossed in what was on television. I gave a thumbs-up to Jordan and Snake to proceed.

Snake handed Jordan a transparent sheet that had two handprints. He carefully placed each fingertip to the film and allowed his body heat to lift each print. Once he had a print lifted onto his fingertip, Snake would carefully make sure it lined up with his finger pads precisely by using a thin instrument that he dipped in a solution. This made the prints mold to Jordan's hands perfectly and undetectable. Snake then fastened a pin light on to a contraption that Jordan was wearing on his head. After he was set, Jordan plugged in the code that he'd deciphered from the embedded detectors on the blueprints. I waited patiently as they worked feverishly to get inside of the safe.

According to Jordan, they only had one time to try the number before a silent alarm would go off and alert a device that he was sure that Easter kept on him. Jordan passed the retina and finger-print scans without any problem, but the number code wasn't as simple. Instead of risking it by trying another sequence, Snake took out another device while Jordan put on some special-looking glasses with a magnifying glass hanging over them and the pen light. I wanted to laugh. He resembled something out of a space movie, but I knew we had to be as quiet as possible.

Jordan and Snake worked in synch. He aimed the pen light at the center while drilling a small hole near the dial. He then accepted the two-way solenoid injection valve from Snake and began slowly pumping in liquid CO_2 to offset the burn mechanism and freeze the safe's contents. To make sure he was on point, he peered inside the dial through the hole made and lined up the three wheels. Just then, I noticed movement on the camera and watched as one of the guards came toward the door of the room. I held up my hand for all action to cease.

The man stopped in front of the door and called over his shoulder. "Say, Reese, what the fuck you think he got in here anyway?"

"Hell if I know," he said from his spot on the couch. "Don't touch that door. It wouldn't surprise me if that runt has an alarm on it. You see the fancy bio lock system he has? Easter, the little midget bastard, trusts no one. I say the best way to get in is when he goes in. After the way he treated Sal in Amsterdam, I'd say the maggot has it coming."

He stared at the door a moment longer. "Hey, what's this?" He bent down to check what I assume to be the tubing to the camera. I began perspiring. Jordan and Snake drew their weapons ready to open fire.

"Say Al, the game's back on!" the other man shouted.

Relieved, I lightly exhaled when he started to gradually back away from the door. Beads of nervous sweat collected on my forehead. I waited until he was occupied by the television again before letting my hand drop. Jordan immediately went back to working the safe.

A few minutes later, I heard a click. The men's faces lit up when they made eye contact. I wanted to see what was going on, but had to watch the video monitor. Snake helped Jordan with the vault's door.

When it was fully opened, I almost dropped the video monitor when I saw a pallet holding gold bricks sitting in the center of the safe. "Oh my God," I whispered.

"Compose yourself, Bianca. I need you to keep your eyes on your targets while I work the shipment below," Seven said in my ear. The sweat from before instantly dried when a blast of cold air coming from inside the safe chilled the room.

Snake opened up one of the bags they'd brought up and took out something folded and black. He went to the hole and gave some hand signals before letting it unroll. Snake fastened the end that he was holding onto some hooks. Seven worked on the other end from the inside of our apartment. He tossed Jordan a pair of really thick gloves from the bag and then he put on some. Jordan and Snake worked diligently moving the iced bricks and letting them slide one at a time down the chute. Transporting the gold took a little over four minutes. Next to follow were a few cylinders and two silver cases.

Once the safe was cleaned out with the exception of the blueprints, Jordan went in the bag and pulled out the 1953 *Playboy* issue with Marilyn Monroe on the cover and left it in the safe. When given the signal, I slowly pulled the tubing from under the door and wrapped it around the monitor that I was holding. The darn thing slipped out of my hands and went crashing to the floor.

Jordan's and Snake's eyes shot straight at me. I stood still wearing a look of shock and fear.

Jordan picked up the camera and guided me toward the hole where the ladder had replaced the chute.

"Go down," Jordan whispered to me. They took out their guns and trained them on the door and waited.

Meanwhile, the Bitch helped me off the ladder. "What's going on?" she asked.

"I accidentally dropped the camera."

Her eyes grew as big as saucers as she grabbed her hair. "Oh shit! Did they hear you?" she asked urgently while pacing and running her hands through her hair.

I shook my head and hunched my shoulders when Snake startled us by coming down the ladder. "Well?" Seven ran over to him.

He threw the gloves on the floor and calmed her by placing his hands on Seven's shoulders. "Not a peep." Snake then helped Jordan with the other equipment they took up with them. They then repaired the ceiling using the original cutout.

Once they were done, Jordan went over and examined the neatly stacked bars of gold. "Let me see . . ." Jordan took in the sight of the pallet and mentally calculated the tally. "Thirteen across, four high and four deep. I'd say we're looking at 208 bricks valued at about 237 million or so easily." He then picked one up and nearly toppled over with laughter.

Alarmed, Snake ran over. "Is something wrong?"

Jordan stopped laughing long enough to swipe at a tear. "Read this." He pointed to the side of the glistening bar.

"Krung Thep?" He looked confused watching Jordan continuing to keel over. "I don't get it, man."

"Krung Thep! In Thai, it means 'Bangkok,' also known as 'City of Angels.'" He laughed again. This time Snake joined in just catching on to whatever it was that Jordan was getting at. "This is what we were after in Bangkok; well, at least half of it. I told you Easter had set us up, and I bet Vicente and Antonio got the bulk of it."

Snake picked up the case and saw that it was guarded by a bio lock as well. Jordan went over and used Easter's fingerprints that were still on the pads of his fingers to open both cases.

"Now that's sexy," he said, examining the contents. "U.S. Treasury certificates in bearer form with the coupons attached." Jordan thumbed through the pages.

"No, my friend, sexy is over here!" Snake pulled out a painting from one of the cylinders. "That bastard had Armando Modigliani's *Woman with Mirror* in his possession. I thought he was lying about the gallery heist last—let's see what the other two are." Seven and Jordan had already beat him to the punch.

"Oh my God ... Fernand Levar's *Life Under a Chandelier*." Seven gasped at the masterpiece she'd just unveiled.

"Matissio's *Pope*," Jordan followed.

Snake quickly rolled his painting and put it back inside the safety of the cylinder. "What was he planning to do with these? Selling them is out of the question unless you want to get caught."

"The Collector," Jordan said more to himself than anyone, causing Snake to look over at him with a puzzled look on his face.

"The who?" Seven blurted out which let me know that I was right in not revealing what I knew to Snake about The Collector. He may have known of him, but he sure as hell didn't know that Jordan was gunning for him.

Instead of answering, Jordan busied himself with getting things ready to go. "Sledge and the Kids will be here to clean this space within the hour. We need to get to the shop as soon as possible."

Chapter 24

After leaving the safe house, we drove to the Golden Triangle area, which was not too far from Trocadéro. I could still see views of the Eiffel Tower, and it gave me a sense of peace in all of this cloak and dagger business that I was engaging in. We arrived at a beautiful chateau that was sitting on many acres coupled with the Seine River serving as its backdrop. The moment we stepped out of the car, a gorgeous man, who could've easily passed for a woman, was waiting.

He ran to greet Jordan by kissing him on both sides of his face. *"Pierre a été de mourir pour savoir si vous étiez en mesure d'accomplir la mission."* (*Pierre has been dying to know if you were able to accomplish the mission.*)

Jordan eyed the man before answering. "Good to see you too, Étienne." Then he immediately started speaking in French. *"Peut-on discuter de ce que nous sommes-nous inside?"* (*Can we discuss that once we're inside?*) He patted him on his back. *"Pourquoi ne pas vous être accueillant envers vos invités et laissez-moi gérer et d'affaires Pierre.* Okay!" (*Why not be friendly to your guest and let me handle business, Pierre.*)

The man shook his head. "*Mais oui ... bien sûr.*" (*But yes, of course*)
He greeted each of us with kisses to both sides of our faces before
leading us into the house.

Once we were in, another man was coming down one side of a
winding, double staircase that reminded me of something out of
Gone with the Wind. He wore his shirt unbuttoned revealing a
hairy chest and gold chains. He was of average height, muscular,
cropped haircut, piercing green eyes, very tanned and for the
most part, decent-looking, if you took away the ode-to-the-'70s
look he had going. The prissy fellow who met us as we got out of
the car hurriedly rushed over to the man kissing him fervently.

The man who just ascended the stairs finished his tongue session
with his lover and held his hands up. "Jordan!" he spoke with a
thick accent.

Jordan did the same. "Pierre! I told you the only way I would be
paying you a visit while on your home turf was as if."

His eyes gleamed over as he rubbed his goatee. "*Si je comprends
bien everythig s'est déroulé selon vos plans? Oui?*" (*I take it everything
went according to your plans! Yes?*) He spoke quickly.

Jordan laughed. "I would say everything went accordingly, and
we even got a couple of cherries on top."

Snake cleared his throat and Pierre's attention went to him and
the rest of us immediately. "Where are my manners? Snake, as you
know, it's always a pleasure!" He walked over and kissed Seven
and me. "Beautiful ladies are always welcomed and treated like
queens à la Maison de Pierre! I'm quite acquainted already with
the lovely Seven. So you must be Bianca?"

"Yes, I am." I beamed.

He grabbed my hands and squeezed them gently, before bringing
them to his lips. "In case you weren't aware, I'm Pierre, and this
is my companion, Étienne."

Étienne sashayed over to Pierre. "*Je vais prendre les dames pour profiter de notre spa tandis que vous et les garçons gèrent les affaires.*" (*I will take the ladies to enjoy our spa while you and the boys manage business.*)

I could do nothing but blush as he stared into my eyes. Étienne was gay, no doubt about it, but something about that androgynous look turned me on like it did whenever I came across an image of Prince. "Thanks for the hospitality, Pierre and Étienne. You have a lovely home."

Pierre kissed him again and then hugged him around the waist, but never took his eyes off of us. "*Je pense que ce serait une merveilleuse idée d'amour!*" (*I think it would be a wonderful idea. love.*)

Jordan interrupted their conversation. "English, Étienne and Pierre; Bianca doesn't understand."

Embarrassed, I was sure I turned a few shades of red. Étienne, however, caressed the side of my arm to reassure me before translating what he had said. "I was telling Pierre to allow me to take you ladies to our spa while they handled business," he replied with a thick accent.

Suddenly, Seven seemed to come alive. "You must've read my mind. I hope Agatha is still with you. She gives the best Swedish massages."

Étienne laughed. "Why of course. Ladies." He gestured with his hand and we followed him willingly.

Jordan caught me before I could leave and gave me a kiss. He then whispered in my ear, "I love you. You know that, don't you?"

At a loss for words, the only reaction I could give him was a head nod as this was not what I was ever expecting to hear from him. Tears spilled out of my eyes before I could stop them. Jordan used his fingers to pat them dry. Étienne and Seven stood patiently wearing goofy expressions on their faces.

"They're waiting on me." I hurriedly left his side.

The next morning, Étienne was a gracious host as he regaled us in his talks of Paris. We enjoyed a lavish breakfast of made-to-order omelets, coffee, mimosas, croissants and fruit on the loggia that was surrounded by lush gardens and a sparkling Olympic-sized pool and spa. Although this was what I envisioned breakfast in Paris to be like, my early morning wakeup call in the form of an orgasm while being pleasured orally before dawn, made this pale in comparison. Jordan leaned over and nibbled on my lip right before kissing me.

"Looks like someone enjoyed their stay at à la Maison de Pierre!" Pierre grinned.

"I would say so," Étienne shared his sentiments, "à la Maison de Pierre is the place to fall in love all over again."

Seven began to choke while Snake patted her on the back. "Are you okay?"

"Yes." Seven cleared her throat. "My mimosa went down the wrong way." The daggers I shot her way didn't go unnoticed by anyone.

At some point during the night, Sledge had rejoined the men as they had worked inside of Pierre's underground garage throughout the night. Sledge was the first to excuse himself. "I'm going to the shop to see how things are progressing along."

"We'll be there shortly," Jordan responded.

Pierre leaned in when Sledge left prompting the rest of us to do the same. "I have my guys finishing up the details on the vehicles. But I don't trust that one." He pointed in the direction that Sledge had gone in.

"I keep my enemies close," was Jordan's response.

With the exception of Snake's tongue darting out and breaking a crispy slice of bacon in half before dragging back inside of his mouth, he was quiet regarding the Sledge issue. It made me wonder what was really going on with this entire operation. Who was really who and better yet, what had I really gotten myself into? It didn't take long for me to find out part of my question.

"The motorbikes should be ready to go by six this evening," Pierre acknowledged. I was trying to figure out what he was talking about, but Snake's response cleared things up.

"Melting all of that gold down was work, but I can't wait to see it all come together in the form of a Ducati Diavel."

Pierre placed his hand on his chest. "It's not going to take Easter long to know of your betrayal, Snake, and that, my friend, worries me."

"Leave Easter to me. I left him a little present, courtesy of our Spanish compadres, Antonio and Vincente, in his vault to deflect Snake's involvement," Jordan said.

Seven seemed to be nervous. "I sure hope he takes the bait."

Snake kissed the top of her head. "Don't worry about me, my love. It's going to take a lot more than a little man like Easter to get me riled up."

"Enough about Easter." Jordan looked at Pierre. "Are we set up?"

Étienne spoke up. "Everything including the jet will be ready by six, but there's still the matter of the paintings."

Jordan cackled. "Is that how it is now, Pierre? You have Étienne conducting business?"

"I give you my resources. I want to be properly compensated," he explained.

Before Jordan and Pierre could continue, there was a lot of racket going on inside of the house. Out of instinct, I screamed and jumped up to run for cover. Jordan caught me when I almost toppled over into the pool. Sledge hurried out with another man on his heels.

"Sledge, what's going on?" Snake asked just as alarmed as me.

When I looked over at Seven, she had her gun drawn and showing no fear. Her chair had been kicked back and she looked like she was ready for whatever was coming her way. While I looked like

I was ready to get away. Unlike her, this wasn't an everyday occurrence for me.

Sledge caught his breath long enough to speak. "The safe house! It's on the news!"

Pierre hit a button on the panel next to him. What I thought was a window on the house powered on. Pierre flipped through the channels until he found the news and there it was. Ambulances, fire trucks and police cars were everywhere. Jordan repeated what was scrolling across the screen.

"*Quatre Quatre ont été retrouvé tué par balles après que la police a reçu des informations d'un corps à corps au sixième étage.*" (*Four were found shot to death after police received reports of a melee on the eighth floor.*) He read slowly.

"He knows," Snake whispered. "I bet the four that were murdered were the guards that were on duty last night."

Sledge's skin was flushed and looked as though he was ready to vomit. "He's coming for us." He started fidgeting with his pockets making me even more nervous.

"Enough!" Jordan yelled and Sledge stopped his ruckus immediately. "Panicking isn't going to do you any good."

Sledge took out a pack of cigarettes and lit one while he paced waiting to see what the instructions were going to be.

Pierre came over to Jordan's side. "I can have the plane ready a lot sooner, but I'm not so sure about the bikes."

Jordan's demeanor made him back up. "Those bikes had better be ready within the next couple of hours. No exceptions." He signaled to Snake and Sledge to follow him. Pierre did the same although he wasn't invited.

Seven finally lowered her weapon and walked over to where I was. "I know we have our differences, but now is not the time for any of that high-end drama that you like giving us. As you see by the gruesome news reports, Easter is a little ruthless motherfucker. That's why Jordan became so upset when you thought of him as not being a threat."

I didn't know what to do, except let bygones be bygones until we were back on familiar grounds. "You're right, Seven, and you'll have no problems out of me for the rest of this trip."

"The rest of the trip, huh?" She sauntered off shaking her head.

There was a series of loud claps stopping Seven in her tracks. "Ladies, even when facing uncertainty, we must always look our best. Let the men do what is needed while we get ourselves together. In case you're worried, Bianca, the man who is out for blood knows nothing of this place nor does he know anything about Pierre and I."

I breathed a sigh of relief. "Thanks for clearing that up, Étienne."

Meanwhile, in the garage, Snake watched as Sledge paced back and forth while he and Jordan were overseeing the completion of the bikes. "Sledge's trouble with the mafia is going to have him going rogue. I was on hiatus, but I still kept my ears to the street."

Jordan stomped the cigarette he'd been smoking into the concrete floor. "You're not the only one who keeps abreast of what's going on. I know all about his debt, so relax."

"A desperate man will do anything. It wouldn't surprise me if he was working us with Easter."

"He's not!" Jordan spoke sharply to Snake.

Snake looked at him not believing his ears and walked off. "All right, it's your funeral," he said over his shoulder.

Chapter 25

A few hours later, Pierre joined Jordan in the garage's lounging area to inform him of the progress. "Never know when you're going to need eighteen-hundred degrees of heat, a shit load of boric acid, and a nice-sized crucible to melt and turn gold into something of a bad ass. Those sexy bitches are finally ready for you to see them." He threw what was left of his cigar into the ashtray on a nearby table and led the way.

Jordan signaled for Snake and Sledge, as they followed Pierre. The bikes were true beauties and bad asses indeed. Jordan had known Pierre for the better part of ten years, but he learned early on in this line of business not to trust anyone but himself. He inspected the chromed-out, black and red bikes before taking his pocket knife out and scratching a part of the rim that wouldn't be so obvious. When he saw the gold behind the color, he was almost satisfied.

"After all of this time, you don't trust me?" Pierre asked, as Jordan repeated the process numerous times on both bikes.

He only stopped to answer his host. "Don't take this personally, Pierre, but you especially should know that much like honor, there is no trust among thieves."

Two hours later at the Paris-Le Bourget airport, after seeing that everything was accounted for, we boarded a private jet. Pierre was satisfied with his portion of the take, and was on his way back to the chauffeured Lincoln Navigator where Étienne was waiting for him. I eased back into the seat and closed my eyes after seeing him off. I couldn't wait to step through the front door of my home.

"Would you like something to drink after takeoff, *beautiful*?" the attendant asked.

My eyes fluttered open to a lovely brunette with a heavy accent that I couldn't place. "No thanks," I mumbled. She gave a weak sneer before walking off. There was something familiar about her eyes that made me take a longer look after her.

The plane began to taxi down the runway. A smile crept onto my face at the thought of finally heading home. Then without warning, a loud explosion occurred. I jerked out of my resting position as my eyes flew wide open to see a roaring fire engulfing the SUVs that had brought us to the airport.

"Oh my God! Étienne! Pierre!" A bloodcurdling scream soon followed when I saw Seven pointing her gun in my direction and pulling the trigger. The gun went off without hesitation. I closed my eyes and braced for impact, but it never came. I turned around to see the attendant who had just asked me if I wanted a drink. She was on the floor, and her white shirt had a red spot that was getting bigger by the second.

I looked in the direction of Seven and her smoking gun. My eyes went back to the attendant, and for the first time, I noticed the gun in her hand. My head immediately swung back around where my eyes made contact with Seven's. No words were needed. Our eyes said everything that our mouths didn't. Our moment was interrupted when the plane began to swerve and more gunshots rang out. Entourages of black SUVs tried to keep us grounded by shooting at the plane. My heart nearly leapt out of my chest. Tears slid down my face as my life flashed before my eyes. "Oh God, please!"

A bullet went through the window across from Seven. "Argh!" She went down clutching her abdomen.

"Baby?!" Snake screamed out as he tried to make his way to her. Seven wiped the sweat off of her brow before giving him her attention. "I'm ... I'm fine," she assured him.

I was harshly pushed forward by Jordan. "Get down now!" he screamed. "Pull up! Pull the fuck up!" he ordered the pilot. "Get this plane in the air, now!"

"I'll do my best, sir, but we may have to land soon. If we try to fly any longer than ten minutes or so, we're going to lose cabin pressure with the window being shot out," the pilot said in panic.

"That's fine with me; just get us out of here," Jordan ordered.

The plane started lifting off of the ground. A few bullets struck the window across from me cracking it. Everything was going in slow motion, but moving so fast at the same time. Snake and Jordan were ready for combat. Seven took cover, but was still in battle mode with her gun poised and ready to unload, all while clutching her abdomen with her other hand. Sledge, on the other hand, was another story. He was still sitting in his seat as if he were in a daze. I couldn't understand why Jordan even had him with us in the first place. Sledge was a coward, simply useless. A sad excuse of a human being, let alone a man.

The gunshots became distant as we ascended further into the sky. I continued to pray for God to save us all. I even promised to leave Jordan and his lifestyle if He allowed me to make it back to the States in one piece, and more importantly, alive.

I slowly rose and eased back into my seat. Tears clouded my vision, but Sledge was still sitting there like nothing had just occurred. "What is wrong with you?" I hollered in his direction. Still there was no response from him. Before I knew what was happening, I was on him swinging and clawing. It took Snake and Jordan to get me off of that fool, but no sooner than they let me go, I was on him again.

"Bianca!" Jordan yelled when he grabbed me from behind. I didn't know why I was so angry with Sledge, but the entire time in Paris, something about him had rubbed me the wrong way. I guessed the shootout and his reaction to it was the last straw. I kept trying to get at him despite being firmly held against my will.

"Get her off of me!" He sprung from his seat like a jack-in-the-box. His fist was about to connect with my face until Snake caught him in midswing.

Jordan pushed me to the side before coldcocking him. Sledge fell back against the window bumping his head. "How the fuck did they know who we were and where to find us? Answer me!" He stared menacingly at Sledge waiting for an answer.

"How the fuck do I know?" He struggled to get up. "After all that we have been through, you're screwing me for this bitch?" He pointed in my direction.

When Sledge was standing upright again, he got in Jordan's face. Neither man was backing down and dared the other to make a move. Snake finally stepped between the two while Seven covered him. "I told you, Jordan. I told you."

"Told him what?" Sledge attempted to jump bad, but backed down just as quickly.

Snake stared at Sledge instead of fanning the flames. They were hot now and cool heads were needed, if they wanted to prevail. "Come on, fellows. We have to be ready when we land, or we may as well sign our own death certificates."

"Sledge, for as long as you have breath in your body—" Jordan stopped when he saw the let-it-slide-for-now look that Snake gave him. "Okay." He held up his hands. "I'm good." Jordan patted Sledge's shoulder. "We good?"

Sledge pushed his hand off. "Yeah, we good."

Jordan went to check with the pilot while Snake checked the girl's body for information before dragging her toward the back of the plane. Sledge was back in his seat giving me dirty looks, but I couldn't be bothered with him. I had something that I needed to say.

"Seven, I want to thank you." I was about to reach over and hug her, but she stopped me.

She unbuttoned her shirt revealing a bulletproof vest. There was a bullet lodged in it close to her navel. "Good thing I decided to wear this, huh?"

My eyes were glued to the bullet. "I'm glad you did. Does that hurt?"

"Burns like hell, but hey, I'd rather the hole to be in the vest than in me. I told you I wasn't the enemy, and neither is Sledge. He's just been through a lot," she said, aiming her attention over to her teammate when Snake came over to tend to her.

I looked over at Sledge who was still giving me the stink eye. "Sledge, look, I overreacted due to the situation. This is all new to me. So, why don't we just let bygones be bygones ... Okay?"

He took out a packet of cigarettes and thumped it against his hand to release one, lit it, and took a long drag before blowing the smoke out in my direction. "No apologies needed. Just don't let it happen again."

He had better been lucky that Jordan had just taken his seat next to me because there would've been another body—for sure. "I have a question."

"What's that?" Jordan asked.

I didn't know what to ask first, so I just went for it. "They could've blown up the plane or at the very least, shot us down. What was that all about?"

"You're right. They could've done all of that, but then the merchandise would have been destroyed. Good thing we were already onboard and going down the strip."

Seven grunted as she adjusted herself in her seat. "Too bad you can't say the same for Pierre and Étienne." She signed the cross over her chest. "May they rest in peace."

Jordan's jaw clenched tightly. "Don't worry; Easter will pay—and dearly. Mark my words."

Chapter 26

A week later, my life had returned to normal. Jordan unloaded the gold motorcycles without a problem to an anonymous multibillionaire who was also a collector of fine and rare things. The paintings were still in his possession, but personally, I didn't care what became of them. The money I'd gotten from the sale of the bikes was payment enough for my troubles in Paris.

It was early in the morning and I was enjoying the comforts of my bed, when I heard someone beating my door down. Deciding to let them knock, I snuggled deeper under the covers, but the insistent knocker wasn't going anywhere. I snatched the covers back and swung my legs to the side to get up and answer. I stuffed my feet into my slippers and put on the housecoat that was draped lazily across the bed.

"Coming!" I yelled, but the knocking wasn't letting up. My footsteps quickened as I ran down the stairs to see who I was about to cuss out. I grabbed my bat in case it was some trouble before peeking through the peephole.

"Ugh!" I groaned when I saw Shelia, Cody and Reggie. I put the bat down and opened the door to let them in.

"Rise and shine, you ole elusive bitch!" Cody sang, prancing through the door uninvited wearing the tightest jeans known to man and a powder-blue blouse that I knew belonged on a woman. His hair was flowing as usual, even though there wasn't any wind to help it along.

I stepped to the side letting them in, and out of habit, looked both ways before shutting the door behind us. "Well, come on in, why don't cha!" Besides, Shelia's big Diana Ross hair hitting me in the face on her way through the door, I shook my head when I saw that she was dressed like she was on her way to the club in a mini-skirt, six-inch stilettos, and a halter top this early in the day. Reggie had his grown man look on in his Polo shirt, and a pair of loose-fitting jeans.

Reggie put a box of Krispy Kreme doughnuts on the table and turned to face me as I walked in. "Girl, bye with all that 'tude and don't be giving us the evil eye, either! You owe us an explanation, hunty, and we ain't leaving until we get one."

"Sure in the hell do," Shelia cosigned while putting the coffees down and pulling out a chair to sit her gigantic video vixen booty on.

I ignored them and went to brush my teeth and wash my face. I grabbed saucers, sugar and creamer before rejoining them at the table. Thank God they'd brought coffee; I had a feeling that it was going to be a long morning. "I hope you got some panties on up under that too-little-ass skirt while you're hoisted all up on my chair, Shelia," I said to deflect the attention from me.

Cody and Reggie fell out, pointing and making fun of Shelia.

"Woo, she read you *down*, chile!" Reggie snickered even louder.

"To hell with y'all and *anyway*, I have on a thong; thank you very much." She snapped her fingers at me like she'd put me in my place. "And don't be trying to wiggle your way out of the discussion at hand, which is you and that mofo you been neglecting us for."

Cody turned his chair so that it was facing me. "Yeah, she's really trying to pull it, but too bad she didn't get up early enough. Now, spill it because you got a lot of nerve, hunty."

Taking a huge bite from one of the doughnuts, I answered with my mouth full. "Why you say that?"

Cody crossed his legs and shook his finger in my direction. "Girl, don't play. You know exactly what this is about."

After stirring some creamer in her coffee, Shelia threw in her two cents. "Mm-hmm, I knew the night we met him that he was nothing but trouble. Arrogant son of a bastard."

I swallowed my food and laughed out loud. "You're just mad because he wasn't checking for you."

Shelia reached over to get a glazed doughnut out of the box. "Mad?" She licked her fingers. "Honey, please, he only chose you because he saw the caution sign warning him about these dangerous curves of mine." She ran her hands over her hourglass figure before popping the side of her big ass that was hanging off of the chair.

Reggie bit into his sugary pastry. "Shelia, shut the hell up. If he would've given your hot behind the time of day, we'd be at your house this morning instead of Bianca's."

We all laughed when Shelia's mouth opened and closed because she couldn't think of a snappy comeback.

After fixing my coffee, I got to the point. "Okay. What's with the early morning visit? It's not even nine yet."

Reggie picked up a napkin to get rid of the glaze on his fingers. "Let me give a brief synopsis of what has become you as of late and why."

This was going to be good, so I leaned back with my cup of coffee and gave Reggie the floor. "Go ahead and tell me a little something about myself, why don't cha."

"Hunty . . ." Reggie began with a dramatic flair. "That tight-eyed-dick ain't nothing but a master of arithmetic."

"What's that?" Cody cupped his ear and leaned in further.

"I said . . ." Reggie looked from Shelia to Cody and then back to me. "That tight-eyed dick ain't nothing but a master of arithmetic."

"Ahh!" Shelia gasped holding the sides of her face paying homage to Macaulay Culkin, during his *Home Alone* days. "Why is that?"

"Hunty, let me tell you what they do. He adds trouble."

"Well!" Cody let roll off of his lips.

"Then multiply your pleasure."

"Well! Well! Welllllll!" Cody sang in quick successions.

Shelia's hot ass wiggled in her seat. "Ooh! Now you're talking."

Reggie really got into it. "He ... he ... I say he, divides your time . . ."

Cody pointed to Reggie, egging him on. "Passa Reg gon' tell it like it T. I. is up in this piece!"

"And subtracts what little common sense you have . . ." Reggie turned, walked off and rushed back over to us. "Then he ... he ... he find the square root of that which equals ignorance because they say it's bliss!" he shouted. "Now, can I get a witness?"

"Amen! Amen!" Cody shouted.

"You ain't speaking nothing but the truth this morning, Passa Reg!" Shelia sang out while getting the Holy Ghost in her seat.

Reggie did a quick shout and finished it off with a James Brown-influenced sidestep before continuing. "Now go forth, my child, and spill that tea, before you get burnt! It's already bubbling; better tend to it, before it boils over! I know you got a testimony this morning, Sista Bianca!" He jumped up and down a few times while clapping. "Now let go, and let have, I say! Tell the congregation what's been ailing you as of late." Reggie picked up a napkin and wiped his brow as though he'd just preached the sermon to end all sermons.

"Yes, because only the truth . . ." Cody flapped his arms like wings and flew around the room. "Shall set you free like a bird. So you can flllllllllyyyyyy! You aint got to be a little caged bird all yo life, girl. Now, come on with it so you can ... flllllllllyyyyy!" Cody sang in a high-pitched voice.

"I believe she can fly, y'all!" Shelia threw in.

Instead of prolonging the inevitable and the buffoonery, I went ahead and decided to give them something to appease their appetites. "Being with Jordan hasn't just been about sex."

Cody stopped flying in midstream. "If not sex, then what else could he possibly have to offer you?"

"Investment advice," I replied.

"*Investment advice*?" they all said in unison.

"Yes, investment advice. I've actually made some sound ventures since I've known Jordan, and in return, I've raked in a ton of money. So much in fact, that I'm taking everyone at Pleasure Principles on a much-needed, all-expenses paid vacation. It was supposed to be a surprise, but since you all are so damned nosey, we're going to fly out to Tahiti and enjoy the beautiful island of Bora Bora. I'm reserving eight private overwater bungalows."

Cody and Reggie were for once speechless while Shelia sat fuming. "I hope y'all have fun." She pouted.

"What do you mean 'y'all'? You know good and damned well I'm not going to Bora Bora without my favorite girl. You may not work for me, but you're still a part of the Pleasure Principles family, and don't you forget it."

"Arrgh!" Shelia screamed and started jumping up and down shouting like she was in church. Leave it to Cody to encourage her more by clapping and humming like the old folks do with Reggie joining in. Before long, all three of them were putting on a show and cracking me up with the synchronized shouting match complete with fancy footwork.

I laughed so hard, that tears were streaming down my face and my stomach began to cramp up. I wasn't even thinking about taking them anywhere, but I knew this would be a way to get them off of my back. Besides, I could surely use a real vacation. "Okay! Okay! Y'all need to stop the madness." I nearly choked from laughing and coughing.

Reggie grabbed his used napkin to dab at his forehead again. "You must've hit it big, hunty, because I know this is going to cost a grip."

I waved him off like it was nothing. "Don't worry about the cost. Trust me, I have it covered. The only thing you all will need to do is pack your luggage because everything else will be provided for you courtesy of *moi*."

"That's why she's been hush-hush while creeping with that tight-eyed dick. Hunty, quiet as it's kept, on the cool, they been out robbing folks," Cody stopped acting a fool long enough to say.

Hearing that made me stop laughing abruptly, but none of them noticed as they were too busy celebrating. If only Cody knew how on the money he was with his statement, all celebrating would have ceased.

"I don't care who they robbed to get enough money, because I'm going to Bora Bora, y'all!" Shelia shimmied some more before breaking out into an impromptu song. "I'm going to Bora Borrrrrrraaaa!"

I downplayed Cody's allegations by laughing and not commenting on it one way or another. "We are going to have so much fun. I was going to act like we had a client there, but it's so much better this way."

In the midst of rejoicing, my phone rang and Cody ran to answer it. "Speak of the devil and he shall appear," he called out and handed me the phone with Jordan on the other end.

Agent Garza stopped the recorder. "What else did you buy with money you received from Jordan Lei? You've mentioned ads and a trip for your employees and friends."

Aliyah held her hand up before I could speak and leaned forward. "Since my client isn't the one under investigation, she doesn't have to answer anything about her uses of the money or anything else that's not about Jordan Lei."

Agent Garza smiled, but took a while to answer in order to tread lightly. "I understand that, counsel. However, Ms. Brooks used stolen money to finance the growth of her company. She also used that same money to take her employees and friends on an extravagant trip. If she doesn't cooperate, I can see to it that her business is placed under investigation immediately to see what else may pop up."

Aliya laughed. "This is going to be my last time warning you, Agent Garza, about my client not being the one under investigation. Nothing she discloses can be used against her as long as she's being cooperative about your target, and she has been. Another thing, my client pays her taxes on her business which is all that Uncle Sam is concerned about. Plus, I don't see you questioning her about this mystery man that got into the car with her which leads me to believe that you're also keeping important information from us as well."

"For all I know, the person that got into the car with her could've been Jordan. Ms. Brooks has already demonstrated amnesia when it serves her best. Furthermore, counsel, I understand your client pays her taxes on Pleasure Principles, but did she do the same for the money she earned being Jordan's concubine, ahem ... I mean ... girl?" Besides being a grade-A asshole, Agent Garza tried it, but he wasn't getting the results he was hoping for.

Rolling her eyes and ignoring the supposed slip of Agent Garza's tongue, Aliyah drew in a sharp breath and slowly exhaled her annoyance before continuing. "Whatever money my client may or may not have received from Jordan Lei isn't up for debate since she has immunity, now is it? Besides, the DA's deal is contingent upon my client's cooperation and she has been nothing but accommodating. Now that I've reminded you for the umpteenth time, care to waste any more of our time with unnecessary stints about the *ill-gotten* money, etcetera, Agent Garza?"

Agent Garza stared at me. His beady eyes then went to Aliyah as if he were trying to come up with something more. "Ms. Brooks, if you will," he responded dejectedly before turning the recorder back on.

Chapter 27

After my trip to Paris, my attitude toward Seven had changed drastically, especially after she'd saved my life. I no longer felt like I needed to be on guard whenever she was around which was becoming a little more frequently than before. Come to find out, she really was in love with Snake, and it wasn't long before I found out why.

It was one evening when Jordan was giving me a crash course on surveillance and uses of the resources around me to pull off just about any skimming job. We sat in the room that resembled a command center at the same house that I'd followed Jordan and Seven to the night of the blueprint job. Mr. Pringley was nowhere to be found. When I asked, I was told that he rarely stayed at the house and that Chicago was his primary home base where he had an even grander estate than the one we were in.

Jordan had some odd items placed in front of him to use for his demonstration. He also had a projection screen to give me visuals.

"This is how I got started on a small-time level, of course, but it's an in, nonetheless. Decoders are used to lift information. A network analyzer can tell you how much someone is accessing and how encoded its encrypting is." He showed me what one looked like with his pointer. "If the person is changing their passcodes often, then that usually means that there's something worth protecting. I'm not talking about love letters or nude pictures, but something of more value." Jordan stopped long enough to see if I was following him. "I see that perplexed look on your face, but let your man school you. These items I have placed before you have value in them beyond their original purpose."

I laughed a bit. "Yes, you can say that I'm a bit curious."

He walked over and picked up a couple of the items. "Well, thanks to the cell phones," he started his spiel, "technology has changed the game making just about everything we do susceptible. For instance, the Bluetooth on a cell phone can be used with an antenna and becomes something else entirely." He held up a Bluetooth and a wire hanger. "Besides conversation, once you combine these two along with a few other easy-to-find items, you can get valuable information over long distances like files from a computer, credit card numbers, etcetera. See, I'll show you how to improvise." Jordan used a bunch of thingamabobs to demonstrate how to make hacking devices out of practically anything.

"Sounds simple."

"It does, but it's not," Jordan answered as if I'd offended him before continuing on. "This contrivance can also be used in parking lots to capture credit card data from the airwaves. Now, you know firsthand why you're warned about using your debit cards at gas stations, etcetera. As you see, it only takes a matter of seconds for someone to snatch your information and wipe out your accounts or assume your identity. Back in the day, I had a very lucrative operation with my carders' market site. People paid good money to have access to valid credit card numbers, personal identification, and checking account information. I got out of it when I realized I was going about it the wrong way. Instead of making it harder for the struggling man, I set my sights on the ones who could afford to take the hit, and they have been my targets ever since."

"We never knew anything about a black carders' site." Agent Garza rounded the table and came face to face with me. "Try to think really hard about this: did he tell you the name of his carders' site or what name he went under as the moderator?" Agent Garza interrupted.

"Not that I can recall. I assumed the name was Carders Market," I answered back.

Agent Garza was about to say something else when Agent Carter bustled back into the room.

"Well?" Agent Garza asked.

Agent Carter placed his files on the table and stood next to me. He purposely made sure that his leg rubbed up against mine. The moment we made contact, I glanced up at him and he didn't outright acknowledge me, but I did notice a smile that left just as quickly as it'd appeared on his handsome face.

"I've got some not so good news regarding Mr. Benavidez, better known as Sledge," he said, picking up his file and flipping through the pages until he came across the one he was looking for. "According to the county clerk, Mr. Benavidez is no longer with us."

Agent Garza swung his fist down on the table outraged. "What the hell do you mean, he's no longer with us? He was just sentenced a few months ago."

Letting out a deep breath, Agent Carter cleared his throat and continued. "Seems like Mr. Benavidez was found dead in his cell a couple of days ago."

That stopped Agent Garza's tirade. "What the hell happened?"

"Appears that he hung himself with his bedsheet," Agent Carter reported.

Agent Garza rubbed his temples to ward off a potential headache. "Are you shitting me, Carter?"

Agent Carter put his file back down. "As I said, *appeared* to have hung himself. From the vibe I was getting, it seemed more like a hit was put out on him than a suicide. The guy was getting sprung in less than six months after the deal he cut, on top of having time served."

"You're right; something doesn't smell right about this. Shit!" Agent Garza almost fell when he kicked his chair.

"What does this mean for my client?" Aliyah broke the tense atmosphere that had suddenly enveloped the room.

"It means that we continue. Sledge wasn't our only ace in the hole." Agent Carter stared at me intensely. "We still have Ms. Brooks."

I took that as my cue to get back to the story.

Jordan pointed out another section that had the same loose items on it. "Now, I want to see you put the same device together."

Before I could begin, I was saved by Snake and Seven, interrupting us when they walked in.

"Sorry we're late." Seven kissed Jordan on both sides of his cheeks and came over to give me a hug. "We were trying to get in some afternoon fun when your call came through instructing us to hurry over." She blushed.

Snake and Jordan looked at Seven, and then me, like we were two slow-roasting chickens on a rotisserie. Jordan tore away his libidinous stare first and cleared his throat for Snake to get it together. "I was giving Bianca a crash course on how to make a hacking device to pass the time until you got here."

Seven walked over to where Jordan was standing. "Oh wow, hacking one-o-one." She laughed. "I remember when I learned these tricks of the trade, no one could tell me anything." She ran her hands over the gadget that Jordan had put together only moments ago.

"Yeah, I had the same sense of pride myself," Snake admitted. He picked up the device and held it in his hands a little longer. His tongue darted in and out a few times whenever he looked in Seven's direction. That's when I noticed he also had an erection.

"Umm ... you might wanna put that thing away," I said, pointing at his pants.

Snake looked down, but didn't seem embarrassed at all. "No, I'd rather put it somewhere soft, hot and wet."

His tongue darted out nearly making me want to vomit. I looked over at Jordan, to see if he was going to check him for his indecent remark, but he had that lust-filled look on his face again. "Jordan?"

He shook out of his trance. "Did you say something, Bianca?"

Not knowing what to say with the situation being so awkward, I decided to let it go. "No, I didn't. You just seemed to be elsewhere."

Jordan walked over to where I was and gripped the back of my hair, pulling my head onto my shoulders. His lips connected with mine followed by his hand traveling to my crotch. I tried to pull away, but his grip was firm. I knew Jordan was a freak, but we had company. Before I could even protest, another set of lips trailed down my exposed neck and a hand began to caress my breasts. From the previous experience, I could tell by the softness of the touch that the hand and lips belonged to Seven. With Snake now in the mix, I was caught up in the raptures of carnal desire. My pants were unbuttoned and slowly tugged until they pooled around my ankles followed by my panties.

Hands were all over my body. My legs parted voluntarily when Jordan's finger work began to feel indescribably good. I felt a head kissing between the soft insides of my thighs that I figured belonged to Seven, but that was impossible since she was suckling my earlobe and Jordan's tongue was currently doing the tango with mine. My momentum almost took a nosedive when Snake pulled my legs over his broad shoulders. I guess my pussy was connected with my brain, because she roared back to life as he began teasing the hell out of her. He licked my outer lips and kissed down my legs, priming me for a good tongue lashing. The moment I felt that darting on my clit, all repulsed feelings about it went away, as my brain was now in synch with my quivering pussy. Snake took his time, alternating his licks on the outside and inside of my pussy lips with broad, flat strokes of his skilled oral tool. He fluttered around my treasure exploring her for the sweet reward that he knew he would be getting. I rotated my hips faster, when he stiffened his tongue like a mini penis and ran it around my pleasure zone, and stuck it in and out of my starving hole.

"Mmm ... " I groaned from deep within. The darting tongue swirled around my clit and was joined by his lips creating a delicious suction feeling.

I was at my wit's end when Jordan abandoned our kiss and began licking my nipples, making them swell and resemble Hershey's chocolate kisses. I bit down on my bottom lip, and closed my eyes to take it all in. Snake's tongue was doing amazing things. I was pulled out of the chair, but that didn't stop Snake; he just went with the flow. Seven trail-kissed down my back and to the crack of my ass. The pleasure was so intense that I was having trouble staying on my feet. I began to sway as an orgasm overtook me. Jordan broke the party up when he led me over to one of the sofas and laid me on it. He then placed my legs over his shoulders, and filled me to the hilt with his delicious dick. Not to be left out of the equation, Seven knelt over my face and I instinctively took ahold of her clit and sucked, licked, and pulled. She leaned forward and gave Snake head while Jordan pumped me into oblivion.

Our moans sounded like a chorus line with Jordan being the leader when he came and shot his hot load all over my stomach.

To finish me off, he got between my legs and massaged my pearl and finger-fucked me until his dick was ready for action again. I was a newbie at eating pussy, but from the way Seven was riding my face, you wouldn't have known it.

"Oooh!" Snake called out as he was claimed by a ferocious nut. Seven wasted no time savoring her milkshake.

Seven fell forward onto Snake's chest trembling uncontrollably. "Ommm! Fuck!" Hot creamy nectar flowed into my mouth, but she didn't have much time to recover. Jordan slid me to the side and out of the way, so that he could hit it from the back while she was still coming.

I got up and went over to Snake. He took a condom from his discarded pants and slipped it on what looked to be about eight inches. Once he was done, I straddled him and rode him like a prized bull rider. From the way Snake was trying to keep up, he'd never had it with a sistah before. He didn't know what to do with my voluptuous ass. He just held on to my waist as though his life depended on it. I was wrong about him that night in Paris; just because he had a few dance moves didn't mean a damned thing. I'd only been on him for less than two minutes, and this bastard had the nerve to be screaming like a bitch and busting a nut.

"Damn it! This cunt is amazing!" he managed to say as he shook and rattled as I rolled off of his tired ass. "I'm getting too old for these young girls," he grunted while trying to catch his breath.

If I didn't think it would be rude, I would've shown my disappointment. I knew next time to only let him eat the box; his dick game was whack. Jordan, however, was delivering Seven the kind of action that I wanted in on. The green monster was starting to rear her ugly head again, and it was as if Seven sensed my mood change. She motioned with her finger for me to come over.

The expression she wore on her face let me know that she was getting it good and I wanted to take her place so bad. I looked over to see if Snake's little snake had regained consciousness and was ready for another round, but found that not only was it still asleep, but so was he. I took Seven up on her offer and lay in front of her where she feasted on me while Jordan fucked her from behind. Our threesome went on into the wee hours of the morning as Snake slept like the old-ass, worn-out buzzard that he was.

Chapter 28

Dear God, I know I said I wouldn't do anything like I'd done in Paris if You got me out alive, but it appears that I'm going back on my word. You know my heart, Lord, and I beg of Your forgiveness because I'm too weak to say no.

I sat in a red Aston Martin Vantage S coupe with tinted windows in the driveway of my home waiting on Jordan to wrap up his phone call. We had plans for a lovely evening out on the town doing what normal couples did like going out for dinner and dancing. I was dressed to the nines and looking good in my deep-purple, one-sleeve, caftan Marchesa cocktail dress and sexy platform slingbacks. My hair was beauty shop fresh, thanks to the Apostle of Beauty being able to fit me in at the last minute since my girl Kyun was touring the country with a hot pop diva. With all the maneuvering that went into me getting myself together, there was no way in hell that I wasn't going somewhere tonight.

I could tell that from the way that his side of the conversation was going, that he was fired up. "I know he's back in the States. What else is new?" Jordan hollered at whomever he was talking to, but from the snatches of conversation that I was getting, I knew it had to be about either Easter or The Collector. "The moment you get some information that I don't already know, is when we can talk further." He clicked the "end" button and threw his cell down. He sat quietly for what seemed like forever, before delivering a single blow to the steering wheel. "Shit!"

I rubbed the side of his arm. "What's wrong, baby?"

From the look on Jordan's face, I could tell it must've been major, but his reaction was as if he was surprised that I was there. "Oh, I'm sorry, baby. I didn't mean for you to see me so upset."

"Don't worry about it. Let's just have a nice dinner and enjoy the rest of the evening."

As Jordan faced me, his anger slowly dissipated. "Can I take a rain check on tonight? Something has come up that requires my immediate and full attention."

"Disappointed" wasn't the word to describe how I was feeling. I'd blown off a meeting with a client to get myself ready for this date, and he wanted to cancel. "Is it about Paris?" I asked, trying to hide the displeasure in my voice and pretend as if I were OK with his decision when I was anything but.

"You'll know soon enough, but in the meantime, I'm going to need you to be available. We may be on our way to China, sooner than I thought."

The trip I'd promised my staff and Shelia came to mind. We were scheduled to leave the following week. There was no way that I was bailing out on them. Then I remembered my promise to God, about not getting involved again. "Jordan, I'm sorry, but I can't go with you this time."

The angered expression returned fast. "Is it going to be this way every single time I need you? What happened to you saying that you were here for me? Was that a lie?"

My nerves were suddenly on edge. "Jordan, you know that I'm leaving for Tahiti with my staff. I can't bail out on them."

"They're grown, and don't need *you* to hold their fucking hands."

At this point, I didn't care about letting him know that I was upset about our plans. His inconsiderateness when it came to what was important to me and his blatant disrespect for my business, made me reevaluate where I stood with him. It was always about Jordan, and what Jordan wanted. Anyone else, be damned. "That's really rich coming from you. Why don't you take your own advice, and go to fucking China without me then?"

"Is that what you really want, because that can certainly be arranged," he shot back.

I had to laugh to keep from crying. "You can do whatever the hell you want, because I will be in Tahiti with my staff as planned next week." I opened the door attempting to get out, but Jordan reached for me and tore the sleeve on my new dress. When I heard the tear without regards for what I was doing, I turned around and slapped him.

"Have you lost your fucking mind?" Jordan lunged for me, but could only get so far since he was strapped in. He gripped my hair and pulled me back toward him.

I clawed and screamed trying to get out of his grip. "You said you'd never do this again." It was only then, that he let go of me.

"Bianca." He reached for me.

"To hell with you!" I screamed as I got out of his car and slammed the door. As I was trying to run in the platform heels, I stumbled, fell, skinned my knee, and lost a shoe. "Damn it!" I cried as if this night couldn't get any worse. I limped to my door and let myself inside.

I locked the door just in time as Jordan tried to get in. He beat the door mercilessly.

"Bianca! Open the damned door." He made threats when I wouldn't obey his request. "I swear if I have to break this door down—"

To avoid my nosey neighbors from calling security, I opened

the door. Jordan came in and instead of going back and forth with an argument, he pulled me into his arms and held me, apologizing profusely for taking his anger out on me.

"You're right. I shouldn't have done that. It'll never happen again," he said.

Instead of allowing him to lie his way back into my good graces, I slapped him for the second time that night across his face. "Isn't that what you told me in Paris, when you hit me the first time, hmm? I shouldn't have believed you then, because I sure as hell, don't believe you now. So take your sorry-ass apologies, and get the hell out of my house!"

He rubbed the side of his face where I had struck. "I deserved that, but know this ... this is the only pass that you'll ever get for putting your hands on me. I'll call you tomorrow once you've had time to come to your fucking senses."

I had nothing left to say as I watched him leave. I locked the door and took off what was left of my $800 dress. There was no telling where my other shoe was. My hair, the dress, the shoes and makeup—I'd spent all day making sure was perfect—was nothing more than money down the fucking drain.

Chapter 29

Since the last blowup, I hadn't heard from Jordan. Surprisingly, I wasn't as hard-pressed about the situation as I thought I would be. Maybe it had something to do with my upcoming vacation that had me so occupied. I was already packed and looking forward to meeting some hunky guy and having a weeklong fling. The last few days had been filled with shopping sprees and hanging out with Cody, Shelia and Reggie. It felt like old times, my life pre-Jordan. They were just as excited as I was to be getting away and having nothing to worry about except for what color beach attire to wear. It was during this time, that I realized how much I really missed my crew and felt like crap for neglecting them to be Jordan's so-called Bond Girl.

I'd just filled my dishwasher and cleared the table of the lunch dishes when I heard someone at my door. I hung the dishrag over the sink that I was about to wipe down the counters with, and went to see who it was. When I looked through the peephole, there was a large bouquet of flowers blocking my view. Figuring that it was Jordan, I opened the door, but to my surprise, it was a very thin, tall, young blonde with the bluest of eyes holding a breathtaking floral arrangement. There was something very familiar about her, but I couldn't put my finger on it.

"Are you Bi-On-ca Bruks?" she asked with a heavy accent that I couldn't place.

"Yes, I'm Bianca."

She waved to someone before handing me the vase. "*Beautiful* flowers for a *beautiful* lady."

Before I could say anything, I saw two men carrying more arrangements coming toward the door. I showed them in so they could put them down, and I did the same with the one that I was holding. When I turned around, she was walking in with another one.

"This is it. You are so much loved," she said before shoving a clipboard into my hands that held a receipt for me to sign. I caught her looking around as if she were casing my home. Feeling my eyes on her, she gave me her full attention. "Your home is very ... *beautiful*."

After I finished signing my John Hancock, I gave her back the clipboard. "Thank you," I commented solemnly.

She stood a little longer than necessary making me feel uncomfortable. "Can I help you with anything else?" I asked.

"You have a very *beautiful* home," she repeated before backing out. The two guys that helped her had already left. I tried looking at her a little more closely to see why she seemed so familiar to me, but she hurriedly turned and left.

I closed the door behind me shaking my head about the bizarre encounter. I walked over to the displays, took a card from one to see who they were from. I had a feeling, but I didn't want to assume. A huge smile covered my face when I saw that my assumption was correct. Instead of staying mad, I decided to give him a call to thank him for the flowers.

The phone only rang once before he was on the line. "I see you got my gift?"

I picked up one of the orchids and sniffed it. "Yes, they're lovely. Thank you."

"Not as lovely as the recipient." His voice was so damned sexy and feelings that I thought were suppressed, resurfaced. That lustful longing was taking over and I just had to have him before I left.

"Would you like to come over so that I can thank you properly before I leave for Bora Bora?"

I heard a car door close before he responded. "I'm way ahead of you. Open the door."

I put the flower down and then ran over to the mirror to make sure that everything was still intact and looking the way it was when I'd dressed. After I was satisfied with what I saw, I went to let Jordan in. The moment I opened the door, my pussy twitched with excitement. The grin I was wearing on my face would not be contained. Our expressions mirrored each other's exactly. He reached for me and I allowed him to envelope me in his embrace. His Creed Royal Oud cologne seduced my nostrils as I inhaled his masculine scent deeply. My eyes closed involuntarily as I was instantly swept back up and into his world surrendering willingly. My need for him was skyrocketing as the seconds ticked by. No longer being able to shield my ferocious desire, I reached inside his pants and led him inside my love nest by his throbbing manhood.

Jordan kicked the door with the back of his foot and swept me up into arms. Our lips clashed as we groped and ripped one another's clothes off. I unbuckled his pants and slid down to my knees. With his pulsating member in my hands charming me like the cobra it was, my tongue and lips were eager to reintroduce themselves.

"Damn, I missed your lips being wrapped around my dick." Jordan groaned when I slowly took him in inch by inch letting my tongue travel the length of his magnificent tool. He fell back against the wall when I started working my magic, then detouring to give his balls some much-needed attention. I let my tongue travel back up his length and stiffened at the tip as it circled his head and dipped between his glistening slit. His eyes closed tighter as I repeated the process, over and over again. I lifted up slightly and opened my lips pausing to exhale deeply over his throbbing phallus before lowering my mouth over the head again.

"Ahh, shit yeah!" Jordan exclaimed as my hot mouth engulfed him. I licked around the head several times feeling the satiny, soft flesh glide across my moist tongue. I lowered my mouth over him again, making sucking noises and letting saliva coat his beautiful dick for an even more enjoyable experience.

My tongue pressed out over my lower lip to massage him as I pleasured more of his wonderfully delicious dick between my lips. He moaned deeply when my tongue slipped between his shaft and balls. My nose nuzzled into his pubic hairs, inhaling his masculine scent, driving myself insane as my hand found its way to my throbbing cunt. My fingers twirled around my clit in the same fashion my tongue curled around his mushroomed head. I felt an orgasm coming from the combination of stimulating myself and hearing Jordan's throaty whispers of encouragement egging me on.

"That's ... it, baby ... aww ... damn."

I took him all the way in relaxing my throat muscles to swallow as much of his golden rod as I could. Tears streamed down my face as I started to gag, but I kept going. Choking to death was not an option, but it felt scary and intoxicating at the same time. I nearly lost it as I felt his dick grow before releasing its buttercream frosting. I grabbed on to his hips so he could fuck my face while enjoying his reward. No sooner than he gave one last pump, his nut burst forward, hitting the back of my tonsils and oozing down the sides of my mouth. I'd reached a climax also and held my fingers up for him to taste. One lick and he'd pushed me onto my back. I lay spread-eagle on the floor as he devoured me with the type of tongue lashing that wet dreams were made of.

After having some intense marathon sex, trying to make up for lost time, we lay intertwined on the living room floor where it all started. Nothing could take away what we just had shared as sex and flowers perfumed the air. The only thing that could be heard was our labored breathing that created a sound of two satisfied lovers. I ran my fingers through his damp chest hairs and wondered what was on his mind.

"Penny for your thoughts," I said.

He turned his head toward me and smiled. I nearly melted like hot candle wax when his smile beamed down on me like the sun. He had a way of making me swoon without even trying, and he knew it. "I missed you."

My hand abandoned his chest and traced his succulent lips. "I missed you too, baby."

"I wouldn't have known, being that you told me to get the hell out."

And just like that, the warm syrupy moment was ruined. "Come on, you know what that was about."

"It was about you acting like a spoiled brat because you couldn't have your way," he had the nerve to say.

I sat up with the quickness. "Excuse me?"

"You heard me. I have a lot of things I need to take care of, and not being able to depend on you fucks up my schedule."

If it were possible, I'm sure my head would've rolled around like Linda Blair's did on the cult classic *The Exorcist*. Judging from the silly look on Jordan's face, I must've accomplished it going all the way around. I was at my wit's end with him being selfish. "I think you got that twisted. When have you ever supported any of my endeavors, Jordan? You speak about my business as if it's an afterthought, or a joke. You take nothing about me besides sex, and what I can do to further your cause, whatever that might be, seriously."

Jordan laughed out loud and that unnerved me because I felt like a fool for not sticking to my guns. "You got it all wrong. I do care about you. Haven't I made you a millionaire?"

I was about to push him when I remembered what he'd said about my last pass for putting my hands on him. "I've earned every damned dime of that money, so don't you even dare go there. When my freedom is on the table, you damn right, I'm going to take every cent of what you give me with pleasure."

Jordan stood and as heated as I was about his behavior, his nakedness had me wanting another round. "Whatever, Bianca. I didn't force you into doing anything you didn't want to do."

I shook out of the trance he had me under, and made a mental note to myself about allowing him to entice me with his body. "Like you gave me a choice with your threats of cutting me off."

He pulled me up from the floor and led me over to the sofa. "I promise to take what's important to you more seriously. I don't want you thinking that what we have is one-sided, because it's not."

That put a smile on my face, but he turned that upside down with his next statement.

"We leave for China next week. I have a trap in place to put Easter out of his misery, and if things go according to plan, I'll catch two birds with one stone."

Chapter 30

"Jordan, you can't be serious."

The look on his face let me know that he was serious. Dead serious. "Does it look like I'm playing?"

My hands instinctively flew to my face to shield the tears that started to flow without my consent. I couldn't believe that I was giving in to him again. My body was racked with uncontrollable shakes as I cried without a care in the world of how I might be perceived by him. Jordan did nothing to console me and I felt as if I'd been sequestered by his dictating magnetism. I had no one that I could confide in without incriminating myself or worse. I had to find a way to rid myself of this hold he had on me.

I dried my tears with the backs of my hands while gathering my composure. "Jordan, you know I have plans already. I can't and I won't abandon them. Not for this. Please don't make me choose because you won't like the outcome." I finally found the strength to wipe those sorry waterworks away and hold my head up high. Well, at least until I saw that there was no compassion coming from neither his eyes nor his body language. He was so austere and icy that I was now afraid of what would happen if I denied him. I wasn't fearful of him hurting me, just him abandoning me. Jordan was like my drug of choice. I realized from the moment I'd heard his voice over the phone, that I wasn't as over him as I thought I was.

The prolonged silent treatment he was torturing me with was tearing me apart. I watched as Jordan slid into his clothes ignoring me until he was finished.

"Again, we leave for China next week." He snatched up his shirt, stuffed his feet into his Gucci driver loafers, and left me alone with my thoughts.

I was so mad at myself for allowing him to see me crying, which was getting old. Sitting back on the sofa, I thought about what I'd allowed myself to get into. My cluttered mind was a mess trying to process the events of my life since Jordan had entered it, but one thing became clear. Suddenly, my backbone had started to develop and I knew what I had to do.

"Did you remember something that could help Agent Garza?" Aliyah asked me.

Thinking quickly, I knew I couldn't show my hand just yet— especially with Agent Garza thinking he had the best of me. I wanted to make him work for what he was after. "Nothing that we hadn't already talked about."

Agent Garza stopped the recorder. "Are you sure?"

I took a sip of the now lukewarm water sitting before me. "Yes, I'm positive." Agent Garza and I made eye contact that was only broken when Aliyah intervened.

"I'd like to take a breather to confer with my client," she said.

"I was just thinking the same thing myself. Everyone, take ten," Agent Garza agreed as he dismissed the rest of the agents. "Ms. Brooks, remember the deal you cut with the D.A., depends on you cooperating a hundred percent. I've already caught you in a few sloppy cover-ups concerning the girl. You don't want to disappoint me by trying to hide more information because I *will* find out."

I made a clucking sound with my tongue before waving Agent Garza away. The moment he left, I went off. "Who does he think he is?"

Aliyah stood and looked around as if we weren't alone. "Not here. Let's take a walk."

Once we were out of the building, we walked down the sidewalk when Aliyah excused herself to take a call. I sat on one of the benches thinking of everything that had led to this point. Aliyah finished up her other business and joined me.

"Is there something more you need to tell me?"

I faced her and tried to hide my true feelings. "Why would you think that?"

She shrugged her shoulders. "You stopped with the story as if you just remembered something pertinent, and I want to know what it is."

The wind blew my hair into my face. I fought with it to get it into a ponytail until we got back inside. "Aliyah, you're my attorney. It would be stupid for me to hold anything from you."

She reached to get a fly-away strand before it made its way into my eye. "It would be very stupid, which is why you should tell me. Better yet, remember what's at stake, Bianca. Hell, Agent Garza already busted you once. If he finds you're withholding information again, he can have the deal thrown off the table and charges brought up against you for obstruction of justice ... or worse. Now, I'm sure you wouldn't want that. Would you?" Aliyah stood, indicating that the meeting was over.

I placed my hand on her shoulder before she walked off, prompting her to contemptuously stare me up and down. "I'm not withholding anything, just betraying my man. I hate doing this, Aliyah, especially when I don't know that he's the one who really set me up."

And that quickly, the look was replaced by a smile before her finger swiped at a tear that rolled down my cheek. "Of course you do."

I followed her back into the building where Agent Garza and the others were waiting with two women who weren't present earlier.

Agent Garza stood when I entered to make introductions. "Ms. Brooks, Ms. Talal, District Attorney Marlow Hayes and Legal Attaché Phoebe Bercherot will be joining us for the duration. They're already up to speed with your statement thus far, as they were listening to you on the other side of the glass."

District Attorney Marlow Hayes, a petite, but curvy woman with smooth, dark-chocolate skin nodded in my direction. Her intense hazel eyes bore a hole through me, as if I should have been intimidated, but I wasn't.

"Good afternoon, Ms. Brooks, it's nice to be meeting you in better surroundings. Aliyah," she said halfheartedly.

Aliyah gave her the same half-assed greeting. "Marlow."

Phoebe's eyes were cold, but her lips held a smile. Her body looked like it belonged to a thirteen-year-old boy. If not for the fact that she was wearing a pencil-skirt suit and sporting a blonde, sharp-edged bob with humongous breasts that made her look as if she would topple over at any minute, I may have mistaken her for one. "Bonjour, Mademoiselles Brooks and Talal. I'm Legal Attaché Phoebe Bercherot, and I work with the American Embassy in Paris. Since a serious and most devastating crime was committed against the Musée du Louvre … well, it's only fitting that I see what you can come up with to make sure that *everyone* involved is brought to justice."

"Yeah, well, nice to meet you too, Legal Bercherot. I only hope that we're able to bring some closure to this catastrophe that took place at Musée du Louvre, and recover your precious treasures while we're at it." Aliyah spoke with concern and passion, but with an undertone of hidden mockery that only I seemed to have caught.

District Attorney Marlow Hayes laughed, breaking the ice. "Now that introductions are out of the way, you may continue, Ms. Brooks."

Guess I wasn't the only one who had detected the sarcasm oozing from Aliyah's so-called speech.

The day of the trip to Bora Bora had finally arrived. Jordan called, stopped by and did everything under the sun to get me to change my mind about going. For the first time in a long time, I was back to my old self, and it felt damned good.

On the drive to the airport, my phone rang, displaying an unknown number. I was going to ignore it, chalking it up to a bill collector, but something prompted me to answer.

"Hello?"

There was static in the background and then Jordan's voice came through. "Where are you? I'm at your house."

I looked at the phone to make sure I'd heard him right. "Excuse me?"

He sighed deeply as if he were annoyed with me. "I guess this means you're on your way to vacation with your *friends*, instead of standing by your man as you promised you would always do?"

"Why is it so hard for you to understand that I had plans already?" I saw the exit for the airport coming up and was almost cut off when I got over. I cringed at the thought of my newly purchased Infiniti QX80 being hit. That was short-lived when the horn of the other driver blared loudly as if I was in the wrong. In response, I gave him the finger and kept it moving.

Instead of showing concern, Jordan's next statement was a demand. "I suggest you turn that car around and get your ass back home. *Now!*"

When he hung up the phone, I decided to power off my cell. I came to a stop at a red light when I thought about the things I had in store while being on the "Pearl of the Pacific" for seven whole days. I wasn't about to be bogged down with Jordan and his drama.

Chapter 31

After making a safe landing on the airstrip in Tahiti, we exited the plane and were greeted with fragrant floral leis and given tropical drinks served in hollowed-out coconuts decorated with little umbrellas and fruit. We journeyed to our private overwater beach bungalows by ferry. Cody, Reggie, Shelia and the three other staff members that made Pleasure Principles stepped off of the boat wearing looks of amazement on their faces. It was the first time that any of us had been there.

Suddenly, it was a bittersweet moment when I thought about the honeymoon that never took place a few short months ago when I was stood up by my fiancé, Michael. We'd been together since the ninth grade which made our union destined to be a marriage made in heaven. The thought of him and this supposedly being our special place caused me to tear up. As quickly as they materialized, they dried up when I realized that I had to get ahold of myself since that chapter in my life was closed. Looking at my closest friends, I couldn't have asked for a better group to experience this tropical paradise with.

"Girl, I think he wants the doll." Cody interrupted my thoughts when he whispered about one of the cabana boys who'd brought us to where we would be lodging. He was a strapping, young Tahitian with sun-kissed skin and a body that only God himself could've sculpted. His thick, black hair cascaded down his back and his accent was ultra-sexy.

The way he devoured Cody with his eyes led me to believe that someone was going to be getting their groove on in the very near future. "Mmm-hmm ... I see him." I snickered softly so he wouldn't know that we were discussing him.

Reggie grunted when he saw the object of his affection was taking a special interest in Cody. "Where is my room so I can go and rest my eyes for a few?" he snapped.

One of the other guides told them to pick out a bungalow of their choice with the exception of the master suite, which belonged to me. They were all the same as far as the décor that provided a romantic theme. The gang all went to claim the spots that they would be calling home for the next seven days.

Another hunk of a guide with my luggage in tow led the way to where I would be. I couldn't help but to look at his well-toned ass and wonder what it would feel like in my hands. Naughty thoughts plagued me until we arrived at our destination.

He stepped to the side and allowed me to enter first. The only way that I could describe the layout and the white décor was ... enchanting. The views were wide open, yet provided private at the same time. I could see the ocean through the glass floor of my bungalow. Seeing the many schools of fish swimming about and the colorful reefs gave the room an ambiance out of this world. I could sit and stare at the beauty of one of God's greatest creations all day. The lie was told when my guide walked past with my luggage proving that Mother Nature couldn't hold my attention too long with him in the vicinity. His bulging muscles beckoned out to me.

My hands were itching to reach out and touch until he caught me staring. Our eyes locked and a knowing grin spread across his face. He flexed pectorals at me that couldn't be contained by his tight-fitting uniform shirt.

"Is there *anything* else that I can do for you?" he wanted to know.

I was still at a loss for words when he boldly led me over to the king-sized canopy bed dressed in the fluffiest of white linens and comforter. He bypassed the stepladder and lifted me onto the high bed.

"Is there *anything* else that you might desire?" This time he allowed me to feel his hardness pressed firmly against my knee.

My hand instinctively caressed his rigid muscle. A soft moan escaped my lips, when I felt that he was working with a fatty. He pulled his shorts down to give me better access. I rubbed him until I saw pre-cum oozing from his slit. I polished his dick with his juices and felt its stickiness coating my hand. He had a musky scent, that would normally drive me wild, but I felt that we needed to get cleaned up before any action was to go down. I pushed him back and used the stepladder to get off of the bed. Never losing eye contact with him, I took off my clothes and stood before him completely naked.

"I would like to shower first."

His smile darn near split his face it was so wide. He eagerly grabbed ahold of my hand and led the way.

Attached to my bungalow was an outside shower with its surrounding resembling a botanic garden. It was out in the open, but still private due to its positioning. We quickly undressed, admiring each other's nakedness. He turned the water on and waited for it to heat up. When he was satisfied with its temperature, he adjusted the shower head and allowed the warm streams to cascade over our bodies. I took the complimentary soap and lathered and explored his most sensitive spots.

The favor was returned when he washed me from head to toe. He took his time giving me pleasure along the way, massaging my nipples and clit. His dick poked me in the belly begging for my attention. I knelt in front of him and was immediately drenched from the gushing waters. My straight hair was now a curly mess, but that didn't bother me as I leaned in and let my tongue glide across his slit to see how he tasted. I don't know what his diet was, but his sap was as sweet as maple syrup. My hungry mouth wanted more and I obliged by engulfing all of him. His tool wasn't as big as I would've liked lengthwise, but it more than made up for its shortcomings in girth.

He grabbed the back of my head while I worked him over, giving him the best tip he would receive all day. As delicious as he was, I didn't want him to cum just yet. I let my tongue wrap around him one last time before standing up to see what his pipe-laying skills were about.

I was quivering with need wanting him to put his mouth on me. Finally, he squatted in front of me, kissed her and then at last, began tonguing her down. I exhaled from the relief as my leg went over his shoulder. I held onto to the shower pole to accommodate him with better access into my sultry oasis. The feeling of his wide tongue as it curled around my clit was indescribable. I fucked his face as though I was in a marathon trying to make it to the finish line. Feeling his soft lips kissing my lips and his tongue doing the bump and grind with my pearl was an ecstasy of a ride. I slowed a bit, paced myself, humping his mouth, slowing every now and then to prolong the inevitable.

"Ooooh!" I moaned to keep from screaming out loud the way I wanted to. In my mind, I pictured the moment of when I would explode inside of his mouth, sending all of my long, pent-up frustrations with Jordan in the form of a creamy tidal wave down his throat. Sensing that I was almost there, I decided that I wanted to feel that fat dick inside of me and backed away.

I rushed back inside the room, trying to think, and became panicked when I couldn't remember which suitcase I had packed my condoms in. Just when I thought I was going to have to send him on his way, he proved to me that he was not only a pussy slayer, but a lifesaver, for he came prepared! He took a couple of condoms out of his wallet and slid one on. I got on the perfectly made bed, grabbed some of the pillows to prop myself up, and tooted my ass in the air for him to hit it from the back.

He was only too willing to take me up on my offer. He massaged himself some more before entering me. His little fatty was just what the doctor had ordered for the time being. He was humping and smacking my ass and serving me right, but the moment it started to get really good. . .

"Oooh, yeeeeah!"

The motherfucker came.

Mad wasn't the word. I was about to cuss his ass out when one of his coworkers barged in without knocking. I looked over my shoulder at him. Cocky and so sure of himself, he grabbed his crotch and walked over to the bed. I couldn't believe that he had such nerve that he thought he could just waltz on in and get in on the action. Without being invited, he hopped on the bed as short-dick rolled off, trying to catch his breath. He pulled his shorts down with me still looking at him and unveiled a whopper! My hand reached back to stroke him while he tore open the last condom his friend had on the bed. Before plunging in, he ate me out from the back and had me speaking in tongues. His friend was good, but this was what I had come to Bora Bora looking to experience— besides the beautiful views.

Once his appetite was sated, he eased himself inside and filled me to the brim. His strokes started out nice and slow, and before long, it became a pounding fest. I played with my clit as the core of my being erupted into a bright explosion of colorful pleasure.

Cum spurted out in what felt like a never-ending climaxing river.

My excitement got him off as he pulled out, snatched his condom off and shot hot rivulets of children that would never be onto my back before collapsing onto the bed.

Being a little gratuitous always went over well. Judging from the wide grins on their faces, I knew they had been tipped generously. Once they were gone, I basked in the aftereffects of the illicit encounter I'd just had. I used one of the pillow cases to wipe off the mess on my back, since I was too lazy to get up and get a towel. Before long, a yawn caught me off guard and with nothing else to do, I pulled the covers back and welcomed the more than deserved nap that was awaiting me.

Chapter 32

Once my luggage was unpacked and put away, I took another shower, dressed, and was about to call the gang to see what we were doing for dinner. The moment I turned my cell phone back on, it started to ring. I hated that I didn't just use the phone provided when I saw who was calling.

"Yes?" I answered drily.

"Why do you continually try to test me, Bianca?"

My eyes rolled heavenward. I cursed myself for not taking international calling temporarily off of my phone. I wanted to hang up so badly, but knew it was best to get it over with then, instead of ruining the entire trip. "I don't want to argue with you, Jordan."

I jumped, nearly dropping the phone when Jordan hollered into it. "I don't appreciate you choosing *them* over me." He then seemed to catch himself and lowered his volume. "But, don't worry; as I've said before, what you won't do, another will. Enjoy your trip." The call was disconnected and then I couldn't stop thinking about the floozy that was taking my place.

Thinking fast, I dialed Seven's phone and got her voicemail. Then I tried Snake's and the same deal. Sledge and I weren't on the best of terms, but he was my last hope.

"This is Sledge," he answered with a deeper voice than I recalled him having.

I signed the cross over me praying that he wouldn't blow me off. "Sledge, it's ... Bianca."

There was a dead silence followed by, "Hmm, Bianca?" he responded like I had some nerve contacting him. "What could *you* possibly want with me?"

I fidgeted with a nearby pillow. "Are you going to China?"

He laughed out loud. "Look here, bitch, I know why you're calling, but let's get something straight: I don't give a damn who Jordan screws just so long as it ain't me, and I mean that literally and figuratively. See where I'm going with this?"

"Yes, but—"

"But fuck you for that little stunt you pulled. If you knew what was best for you, you'd stay away from those people."

I sighed deeply. "Sledge, look—"

"And since you don't know a gift horse when it's staring you in the mouth ... while you're at it, lose my fucking number." The phone went dead.

My heart was telling me to get on the first thing smoking, but my head was telling me to let it go. I tried calling Jordan back, but got his voicemail three times in a row. On the fourth call, I left him a threatening message, but then I erased it after listening to how pathetic I sounded.

I sat on the bed with my knees drawn to my chest willing the phone to ring with Jordan, saying that he was just playing. I didn't realize that Shelia had come into the room until I felt her hand on my shoulder. It nearly scared the hell out of me.

"Are you okay?" She took a napkin that she was using to catch the perspiration from her drink to dab at the tears falling from my eyes. "What's wrong, B?" She sat down on the bed next to me.

I looked at her, not wanting to reveal how much I was in over my head when it came to my feelings for Jordan. Then again, I figured that she would understand more so than anyone. "I don't know what to do."

"Do about what?" Shelia asked as she stood. It was then that I took in her attire. She was dressed appropriately considering her normal taste. She wore a leopard-print, strapless maxi dress that swept the floor and red accessories. Her hair was in a playful ponytail and her makeup was not as heavy as she normally preferred it. She was absolutely stunning when she wasn't so overdone.

I dried my tears and blew my nose before spilling. "It's Jordan."

Shelia placed her drink down and threw her hands up in the air. "What in the hell has he done now? You bet not let him come here and ruin our time with you. Hell, we barely get to see you anymore, thanks to his selfish ass, as it is."

Now, I really felt bad—not because Jordan was coming, but that I was considering leaving them behind to be with him. "No, it's nothing like that. I ... I can't explain the way that I'm feeling without coming off as sprung."

Shelia tilted her head back in laughter and sat back down. "Oh! Now I see." She hit the side of my arm. "Bianca's in love!"

"Who's in lust, confusing it with love?"

Cody interrupted when he walked in with Reggie and the others in tow.

"Do any of you know how to knock? I could've been in here naked."

"Chile, it ain't like we have never seen you in your birthday suit before," Reggie said as he claimed a seat on the bed next to Shelia. "Trust, hunty, none of us do fish unless it's from the ocean, Ms. Thing." He snapped his fingers as the rest of the guys cosigned.

I didn't mind Reggie, Cody, and Shelia being all up in my business, but I didn't feel comfortable divulging any of my personal going-ons in front of the others. I was glad when Reggie interjected because I didn't feel like explaining my current state of mind.

"We don't have time to sit around twiddling our thumbs. I've made reservations and we only have twenty minutes to get there, so brang ya asses." Reggie got up and the rest of us followed him to a chauffeured motorboat that took us to one of the nearby restaurants.

After tossing and turning throughout the night, I decided that I was going to head back to the States to assist Jordan on his China mission. I knew all of this went against the promise I'd made to God, but I had to go. I only prayed that He would forgive me, for I was admittedly weak, when it came to this man. What was important to him should be just as equally important to me since I was, after all, his woman. There was no way that I was going to face my friends with what I was about to do. I took the chicken way out and I'd left a note with one of the on-call wait staff. There was also information regarding a wire transfer to Reggie with more than enough money to take care of anything that they would need.

A flight was due to leave within the next couple hours to Los Angeles and like that, I'd left Bora Bora with my tail tucked between my legs, abandoning my friends.

Chapter 33

Aboard a jetliner, Jordan bobbed his head to whatever music that was playing on his Beats headphones while staring blankly out of the window and paying me no mind. He had a lot of gall to be ignoring me after I'd ditched my friends to be here for him. Once I'd made it back to Dallas, I learned that there wasn't anyone else. He knew my jealousy would get me back to him where he said I belonged. Every time my eyes wandered over to Sledge, I would catch him smirking at me, shaking his head and making it known that he thought I was a damn fool. I didn't even bother to confront him; it was the truth. Seven and Snake were their usual selves, but I still felt like they were all laughing at me for being so weak. My phone rang constantly with the numbers of those that I'd left behind in Bora Bora. I didn't have the courage to face them in person, let alone over the phone.

I was leery of flight attendants on private planes after that last fiasco. Paying close attention to the tall, but petite brunette, I couldn't help but think that there was something oddly familiar about her. Her blue eyes were icy, haunting, and her accent I couldn't place. Her presence was driving me insane. Or could it be that I was finally losing it?

"Would you like something to drink, *beautiful*?" she asked me.

I was taken aback for a second and she seemed to have noticed the change in my demeanor. "No. No, thank you," I answered, still unsure why she irked me.

Six pairs of eyes seemed as if they were burning a hole through me. It was as if they suspected something. To play it off, I yawned and pulled my shades over my eyes. Suddenly, I felt uncomfortable, or was it my conscience playing tricks on me, making me see, and hear things, that were impossible.

According to what Jordan had told me, Easter was set to meet up with The Collector to discuss the Louvre and taking out their number one enemy, which was him. Jordan's head on a platter was their main priority for the moment. Once the pilot let us know that we were at cruising altitude, only then did Jordan take off his earphones to address us.

After he got our attention, he didn't waste a minute. "As you all know, this could go either way, but I don't plan on being the one that it goes badly for. Easter is planning to meet with a Mr. Novikov, a Russian spy, that I've had a few run-ins with some years back. Where I have the upper hand is that Easter doesn't know that the beef Novikov and I had has long since been squashed. I tipped him off on an ambush, which resulted in him being able to get rid of a few enemies and saved him from an untimely death. For that information, he now practically owes me his life."

"How do you know he's as indebted to you as you think he is? That setup could've been a ploy to make you think you have an ally in him." Snake hurriedly spoke up out of turn.

"He's right, Jordan. How can we trust that Novikov isn't in on what Easter and The Collector is planning?"

"I've known Easter for years. I know how he thinks. He wants to be me and there's nobody who knows Jordan Lei better than I do." He chuckled as he displayed his arrogance. "Easter has a bad habit of trusting those that he feels have an axe to grind with me, and Novikov is no different. Snake, when you went to him that night in Paris, you saw it firsthand. He was more interested in your hate for me, than he was in conducting business. His obsession with me is to the point that he literally let you take over his operation when he allowed you to choose who *you* wanted to work with. I would have never allowed an idiotic move like that. I would've found another man for the job. Nor would I have disclosed that much information on a first meeting. Like with you, Snake, he feels that he has a friend in Novikov, and that's what I want him to think."

Seven interrupted Jordan's self-absorbed speech. "You're so sure of yourself. Are you certain that you're not the one who's being played?" She smirked.

Jordan rubbed his goatee that he'd recently started sporting. "To answer your question, I've placed Novikov in a number of situations to see where his loyalties were. He's passed them all with flying colors each and every time, proving to be a man of integrity. It doesn't hurt that just about everyone on Easter's payroll is beholden to me in some way or another. Besides, his constant contact with Snake; how do you think I'm able to stay on top of everything that he has going?"

Sledge laughed out loud while slapping his knee. His actions were misplaced since no humor could be found in what was being said. To me, it's like that jab was directed at me. "That Giovanna sure is one of a kind. When are you going to stop playing games with these little *girls* . . .," he pointed at me, "and make an honest woman out of *her*, my man?"

Jordan's eyes narrowed and he was about to say something slick when the flight attendant seemed to appear from out of nowhere.

"Is there anything I can get for any of you?" Sledge raised his empty glass that once contained scotch. She then looked at me. "Anything for you, *beautiful*?" That eerie feeling came over me again when I gazed up at her, but before I could respond, Jordan dismissed her.

"We're fine," he practically snapped. "Sledge, make this the last time you disrespect Bianca."

Sledge threw his hands up in surrender. "Chill out, man. I was just fucking with you."

"Now is not the time. We need to be focused!" Jordan's eyes connected with mine. I could tell that he wanted me not to react to what was just said, but how could I not.

"Who in the hell is Gio—" And there it was, the bitch on the magazine covers and the woman who Easter was going on and on about. It was something about her that I didn't like, but to find out that she'd been with my man, intensified my displeasure for her. I felt like such an ass. Was I just keeping Jordan company until her mission was complete? I buried my face in my hands and didn't pay the rest of the trip any mind until the pilot announced that we were about to land.

From the Shek Kong private airport in Hong Kong, we were swiftly whisked away by helicopter and landed on an estate that had its own heliport pad. From the glass rooftop, I could see a beautiful view of an indoor swimming pool. The house was huge with fifteen fireplaces, Scandinavian marble flooring, a four-story solarium, twenty-four-karat-gold gilded ceilings, a glass elevator, and an array of other high-end features. It was amazing to me how Jordan knew people that lived so lavishly, yet I'd never seen where he called home. I was beginning to wonder more and more about whom was I really dealing with.

Jordan led me by the small of my back to one of the two master suites. Once we were alone, he pulled me into him and kissed me passionately. Normally, I would have been on fire from his touch, but with all of the questions swimming around in my head, sex was surprisingly, the last thing on my mind, if at all. Jordan noticed my hesitant demeanor.

"What's wrong, baby?"

I shrugged my shoulders while looking down at the beautiful floor. I couldn't give him eye contact for fear of what would be revealed. "Jet lag, I guess."

He led me over to the king-sized sleigh bed and pulled back the duvet. He slipped out of his Gucci loafers, climbed into bed and pulled me in with him. In the spooning position, he held me close while alternating between caressing my body and placing feather-light kisses along my neckline and earlobe.

"Are you going to tell me what's bothering you?" he asked for the second time.

I took in a deep breath and stuck to my lie. "Like I said, jet-lagged."

Jordan rose up on his side and nudged me until I was facing him. He cupped my chin and did what I didn't want him to do. He stared into my all-revealing eyes. "What Sledge said is bothering you. I know it is. You've been quiet ever since."

The waterworks started and I wanted to kick myself for being so weak in front of him. "I can't—I just can't do this anymore. I'm sorry." I made an attempt to get out of the bed, but Jordan wasn't letting me out of his reach. He held on to me tightly as the pain that I'd been holding in for so long finally took over and ravaged my body. Tears and foreign-sounding sobs escaped me for what seemed like an eternity.

Chapter 34

*A*gent Garza stopped the recorder. "It took you that long to figure out that the bastard didn't give a damn about you?"

The memory caused a sudden sadness and Agent Garza's wisecrack didn't make matters any better.

District Attorney Marlow Hayes waved him off. "Ms. Brooks, you must excuse Agent Garza, for his injudicious behavior. Your deal is with me, and I want to see The Tarantula—"

"Uh, we're referring to him as Jordan Lei, per Ms. Brooks' request. She just hates it when we call him the latter," Agent Garza interrupted with a condescending remark.

"Duly noted, Agent." District Attorney Hayes gave him a contemptuous look, then focused her attention back on me. "Ms. Brooks, I see that you're experiencing some difficulty carrying on. If you need another break, we can reconvene at a later time. Just remember our terms and you should be fine."

"No, we'll finish this now, Marlow," Aliyah spoke on my behalf.

"I believe I was speaking to Ms. Brooks," the DA said, never giving Aliyah any eye contact.

Aliyah stood in the DA's line of vision, making her have no

choice but to give her the attention she felt she deserved. "And I believe that I'm the one she's paying five hundred bucks an hour to represent her."

District Attorney Hayes crossed her arms over her voluptuous breasts. "Is there a reason for the hurry, Aliyah?"

Aliyah sucked her teeth while tapping her pen against the table. "My client isn't the one under investigation or have you forgotten that, Marlow? Once she's done, she's free to do as she pleases so long as it's in accordance with the law."

"This is my show and until I'm satisfied with Ms. Brooks' deposition, and anything else that I deem as necessary, she's not to leave the state of Texas." District Attorney Hayes didn't give Aliyah time to respond. She signaled for Agent Garza, who couldn't hide the enormous grin on his face if he wanted to, to start the recorder back up.

After much cajoling, I had convinced Jordan that I was OK and only needed to take a walk to clear my mind.

"There's a lot of land here for you to get that done on, but don't leave these grounds, Bianca, and I mean it."

I offered him a smile that belied what I was really feeling. "I won't, especially since I don't speak Chinese, let alone know my way around Hong Kong."

"Cantonese," he called after me.

I stopped to understand what he was talking about. "What?"

"Most of the people speak Cantonese, not Chinese, but you'll need to learn both languages if you plan to reside here with me."

"What happened to the sandy white beaches of Anguilla? I thought you were thinking of retiring some place like that."

"I never said I was going to retire here. This is only *one* of my homes," he revealed.

Just when I was beginning to wonder about where he resided, he'd floored me with this news. "Are you serious, Jordan?"

"This was one of the homes that belonged to my family until my father gambled it away. I bought it right from under The Collector's nose at an auction for next to nothing. He never wanted this place. He only wanted to further humiliate my family."

I leaned against the wall thinking of all the things Jordan was going through to restore his family's name. "He must've been pissed when he learned that it was you who got it back."

Jordan laughed slightly. "That would've been sweet, but I acquired it under a fictitious name so that nothing would happen to it. The Collector's a vengeful man and he would've rather had it burnt to the ground than letting it fall back into the hands of the Leis."

"I see." I went for the door and blew Jordan a kiss before leaving.

The sprawling estate grounds were awe-inspiring with nothing but lush, green manicured lawns, vibrant flowers, trees and other vegetation for as far as my eyes could see. During my walk, I came upon a sitting area that was surrounded by a small lake filled with ducks and swans floating around it without a care in the world. I sat down on one of the wrought-iron chairs, pissed at myself for not bringing a glass of wine or something to help me enjoy this area of seclusion. The birds chirping and other sounds coming from nature lulled me into a peaceful slumber.

What later turned out to be a beautiful dream turned into a nightmare. Jordan and I were married with children and had moved to Hong Kong to live in his family's home. Everything was perfect, as it should've been. Our son looked like me while our precious daughter resembled her father. Both were as cute as they wanted to be. We doted on them making sure they never knew what a hard day looked like. In the fantasy, we had just put the kids to bed and settled into our own. As Jordan caressed my burning flesh with his soothing lips, I recalled being so hot for him and needing his touch. I begged for him to give me what I wanted, when all of a sudden, I was in the lake trying to stay above water. The ducks and the swans were doing their best to get to safety as I fought with someone that I could not see. A woman's hand with long, lacquered fingernails closed around my mouth and nose while trying to hold me under. The more I struggled, the more the person who was restraining me fought. I bit down hard on the hand of my captor who momentarily let go to nurse her wound.

Finally, I was able to come up for air. Taking in deep breaths, I choked while trying to get as much oxygen as I could, all while screaming for help and throwing up water. The perpetrator now resembled a man as he tried to put a stop to my pleas, slapping me repeatedly, before once again dunking me under water. This time, I fought because my life depended on it.

"Bianca!" I heard a distant voice calling me.

Water was being sucked in through my mouth and nostrils as I struggled to defend myself and take in breaths of fresh air, but it was a losing battle. I prayed that my cries could be heard as I called out before I was submerged again.

"Bianca! Bianca!"

I took in a deep breath. "ARRGGH!" I hollered to the top of my lungs.

"Bianca! Bianca!" I felt a stinging sensation across my face. "Wake up!" My eyes flew open, and Jordan was standing over me where I'd fallen asleep ... on the bench.

"Where am I?!" I looked around wide-eyed and unsure of what was going on, especially since I wasn't wet and still seated where I'd found this little slice of tranquility. "What ... what happened?!"

Jordan straightened up and looked at me as if he wasn't sure if

I was stable or not. "You're in Hong Kong, at my family's estate. I came out looking for you, when I heard you screaming."

I noticed that my breathing was somewhat erratic and that my heart was racing. "I feel like I'm going mad."

Jordan took the seat next to mine. "Care to tell me about it?"

He seemed genuine in wanting to know, but something told me to tread lightly. That something also angered me. "Exhaustion. The conversation on the plane. Leaving my friends in Bora Bora. I don't know. You tell me, because lately, I don't know if I'm coming or going, thanks to you!" With that, I left him where he sat as I started back toward the house.

Chapter 35

My phone indicated that I had messages. When I called in to check them, my mailbox was full. I pushed one to listen and confirmed my suspicions. It was Reggie. The rest were also from Reggie, Cody, Shelia and even my employees who had accompanied us on the trip. I didn't have the energy to explain things to them, so instead of calling, I sent out a mass group text to ease their minds, at least for the time being.

Hey guys, sorry I ducked out on you the way that I did, but something came up that needed my undivided attention. I promise you all that we will reschedule to do the trip in style, as planned, another time in the near future. I hope you all are enjoying yourselves, on me of course, and if you need anything, please don't hesitate to charge it. In addition to the money that I left, I have an open line of credit with the resort and they are aware that it's for my party to use however they choose. Love you all, smooches! ☺

I hit the *send* key and then powered off my phone. Knowing them, they were going to still demand answers that I wasn't ready to deal with. I had bigger issues to concern myself with at the moment.

Just as I was putting my phone away, Jordan walked in. "Am I interrupting?"

"No. I sent a text to my *abandoned* friends letting them know that I was okay." I was sure my sarcasm wasn't lost on Jordan, from the look on his face.

Jordan clasped his hands together and bowed his head. He looked to be saying a silent prayer. Then he trained unflinching, forbidding eyes on me. "Bianca, if you knew what was best for you, you wouldn't bring up those faggots to my face ever again. I gave you more than enough time to sulk and have your pity party. Now get yourself together, and meet me downstairs in the library within the next five minutes and not a second later," he said before walking off.

His departure didn't leave me with a chance to respond to the disrespectful way he had just regarded my friends.

I was the last one to walk through the beautiful wooden double doors of the library that bared a crest that I guessed belonged to Jordan's family. The room not only displayed books on the impeccable shelves complete with a ladder, but heirlooms, accent pieces, expensive furnishings, priceless art, and family portraits. I should've known by how exquisite the rest of the house was decorated that I shouldn't have expected anything less with the library.

Judging by the nasty stare I got from Jordan, he wasn't too pleased with me holding up his precious meeting. As usual, Seven and Snake sat side by side while Sledge sat off to himself. When I took the empty seat next to Seven, Sledge snickered loud enough for it to be heard.

"Is there something funny, besides you?" I asked.

Sledge reacted as though he was about to come across the table at me, but slowed his roll when he caught sight of Jordan. "You need to control your—"

the States and forget about me. Or B, get a few cuts and go for a swim with the sharks. It's your choice, but know this, if you choose A, don't even let the word *double-cross* enter your mind because if you do, I'll more than make good on my threat, starting with that foul mouthed-ass mother of yours. There won't be a rock for you to hide under. Trust me, you're going to wish that you had chosen B, by the time that I'm done with you." Jordan pulled the gun back from Sledge's temple. "So, what's it going to be?"

Sledge was shivering with tears and snot running out of his nose. "You ... you know that I woo ... would never double-cr ... cross you, you, mm—man."

Jordan punched him one more time before relenting from the domineering stance he had over him. "That's what I thought." He returned to his spot at the head of the table. "Seven, book this sorry sack of shit on the next thing to the States. I don't care where it is, just so long as it's on U.S. soil."

I almost felt sorry for Sledge ... almost. There was no way I was going to say something slick to get Jordan riled up at me. Snake snatched him up and led him out of the library. Seven followed.

When we were alone, Jordan went from being a menacing pit bull to playful cocker spaniel, within a matter of seconds. He walked over to where I was and tickled me. We playfully wrestled for a minute before ending our squabble in climactic kisses. Jordan stood up and looked down at me as I was trying to contain myself from the abrupt ending of our frisky romp.

"Bianca, I apologize for having you go through that, but you don't have to worry about Sledge, anymore. Now is not the time for his bullshit, especially when I'm so close to avenging my family's honor. What I said earlier about your friends was uncalled for. I'm guilty of being jealous of your relationship with them. I sometimes wonder why we can't share the same closeness."

"Sledge!" Snake gestured for him to cool it.

He looked at everyone, and eased back into his seat. "I
Snake."

"Are you two done?" Jordan asked.

Neither of us said anything.

"I said ... are you two done?" he asked again.

"Why don't you ask your *girlfriend*?" Sledge's bitter r
made me wonder who the real faggot was since he'd bel
though Jordan was his man, instead of mine.

With the speed of a cheetah and the sleekness of a
Jordan was on Sledge pointing at his head with a gun that
even know he had on him.

"You were right, Snake, but hey, I tried," Jordan shout
his shoulder. "This motherfucker has forgotten who he's
with. I wouldn't be surprised if he's the reason we alm
popped in Paris." Jordan punched Sledge in the gut.

"Oomph!" Sledge mumbled when the blow connected w
abdomen. "Come on, man. I was ... I was just joking."

Jordan, hit him again. "And you of all people should kno
I'm not the joking type."

"I think he needs a reminder." Snake stood and walked
where Jordan held Sledge hostage.

Seven got up to try and diffuse the situation. "Come on,
is all of this even necessary?" she tried to reason.

Snake held up his hand to stop Seven from coming any
"Stay out of this."

She sat back down next to me. I wanted Jordan to pistol-
his ass so I was all in and wasn't stopping a damned thing.

"Now, I'm going to give you a couple of options that I nor
wouldn't, but since I consider you a friend, I'll make a one
exception. You can either A, get on the next plane heading ba

The anger I felt earlier started to melt away. I can't say that I'd waited to hear Jordan express some kind of feelings for me, but it felt good just to know that he did care. "Apology accepted."

He cupped my chin in his hands. "Once this is over, I promise to do better by giving you all of me, instead of just pieces."

That got a smile out of me. Suddenly, I felt better about the decision I'd made to leave Bora Bora. "I would like that very much, Mr. Lei."

Just as we were about to kiss, Seven came back interrupting what could've turned into something X-rated on top of the massive table.

"There's a flight scheduled to leave within the next couple of hours nonstop to San Francisco."

"Did you book him on it?"

Seven took a seat at the table while giving us a knowing look. "Yes, Snake is accompanying the driver to the airport to make sure he gets on it."

Jordan went back to his chair. After reclining back as far as it would go, he covered his face with his hands. "I should've listened to Snake in Paris. This impromptu trip to the airport is going to delay us. Now, I have to find a replacement on the fly." He rose back up and slapped the table with his hand. "Fuck!"

"Let me take over what Sledge was going to do and let Bianca man the computers," Seven suggested.

Jordan sat considering Seven's idea for a split-second. "No. No. No ... I need you on those computers." He ran his hands over his head, then stopped when he seemed to have had a light bulb moment. He picked up his phone and dialed a number.

Seven and I sat patiently waiting on him to wrap up his call.

"Jim, it's me." He drummed his fingers while listening to his caller on the other end. "Okay, that's not important right now. I need you to get on the next flight to Hong Kong and meet me at the place like yesterday. Seven can schedule it and call you back with your itinerary." He listened some more. "Good. Good. I'll see you when you touch down."

"Was that Jim on that call, Jim Reynolds?" Agent Garza asked.

"Yes, it was him," I answered.

DA Hayes spoke up. "Seems like our boy Jim, has been knee-deep in scandal. I'm going to have a ball putting his bigoted ass behind bars. You're doing well so far, Ms. Brooks. I'm pleased with information you're giving us. If not for your cooperation, we would be still at square one."

"I'm glad someone is finally treating my client with the respect she deserves, even if it's you, Marlow."

To prevent the claws from coming out, I jumped in. "Thank you, District Attorney Hayes. I'm only doing what I should've done from the beginning."

"Aww, that's sweet. Now, can we continue with the task at hand, please?" Agent Garza interrupted.

Chapter 36

Three days later, we arrived at an abandoned old building in the middle of nowhere. Jordan shook hands with a man who introduced himself as Novikov. He was Russian, tall, ruggedly handsome with a blond, military crew cut. He was sporting a noticeable scar on the left side of his face. He caught me staring a few times and from what I could see, he didn't mind me looking one bit.

Once Jordan was seated comfortably, he read over the details he had on Easter and The Collector before addressing the rest of the group. Snake walked in with coffee and bagels. I was glad that someone had thought of food since we didn't have breakfast at the house. During this time, Jim Reynolds joined us fresh from his flight. He greeted everyone with only a nod and took the only seat left.

Jordan stood to address us. "Now that we have everyone assembled, we can officially begin. As you all know, I only do things pertaining to business and rarely do I focus on personal, but this time it's an intimate matter that's driving me. I won't go into details, but you all know where I stand with The Collector, and why this is so important to me. Easter, on the other hand, is business. He's tried to infiltrate my organization for years, even before the fallout in Bangkok. For some reason or another, Easter has always had it out for me. I can't continue on the way I have with having to have eyes on him twenty-four-seven. What we do depends on all bases being covered, and we can't afford to be lax, especially with someone like Easter, lurking around. The setup in Bangkok could've proved deadly, and for that, Easter, must suffer the same fate that he had in store for all of us."

Jim threw in his two cents when he cut in. "I'd love to get my hands on the little rotten scoundrel. I was depending on that score to get this yacht I had my eye on."

"Speaking of yachts, Snake and I were planning to take some much needed time off to sail the Mediterranean, Seychelles, Hawaii and Tahiti among other places. We'd planned to even maybe start working on starting a family during the time off and that little imp of a man ruined it for us," Seven argued.

Snake took over Seven's rant. "When I think about what we lost in Bangkok, when it comes to Easter, I have thoughts of putting my hands on him in the worst way." That evoked a laugh from all that was in attendance, including Jordan.

"As would we all, but luckily or unluckily, depending on how you look at it, The Collector's people will be the ones doing the laying of the hands. As most of you know, Snake has been in on Easter's Louvre heist plans for the past few months. It has been confirmed that this will be *the* weekend. The Louvre will be undergoing roof repairs since a leak was discovered due to all of the rain damage. What that means is that the glass that's usually triggered with an alarm won't be. There will be guards watching the repairmen on duty, but no need to worry. We can overpower from a distance with these ... " Jordan held up a small, thin object.

"Tranquilizing darts. First, we'll need to find out what time the workers will be ending or going on break. I don't want to chance anyone dying by falling. However, this must be a synchronized attack done succinctly with no breaks for them to be able to react. No need in wasting precious time in combat. The men inside will be even easier to subdue since we've been made aware of their routines.

"As for the treasures," he continued, "The Collector has his eyes on the museum's European collection. Including works by Brueghel and Rubens with the most valuable being Remington's *The Wrath Angel*, *Lilith*, and *The Silence of Bathsheba*. He's very specific in what he wants and we'll have the rest of the details after Snake's briefing with Easter in Paris. Mother Nature has made Easter's job a hell of a lot easier, but with the tarps covering the repair zone, ours will practically be a foolproof victory. Once I get all of the names of the paintings that The Collector wants, I'll have prints made. After all is done, the way it's going to be received by The Collector is that Easter has once again pulled another of his stunts like the one in Bangkok."

"Isn't The Collector going to be there?" Seven asked. "I don't get it."

"No, he won't be, but Easter is scheduled to meet him the same night at an undisclosed location for now with the masterpieces that he has hand-selected for his compendium. The Collector doesn't want to take any chances of having something happen to his precious works of art. The man's a hands-on-multitasking maniac. Of course he's still searching high and low to recover the Joie De Vivre diamond that I relieved him of." Jordan chuckled. "I have to admit that I've enjoyed toying with him with pictures and false leads which make him want to retaliate even more. The more focused that he and Easter are on my demise means mistakes that I plan to capitalize on."

Novikov laughed out loud. "Keeping him on his toes, eh?" Even though he had a very sexy, but thick Russian accent, he spoke perfect English. I found myself watching him again and this time, when he caught me, I didn't look away.

"Exactly, Novikov!" Jordan shouted before he addressed Jim.

"Jim, I need you to make a little impromptu visit to Ming-Hua Wang. He has been tracked to the south side and is currently staying at his luxury high-rise apartment. I want for you to send a coordinated message to The Collector to rattle his cages a bit. Ming-Hau has a concert the day following the heist that I'm going to need for him to cancel indefinitely. However, do not harm a single hair on his wife's—" Jordan cleared his throat when he caught me gawping at Novikov. "Ahem ... Bianca, can I get you to focus over here, please?"

I reluctantly gave Jordan my undivided attention. I knew he would have a few choice words for me later by the way that he'd called me out. "Sorry," I mumbled as I nervously shifted in my seat.

Once he was satisfied, he picked up where he left off. "Jim, I'll give you the final details before you leave along with an address and precise instructions that you are to follow to the letter."

"Not a hair on her beautiful head will I harm," Jim said as he rubbed his hands together. "You know I have a weakness when it comes to the ladies."

Jordan shook his head in response. "Now getting back to Easter; he has a crew of four besides himself. After a short briefing, Snake is the one that he placed in charge of transport and that's where we'll come in. On the way to the Louvre, we'll switch in the van. The crew that will emerge to do the deed will be us plus Delilah."

"This sounds safe enough, but what about Johnny and Tony? They were at Easter's the night Snake and Bianca met with him," Seven questioned.

"Easter has them on as the hired muscle for when the exchange is made with The Collector. You know as well as I do, that their big asses wouldn't work for this type of job."

Seven didn't see anything funny about the situation. "The Collector is going to more than likely kill Easter. Tony and Johnny don't deserve the same fate, Jordan. They're our friends, for crying out loud!"

Jordan quieted her down. "You're right. He is going to take Easter out and anyone that is with him the night the drop is made. When Easter arrives at the exchange point, we're going to create a diversion to get them out of there. That will leave Easter to go on his own which he will without question, because he's a fool and desperate. What that diversion will be is still being worked out, but don't worry; we will have it under control."

"And if you don't?" she questioned.

Jordan ran his hands over his head and face. "Then plan B it is. We go in guns blazing and take The Collector and his men out. Only thing, I won't get the satisfaction of him seeing me reclaim my family's honor, but that's just something that I will have to live with."

Seven stood and paced back and forth. "I don't know, Jordan. This was supposed to be foolproof. I can't stand to think of what may happen. Nor am I ready to handle the what-ifs, if things go wrong."

Jordan walked over to Seven and placed his hands on her shoulders. "Remember Hawaii? This is a cakewalk compared to that. Easter is an idiot. He runs on emotions. Being in this line of work, you all know just as well as I do, that letting feelings dictate your next move is the kiss of death. It's all about strategy. Get it together. We can't afford for you to be on some PMS-type shit." He patted her on the back as he gestured for her to sit back down. "Not today."

We stayed in Hong Kong for a little less than a week and

was off to Paris bypassing U.S. soil altogether. Jordan said he'd accomplished what he'd come for, but I don't know what my purpose was for being there. I just think he loved seeing me jump through his hoops and like a trained seal, I did it every time. Even if that meant leaving my friends in a tropical paradise.

Chapter 37
Easter's Plan

Later in the week, Snake met up with Easter at 10 Place de la Concorde, which was the address of the luxurious Hôtel de Crillon in Paris. This was now where he called home since the previous residence was destroyed when Easter decided to go on a mini killing spree. The four sentinels, who were left in charge of his safe while he entertained Giovanna at the Opera, met untimely and gruesome deaths. Snake was led to the Batailles meeting room that looked more like a sumptuous banquet hall instead of the Louis XV suite that he was currently staying in.

The little man with an ego the size of the Empire State Building stood before the hand-selected crew to go over a few final details. Wearing a suit made out of the fabric that was patterned after a picnic table, Snake suppressed his laughter, which was a hard task within itself.

"Snake!" He stretched his stumpy arms out as far as they would go. "Good to see you, my friend." Easter moved as though he were modeling the monstrosity he wore as he talked. It took every ounce of resolve that Snake had not to lose it in a cackling fit.

"Meet another good friend of mine, all the way from Russia, Novikov."

"At last, we meet. I've heard good things." Novikov shook Snake's hand.

Snake played it off and smiled tightly. "No offense, Novikov; while I'm glad to meet who I'll be working this job with, I need to get some fuel in this system first." He rubbed his stomach for emphasis. "I'm hungry after such a long flight."

Novikov stepped back. "Don't let me stand in your way. We have plenty of time to get acquainted after you've *fueled* your system, as you say."

Easter pointed in the direction of the extravagant buffet he had prepared for his meeting. There was a never-ending assortment of breads, a variety of egg dishes, bacon, sausages, casseroles, juices, fruits and cereals, hot and cold. The layout was fit for a king and knowing Easter, that's exactly the image he wanted to portray. "Please, help yourself. There's plenty to choose from. Why don't you two go ahead, eat and mingle with the others while I tie up a few loose ends?"

Snake extended his hand gesturing for Novikov to lead the way. *This was going to be easier than I thought*, he contemplated to himself.

After everyone was done with eating and making small talk, Easter stood at the lectern and started the meeting that would place him in high demand, *if* the job was a success.

"Palais du Louvre. . .," he stated louder than necessary, "dates primarily from the late sixteenth century and has since acquired many of the world's most treasured pieces of art. To the right of the pyramid in the center of the main courtyard is where the water damages have occurred. This side and not the south, which faces the Seine River will serve as our entrance from the rooftop. There are multiple floors, which can make navigation confusing." He passed out some maps with highlighted areas. "Here's a copy of the official map and not the piece of shits that they hand out to tourists. This here is the real deal. I've highlighted evacuation points if the need arises, and for your sakes, I hope it doesn't. There's a lot of money on the line and we can't afford to fuck it up."

Snake became unnerved. "What do you mean for *our* sakes? Easter, must I remind you that without our help, you're fucked? Try and remember that instead of talking down to us like we need you when we all know it's the other way around."

The others seconded Snake's point by openly agreeing with him. Easter blushed red from embarrassment knowing he could never take Snake, who'd earned his name and rightfully so. He didn't want the others, especially Novikov, to see him in any way other than a man who was in charge, but now that had been ruined. "Another opportunity like this will never present itself again." Instead of showing fear, he decided by not addressing Snake directly may have saved him face. The uncomfortable stare down caused him to perspire. He took off the jacket to his suit, laid it on a nearby chair and loosened his tie.

Without having to say anything else, Snake was pleased that his message had been received loud and clear. Snake ended the stand-off with a slight nod of his head, relieving Easter of the hold his warning had on him.

"We ... we're ddddeal-ing with. . ." Easter took a deep breath to calm his mounting stress that was brought on by being called out. "We're dealing with a very important, and demanding man. For your sakes and *mine* . . ." His eyes met back up with Snake's. "Let's just get the job done without incident, okay."

Easter picked up the glass of cold water that was on the podium in front of him and nearly drained it empty. Once his thirst was quenched, he used the napkin to wipe the sweat from his brow.

He knew from looking at their faces that he had lost his power and become one of them. The only difference was that he was the one with the plan. The best thing for him to do was to focus on the task at hand, but he'd be fooling himself trying to do just that. Easter wanted to be revered as someone to be respected, if not feared. It was bad enough that he suffered from Napoleon Complex. If he was honest with himself, he'd have no problem admitting that his issue with Jordan stemmed from his own insecurities about his shortcomings, and literally, at that. Jordan's presence when he entered a room. His athleticism. The way women reacted to him. The way people around the world in this line of business considered him the one to call on if you wanted a job done. Why couldn't his mere presence command that same effect on people? Easter tried extra hard to be seen as the world viewed Jordan Lei aka The Tarantula.

Jordan's looks guaranteed him an easy stride in life unlike his own miserable existence. Easter was the polar opposite of everything that was him. Jordan would never have to find ways to compensate for his shortcomings; everybody loved him. No one was exempt from his magnetism and charm, not even men. Why did he have to have the full package? Was this God's way of playing a cruel joke on him? If so, when was the punch line coming because he was tired of waiting for it. Since God had already forsaken him, he would make his own way to best Jordan. The only way he was going to gain respect was to be the one who crushed the spider since his small stature couldn't be helped. When he learned of The Collector's disdain for his nemesis, he practically signed his name on the dotted line without batting an eyelash to even consider the dire consequences that may befall him. Having an alliance in his mission to rid the universe of The Tarantula was motivation enough and all that mattered as far as he was concerned.

"The exhibits," he continued, "are well lit and labeled. There shouldn't be an issue with nabbing the right pieces." He handed out more papers that were in color of the intended pieces and their exact locations. "However, this isn't the case with the paintings department. The departments and room numbers are clearly marked with signs, which I have also taken the liberty of duplicating on the papers that I've just given you. The collections are divided into eight departments, plus the Medieval Louvre, which we won't be getting anything out of. These are spread over four floors, lower ground through the second floor and three wings. Our focus will be the Denon and Richelieu wings. Our benefactor is no longer interested in the initial pieces in the European collection that we discussed during earlier talks. So here goes ... we are to acquire the following pieces *only*. The *La Belle Ferroniere*, the portrait of an unknown woman, *Louis XVI* in his coronation costume, *The Virgin with Child* and *Birth of a Goddess*. Four pieces for a crew of four. I will tell you which piece you are responsible for to avoid confusion at a later time. It is crucial that we acquire these pieces only. Our client has no need for the *Mona Lisa* or any other treasures housed there. Nor are you to take anything for yourself. I don't have to remind you that these will not be easy to move without a buyer already on deck."

A black man who appeared to be in his late twenties with a low Caesar cut and goatee giggled softly to himself. Easter immediately felt that he was being made fun of.

"Did I just tell a joke, Kirk?"

"Just thought we'd be swinging by Napoleon's Apartments." Everyone in the room doubled over with laughter.

Easter wanted to pull out his gun and instantly shut him up, but knew the job depended on every man that he had in the room. A replacement at this late date would not be feasible. Well, for that reason and having Snake to contend with, since this was after all, his "boy." There were things that Easter admired about Napoleon like seeking power, war, and conquest to make up for his stature and he did so without apologies to anyone. "Ha! Ha! Ha ... very funny."

Kirk stopped laughing when he glanced over at Snake and decided to apologize to put Easter at ease. "Sorry, dude. I just couldn't resist. You know with—"

"Power. Luxury. Opulence. Grandeur. Are just a few words used to describe myself and the man you make fun of," Easter said, cutting him off as he pinned him with a deadly stare.

Sensing something menacing beneath Easter's penetrating scowl, he withdrew from saying another word and relented.

"Now back to what's important." Just that quick Easter had regained control of the room by using what he'd learned about transference in psychology and judging from Kirk's discomfited demeanor, it worked like a charm. "The address, which should be ingrained into your brains already, but just for the avoidance of mistakes, is Rue de Rivoli, 75001 Paris, France." He watched as they took notes. "The coordinates that we're working in are 48.860868° N, and 2.336655° E. If your Z Compass says different, then you're going the wrong way, so pay strict attention, please."

"Are you sure that there's going to be only two guards on duty with the repairs going on?" Snake stopped writing long enough to ask.

"According to my sources, there will be only two guards for those particular wings of the building. So we're talking about four in total. Not to trust sources completely, I've also done my home-work by studying them for the last year. They're pretty predictable which is why I chose four a.m. for us to strike. From what I've observed, it is around that time that they become indolent and do other things like, meet for extended smoke breaks and to goof around," Easter explained.

"Who are we up against? Old? Young? Buffed? Fat? This information is just as crucial," Kirk, no longer in a joking mood, asked.

Easter cleared his throat. "Two of the guards appear to be middle-aged, while two are young, maybe mid-twenties or so, if I were to make a guess. One muscular and the other is a bit out of shape. The two middle-aged men look to be in great shape, but judging the excessive rest breaks they take to smoke, with one having a chronic cough and the other nursing his knee, I don't think we will have any problems subduing them, if it comes to that. The other two are more concerned with who has the most notches in his bedpost with the ladies to not be taken by the element of surprise."

A slender woman with catlike moves, the most piercing of bright green eyes and long dark hair, stood and stretched. "And how would you know what their conversations were about?"

Easter's eyes were glued to her voluptuous breasts, but his ego was offended by her asinine question. "Ever heard of a bionic ear? In this line of business, it would behoove you to keep *abreast* with the latest in technology. In case you didn't know, beauty will only take you but so far."

Instead of responding to his dig, she focused on his staring, but didn't try to cover herself like most women would have after being put down over their aesthetics. She embraced and encouraged his taking pleasure in her body. It's how she achieved taking down her opponents—past, present and future. She caught every eye in the room on her which was to be expected, being the only female present. "This weapon . . ." She ran her hands over her shapely frame, making sure to accentuate her breasts. ". . .has a proven track record throughout history of overpowering men, no matter how great they *thought* themselves to be. Adam bit into that apple because of Eve. Sampson was set up by my namesake, Delilah.

Hell, both Julius Caesar and Mark Anthony gave in to the seductive talents of Cleopatra. That was during the times of old, but men are still being brought down to their knees and near ruin behind the bewitching of a woman's feminine wiles." Delilah laughed driving Easter insane as the others looked on in amusement. "Clarence Thomas had us all trying to figure out the correct way to say the word *harassment*, when Anita Hill nearly cost him his seat on the bench. Tiger Woods caused uproar in the world of golf when his wife tried to beat him with a club after discovering that he was messing around with not one, but a harem of women. Jimmy Swaggart broke down on national television boohooing and carrying on with his '*I have sinned*' speech" all because he couldn't' resist being tempted by the lure of a woman—even if she was one of the night, she was still a woman, nonetheless. Shall I go on?"

Easter flagrantly wiped the drool that had begun to collect on the sides of his mouth. He loved nothing more than his revenge for Jordan, than a feisty and provocative woman who knew her power. "No, you've more than proven your point, *Delilah*." Although embarrassed yet again, he laughed and to his relief, so did the other men. "As I was saying, the guards shouldn't pose too much of a threat. And Delilah, I know their conversations because I listened to them for over a year. Their top of choice has never really varied into much else."

Delilah sat down, giving Easter the ease of having satisfied her curiosity when unbeknownst to him, he had done anything but.

Easter wrapped up the rest of the meeting with them making plans to go over everything in detail now that they had the logistics needed in order to pull the job off. He didn't want to give out all of the particulars too soon. No way was he going to let what he'd done to Jordan on the Bangkok assignment be done to him.

Chapter 38
Three Days Later
Back in Paris

*M*eeting up with Jordan directly could have blown everything, so instead of a face-to-face or phone call, they had other communicating methods in place. Snake reclined on the king-sized bed in his suite at Hotel Britannique. After he turned on the computer, he plugged another device into it, and put on a pair of what looked to be regular reading glasses. The computer pulled up his Yahoo! account, but the glasses displayed Jordan on the lenses back at Le Meurice. Jordan was luxuriating in its Belle Etoile Suite with a rooftop retreat on the seventh floor. The suite had a private terrace that offered 360-degree views from Notre Dame to the Musée d'Orsay, and the Eiffel Tower, the Grand Palais and the Sacré Coeur were just a few of the sights that he could take in without ever leaving his room. As extraordinary as his views were, none were better than having Easter right in his sight. Thanks to the high-powered Celestron Edge Aplanatic SCT telescope, he had optimum spying advantage.

If he wanted to simply take him out, he could, but where was the fun in that? Unlike Easter, he wasn't the behind-the-scenes type, which equated to being a coward in his book. He took pleasure in being up-close-in-your-face and personal so there would be no mistake about who had sent them to meet their maker.

Getting straight to the point, Jordan asked, "Are we set?"

"Ready, locked and loaded, baby," was Snake's reply.

Jordan eased back in his chair and kicked his legs upon the table and locked his hands behind his head. While overlooking the heart of historic surroundings of Paris, like the Seine River, theaters, and bistros, he smiled knowing that one of his problems wasn't going to be an issue for much longer. "Show time!"

"Got my popcorn and beer! You have no idea of how long I've waited for this day." Snake rubbed his hands together in anticipation.

Jordan picked up the throwaway he had sitting next to him and dialed a number after pulling a camera into view of Jim giving him and Snake the thumbs-up. It rang only once before it was answered.

"I didn't know that dead men made calls." The Collector recognized the 214 area code.

Jordan ignored the threat. "Your Joie De Vivre diamond looks exquisite on my lady's delicate finger. Looking at how beautiful it is makes me want to do right by her and settle down. Thank you for acquiring it for me."

The Collector couldn't contain his anger. "Death for you will be excruciatingly painful and very deliberate. I hate that I—" He stopped abruptly while breathing heavily into the phone.

Jordan laughed, further infuriating him. "Speaking of painful ... you should be receiving a call right ... about—"

Another phone began to ring. The Collector answered it immediately. There were a series of rushed words both in Chinese and English followed by screaming. "No! My son—"

"As you see, you're not as invincible as you thought you were. This time, your beloved heir will live to see another day, but *next time*, I won't be so merciful." Jordan disconnected the call, leaving just seconds from his whereabouts being traced. He disposed of the phone by throwing it into a bag that would scramble its signal.

"Looks like you got company," Jordan replied when he saw Seven carrying a tray toward Snake. He decided to let his coconspirator fuel up because he would need it. "Enjoy your meal. I have other business to attend to."

The lenses in Snake's frames went blank, signaling the end of the connection. "The end is near, my dear."

"Thank God we'll be free of him, and to think, he's doing all the work to make it possible," Seven agreed.

They both laughed as Snake relieved Seven of the tray that she was carrying with an assortment of pastries and a tea set, and then put it to the side. He was hungry, but it wasn't for food.

I lay in bed watching Jordan out on the terrace. Thank God the rain had stopped long enough to enjoy the beautiful view from the terrace. When I saw him toss the phone into the bag, I decided to go out and join him. Before doing so, I removed all clothing with the exception of my bra and panties. Detecting that he wasn't alone, he removed his legs from the table and pulled me into his lap. Our lips met in a frenzy of starved kisses as our hands groped one another hungrily.

I pulled back from him. "So this is it? It's going to finally be over."

"After tomorrow night, this whole ordeal and Easter will be an afterthought." He ran his hand through my hair and stared at me longingly.

I stood and pulled him up from his seat by the hand, leading him over to one of the chaise lounges.

The soft and gentle breeze felt good as it cooled my heated flesh. Since I hadn't been home, I missed the simple pleasure of fucking on my terrace. The thought that someone could be watching did something wicked to my libido and caused me to become as wet as the ocean.

Jordan removed my bra and panties. I stood before him naked. "Damn, you're beautiful," he complimented. I admiringly watched as he took off his clothing, revealing the breathtaking sculpture that was his body. None of Michelangelo's statues could compare to what was standing before me.

My breasts were perky and my nipples hardened at his touch. He turned me around, raised my flowing hair from around my shoulders and neck before making a trail of kisses that stopped at my buttocks. Jordan leaned me over the lounge and spread my legs, pressing his lips against my naked flesh. He kissed the insides of my thighs and suckled on my plump love lips before diving between licking me ferociously with the tip of his tongue. My wetness percolated as I rode his face hard, trying to take in as much of it as I could.

Jordan marveled at how wonderful my pussy felt and tasted on his tongue. He abandoned my saturated goodness long enough to make a demand. "Scream my name," he ordered.

"Jordan," I said, but not enthusiastically enough for him.

He smacked me my on my ass and began massaging my clit between his forefinger and thumb. "I said, say my name, bitch!"

"Aww, yeah! Jordan! Joooordan!" I screamed with the release I needed, but he wasn't done with me yet. His fingers reconnected with my engorged and sensitive clit with his tongue joining in on the party for what seemed to go on forever. I moaned and squirmed, trying to get away as he continued without mercy to feast on me.

"*Yes*, Jordan! Oh my gawd, *yes!*" I shouted as hot cum squirted hard onto his tongue when I exploded into his mouth with the force of a hurricane.

I turned over and grabbed his dick to return the favor. His large balls were hanging low, heavy with cum. I didn't neglect them as I massaged, licked and sucked him into nearly a state of unconsciousness.

He threw his head back and closed his eyes, trying to prolong the inevitable. "Ahh! Shh . . ."

Jordan pushed me back, pulling me along by the ankles so my pussy could meet him halfway. He angled himself on top, straddling me with his huge, fat dick pressed against the opening of my slit. I took ahold of his magic stick and massaged it before welcoming it inside of my paradise. Jordan moved in and out with ease at a steady rhythm before picking up the pace and showing me who was really the boss. My head moved from side to side as he began kissing my shoulders and sucking my breasts. I pushed myself up with my arms, so that he could have better access to my perky, yet voluptuous round fruits. My nipples became even fuller and harder in his juicy, hot mouth. I met him stroke for stroke, wrapping my legs around his waist. He was definitely giving me something that I could feel with the phenomenon of his magnificent and always pleasurable dick. My hands roamed over his exquisite, sweat-soaked body. Oh my God, he felt so warm, drenched and smooth to the touch. I leaned back and raised my legs high into a "V" shape. He never lost the momentum as he continued to plow me like a field hand would his crop.

"Harder! Hurt me, daddy. *Yes*, like that! Oh Jordan, yes, fuck me like your life depends on it!"

Jordan grunted, trying to hold back, but he was clearly losing the battle. The wetness my hot love tunnel had produced wouldn't be denied mixing with his sweet, creamy nectar, no matter how hard he tried to control the situation.

"Damn ... didn't I ... ever ... tell you ... aww!!!" he roared like a lion as he exploded deep within me.

I wasn't too far behind when the sweet satisfaction of being fucked royally trounced me, making this time in Paris really unforgettable.

Chapter 39

The night had a chill in the air due to the relentless rain that fell for almost a week straight. It wasn't the best condition to be scaling glass in, but they would have to make due. Snake had prayed for the best concerning him and his friends' safety, but prepared for the worst since he was dealing with a slime ball like Easter, not to mention his own treachery.

After being dropped off by taxi, Snake met Novikov, Easter and crew at the designated spot to commit the biggest heist of the century, *if* it was a success. He was ready to get the job done so he wouldn't have to see Easter's conniving face or any other person he deemed as an enemy ever again in life. Being the fool that he was, Easter either didn't realize or maybe he just didn't give a damn that he had not only put Jordan's life in jeopardy with the Bangkok job, but his and Seven's as well. For that reason alone, Snake was going to take pleasure in watching the midget try and squirm his way out of this one. Unlike Jordan, The Collector wasn't going to be as forgiving—not after helplessly listening in agony as his award-winning pianist son's hands were being broken. No, he wasn't going to be in the mood to hear Easter's reasoning on why he was handing him invaluable prints instead of the real deal.

He would, however, refer back to the information given to him months prior after having Easter investigated. He'd learned of his underhanded schemes after receiving an anonymous packet detailing his betrayal on the Bangkok job and others. That was all The Collector needed to know that Easter was not to be trusted. Besides, being born with a silver spoon in his mouth, The Collector had acquired most of his fortune through means of blackmail, intimidation, and other unscrupulous methods. Having some want-to-be-runt like Easter undermine him wasn't happening.

Snake walked over and shook everyone's hands. Easter was dressed to work in all black as discussed, until Snake peeped his Evolv Defy climbing shoes.

"How in the hell are you *not* going to stand out in snakeskin shoes?" Snake pointed out.

Easter gladly showed off his kicks. "I had them specially made for this assignment. This job will always be linked to the mysterious thief in *snake*skin shoes."

Delilah stepped forth and inspected the kicks. "Specially made as in the person who designed them will know who to point the finger at. Oh my gawd ... how could you be so—" She shook her head at Easter's obvious stupidity. "Let's just get this over with, please."

The other two men, one being Kirk, who'd made fun of Easter's height the day before, laughed unashamedly at his expense. "Good thing you're not scaling that son-of-a-bitch with us in those ridiculous shits."

Before Easter could speak on his behalf, Snake put an end to what would otherwise have turned into something else and messed up everything. He also made a mental note on how Easter emphasized *snake*skin shoes. "Delilah's right; let's stop bickering like little schoolgirls and get this show on the road."

Easter walked over to one of the black vans and climbed in. He had Giovanna already seated on the passenger side waiting patiently for him. The others followed Snake to the other van. After Easter had driven off, two more shadows emerged. The facades were replaced with happy greetings all around.

"Tarantulaaaaa!" Kirk practically sang.

"How's it going, my man?" Jordan gave him and the other guys dap.

"This is going to be ... umm, candy ... umm, yes. Candy and babies!" Novikov kidded, and although he said the phrase wrong, everyone got his point.

"Easter could definitely go for a baby dressed like a miniature pimp," Jordan chided as they got inside of the waiting van. "Oh, and good work on those hands, by the way, Jim. The Collector is out for blood already, but when he gets those prints ... watch out."

"I felt like I was breaking my mother's favorite crystal vase," Jim responded with an undetected wink by anyone but Jordan. "I happen to like his music. Pity he's going to be out of commission for a while."

"Our little buddy Easter is in for one rough night," Stephan threw in for good measure.

Everyone laughed as they thought about Easter's impending demise.

As they were traveling down Boulevard du Palais, Snake lowered the petition and saw that the switch had been made. Delilah was the only member from Easter's original and so-called hand-picked crew that would be seen by him once they made it to the location. The other two were replaced by Jordan and Jim. When the coast was clear, Kirk and Stephan would join them on the ambush point. Kirk would rejoin the others after taking care of the guards and construction workers since Easter was expecting to see five people scaling the Louvre. Stephan would assist Jim on the ground. It didn't take much for Snake to convince Easter that using his crew was the smartest way to go to avoid ego trips, and most importantly, screwups.

Seven and I were a few hours ahead of everyone involved in the take. They were in another Sprinter van equipped with computers and other high-tech gadgets. Seven made it a point to stop every so often, once they were within sight of the museum, to place projection portals. When she pulled into the bushy area that would provide the security she needed to be undetectable, Seven killed the engine and turned off the headlights.

She placed a reassuring hand on my leg and gave me a cell phone. "Bianca, I hope you remember everything we've been going over because this is it. Now, go to the back and look at the monitors so you can tell me how things are focusing in from this end. I'm going to need clear visuals to make sure everything is copasetic while communicating with Jim and Stephan, who'll be working from the outside." After making sure I understood what was needed, she jumped out of the van with a large bag to do her part in putting the final pieces in place.

Two black Mercedes-Benz Sprinter vans pulled into the dark foliage on the side of the repair zone of the museum. Snake got out first and the rest of the crew spilled out of the other vehicle shortly afterward. Easter and his beautiful companion met up with them at the halfway mark between the vans.

Easter was overly anxious as the words, "Carpe Diem," slithered quietly from his lips. He'd planned to do just that, seize the day ... and the take.

"All right, gents and ... lady. This is it! No turning back or getting cold feet. It's do-or-die time."

"Enough with the stupid sayings already," Delilah retorted.

Easter was put off being told to basically shut up. Especially in front of his woman. "As I was saying, let's get the job done."

Everyone turned in the direction of another set of headlights coming their way. Snake withdrew his gun, but Easter calmed him.

"Relax, my friend. It's just Tony and Johnny, my hired guns for the night."

Although Snake knew that already, he was putting a little extra on it for Easter's benefit.

"Sorry we're late, but we're here now," Johnny explained nonchalantly.

"Remember you're on my dime and I won't tolerate anything less than your best," Easter countered as though he were putting the two big guys in their places.

"Sorry, Easter, but it wasn't the easiest thing driving a car through the marsh." Tony tried to quell the tension that was thickening the air.

"Maybe if you two overgrown apes had gotten a sports utility or an off-road vehicle to transport your fat asses, it wouldn't have been as hard. I told you that a car wouldn't be wise because of the rain. What if it had gotten stuck in the mud? Then what?"

"But it didn't. Now, can we get this done instead of standing here arguing over what-ifs?" Snake's agitation was showing even in the darkness of night.

For that reason, Easter decided not to make a big deal out of Tony's and Johnny's tardiness. "Okay . . ." he conceded. "But before we begin, I'd like to say a prayer."

"Are you for real?" Delilah was two minutes from getting back inside of the van. "We are about to *steal*, not sell Girl Scout cookies, and you want God's blessings. Let's go. Let's go now, before I change my fucking mind!"

"Have you forgotten who is in charge?" Giovanna challenged Delilah.

"Have you not been told that I'll rip every strand of hair out of your fucking head without breaking a sweat or a nail?" Delilah threw back at Giovanna.

"Ladies! Ladies! Although I'm sure us men will be thoroughly entertained, now is not the time for a catfight. Giovanna, please go back and wait for me in the van, sweetheart."

Giovanna stood for a minute longer, wearing a scowl on her pretty face. She weighed her options to either take the woman who dared challenge her out or get in the van. Finally, she relented—somewhat. "You do not know who you speak to, *Beautiful*."

"Beautiful? Is this bitch for real?" Delilah pointed after her newly made nemesis, but no one answered as they got in position.

Chapter 40
The Louvre Job

Jim gave Seven the signal all was clear on his end. Through a well-hidden camera, Seven spied two middle-aged guards as they casually walked the museum oblivious to what was going on as they were deeply involved in their conversation. One of them was smoking a smokeless pipe while engaging in a heavy dispute with his coworker. Through technology, she gave the crew the go-ahead as she coordinated with Jim and Stephan.

Their intended target loomed largely ahead. It was four o'clock in the morning, dense fog, and thankfully, minimal life in the vicinity of one of the world's greatest treasures. They would be practically invisible to the naked eye, which worked to their advantage in more ways than one. After receiving Seven's signal, Jordan and his crew took in the sight of the guards and workers standing outside and around the construction site. On cue, he gestured the signal and one by one, each person fell, holding onto their necks upon impact of the tranquilizing dart with no time to respond for help. After making sure each man was down, they all ran toward their mark and got into position to conquer it.

Before doing any scaling, they covered the grounds to make sure there were no lingering people they missed. Novikov took down two more guards as Delilah got a construction worker who was crawling toward the vehicles to call for help. Snake called "clear" on his end, followed by Jordan and Kirk. They all met back at the rendezvous point ready to get the job done.

Like his namesake, The Tarantula, Jordan inched his way up the steel and glass surface of the museum with little to no effort on his part. The rest of the team followed, dressed in all black and wearing sleek visored helmets that concealed their faces. They all carried oblong backpacks and climbing ropes. Lightweight tool belts adorned their waists and harnesses across their backs. Everyone was sporting night-vision goggles. Since he wasn't as agile as the rest, Jim, along with Stephan, stayed on the ground, hidden from Easter's prying eyes. Their job was to assist Seven with any unforeseen issues that might arise.

I watched the monitor screens on pins and needles praying that no one fell. They made climbing the slippery glass look effortless, but that did little to calm my nerves. Seven looked crazy typing the air which was really a digital keyboard displaying coordinates on the floating monitors. I was amazed at the touchscreen hologram computers she had set up in the van. She was only too glad to let me know that *her baby*, as she called it, wasn't even on the market. Her hands swiped and moved things around all while closely paying strict attention to what was going on at the museum. Her magic was something I didn't mind watching her perform because she was good at what she did. I could see why Jordan admired her; she had sex and savvy technical skills to offer. Watching her made me wonder what other talent I had besides lying on my back and being the eye candy that could prove useful to my man. *Well, I am one hell of an event planner and maybe those proficiencies will come in handy one day*, I thought to myself.

Meanwhile, Easter watched through his high-powered, heat-seeking binoculars as his very own assembled team climbed their way up the slippery slope to make him a very wealthy man. He didn't quite know how he would overthrow them, but he had his ways. His hands were sweating in anticipation to make contact with the treasures that would be in his possession shortly.

"Baby?"

"Yes, my love." Giovanna looked over at Easter with a false look of admiration plastered on her exquisite face.

"I was going to make it a surprise, but you know that chalet that you couldn't get enough of?"

"You didn't!" she squealed.

"I did. The sale will be finalized by the end of the week, paid in full. I want nothing but the best for you. I know you're able to buy whatever you want, but after this, you won't have to. I'll have more money than The Collector himself, and I plan to be the one to spoil you rotten." He reached over and kissed her longingly.

"You make me so happy, my *beautiful* and handsome love." She tilted her head, coquettishly smiling at Easter and making him get an instant hard-on. If the task at hand wasn't so vital, he would've taken her right there and then, but after this, he would have plenty of time to satisfy his loins.

They were almost at the point of entry. Jordan used the piton-like bolts one last time as the electromagnetic force stuck to the steel to support his weight. After the bolt was pulled up by the cords to its last intended position, he clicked a button to release the magnetic charge. Remarkably strong and agile, Jordan scaled the rest of the way with fluid precision. Once there, he helped Delilah up. Snake, Kirk and Novikov soon followed. Now at the rendezvous point, they slithered their way in undetected. No sooner than the moment they hit the floor that they took out their compasses already set for the destination of the pieces they were to take. They synchronized their watches and deftly, but carefully, made their way through the museum.

Delilah was the first to make contact with her assigned piece, *La Belle*, the portrait of an unknown woman. Just as she reached out to touch it, she heard the guards in the nearby vicinity. She gathered that from the nearness of their voices, that they were closer than she first assumed. She ducked behind the shadow of a glass casing that was close by. She sized the men up to see if she would be able to take them if need be.

"I'm telling you, bloke, I could've shagged her if I wanted. She was hot for me," the muscular one said.

"The way to a girl's key to unlock her chastity belt is in the approach." The heavier one demonstrated by doing a smooth dance move.

"Ha! Ha! Ha!" His coworker doubled over, laughing and pointing. "With moves like that, you'll never get shagged."

Delilah thought they were going to keep it moving, but the muscular one had something to prove and he was going to do just that. Glancing at her watch, she knew she didn't have time for their tomfoolery. Hitting a few keystrokes on her iPhone, she was able to get a message to Seven. Within mere seconds, a crashing sound got their attention immediately.

"Bloody hell! You hear that, bloke?"

"You bet your ass I did!" the muscular one answered.

"Holy crap! What are we supposed to do? I'm not ready for this. You said this was an easy, no-hands-on type of job," the fat one complained as he looked about nervously.

"Shut your blubbering pothole, why don't cha." The muscular one tried to act as though he wasn't scared shitless by whatever it was. "Come on. Let's go check it out." They both ran in the direction of the sound.

Delilah breathed a sigh of relief and went about her mission.

Jordan heard running in his direction. Thinking quickly, he threw out a device on the floor to the farthest end from where from he was. Once the device landed, he hit a button and instantly, an armed, muscular man who stood at least six feet seven inches, dressed in black, appeared. The guards stopped dead in their tracks.

"Get on de floor. Now!" a voice with a thick accent demanded. Both guards took one look at the heavy artillery the man had and then at their own flimsy pieces and immediately dropped without hesitation. The man then started pacing back and forth every now and again saying something to them. Once Jordan saw that they were occupied out of fear, he went about his business.

A softly lit area housed what Novikov was looking for. It was like the heavens themselves had opened up and started to sing *HALLELUJAH!* when he feasted his eyes upon *Louis XVI* in his coronation costume. He took out the photograph to make sure it was the right one before doing a sweep to make sure there were no silent alarms or otherwise. With the speed of lightning, he took the piece out of its frame with meticulousness. As soon as he made a move, he felt a hard object pointed in his back.

"Make one bloody—arrgh!"

In one swift move, Novikov flipped the assailant over his shoulder and subdued him with the sleep hold. His partner, an older man with winded breath, tried to go for his gun, but was taken down just as swiftly.

Novikov looked at the men, wishing he could've gotten the painting in peace. Time was wasting and he had to work quickly in order to meet the others back at the exit point. He did a quick sweep on the perimeter of the painting. Not detecting anything, he took out what appeared to be an ink pen, clicked it and produced a red gleaming light. Sticking a balancer on the frame, another green light outlined it to guarantee a perfect cut. Just before he made contact, Novikov wondered about the amount of the painting cloth that would be left behind the frame once cut from the front. Even though it would mean time, Novikov put the brandishing laser down and hurriedly removed the painting from the wall which was a task within itself. After seeing it, he was glad he'd followed his first mind.

"Oooh . . ." One of the dazed guards regaining consciousness prompted Novikov to get a move-on. He removed the painting from its frame and loosely rolled it in foam and left the groaning men to themselves.

As Jordan was making his way back to the exit point, he caught sight of Snake who nearly collided into him.

"Did you run into any problems?"

"No. Like Novikov said, it was like taking candy from a baby."

"Hey, guys, let's get the hell out of here. I nearly got caught," Delilah murmured.

They saw Novikov making his way toward them. "No time!" he said, letting the others know that something had taken place.

Kirk soon caught up. "Let's bounce!"

They quickly secured the paintings and then put their electromagnetic gloves back. Jordan fired a shot that rigged an electro-magnetic suction-mounted harness to the steel casing above the opening that was the entry point. Pulleys, metal carabiner clips and Kevlar ropes pulled him up safely. The others followed Jordan superbly as if they'd done it countless of times before.

Easter watched in awe with his high-powered, heat-seeking binoculars as they were scaling down the Louvre using the huge suction cups pressed to the surface of the glass. His palms twitched with anticipation, longing to feel the millions that would soon be gracing them.

Chapter 41

"What happened back there?" Jordan asked Novikov as they ran through the thick marsh. The darkness and fog was blinding, but with night-vision goggles, it was if they were running in the daylight. Novikov let them know what had taken place, and from the way he was talking, one would've thought that he was walking instead of running. His breathing was even as was the rest of the crew. They'd all trained extensively, running for miles and holding water in their mouths. Over time, their lung capacity had expanded, making it possible to endure long treks such as this one.

Looking on the hologram monitors with Seven, I breathed a sigh of relief when I saw them making their way back.

"Thank God, no one fell."

Seven's eyes stayed fixed on the monitor that had Easter's van in view.

"So what do we do now?" I asked.

"We wait. The fireworks are about to begin shortly," Seven answered, never taking her eyes off from what she was doing. Her hands fluttered over the images as if she were putting things into a queue. The images flipped back and forth as she slapped them around.

My eyes went back to the image that had Jordan and crew on it. I saw that they'd stopped, and instead of five, there were two extra men. "Oh my God." I gasped.

"What's wrong?" Seven suddenly stopped what she was doing and gave me her undivided attention.

I pointed to the screen and the tension drained off of Seven's face immediately.

"That's Kirk and Stephan making the switch with Jordan and Jim." She blew out an exasperated breath as though I were getting on her nerves.

Meanwhile, back at the vans, Easter got out when he saw the crew reemerging. His rapacious hands couldn't wait to have the paintings in his possession. He made contact with his well-hidden pistol and signaled for Tony and Johnny, who begrudgingly got out of their car nearby. The three men stood as Snake and the chosen four were within talking distance.

"It's only going to be a matter of time before the two guards that Novikov took out come too, and the others to realize that they've been duped. The guards shot with the darts should also be coming around shortly," Snake shouted as they made their way back to their van.

"Not so fast, Snake." Easter stopped them in their tracks and held out his hand. "I need those paintings."

Snake glared at the little man. "Didn't you just hear what I said?"

Easter signaled with his hand again for Snake to hand over what was to be his, while keeping his finger close to the trigger of his hidden gun.

"Don't you think that's a bit unceremonious of you being that we need to get the hell out of here, Easter?" Snake stood firm not giving in to Easter's demand to hand over the paintings.

Easter produced his gun into view while wearing a devious smirk on his face. "No, I don't. In fact, until I get those paintings in my hands, we're not going anywhere. You don't think I've been this successful by trusting a *snake*, do you? Now, hand them over or I won't hesitate."

Snake looked defeated as he took in Easter and the gun. "I should've known you would pull something like this."

"I was surprised you took the *I'm innocent, my friend* act after Bangkok. What a fool you must feel?" Easter admonished his guilt without flinching. "Now, I'm not going to ask you again—"

"Kirk!" Snake called out over his shoulder. "Give him the paintings."

Kirk reluctantly handed over the bounty.

"I don't see you laughing now, punk," Easter mocked as he snatched the oblong bag containing the precious works. Upon contact, he felt giddy inside. "Like Napoleon, so many years ago, looks like I've conquered here tonight, gentlemen. Oh, and you too, Delilah."

Back in our van, listening to the conversation unfold, Seven let the fireworks fly when she saw Easter brandishing his gun. The projection portals she'd dropped along the way earlier were activated with sirens being heard from the distance.

Upon hearing the sirens, everyone became fidgety. "Easter, what good is all of this if we get caught?" Snake was seething on the outside, but laughing out loud on the inside.

"*We*?" Easter threw his head back as he chuckled. "I'm only concerned about *me*," Easter threw back at Snake.

"You have the paintings. Do something worthwhile in your miserable little life and let us have a chance to get out of here!" Delilah screamed.

"I've been waiting to shut that pothole in your face since the day I met you. You dare talk to me with such disdain when I'm the one who's holding a gun, you dumb bitch!" Easter pointed the gun at Delilah with his finger steadily easing back the trigger. Thinking quickly, Snake pushed her out of the way and went for Easter.

As they struggled, the sirens were getting louder and headlights were now thrown into the mix. The gun shot into the night air twice before Snake collapsed to the ground holding his stomach. Crimson liquid spilled between his fingers at a rapid pace. Still in control of the gun, Easter pointed it at the remaining party as he backed slowly toward his van. When he called out for Johnny and Tony, they were nowhere to be found. Neither was Giovanna once he made it back into the safety of his vehicle.

Easter looked around frantically for his love, but time wouldn't allow him to dwell on her whereabouts. He put the van in drive and drove as fast as he could through the muddy, wet mess. He wondered if Giovanna had been kidnapped by his supposed hired guns. They knew what he stood to gain from this job and if he were in their position, he would've done the same thing. His worries dissipated once he realized what he had in his possession.

"I did it! I got the paintings! ... I got the fucking paintings!" Loud cackling vibrated throughout the van as he drove to his destination to collect his largest payout ever in his career from The Collector. With no one to split it with, he was about to become a very wealthy man beyond anything that he ever could have imagined. He laughed himself to tears as he drove down the wet streets of Paris.

Chapter 42
All Be Damned

The more popular streets of Paris were ruthless, regardless the time of night with crowds of tourists looking for that Parisian experience while on vacation. Even though Easter knew the route to the meet-up spot at the Père Lachaise Cemetery, he was lost. With his mind being a mess of convoluted thoughts, concentration was out the window. He couldn't believe he was really perplexed after having driven the planned route to the cemetery countless times over the past year. He couldn't seem to focus on anything but shooting Snake and wishing it were The Tarantula, instead. Giovanna's disappearance. His hired guns' obvious betrayal. All of these things afflicted his mind like the Plague, but could be dealt with later. His first and foremost priority was making the trade with The Collector. He would hire the best snipers that money could buy to seek out those who'd betrayed him and then pay extra to have Jordan taken out. Once he set those dogs loose on his foes, he would scour the earth looking for his beloved Giovanna. They had a life of privilege waiting for them, and he couldn't see experiencing it with anyone but her.

"No! No! No! No! Not this shit. Not right now!" Easter was thrown out of his plotting abruptly after having to come to a complete stop. As luck would have it, it was right before he finally remembered the name of the street for his destination, *Boulevard de Ménilmontant*! A crowd had gathered in the middle of the road to watch a flash mob of women in wedding dresses for an unknown designer trying to make his mark.

"Fuck!" Easter slammed his hands down repeatedly on the steering wheel causing people to look his way because of the blaring horn.

Seven jumped in the driver's seat and took off driving as fast as the muddy condition would allow upon seeing Snake go down.

"Oh no! Please, God. Not like this," she cried at the realization of the devastating news that could be awaiting her.

I was too numb to speak. Everything was beyond real at this point. Someone had been shot and that someone was Snake. Snake, I considered to be a ... a friend. My eyes misted as the van hit every bump, lump, log and pothole as Seven drove frantically to get to her man.

Agent Garza stopped the recording. "Here's a tissue." For the first time today, I'd seen a hint of compassion in his eyes if only fleeting, but it was there.

Aliyah sat stone-faced, mechanically drumming her clear nails with a hint of pink lacquer on the laptop's keyboard as I was being made a fuss over. Everyone was hovering over me offering condolences for what I must've been going through being thrust into Jordan's world. It was at this point that I made a brazen move that went undetected by all except the one it was meant for. Our eyes locked briefly as he straightened his tie and walked away, concealing the note I'd given him.

"I'm sorry. I didn't expect that to make me so emotional. I mean, I hardly knew him, but he was a good man who didn't deserve what he got." I peered over at Aliyah before clearing my throat and continuing with the story.

Not wanting to chance the marsh, Seven stopped just short of where the other Sprinter van was parked and jumped out, leaving me to my own vices. I sat a second longer before taking that as my cue to either stay put or come with her. I decided the latter. I caught up quickly to Seven as we made it in record time.

Jordan met Seven before she could make it anywhere near Snake's slain body.

"No!" she cried as if she already knew the answer to her unasked question.

Jordan tried to comfort her, but she wasn't having it. "I'm sorry. I'm so sorry," he repeated.

I stared at Jordan and then at the rest of the team as the men picked up Snake's remains and loaded him into the van.

"Damn it, Jordan, nooo! You have no right!" Seven continued to cry as she hit him repeatedly in the chest. "I ... I need to see him, pleeeaaase!" Seven's shoulders shook violently as misery consumed her. I wanted to console her, but couldn't get my legs to take another step toward the carnage.

"Jordan," Stephan hollered out. "According to the scanners, the real police are in very close range to the museum." A piercing alarm went off signaling a breach at the museum.

"Seven, meet us back at the location. You can see him then."

"He needs to go to a hospital, Jordan!" she snapped as her knees buckled.

The light coming from Jordan's visored helmet showed his demeanor that said all that he didn't. "Unless you want to spend the rest of your days rotting away in a Parisian prison cell, and trust me, there's nothing chic about it, I suggest you snap the hell out of it and come on." Upon hearing Jordan speak those words, a look passed between them; her undoing was short-lived. It was like someone else had taken over her body as she composed herself instantly and without saying a word, turned and sprinted back toward the van.

Jordan gave me a quick peck before my legs decided to finally move. I hurriedly trotted off to catch up with Seven. I felt as if I were living in the Twilight Zone after witnessing everything that had taken place. I didn't realize it at the time, but it would be the last time that I would have any connection to Jordan in the flesh. I watched him fade into the night as Seven sped away into the darkness as a flowing spring of tears blanketed her face.

"Where are we going?" I asked Seven as we drove aimlessly through the streets of Paris until she came upon a cemetery.

"To see Easter go to hell," she spoke between gritted teeth. We came to a stop just after passing the entrance of the cemetery and pulled into some more bushes. She put the van in park and reached for a bag.

"But Jordan told us to meet him back at the place." I knew she was hurting, but I had to remind her of the plans.

Seven turned menacing eyes on me. "My man was just gutted like a fucking pig out there." Her neck swiveled at a pace so fast that she almost resembled Linda Blair. All that was missing was the split-green pea soup spewing from her mouth. "Now, you may jump to Jordan's pipe, but I don't." She took out some binoculars, earpieces, a .45 and attached a suppressor to it. After making sure she was locked and loaded, she tossed me a pair of the same items, less the .45.

I looked at the Bluetooth-looking contraption waiting on her to hand me and the phone, which never came. "What is this for and how am I supposed to use it with no phone?"

Without giving me any face time, she got out of the van once again, leaving me to my own vices. "You can either sit there and ask questions or follow me," she called out over her shoulder.

We crept through the dark cemetery, taking special care to be as quiet as possible. Although the Père Lachaise Cemetery was a major tourist attraction, at this time of night, it was deserted and spooky. Thank God, there were actual paved roads and sidewalks, but leave it to Seven to want to traipse through the lawns and mazes of trees. There were mausoleums everywhere from small to some that looked like cathedrals. The statues, although perfectly sculpted, gave me the creeps.

Every shadow made me think that we were being followed. I couldn't help but think of the video *Thriller* with all the zombies awakening from their eternal slumber and Michael Jackson turning into a werewolf. Let's just say that being in a cemetery definitely had my mind playing tricks on me. I was so worked up that when something ran across my shoe, I totally freaked out.

"Arrggh shit! Something just grabbed my foot!" I was sure I screamed as loud and acted as badly as one of those women on the scary movies running and falling while trying to save their lives. My bad rendition didn't stop until I slipped and fell again into a pile of wet leaves. "Oh my God!" I continued to act a fool, swinging at the air and fighting the leaves like something was on me.

Seven rushed over, snatched me up, and slapped the scream out of my mouth. "Will you shut the hell up?" she hissed. "You're going to get us killed out here."

My mouth hung open. I was speechless because she'd hit me. Couldn't believe that she fucking hit me was all that was on my mind as I swiped at wet leaves and hair stuck to my face. After I recovered from making an ass out of myself, we continued on until we came upon a statue of a woman in a flowing dress.

Seven scoped out the surroundings. She would do that every so many feet until we came upon the location she had circled on her map.

"This is where—" Before the words were given time to leave her mouth, we saw a bewildered-looking Easter stumbling toward the mausoleum, not too far from where we were standing. We ducked to avoid being detected.

Once it was clear that our cover hadn't been blown, Seven got him in her line of sight and was about to pull the trigger.

I placed a calming hand on Seven's arm that was holding the gun aimed at Easter. "You can't shoot him. Not now and damn sure not here!" I whispered agitatedly.

As if she were weighing her options, she dropped her arm down to her side with the gun still locked in her grasp. She dabbed at her eyes at what I assumed to be tears. I felt bad for her. Lord only knew what state of mind I would have been in had it been Jordan, instead of Snake. Seven slumped down, placed her head between her legs, and took deep breaths.

I caressed the nape of her neck trying to be nurturing since I didn't know what else to do. "Are you going to be okay?" I asked, until the moment was interrupted just as soon as it began.

"What story did he force-feed you about his dealings with The Collector?"

"I wasn't ... force-fed anything."

Seven raised her head and looked at me before laughing more to herself than directly at me. "He's always force-feeding that horse shit of a story only with different variations of the truth down you simple bitches' throats. If only—"

"Seven, you are way out of line. Jordan, would never—" I cut her off, but she regained control of the conversation just as quickly.

"It's Seventhia! I never did like that Seven shit," she scolded me. Her everchanging attitude felt like a slap across the face. However, I decided to keep my cool since she was the one with the gun.

"I understand that you're hurting. I would be too had it been—"

"Would you listen to how stupid you sound? Do you really think that Jordan loves you? That he would never lie to you?" She laughed again. "I got a newsflash for you sweetie. He's not capable of that emotion. Hell, he's not capable of anything, unless it's to serve his own overinflated ego. He's a user! A got-damned user!"

From my peripheral view, I saw movement and focused back on the mausoleum. Seventhia, Seven, or whatever the hell she wanted to call herself, was not going to rattle my cage.

"They're here," I said.

Seven immediately stood from her crouching position and became engrossed in what was happening as if she weren't just trying to let me know that she cared for Jordan in a way that went into more-than-friends category. Now that I looked back on it, I thought Seven was not only bipolar, but jealous. She'd always had it in for me and I should've stayed with my first impression regarding her. I stared at her and it was like looking at a different woman. She took extreme pleasure in watching Easter get what was coming to him. It didn't take a rocket scientist to know that she wouldn't mind seeing me meet the same fate.

Chapter 43

*T*he Collector didn't waste any time walking out into view followed by two of his men when he saw that Easter had finally arrived. He was beginning to wonder if he had pulled the wool over his eyes as he'd been known to do, but that would've been a fool's move on his part.

Wet and with ashen skin, Easter had the appearance of belonging in one of the freshly dug plots. "I have the paintings" were the first words out of his weary mouth. He tried to betray the way he looked with a strong and confident voice. After handing over the case containing the priceless pieces of art, he started feeling like his old self, knowing that all of the planning and manipulating was about to finally pay off. This time tomorrow, he would be rich beyond his wildest dreams. Then Giovanna filtered into his mind and the feeling of melancholy returned. He shook it off as he watched The Collector with a keen eye as he took the merchandise from him.

"Pat him down," The Collector ordered one of his henchmen. After Easter was fully searched and relieved of his weapons, only then did business begin to be conducted. "Now that you've been properly looked over, you can follow me inside," The Collector said.

Easter eagerly, but hesitantly, followed The Collector and his guard inside of the mausoleum. He didn't think of it until then, but this was after all, a cemetery, and now he was without a weapon—in case things got ugly. *What if this is a setup?* He couldn't let fear and second-guessing come into play and get him off-kilter. Hell, if he were in The Collector's shoes, he'd have people frisked too.

"What do we do now?" I asked Seven, who appeared to be in another world.

She shook her head as if she were coming back into the present. "We ... we listen and ... and we wait for the perfect opportunity. Turn on your bionic ear, if you haven't already, and use your binoculars." She dismissed me and went back wherever in her mind she was before I'd interrupted her.

Not more than a minute after fumbling with the device, I saw Jordan followed by five others—two of them sticking out like sore thumbs due to their large frames and height. They surrounded the mausoleum giving a series of hand signals before they disturbed the meeting going on inside. The two towering figures stood guard to avoid any surprises from the outside.

Once I got my binoculars adjusted, the inside of the mausoleum was a work of art in itself. It had to belong to a very rich and influential family for it was a golden masterpiece. There were three over-the-top lounging areas, large bronzed letters depicting the family's name, *Laffitte*, above their crest. A plaque was set in a deep-mahogany, black-cherrywood finish with a custom Mayfair border that included full names, dates and cameo photos of the deceased. Breathtaking arrangements were strategically placed throughout. There was a crypt that was the focal point of every-thing that must've belonged to the patriarch of the family.

While spying, I saw The Collector examine the paintings using a loupe. He frowned and spoke in Chinese to the men who were with him. Easter stood, unsuspecting of the brewing problem since The Collector's demeanor didn't give anything away.

"Exactly what did occur during the heist?" he calculatingly but calmly asked Easter.

Still oblivious, Easter told a colorful story of how he'd scaled the slick glass of the Louvre in his specially designed shoes that he'd proudly showed off to everyone. He then went on to say that he only had a two-man crew when a job of this magnitude would normally call for at least five. He continued to overindulge his story some more by telling The Collector how they took down eight guards before finally being able to get the paintings out of the museum.

"We were in and out of the Louvre within seven minutes when it should've been more like twenty, but as you see, we were very efficient," he lied.

"Hmm ... I see." The Collector then turned and gave a short but slender man, who had a nerdy disposition about him, an additional loupe to examine the paintings. The man frowned as he inspected the first painting. With each painting he observed, his frown deepened. Looking at The Collector, they spoke frantic Chinese to each other. The exchange seemed to go on forever.

Easter watched them closely as they looked over each painting. He wore a smug expression on his face while thinking of the glamorous life he and Giovanna would lead. The idea of never having to do another job had him beginning to feel like a kid on Christmas morning. He could see it all, a grand wedding that would make the royals of England seem like low-budget affairs. The chalet filled with children who would take after their mother and have her height and model good looks. The snipers he would hire to track down and cause The Tarantula serious harm and then bring him to view his battered body and allow him the pleasure of delivering the final blow ... a bullet to the center of his conceited head. He couldn't dare forget those two big ogres whom he knew had to have abducted Giovanna against her will, for she would never leave on her own accord, not without informing him. Yes, they too would meet untimely and gruesome deaths. Now, that would be the life. Easter breathed in a gulp of stale air and had to fight the urge to give himself a pat on the back for masterminding a plan well done.

"Print," the nerdy man said.

"A print?" The Collector questioned.

Upon hearing the word "print," his gloating was suddenly cut short as his face hit the floor with disbelief shattering his dreams. The Collector grabbed his head as if he were in pain and then hit the crypt that was being used as a makeshift table to cause a violent echo.

Easter's mouth filled with saliva. His stomach tightened, causing him to clench his butt cheeks. Not knowing which end the lava stirring in his intestines would spill out of if things got out of control, he quickly placed his hand over his mouth. Now was not the time to be a sitting duck, so he did the only logical thing he could do: slowly remove his hand and talk. His life depended on his gift of gab.

"Is ... is ... there a ... a problem?" he asked while still trying to hold on to what little nerves he had left.

The Collector finally gave Easter his attention. "Did you think you could fool me with worthless prints?" He slapped one of the paintings onto the floor.

Sensing danger, Easter took several steps back before feeling his back rest against a wall. "But ... but ... but, I don't ... I don't understand. I ... I never let those paintings leave my sight once

they. . . I mean, *we*, had them in our ... our ... umm possession."
Easter's so-called gift of gab failed him miserably. He stammered
for the first time allowing what he was feeling on the inside, show
on the outside.

The Collector grabbed Easter by his neck and literally stooped
to his level. "You waste my time with your lies and grandstanding
with talks of besting Tarantula! I should've ended your dismal
existence after our first meeting with that nonsense." Hot spittle
flew in Easter's face as The Collector continued his tirade. "Now,
you insult my intelligence by bringing me invaluable replicas!"
He swung on Easter, causing him to stumble and knock over a
flower arrangement before collapsing onto the floor.

Apologizing as he struggled to get up proved to be a difficult
task when fear had his heart in a choke hold. "No! Th ... those are
real! I swear on it with my life!" He wanted to kick himself for
saying the last part. Of course they were real! He saw them go
into the Louvre with his own eyes. Hadn't he?

The Collector was not swayed nor was he amused by this weak-
ling trying to swindle him. "And that is one promise that you're
going to deliver on, *Easter*." He gave his men the signal.

Easter racked his brain trying to figure out what could've gone
wrong, and more importantly, when. *I saw my crew go into the
Louvre and come back out with those paintings with my own eyes. Or
was it all an illusion?* he thought for the millionth time. Then he
recalled how easily one of the members from the crew scaled up
the structure as if it were dried concrete instead of slippery glass.
He'd never seen anything like it except ... *The Tarantula!* Easter
screamed inside of his aching skull. He should've known Snake
was called "snake" for a reason. If he were a strategizing man, he
would've taken heed about not being trusting of a snake. It didn't
matter if it slithered on its belly or walked upright. A snake was a

snake! Was a fucking snake! Point. Blank. Period. *Looks like I'll be seeing that conniving son of a bitch in hell a lot sooner than I thought.*

"Wait!" Easter made an attempt to spare his life. "I ... I know who has your paintings! The Tarantula, he ... he ... he somehow tricked me. You gotta believe me!"

The Collector walked back toward the crypt and stopped midway. "The Tarantula?" he answered with his back to Easter. "I thought no one knew of your plans except for your crew?" He shook his head, thinking that Easter had to be the dumbest criminal alive. "You're telling me that you were unintelligible enough to hire a crew that you didn't trust or check out?"

Easter squirmed and cowered like a child when the burly men approached him. "He must've gotten to one of them. Otherwise, I don't know how he knew, but it was him! I swear it was! No one can move up surfaces better than he can. Please, I will get your paintings ... just give me the chance to prove myself!" Easter couldn't remember a time he was ever more desperate than he was at the moment.

The Collector picked up a briefcase that was sitting on the floor next to the crypt, opened it and pulled out a manila folder. The two men parted like the Red Sea when The Collector walked back over to where Easter trembled. He looked through it, examining the pictures and other information that had been sent to him anonymously, or so it seemed. "According to what I hold in my hands, this is how you operate. Give me one good reason as to why I should go against your stellar track record of being underhanded?" The Collector paused, but not long enough to give Easter time to come up with a lie. "Let's see ... we have Mexico, Washington, The Caymans, Capital Bank, Liberty Bank, Kingdom Bank, Bank of USA, The Bierman and Bierman, The Hackensack, New York, and that's only a short list of your transgressions. Will the deceit you operated under during those missions give me reason to believe that you will be any different than what's clearly been your M.O. all along?" As The Collector flicked through the pages of misdeeds, one by one, he threw them in Easter's face. "Ah, better yet, how about *Bangkok*? Yes, the now infamous Bangkok job where you didn't give a damn about the repercussions as long as you made out. The gold you stole. Blackmailing your own team? Does any of that jog your pathetic memory?"

Easter pushed the papers out of the way like they were laying on him. "I can explain—"

The Collector cut Easter short. "You can't explain anything! I will, however, take great pleasure in watching you suffer."

"Wait! I can—oomph!" Easter was met by a swift blow to the gut that knocked the wind out of his sail. "Oomph. . ." He fell back down to the floor as a barrage of punches hammered down on his tiny physique. As Easter was trying his best to shield himself from a certain, and most painful death, there was a distraction when a figure emerged through the doors of the gilded mausoleum.

Before I could see that Jordan wouldn't become maggot food, I suddenly felt cold steel against my temple. I slowly put the binoculars down when another figure came into view.

"Hello, *beautiful*."

"Okay, show's over, toots. You've seen enough. Let's go." Seven stood.

It took me a minute to realize that she was serious and the other figure was ... Giovanna. "Seven ... I mean, Sevenchi—"

Seven kicked me in the stomach as Giovanna laughed. "It's Seventhia, you disgusting cunt!"

I doubled over in pain frantically looking for something to knock her ass out with. I grabbed a rock, but Giovanna was quicker than me. "Arrgh!" I fell to the ground when her boot, propelled by a roundhouse kick, connected with my face.

"I'm going to enjoy fucking you up, *beautiful*."

Before I could recover, Seven's gun was damn near down my throat. "Bitch, I'm only going to say this one more time. Let's go ... now!"

Chapter 44
What Bianca Didn't See

"Looks like I made it just in time for the party," Jordan interrupted the men at work.

"You!" The Collector shouted as sputum flew from his foaming and angry mouth.

"Ttt ... T-T-Tarantula . . ." Easter got past his swollen and bloodied lips.

Before The Collector's two men could make a move, Jordan's backup stampeded in behind him, ready for battle.

"Easter—" Jordan looked down on him with mock pity. "Let me guess; you tried to pull another stunt like you did in Bangkok. Good thing this job didn't take place in Malibu." Jordan made a shuddering gesture as if recalling something gruesome that had happened. "The last guy that tried to double-cross the old man was given tiny cuts all over his body, especially his ... ahem— lower region. The old man wasn't satisfied with just the cuts; he then had him beat with hot chains. That was just the beginning;

he had salt and battery acid poured into the wounds. If that wasn't bad enough ... you know what I heard the grand finale to his suffering was?" Jordan didn't give Easter time to respond. "Sharks. Yes, the old man here has a shark tank in his Malibu home and after a torturous, hell-filled night, the poor sap became dinner. Or was it breakfast? Hmm ... I can't remember. Anyway, let's just say that whatever they have planned for you here is a walk in the park compared to that. It was a nasty situation, I tell you. Just imagine those iron jaws clamping down on you and tearing you to shreds on top of suffocating on your own bloodcurdling screams and water filling your lungs, unless the shark rips your torso apart first. Tsk. Tsk. Tsk. Yes, you should definitely consider yourself lucky." Jordan shivered at the memory.

"Tarantula, help ... help me. . . please. I will give you the gold bars from Bangkok. You can ... can have all of it." Never did Easter think that there would be a day that he would beg The Tarantula, of all people, to save his life.

Jordan couldn't believe that the little imp thought him a fool. "You'll give me the Bangkok gold?"

"Yes, you can have it all. I swear!"

"I don't understand how that's even possible, being that I already took it from your place in Paris."

Now Easter really felt the sting of Snake's betrayal. The bastard was casing his flat that night, and there he was giving him complete access to it all. To think that he was thinking that he was the puppeteer, but the entire time he was the one wearing the strings jumping to Tarantula's commands. His mind began to play back certain events over the past few months that had taken place. *Four of my best and most trustworthy men were killed execution style when my flat was robbed. Then, as if on cue, Tony and Johnny showed up claiming to have seen Novikov running from my building.*

That's when the plan was to hire Novikov, make him think I didn't know of his treachery, and then take him out after the heist mission was complete. Without question, I hired those two ingrates who were more than likely responsible for the theft and killings, now that I think about it. Then they sucker-punched me again when they betrayed me and kidnapped Giovanna, all probably at Tarantula's urging. How stupid of me? Why had I let my trying-to- prove-myself-to-be better than Tarantula cloud my better judgment? he silently berated himself. *Snake is already taking an eternal dirt nap, but if I live to see another day, The Tarantula, Novikov, Tony, and that fat bastard Johnny, will be joining him very soon. They will all die the most grisly of deaths that I can think of when the time comes,* he vowed.

"So even in this situation, you're still trying ... to . . ." Now Jordan was the one caught off guard. "Pull a fast one?" *So that's who was behind the shooting at the airport and not Easter. Snake had better be damned lucky Easter got to him first.* The sting of the betrayal stung like a million angry hornets.

"Anything I have is yours. Please!" Easter cried, ignoring his stupid question since admitting that he was lying about the gold wouldn't go over too well. Plus, had he known The Tarantula was involved, would he have been foolish enough to continue working with Snake!

"Shut him up!" The Collector ordered before turning his attention back to Jordan as the two men attempted to put Easter in a sleep hold. "I knew you would come."

Jordan laughed. "Nothing could've kept me away for such a momentous occasion."

The Collector took a few steps in Jordan's direction with his hands being where he could see them. "Help me to understand ... I give you the world. Send you to the finest schools ... and you still dishonor me."

"What is he talking about?" Delilah spoke out of turn. "That old crazy bastard is delirious."

"You let her die!" Jordan shouted back with enough emotion worthy of an Oscar-winning performance.

"How many times do I have to tell you that she made her choice, and it wasn't me?" The Collector signaled for his men to fall back. His chest was jutted out, showing Jordan that he was unafraid. "Look at this. Me. You. Us. Why?"

Jordan became agitated and went for his gun, which found its way in The Collector's unflinching face. "You know why." Tears threatened to break, but crying was not an option. He'd waited a long time for this day to finally arrive. The day of retribution.

"Tarantula, are we going to kill two birds with one stone or what?" Jim asked impatiently with his gun poised as he kept watch on The Collector's men.

"You're getting pretty good at this." The Collector laughingly admitted.

"Yeah, I guess I am." Jordan's scowl was replaced by a big, loopy grin as he went in for a one-arm hug.

Everyone in the room was stunned, but none more so than Easter, who was faking being unconscious. Ignoring Jim, he continued his revelation.

"We make a great team don't we, *Father*?" Jordan took pleasure in watching the looks of confusion on everyone's faces except for Jim's and Delilah's.

"*Father*?" was the only word everyone was able to get out before Delilah and Jim opened fire. Once the smoke cleared, the only ones standing were The Collector, Jordan, Delilah and Jim. Easter took the opportunity given and bolted out of the door.

There were a series of shots heard outside. "Oh, what a shame; Easter thought he was in the clear," Delilah joked.

"Yes indeed, what a shame," The Collector said right before ending Delilah's life when he shot her in the center of her pretty head. "Can't have too many loose ends. I'm sure you understand, Son."

Jordan shrugged his shoulders. "You saved me the trouble of having to do it. She was too damned stubborn and mouthy for her own good, anyway."

"What about the other girl?"

"Bianca? She's not a problem that you should worry yourself with, Father."

They turned their attention toward the door when Tony walked in. "Easter was too quick, boss, but he is wounded. Johnny's out searching for him now," Tony let it be known.

"Have Johnny to fall back; I'm sure Easter won't get very far," Jordan said knowingly.

"This is such a lovely mausoleum; too bad it had to be desecrated, but this was the only way," The Collector said as he looked around at the remains of their former crews.

"You want us to bag them when I get back with Johnny, boss?" Tony asked as he looked around at the mass massacre.

Jordan stepped over Delilah's body. He made the mistake of looking into her opened and shocked eyes and instantly regretted her fate. She was good at her job and in the bedroom, but remembering her mouth suddenly dismissed any regrets. "No, leave them, but make them unidentifiable. We don't have the time nor the man power to do more."

"At least let us sweep the place, making sure no prints are left behind that belong to you or Wang," Tony said.

Jordan held up his gloved hands and The Collector followed suit. "Looks like we're covered."

Easter saw his van not too far in the distance. If he could just make it to his vehicle where he had another gun, he would live to plot both The Tarantula's and The Collector's demises. As soon as he was almost in the clear, a black van rolled to a stop, cutting him off. He was about to go for his gun, but cursed when he remembered that he was relieved of it. Looking for an out, Easter was about to run back through the cemetery when the voice calling out to him halted him.

"Giovanna?"

Chapter 45

"*E*ven though you didn't see what happened, at least now we have information on the carnage that the groundskeeper had the misfortune of discovering at Père Lachaise Cemetery," Phoebe Bercherot stated. Since her introduction, she'd been sitting and observing quietly.

I cleared my throat and stole a quick glance at Aliyah. She nodded her head that it was OK for me to go on. "I didn't see what happened after I ... I was taken and—"

Marlow stood and came closer to where I was seated. "I'm going to need you to really think back to that night."

"But I've told you everything that I know up until the point that Jordan—" Then without warning, incidents that had occurred that didn't mean much to me that left me wondering, started to make sense: *The first encounter with Seven telling her that she would always be in Jordan's life after she was long gone. Her statement at the cemetery about Jordan's story concerning The Collector changing with every gullible bitch that he got with. How close Jordan and Seven seemed to be even in the company of Snake. Snake trying to always talk Jordan into believing that Sledge was the leak in the group when it was really him, Seven and Giovanna. Sledge, although he made my life hell, was really trying to warn me about Jordan's intentions and his relationship with Giovanna, especially in Paris when they'd hurriedly put him on a plane back to wherever. Now Sledge was silenced forever. Giovanna's dreadful accent sounded just like the one from the flight attendant both times and the delivery person who kept saying the word "beautiful" with her enunciation making it sound dreadful. The dream she had of being drowned with the person talking with the same accent. Seven was always beyond jealous of Jordan and I showing any kind of romantic affection toward one another, except for when we were all engaging together. Jordan always made sure to pay close attention to satisfying Seven's needs sometimes even more than mine. The way Seven and Snake reacted when she shot the flight attendant. Snake made it his mission to take care of the body. Jordan's reaction to Sledge on the plane and never dealing with the body was strange as it would've given him a clue as to who was after them. I dismissed all of that because I believed that it was Easter, so why would I question it. How would Easter know where to come? They were at a private airport. That meant that it had to be Seven, Giovanna, and Snake who were behind it all. Was the plan to use me as the one who took the fall? How did Easter get in that hotel room bed with me?*

The memories slamming into me like a runaway Mack truck began to make me question everything about the relationship with Jordan. Easter shooting Snake had to be a mistake since he was probably in on whatever that was really going on. "Oh my God. I think I'm going to be sick." I grasped my chest and nearly knocked Marlow over trying to get out of there as fast as my legs would carry me while wearing six-inch stilettos to find the nearest men's or ladies room.

Marlow made a move to go after me, but was nearly trampled by Aliyah. "She's *my* client and *I* will see after her!"

I was disgusted as I'd made it to the toilet just in time to throw up. It became uncontrollable vomiting, as more reminiscences flooded my delusional brain. *Hadn't I done everything that he'd asked of me? Risked my life. My freedom. My business. Jeopardized friendships, all to be with him.* I heaved and cried, wondering how Jordan could have betrayed me as he had.

The door to my stall flew open.

"Get out!" I screamed, knowing that it was nobody but Aliyah.

She grabbed my hair and held it back to keep it from getting vomit in it. "Are you okay?" she asked.

More contents left my body before I could answer her. "Did Jordan set me up?" I asked, needing to know the truth.

Aliyah laughed. "Why stop being the gullible, dick-starved bitch you've always been when it comes to Jordan now, huh? Are you finally starting to use that thing you call a brain?" Aliya laughed. "We're almost in the homestretch, Bianca. Don't ruin it because then, I won't be able to protect you."

I cleared my throat. "Is that what you call this? Protecting me? I just need to know if Jordan is in on what's happening to me." I panicked.

"When was the last time you heard from Jordan? Has he made a call to you? Come to visit? Sent a postcard? Email? Carrier pigeon? Are you that fucking stupid, Bianca?"

I hated that I was bent over a toilet which gave her the advantage to drown me in my own puke if she wanted to. "Easter was found dead in my bed and I don't know how he got there, or even me, for that matter. Last thing I remembered is being in Paris with your crazy ass holding a gun to my head while that other crazy bitch drove."

"Damn, I at least took you for having half a brain to figure this shit out. Since you're still having a hard time deciphering it, let me break it down to you. Besides his wannabe emperor father, The Collector, Jordan cares only about Jordan."

"But I overheard him having The Collector's son's fingers broken over the phone. That can't be true."

"You're not the first stupid bitch he's used and unfortunately, probably won't be the last. Do you think he would actually hurt his baby brother? Jordan tried to play us. We got the memo long ago that The Collector was Jordan's father. He wanted us to think that he was working against The Collector when all along he was working with him. You see Snake never took Sledge to the airport. With a little persuasion, my girl Giovanna got him to talking real good and confirmed what we were already suspecting." She laughed. "I remember telling you in Paris that I was here before you and would be after you're gone. I guess I lied since Jordan was planning to take us all out and ride off into the sunset with the take and his father."

"I still don't believe you."

"Then don't. Either way it's your funeral, *bitch*." Her demeanor went back to being my lawyer when she heard the door to the ladies room open. "Are you sure you're feeling okay, Ms. Brooks?"

"Must be something I ate," I answered.

Suddenly, the grip on my hair tightened as she came closer to me and whispered, "Or it could be something you're thinking of telling? Don't fuck with me, Bianca." She released my head and shoved it forward.

After she left my stall, I overheard her talking to Marlow.

"Poor thing is puking her guts up. I hope it's nothing contagious from that *water* the department gave her before the interview."

"I doubt that very seriously, Aliyah. I drink water from here all the time."

"Which proves nothing since you also can drink any man under the table, Marlow." Aliyah enjoyed the surprised look that crossed

Marlow's face. "Oh, you thought your being an alcoholic was a private matter? Shame on you, Marlow. For a district attorney, you're quite clueless."

Flushed, Marlow ignored her taunting. "Maybe we should postpone and reconvene tomorrow. I don't want you putting her testimony at risk by saying she was forced to cooperate under duress. I know how you operate, Aliyah."

"Do you now?" Aliyah laughed. "Like I said, must be the water they served to her in that beautiful glass pitcher. I wonder who it belongs to."

Then the bathroom door closed as I heard their heels clacking against the hard floors going toward the direction of the conference room.

I lurched, trying to throw up more, but there was nothing left. The way Aliyah kept mentioning the water and pitcher made me suspicious, especially since it had been her idea for me to make such an outlandish request in the first place.

"Ask for some water before we begin, but not just any old bottle of water. Ask for it to be served in a nice glass and watch how they jump through hoops to meet your request. That's how you'll know that they need you more than the weight of their futile threats really carries. Take advantage of your power and remember that I will be with you every step of the way just as we talked about."

"But what if they don't?" I asked.

"Then I threaten to pull you. They know that there's neither a judge nor jury alive that will ever convict you with the flimsy evidence that they have against you. Besides being a straight shooter, I know how to manipulate the law as well." After recalling that conversation, I knew the use of the double entendre was meant more for me than law enforcement. I stayed leaning over the toilet, trying to digest everything before finally getting up, flushing the toilet and going to take a look in the mirror to see what a real fool looked like.

Chapter 46

After nearly twenty minutes of reflecting, I rejoined everyone who was eagerly awaiting my return.

"Are you feeling up to continuing?" Agent Garza asked.

I took my seat and pushed the water away from me. "Yes, I'm sure. It must've been the seafood salad I had before coming here." I stared at Aliyah with daggers in my eyes, but no one noticed, especially when she smirked back at me.

Phoebe Bercherot had a few questions of her own that she needed answers to. "Have you any idea of how to locate this woman whom you call Seven? Whatever became of Giovanna? She seems to have suddenly vanished off of the face of the earth which is hard being a world-famous supermodel. This Snake person, you say you saw him shot, but did you actually ever see them get rid of the body?" She fired off one question after the other, not giving me time to answer. I looked over at Aliyah who pretended to be studying on her laptop, but was really giving me death looks.

"Umm ... no. I have no idea on how to get in contact with any of these people. As for Snake, I told you what I saw. Easter shot him."

Phoebe snorted out a condescending laugh. "Luckily for you,

you're on American soil. This oversexed, poor-is-me story wouldn't fly in Paris. Your participation in all of this is just as guilty as the ones who actually stormed our beautiful treasure and violated her! And you should pay for your part in all of this." Her once alabaster skin was now a flushed crimson red.

"Phoebe, as you said, *if* we were in Paris, but we're not. So watch how you speak to my client." Aliyah's voice was professional, but carried heavy undertones of a threat. She cleared her throat before continuing in case someone picked up on it. "Ahem, I understand your frustrations. Hell, we're all frustrated, but Ms. Brooks is giving you information that, until she decided to talk, you didn't have."

Phoebe's bark calmed down a bit. "Understood, but I'm not buying her story on not knowing where The Tarantula is hiding out. The others maybe, but from what I've heard on the other side of that glass, she's in love with that man. Never would she let him out of her reach!"

"Her being in love is besides the point, Agent Bercherot," Aliyah challenged with a hot stare.

Marlow jumped in. "You know if not for this deal, your client would be behind bars. If she's withholding any information, then I suggest you inform her to be forthcoming with it."

"Marlow, you and I both know that the evidence you have against her will do nothing but piss a judge off for wasting his and the taxpayers' time and money. You got a tip that she was in a hotel room and with a dead man. How convenient was that?" Aliyah laughed and shook her head. "Who made the call? Did you ever figure that one out? It screams a setup and you know it. At best, my client would receive nothing more than a slap on the wrist and be made to pay restitution, but for what? You have no records of what she actually collected from the man you want, if she ever got anything."

"She admitted to receiving money from the Tar ... I mean, Jordan Lei on a few occasions, even taking her Pleasure Principles staff on an extravagant vacation that she left behind to go and commit yet another crime," Phoebe reminded the room.

"Great listening skills, Agent Bercherot ..." Aliyah clapped. "But do you have proof of this influx of cash? Bank statements? Wire transfers? Or maybe even evidence of money laundering?"

Agent Garza stopped the recording. "We don't have proof, but it's not like we can't obtain it."

Aliyah laughed out loud this time. "You're just hell-bent on wasting taxpayers' dollars when my client has been exonerated for cooperating. What good would that do you all now?"

By this time, Phoebe was burning with rage. Agent Garza got her attention to step outside with him and DA Marlow Hayes. He came back in a few minutes later minus them.

"Did Special Agent Bercherot and Marlow decide to leave us?" Aliyah asked before Agent Garza could make it back to his seat.

"I let them know that we could handle it from here," he answered back curtly while deadpanning Aliyah.

To stop what I knew would turn into another heated debate, I grimaced and rubbed my stomach for show. "On second thought, Agent Garza, I think I do need to call it a day. I'm not feeling too good, after all."

Aliyah stood and protested, her eyes darting about wildly. "But Ms. Brooks, I thought you wanted to get this over with as quickly as possible?"

I continued massaging my stomach and spoke in the sickliest voice I could muster. "I did, but whatever I'm coming down with has other ideas. Now that I think of it, I've missed my period again this month."

The men in the room quickly took that as their cue to go about their business. No way did they want to listen to a woman, no matter how fine, complain about missing her menses.

Agent Garza shook his head while watching the men go at breakneck speed to try and clear the room. It was almost comical to him, but the matter at hand was serious. "I think that would be a good idea, Ms. Brooks. I can't have your attorney trying to sue us on your behalf saying we forced you to finish this interrogation under duress."

Aliyah reluctantly stood and stretched before gathering her things. "You know, Marlow said the same thing, so I just might do that, anyway, Agent Garza."

"I wouldn't expect anything less from you, Ms. Talal." He went about clearing the room of the water bottles and other items that the others had left behind. He then took the day's session out of the recorder to prevent it from mysteriously disappearing.

"I'll give you a ride home so you won't have to worry about driving since you're not feeling too well," she offered a little too graciously, instantly putting me on edge.

"I think I can manage. Besides, now that I just realized my dilemma, I need to make a quick stop to the drug store for a pregnancy test and a few other items." Aliyah's head looked as if it were about to explode. Just the thought of me carrying Jordan's child was enough to make her blow her cover.

Agent Garza walked us out making small talk along the way. After giving the tape and video to that fine-ass Agent Carter that went to get the goods on Ramon Benavidez aka Sledge, he walked us out to the parking garage.

"Well, ladies, I will see you around nine a.m. Don't be late, Ms. Brooks; we still have a lot of ground to cover. Don't try anything tricky as we have our eyes on you," he said, eyeing me suspiciously.

I looked at him and shook my head for emphasis. "You don't have to remind me, Agent. I'm well aware that big brother is always watching."

"As long as you remember that, Ms. Brooks, and don't try anything rash."

"Enough already, Agent Garza. I will see to it that my client is here at nine a.m. sharp and not a minute later," Aliyah announced tartly.

"Yeah, you see to it that she is," he answered back just as nastily.

They went back and forth like I wasn't even standing there. While they were trying to see who had the biggest balls, Agent Carter walked out to his car. When he noticed that he was being watched, he winked and gave me a smile that had my thong about to disappear even further up my ass. Oh, he just didn't know how much I wanted to jump in with him and head to the nearest hotel, or did he? I exhaled and digressed from my wayward thoughts. Hell, being shot in the ass is what had gotten me in my current mess. Hating to leave all of that sexy behind, I climbed into my car, and then gave Aliyah and Agent Garza one more pathetic look before pulling off.

For good measure of the lie I'd just told about missing my cycle, I actually decided to make a trip to Walgreens. Thank goodness it was only around the corner from my house. I purchased a pregnancy test along with something to soothe my nauseous stomach. One never knew what that sneaky bitch Aliyah was up to, and I needed to cover my ass in case she was watching.

Chapter 47

The moment I walked inside of my dark house, I had a feeling that I wasn't alone. Thinking quickly, I decided that leaving was the best decision. The moment my foot was nearly out of the door, the lights came on and his voice stopped me.

"Don't be afraid," he spoke barely above a whisper.

It was then that his cologne filled my nostrils instantly making me want him. I forgot all about the masturbating session I had planned with that fine-ass Agent Carter being the star of my thoughts. I inhaled his scent and held it for as long as I could before exhaling and speaking his name, "*Jordan*."

"Please, close the door and come back in." He was being unusually gentlemanly and not cocky like he normally was. That gave me a cause of concern.

I slowly shut the door, and turned to face him. He walked up to me and relieved me of the bag from Walgreens and my purse. When he hastily set the bag on the floor, the pregnancy test fell out. Jordan looked at the test, and then at me. "I know everything," Jordan explained, ignoring what he'd just seen. "I know you spent the day being questioned. I know Seventhia, better known as Seven to you, represented you using her first name, Aliyah."

"So what she said about you setting them all up to kill them ... and me ... is true?"

Jordan quieted me once more. His face was a mask of seriousness that I'd never seen before or was it fear that I was detecting. "You can't believe a thing she says. She's dangerous, Bianca. Do not, under any circumstances, take anything about her lightly."

Then another revelation hit me. "O ... kay. So, what Snake was saying to Easter about you and her was true?"

Jordan took my hand and led me to the sofa. "Yes, and no. Seven and I was long before Snake ever came into the picture. Snake knew that no matter how hard he tried, that her heart would never belong to him. She loved him, but she wasn't in love with him. Seven used him as a way to make me jealous, and for a while, I'll admit that it worked. We saw each other behind Snake's back for years until I broke things off with her permanently. Every woman that I've ever gotten close to, she would give a hard time. Snake couldn't stand it, but as time went on, he learned to deal with it."

"A triangle, I see. Why are you risking everything to—"

He put his hand over my mouth. "Shh!"

That instantly got me beyond nervous. Was he alone? My heart was beating an up-tempo beat that synchronized perfectly with the rhythm of the ball of nerves that danced in my stomach. He then pointed toward the stairs, which led up to my bedroom.

He led me by the small of my back up the steps. "I think we would be better off just in case someone is at your door listening. There was someone watching your place earlier, but I had Tony and Johnny take care of him. He was one of Giovanna's go-to guys."

"Why was he here?" I let the words slip out of my mouth smooth and without surprisingly throwing up everywhere due to being on edge about my current situation. Although I was a panicky mess, my libido was in overdrive and had me wanting to jump his bones.

"He was just doing what he was told to do. I wouldn't be surprised if he hasn't been watching you since you've made bail."

As he stood next to my bed, I could see how devastatingly sexy he was. Oh, how I missed those eyes. Those lips. Those hands. Those—

Jordan's bass-filled voice startled me back into reality. "Bianca, did you hear what I'd just said?"

I didn't know what he'd just said, but I guessed it was crucial—whatever it was. "I'm still stuck on you saying that I was being watched." Jordan knew that I was lying. I should have been ashamed of myself for the direction my ill-conceived thoughts were taking me instead of focusing on the imminent danger that I could've been in.

There was an uncomfortable silence in the room. Our eyes locked and at that moment, I didn't give a damn as I went in for a kiss. It was tender and filled with everything that I'd been missing. Maybe seduction would have bought me a ticket to live past that day.

Jordan ended the kiss abruptly. "Bianca, now is not the time for that."

I looked down at his pole that was straining to break free from his jeans. I groped and massaged it, loving the way it felt growing at the touch of my hand. "Why don't you tell him that?" I went in for another kiss.

Jordan was swept up in emotions trying to fight the urge. I knew it wouldn't be long before I got what I was working for. Maybe, just maybe, he would be so caught up that he would forget if he was there to kill me.

Jordan bit his bottom lip, but not before a lustful moan escaped. His eyes became tighter as his breathing labored. To not be overcome, he pushed me back and held me at arm's length. "Bianca ... as much as I want you . . ." He had to compose himself before going on. "As much as I want you, we need to talk. Can you behave while we do that? Besides, someone could be watching us at this very moment."

I lurched forward again only to be stopped in my tracks. "Hmm, that's never stopped us before. In case you forgot, and thanks to you, I just *love* an audience."

Jordan did his best to ignore me and started back talking. "I know that Snake, and Seven, along with Giovanna, were behind the shooting at the airport. It was Seven who set you up with Easter in that hotel."

I stopped long enough to look at Jordan. "But I thought you killed Easter when you went into the mausoleum?"

"That was the plan, but he got away." Jordan placed his hands on my shoulders to get me to calm down and so that he could finish. "Easter revealed more to me than he realized. He tried to bargain for his life with the luring promise, or shall I say lie, of letting me have the Bangkok gold. It was then that I knew Seven, and Snake, were behind the airport shooting and killing Pierre and Étienne."

"That makes sense because surely he wouldn't be fool enough to use a barter that he knew was defunct."

"Now you're thinking with your head instead of what's between your legs. Had Snake been there at the moment—" Jordan rubbed his temples like simply thinking of Snake's betrayal was painful. "My father said that I had enemies in my camp. I never would've thought that it would've been those three."

"So whose fingers did Jim break?"

"No one's. It was to make everyone involved more at ease. The wedding and taking the ring was one thing, but I had to go even further by doing something even more drastic. Once I learned of Snake's and Seven's betrayal, I had no choice but to take out his entire team with the exception of Jim. Adding Snake, Giovanna, and Seven to that body count and giving them a one-way ticket to hell would've been icing on the cake had they been there."

Now I was dumbfounded. "Question. How was Easter able to get away? More importantly, how did he end up in a Dallas hotel bed with me and with a bullet in his head?"

Jordan sat down on the bed, pulling me along with him. I straddled his lap and tried to listen when I felt his bulge greet my pleasure zone. "Easter was wounded. Being that Seven wanted revenge for Snake, I knew it wouldn't be long before he was taken care of. Giovanna was his weakness, and I'll put my last dollar on it that she was the cause of his demise." Jordan laughed like he'd just remembered something.

"What's so damned funny?"

"Delilah said something about women being the cause of many powerful men's downfall. To think that Easter, being the chauvinist that he was, fell for a woman's beguiling lure. He never stopped to think that it could be a trap, being that she suddenly went missing after the heist and then just magically reappeared like she'd gone shopping or to the spa."

"I really didn't get to know Delilah, but from what I saw, she seemed like she would be your type. I mean, is it a prerequisite for all of the women in your circle to be stunningly beyond gorgeous?" A deadpan expression marred my face, but inquiring minds, mainly mine, had one more pressing question needing to be answered. "Never mind that; I guess what I really want to know is ... did you fuck her too?"

Jordan let off a nervous chuckle this time instead of the confident one he'd had a minute earlier. "Bianca, don't be ridiculous. I never met the girl until this job. She was one of Snake's people and got her due just like the rest of them," he lied.

"Umm-hmm ... whatever, Jordan." I rolled my eyes. "Does it look like I have the word *stupid* stamped across my forehead?"

"Now is not the time for one of your jealous temper-tantrums." I reluctantly got off of Jordan's lap and made my way to the other side of the room. "I can't get mad over what I can't prove. I didn't know Delilah, or what she was about. However, I do know that Giovanna is a supermodel, so how does she fit in all of this?" I exhaled loudly and ran my hands across my face and exhaled again. "Oh my God, what have I gotten myself into?" I paced back and forth shaking my head. "I can't believe I was so blinded by your bullshit, Jordan. I've never had a run-in with the law." I looked at Jordan still filled with questions.

Jordan sat stone-faced, watching me become unraveled before speaking a couple of minutes later. "I wouldn't stand in front of that window, if I were you."

I hurriedly moved away from the window and into a corner where I couldn't be seen from the outside.

"Now to answer your question, being a model is her cover. Giovanna is a chameleon, a merciless killer. She and Seven met in the military and are longtime lovers. Snake was fine with the relationship because it also benefited him."

"Bullshit! Sledge said that Giovanna was the one you needed to make an honest woman out of. So I don't buy that she's in a relationship with Seven and Snake."

"Yes, I did sleep with her more times than I can count, but it was nothing like what I have with you. It was purely physical between us. I can't even fathom sending you to sleep with another man. It would drive me insane because you mean *something* to me. Giovanna is ... very skilled and just as calculating and deadly as Seven. If that were the case, I certainly wouldn't have sent her to seduce Easter. I needed someone who could handle herself, and when Snake suggested Giovanna, let's just say that I was sold. Easter never knew about Giovanna's relationship with Seven."

That extinguished my fire, but then another revelation reignited it. "That accent ... so it was Giovanna that tried to shoot me on that airplane! Did you know it was her? Oh my God, Jordan! She ... she delivered your flowers to my house!"

Jordan averted his eyes away from me and for the first time, he was speechless. I walked over and slapped him as hard as I could. "Did you know that it was her on that plane?"

He didn't flinch, but the homicidal look in his eyes retreated and was replaced with one of remorse. "Yes, I knew, but ... it's complicated."

"Complicated my ass! That bitch tried to kill me and you reward her with the address to my house!" The realization of Jordan's disregard continued to fall on me like a ton of bricks. "You invited a stone-cold killer to my house. My house, Jordan! What kind of *something* is that you have for me?"

Jordan stood and grabbed me by the shoulders as if he were about to shake me like a rag doll. Instead of rattling my cage, he let go and placed his finger on my lips. "There's a lot that I kept you in the dark about, but I had to know if I could trust you. I had to know if you were the one."

Oh no! Jordan wasn't throwing that *if you're the one* crap on me again. His time for ruling me was over. I was taking a lot of heat behind his mess. Not to mention being controlled like a lab monkey by Seven's crazy ass. I was going to get the answers I wanted once and for all. "My life was in danger, and you're trying to justify it with that nonsense?"

He hung his head and exhaled like he were trying to come up with something that would get me off of his case. "I should've handled that situation a lot better than what I did. I didn't find out that it was Giovanna on the plane until afterwards. She called me and told me that she could've taken you out if she wanted to, but Seven had talked her out of it."

"What was up with the whole situation, anyway? Why would Seven act like she killed her if she didn't?"

"Seven wanted to gain your trust. Before the shooting, you must admit that you and she were like oil and water. Not that you became best friends afterwards, but you loosened your jealousy reins up a bit on her."

"Okay, I'll give her that, but why was Giovanna trying to shoot me in the first place?"

Jordan looked like he was getting tired of playing Twenty One Questions, but I didn't give a damn. "I told you that already. Seven can handle the one-night stands, but when she feels threatened ... well, let's just say that Giovanna was willing to get rid of that threat."

"That bitch! You ... you people have a lot of damn nerve," I screamed in Jordan's face.

After wiping the side of his face where spittle from me yelling at him landed, Jordan tried to embrace me, but I wasn't done with his ass yet.

"Where have you been all of this time while I was going through hell and high water with those crazy-ass, vindictive bitches?" I asked again since he'd avoided the question like the plague.

Instead of answering, he rested his hand on my belly and caressed it. When he looked into my eyes, I knew what he wanted to know.

"There's a strong possibility," I lied, thinking that if his plans were to kill me, maybe having him think that I was carrying his child might give him a change of heart. Since me trying to seduce him was falling flat.

Jordan closed his eyes and took a deep breath as his hand continued to caress my flat stomach. When he opened them, they were filled with tears. "I'm sorry for putting you in harm's way. I should've been more protective of you, knowing how Seven feels. I've been in denial about my lifestyle for so long, that I never once took a moment to really consider anyone else's feelings, but my own. It was wrong for me to mislead you about me and my father's relationship. Letting others think that he's my enemy is one thing, but you didn't deserve to be lied to."

The sincerity in his voice moved me to second-guess not only him, but myself. I didn't know what to believe. Jordan was, after all, a master manipulator. He made a living out of making people think and feel one way when he was on a "job." Why would this be any different?

Chapter 48

"*S*hit just got real, huh?" Jordan said out of the blue.

I was caught off guard, but tried to act as though I wasn't afraid of what might have been about to happen. "What do you mean by that?"

His hand found its way back to my belly. "You might be carrying my son."

I moved from his touch. "Or daughter," I countered.

"Why are you backing away from me?"

I took a deep breath and looked at Jordan to see if I could get a read on what was going through his conniving mind. "I know you came back for a reason and it damn sure wasn't to play daddy."

He laughed and rubbed his goatee while shaking his head. "Didn't I tell you that I would never hurt you again?"

"But things are different now. People are dead, Jordan. People that I thought were your trusted allies, you killed. What makes me any different from any of them?"

He tried to touch my face, but I pushed his hand away. I wanted him, but now that *shit just got real* as he said, I wanted my life even more.

"I'll give you that. Truth is when I learned of Seven, Giovanna and Snake's betrayal, I knew your life was in danger. And as they know me, they used you to draw me out. Seven knew that I would come running to your rescue. You've touched me in ways that she never could and that kills her."

I wanted to believe what he was saying, but my brain kept telling me not to be a fool, while my heart was falling for his words—hook, line and sinker. "I don't know what to believe, Jordan."

"I promise to let you in on everything when the time is right."

"Including the real truth about your father ... The Collector?"

Jordan took a deep breath. "I know I wasn't forthcoming with you concerning him, but to make things look legit, we had to play our parts. I want you to meet him, because I know you're the one. With you possibly carrying my child, I want to do the right thing by you."

My heart nearly melted. *Jordan wanted me! Not Seven! Not Giovanna, or any of those other women, but me!* I wanted to jump for joy, but the lies, deceit and the abuse was all that I could think about. *What would I really be getting myself into being "the one"?*

Jordan must've picked up on my thoughts and took my trembling hands into his. "My father, Xing Ho Wang, our relationship did start out as I told you, but over the years, we hashed out our differences and used what everyone else assumed as hate to our advantage. When he told me of his dealings in obtaining the finest and rarest treasures in the world, I was immediately intrigued, Bianca. Since my brother, Ming-Hua, was solely into his music, I wanted to work by my father's side. I love my father, Bianca. He saved me from a life of pain and gave me one of privilege. I owe him my life and I will give it gladly as he would do the same for me."

I stared at him with unbelieving eyes. "So what was all of this for, if not to get back at your father?"

"He told me that there were enemies in my camp. I didn't want to believe him, but he has never been wrong about that sort of thing before. Easter had it coming for the Bangkok job; now that part of it was true. I misjudged Sledge, and will regret that for the rest of my life. I should've known that Snake was up to something. Being a snitch wasn't Sledge's style."

I sat with my thoughts on how things had occurred. Snake was always in his ear about Sledge. Sledge went out of his way to be nasty to me, but now I felt like shit wondering if that was his way of trying to warn me about the company that I was keeping. He played the making-me-jealous role really well and I fell for it every single time. I even grew to detest him. Seven's words slammed back into me. *"He's always force-feeding that horse shit of a story only with different variations of the truth down you simple bitches' throats."*

Jordan snuck a kiss. I was instantly wet, ready, willing and able to rock his world. I was playing with fire and was well aware of the third-degree burns that I would receive by messing with this man. With that being the case, I needed him to understand that everything I'd done up until this point was for him. My back was up against the wall when I was taken against my will. I had no choice in the matter, but to cooperate or meet the torturous death that my captors had threatened me with. My friends. My life. My everything was at stake if I didn't go along with the program. The only silver lining was that Jordan knew nothing about my family and neither did they since they never mentioned going after them. At least I hoped they didn't.

Jordan led me back to the bed. He sat down and I straddled him and ran my hands up and down his body. I was in a zone when he stopped me and hurriedly helped me out of my jacket. He impatiently tried to unbutton the pink ruffled blouse that I wore before becoming frustrated with the task and ripping it open, causing buttons to fly everywhere. His eyes widened in delight when he took in the sight of my beautiful cleavage beckoning him to please them. His hands caressed the delicate lace fabric of my La Perla Baronessa bra before taking on the task of unhooking the clasps and helping me out of it. He fondled my begging-to-be-touched breasts, pushed them together and suckled my taut nipples. My head fell back as moistness pooled between my thighs.

"Let me help you take off the rest," he stopped licking my nipples long enough to say. I raised my body up as he wrestled my skirt off. While he was doing that, I was trying to get his pants undone. I was in need of feeling him inside of me, even if it was for the last time. His shirt was next as it met the same ending as mine with buttons flying everywhere. Those pecs and abs were as magnificent as I remembered them being. My hands hungrily ran all over his torso. I applied shiatsu techniques along the way to his taught muscles. He soon began to relax as I applied the right amount of pressure.

"Ahh, baby . . ." Jordan exhaled loudly. "That feels so damned good."

Not wanting to wait another minute longer, he raised his hips and slid his pants and boxers down. To my utter delight, I was greeted in the best way when that pipe of his sprung forward ready for action. After feeling my juices on his fingers, Jordan guided me down on him as he thrust himself deep inside of my deprived tunnel.

"Ooh . . ." I moaned as I tilted my head back again with my eyes half closed. I took pleasure in each stroke that he delivered and tried my best to match him on each one.

"I miss you so much. I miss this. Ahh ... you just don't know ... how much. You trust me, baby?" Jordan whispered as he brought my face to his and engaged me in a kiss to end all kisses.

"Yes, Jordan ... I do," I said between kisses.

Jordan stood with me, still riding his shaft, and laid me on my back. He looked into my eyes and answered all of the lingering questions without saying a thing. His forehead rested on mine as we stared deeply into each other's eyes searching for the connection that we knew still had to be there, and it was. Through mental telepathy, we received every word. I was immediately swept back up into his world again just that easily. I knew that if we wanted to, we could have the outcome I always dreamed of. We could make our home and start a family anywhere in the world. We could have a little boy that looked like him and a daughter who would be my mini me. All that mattered was him knowing that we could have that and more. Our lives could be beautiful, fulfilling and meaningful if only he felt the same way about me as I did him. From our connection, I didn't feel that he had cruel intentions, and I could only pray that what was coming down the pike would be the fairy tale that I envisioned for us. From the way he was sexing me, I hoped he could feel how much I cherished our time together. In a true expression of love, honesty and loyalty, I sang his praises in a series of moans. I had no doubt that Jordan felt something for me deep within his heart, but was it love?

For all the goodness I was feeling, my conscience was screaming for me to take off the rose-colored glasses, but my heart overruled. "Let me ride him, baby."

Jordan didn't waste any time flipping me over to where I was on top of him. I rode him like he was a runaway wild stud that couldn't be tamed. My hair swung all around us as I bucked my hips wildly back and forth. Up and down. Round and round. I swirled my hips with vigor like a belly dancer that was putting on the show of a lifetime as she performed for her master. I thrust them faster. I worked them harder than ever before. It was my mission to cast this devil of a man into the depths of the oblivion that was me.

But as fate would have it, Jordan wasn't about to surrender and let me have that type of power over him. He grabbed me by the waist to put a stop to my magical, gyrating hips that had him spellbound. No way was he going to the point of no return without putting up a fight like the true warrior in the bed that he was.

"What are you trying to do to me, girl?" he asked as he tossed me onto my side and got behind me. Jordan lifted my leg up high and power-drilled with sweet, slow, agonizing, commanding strokes that had me losing the hold that I had over him only seconds ago.

My walls constricted around Jordan's shaft trying to savor all that he had to give. "I'm ... trying to ... bewitch you with ... this pussy," I managed to cry out.

"You've already done that," Jordan admitted as he hit my sweet spot causing me to yell out. It didn't take much for me to surrender to him once again as my creamy nectar coated him and dripped down my leg.

"You like the way I'm putting in work ... huh?"

"Yes, baby! Give ... it ... to me just ... like ... that. Make me cum for ... you—ooh!"

With my leg still suspended in the air, Jordan eased out of me and reacquainted himself with my lower lips. I nearly lost control when his tongue swirled my clit around like a cherry on a stem. "Umm ... you taste so damn good, baby."

Jordan was being extra attentive and I loved it. He had yet to have a release of his own, while I'd had a few. He pushed my legs back and spread them as far as they would go and devoured me like I was his last meal. The momentum of the impending orgasm was coming fast and it was going to be the undoing of me.

"Oohh!!!! I ... my oohh! Yes! Yes!" I caressed Jordan's head as he continued to drive me into another atmosphere. He introduced two of his fingers into the mix and when they made contact with my g-spot, it was over. Bright colors and stars exploded before my eyes as my milky goodness flowed over his fingers like a river while his tongue continued to tap dance on my clit and savor my creamy slit. Jordan delicately handled my oversaturated canal with gentle bites that alternated between my clit and outer lips. He eased his fingers out and released my nub long enough to savor my sticky essence. From the look on his face, he was enjoying every bit of the award he'd received for the hard work he'd put in.

Without notice, Jordan went in balls deep while I was in the middle of a climax, which only heightened the intensity of the moment. He positioned me to where he was hitting it from the back. As our bodies connected, you could hear one delicious smack after another. Jordan slapped me on my ass repeatedly as he neared nirvana. I could tell that he was getting close as he thrust with harder, deeper and longer strokes. While in the midst of trying to help him make it to the promise land, I found myself in close proximity of joining him there. We arrived at our destination at the same time. When it was over, we crashed like waves onto the bed, panting while trying to catch our breaths.

Chapter 49

Mentally and physically drained, Jordan and I dragged ourselves into the shower. The hot jetting streams from the water reinvigorated us and once again, I found myself stuffed to capacity with Jordan knocking my back out.

"Fuck me ... yes! Ooh yeah!" Jordan fondled my clit, never missing a beat and nearly causing my legs to buckle.

I gripped the towel rack, nearly breaking a nail. "Ooh ... that's my spot!" He propped my right leg up on the seating area of the massive shower, for more access into my pleasure zone. Jordan held me firm around my waist and continued fingering my clit and creating a delicious, stimulating feeling.

"Ummmmm ... that feels so ... got ... damn ... good!" I managed to say between gasps and moans.

Jordan spanked my ass. "I'mma tear ... this cunt ... up! Come on ... work that ... fat ass!" *Smack*! Jordan took his dick out momentarily and spanked me on the ass with it and ran it through my hungry slit, connecting with my love nub a few times.

"Umm ... ooh fuck!"

"Yeah, that's it! Handle that shit, baby. Give me that freak I know and love," Jordan commanded.

I turned, facing him wearing a devilish grin on my face as the water continued to cascade all around us. I wrapped my legs around him and held on tight to his neck as I rode the shit out of him. "Is this . . .umm ... what ... you want? You ... want ... umm yes ... me to ... take ... control and command that dick."

"Yes ... throw that pussy. Arrgggh! Make me ... be ... believe that you missed me putting ... it on you," he grunted as the curve of his dick hit my spot.

"Aoooh! Oh my gawd! Umm ... Yes, daddy!" Once again, I was being conquered and losing the power that I so desperately wanted to maintain. I had to gain control of the situation. I eased him out of me and slid down to my knees. The water was becoming cold, but I didn't care about the fact that my hair was a drenched mess. The only thing I cared about was going deep-throat dicking.

There was no denying that Jordan's dick was one of my indulgences. The moment his pre-cum landed on my tongue, I nearly lost it. I relaxed my throat and took my time devouring him inch by delectable inch. I became consumed with licking and sucking as if he were a melting Popsicle on a hot summer's day. Suddenly, Jordan grabbed both sides of my head, gathering handfuls of my hair, and began thrusting his pelvis into my mouth with the same vigor as he had my pussy only moments ago. His climax was thick, sweet and never-ending. The sound of coming from him couldn't be described as nothing but barbaric. I knew from the buckling in his knees and watching the towering giant collapse that I had conquered. The now freezing water had us shivering as we descended back to earth.

"Arrrggght! Sheiit!"

"Damn, that was good."

After cutting off the water to get out of the tub, I smiled, showing him now that I agreed. "So, what now?"

Jordan reached a towel and started to dry me off. "Sleep."

Suddenly, I felt the day catching up with me. "I couldn't agree with you more, but what about Seven? Plus, I have to be at the police station tomorrow at nine a.m."

"We'll cross that bridge in a few hours, after I catch a couple of Z's. But, to ease your mind, I'm here now. You don't have anything to worry about concerning Seven and Giovanna, ever again. Let me worry about them bitches."

I woke up to find Jordan draped across me like a cheap suit. Normally, I would have welcomed being in this position, but I was uncomfortable and thirsty. I eased up from under him, put on a robe and made my way downstairs to the kitchen.

When I opened the fridge, there was a bottle of frosted Evian water that was calling out my name. I stood with the fridge still open while gulping the water down. The bottle was darn near empty when I turned it away from my lips and put the cap back on for later consumption. After putting the bottle of water back in, I spotted a glass bowl with some strawberries in it.

I closed the door to the fridge, but not before plopping a juicy berry into my mouth. As soon as I turned around, I dropped the glass bowl when my eyes caught Seven, sitting on one of the stools at the bar holding a gun.

"Oh, did I startle you?" she asked as if she were concerned.

Glass was everywhere. I felt a slight sting and saw blood on my foot. I swallowed the rest of the strawberry and the lump that had formed in my throat. "What are you doing here?"

Seven laughed. "Isn't it obvious?" She looked at me through squinted eyes. "I'm here to kill you, bitch. I was hoping you would've ended the damn briefing today, so we could've moved on, but you had to fuck it up by stopping it."

The pain in my foot was bad, but the bullet hole she was threatening to put in me would have been worse. "Seven." My nerves were frazzled, but now was not the time to be letting them get the best of me. I straightened up and squared my shoulders. "You're the one who poisoned me with tainted water, remember? What's going to happen when I don't show up tomorrow?"

Seven jumped off of the stool and came near me. "Last I checked, I'm the one holding the gun, which means that I'm the one that's in control, bitch! You don't get to ask me any questions."

I retreated until my back hit the refrigerator. There was nowhere else for me to go. "Seven, please don't do this. There's no need for this to get ugly."

Seven stood in front of me wearing a wicked grin. After a few uncomfortable moments, she slapped me so fast that I didn't realize it had happened until I was met with a swift upper cut to the chin. Her wrath continued with a blow to the stomach. "It's already ugly, bitch! You can forget about having that bastard because neither of you will be alive come the next hour."

"Oomph!" I slid down, holding my stomach and praying that Jordan would come and rescue me.

Seven raised her foot and brought it down on my shoulder. "Get up, bitch!"

I spat the blood filling my mouth onto the floor. I knew that pleading wasn't going to save my life, and it was at this moment that I decided that if I was going to die, I would go out fighting. "Arrrgh!" I charged at her, knocking her over by surprise. I screamed as loud as I could, praying that Jordan would hear.

"You bitch!" Seven tried to grab at the gun again that flew out of her hand and skidded across the floor.

We tussled on the floor. I tried to keep her pinned down, but the military training she had, I could not compete with. This was a different fight from when we were in Paris. A damsel in distress, she was not; she was on some *Xena: Warrior Princess*-type shit. The only way I knew to neutralize her was to pick up something and try to knock the shit out of her with it.

She grabbed a fistful of my hair with her free hand. I was able to push her back enough to kick her into the island where the butcher block fell close to us. We both looked at the knives and then at each other. Luckily, I was much faster since I was on top and grabbed the biggest knife that I could get within my grasp. My knife-wielding hand lashed out, immediately cutting Seven on her right arm. I followed that up by plunging it into her back. I was unable to land another blow, but I held on to the knife waiting for another chance.

Her pain was evident from the intolerable screams that erupted from her throat. "You fucking cunt!" she hollered at me as she retreated to a safe distance from the knife and checked the bloody damage I'd done to her arm and back.

With the knife in hand, I rushed her again, but this time, I stopped in my tracks when I was clotheslined and knocked back onto the floor. I looked up to see who else was in my house and got the shock of my life when the second attacker was none other than Jordan.

"Didn't I tell you to make it simple and sweet!" he yelled at Seven.

"That's easy for you to say. I could've offed her when she was riding *my* dick, but you had to wave me off. I guess getting one last nut was more important than getting on that plane," Seven admitted to being in the house all along as she got up, still wincing in pain.

Jordan stormed over to her and slapped her so hard she spun in a circle, lost her balance and fell back onto the floor. "What I tell you about letting your emotions get in the way when doing a job?"

"A job," I blurted without thinking.

"Did you really think I was going to let a nutcase like you live with all that you know about me?"

I clutched my belly and tried to plead my case. "What about our baby?"

Jordan laughed out loud as if I what I'd said was the most ridiculous thing he'd ever heard. "Bianca, if you have a baby growing in that cesspool, then call me Jesus, because that means I am a miracle worker. There is no way you're carrying a baby, and if you are, it's not mine which makes killing *it*, along with you, even more satisfying for giving my pussy away."

"But, you're the only one that I've been with since the night we met in Chicago."

"Jordan, just do it so we can get out of here! The plane is waiting and our window is closing," Seven barked as she slowly got up from the floor for the second time. Her breathing was labored, but she was still faring well despite the pained expression on her face.

"Oh well, I guess I should consider myself lucky that you stayed faithful, but you're a lying, 'no good for nothing but laying on her back' whore of a bitch. You see, I know you're not pregnant because I had a vasectomy years ago. I've never wanted rug rats, Bianca, and since I like fucking simple bitches like you, I made that possibility impossible."

And there it was. I saw my only bargaining chip fly out the window. "But I'm having symptoms. I missed my cycle." I kept the myth going, anyway since at this point, I had nothing else to lose. "I don't understand."

Jordan scratched his head with the hand that was holding the gun. "The good news is that whatever is going on with you won't be an issue in a few minutes."

"But I love you! I thought you loved me too? We can put all of this behind us and still go on with our lives just as we planned."

"Love? Don't you recall me saying that I don't love nobody more than I love Jordan Lei? And to show you . . ." He turned the gun on Seven and shot her in the center of her forehead before she ever knew that she was in danger. "One down and one more to go. Oh, and Sledge wasn't lying about me and Giovanna, by the way."

On cue, Giovanna stepped out of the darkness and stood by Jordan. "Hello, *beautiful.*"

Jordan pulled her in for a kiss. "It is time that I made an honest woman out of her. She would make a breathtaking bride. Don't you think so, Bianca?"

That's all it took for me to be up and on them, but Giovanna put those long-ass legs to use. I received a round-house kick that knocked the wind out of me. Since I hit my head, my vision was distorted as I tried to gather my faculties.

Jordan came closer to where I was and knelt in front of me. "Bianca, I really didn't want to do this. Remember when I said that I needed complete trust. Your loyalty has to be to me regardless of the situation?" He wiped the blood that had trickled down my chin with his thumb. "Hmm, do you?" he asked as he took in my exposed breasts before fixing my robe and tying it securely.

"I was ... Seven." Jordan put his finger up to my lips to quiet me. "Shh ... I know. They threatened you, right?"

"Do it," Giovanna demanded through clenched teeth.

I shook my head yes as tears fell down my cheeks in currents. "Please." Remembering that I still had the knife, I attempted to use it. Jordan was quick as he caught me by the wrist before I even made contact, squeezing it until I dropped it on the floor. "Oww," I cried.

Jordan exhaled and closed his eyes. When he reopened them, there was nothing there but a stone-cold killer staring back at me. He stood and pointed the gun. I closed my eyes for the last time.

Chapter 50

"Aaargh!" I heard Jordan scream and felt him fall near me. Then I felt another presence rush over to Jordan.

My eyes flew open and to my delightful surprise, Agent Carter was in my view kicking Jordan's gun away from his reach and checking his pulse. After checking Jordan's vitals and signaling with his hand, he gave me his undivided attention.

Immediately, I heard Prince in my head singing, *u sexy motherfucker*. That hook played over and over as we stared each other down until I heard a familiar but nerve-racking voice.

"Let go of me dis instance. Don't chu know who I am?" the voice questioned as it became closer to where I was. "I'm Giovanna, and I'm—"

"About to be a dead bitch!" I leapt up from the floor with the speed of a cheetah, but Agent Carter blocked me as if he moonlighted as the linebacker for the Dallas Cowboys, relieving me of the knife in the process.

Giovanna was taken aback by my challenging her after the many threats she'd warned me with since knowing Jordan. "Chu dare go against me? Tell dem dis is a mistake, at once," she screamed.

"Unhand me, chu brutes! I'm Giovanna, supermodel of de world!" She continued to struggle against the two officers that had her in their custody.

I took in the pitiful sight of her. What a beautiful waste of a woman. Even on a deadly mission, she was dressed to kill, pun intended. Adorning her from head to toe was designer everything down to the kick-ass stilettos she wore.

"It's all over now. Let the law deal with her." Agent Carter held me in his arms, trying to calm me down.

After hearing those words, I broke down crying for the love I'd lost and for how happy I was to have been spared. "Thank you. Thank you so much." I cried unashamedly, but more so that I could get back to being me and doing what I loved.

Agent Carter didn't say a word as he continued to console me. Agent Garza, followed by DA Hayes and Legal Attaché Phoebe Bercherot, walked in.

"Bianca!"

I jumped at the sound of Jordan's voice. He was still on the floor drenched in blood. Our eyes connected and for the first time, I saw something in Jordan's that I'd never thought I'd see ... fear.

"Bianca ... I need you," he pleaded.

My heart was torn, but my brain wasn't. I led with my brain and didn't give in to the conflict my heart was trying to create. If not for Agent Carter, I would've been dead and that was more than enough irony for me.

I turned my back on him and allowed Agent Carter to lead me into another part of the house.

"Bianca! Bianca! Biaaaaanca!" Jordan called after me.

Tears fell in torrents down my face as I closed that chapter of my life for good. I couldn't help but think about the way he made me feel; whether it was good or bad, it was always intense.

Once we were alone, I was about to speak, but he interjected, already knowing what I was about to ask.

He looked around and went into a spiel of his own. "We had a tail on you. Had it not been for them taking out the tail, we would've never known what was going on here. When we didn't hear from officers Simon and Travis, we knew something wasn't right and came just in time to see de supermodel of the world," Agent Carter mocked Giovanna to lighten the mood, "brazenly walking into your residence with her gun drawn. There was a van parked with two buffalos in it that we also have in our custody. They told our men that two more were inside, and that's when I knew that one of them had to be Aliyah, and the other, Jordan. It was a good move with you handing Agent Garza that note. Otherwise, we would have never known that your attorney was involved. Especially, that she was the infamous Seven." He winked at me with those gorgeous eyes before continuing. "You don't have to go into detail now, but in the near future, we're going to need you to come down to the station."

"No, I need to get all of this over with as soon as possible. I'm ready to get on with my life . . ." I smiled at him and swiped at the leftover tears that ran down my face. "And Pleasure Principles."

Chapter 51
Three Months Later

*T*he Collector made sure to stay where he couldn't be extradited back to the States for his involvement. Being that he was considered a dignitary, none of the countries he was said to be in would assist in his capture. Of course Jordan rather would've rotted in prison for the rest of his days before he'd go against his father.

Anyway, Jordan had said that he'd loved to have seen me on the white sands of Anguilla looking sexy in a two-piece sipping on something sweet. Well, here I was with my Pleasure Principles staff enjoying a tropical drink. After I let Cody, Reggie and Shelia know everything, surprisingly, they didn't judge or give me any grief behind it. That stunned the hell out of me. However, they didn't waste any time reminding me that I owed them an all-expense paid trip to paradise. So here we were on day four of a fourteen-day retreat having the time of our lives.

"Ooh, y'all see my baby father over there." Cody pointed to this Greek god of a man that had us all wishing he was our baby's daddy.

His dark, wavy hair, oiled olive complexion, exotic features and his ... his manhood was just begging to be sucked. When he turned around, I liked to have died. For a moment there, I was reminded of Jordan—not that the man looked anything like him, but I got the message loud and clear.

Reggie nudged me out of my reverie. "Bianca, did you see him?"

I took off my shades and looked at Reggie. "I couldn't miss him if I tried."

Reggie passed Shelia the suntan lotion. "Chile, she's still going through it behind that tight-eyed dick motherfucker, Jordan. I knew it was a reason I didn't like his ass. He better be glad that he's on lockdown because otherwise, I'd fuck his ass up on sight."

"Aww, bitch, you ain't go do shit." Shelia laughed as she slathered on the tanning lotion. As usual, she was skimpily dressed in a two-piece with a thong bottom giving all the men on the island a heart attack with that big, yellow ass of hers on display.

"Y'all know Bianca is an 'on to the next one' type of bitch, so I don't know why y'all tripping on her not paying that man no mind. Hell, I wouldn't either if I—" Cody was cut short.

"Here ya go, baby."

A huge smile graced my lips as I reached up and took my refreshed drink from Maseo aka Agent Carter. "Thank you, baby."

About the Author

Lesley E. Hal resides in Dallas, Texas where she continues to write and create independent, but beautifully flawed heroines in her stories. She's a firm believer in the power of women, the true rulers of this world. Aside from that, Lesley E. Hal is the author of *Blind Temptations: The Seduction of Sex, Lies & Betrayal, Pleasure Principles* and is a contributing author of *New York Times* bestselling author Zane's *Succulent: Chocolate Flava II*. She's currently putting the finishing touches on *Blind Temptations: The Seduction of Sex, Lies & Betrayal II* and her fourth novel, *Deception*. For more information, please visit Lesley E. Hal at:

www.Lesleyhal.com
https://www.facebook.com/LesleyEHal/
https://www.twitter.com/mslediva